Return of the Malevolents

This book is
dedicated to my
loving family and
friends who have
showed me the
power of stories.

The Kingdoms

Hunter   controller of plants with connection to animals

Sorcerer   elementals, can do spells and charms

Scholar   conjure potions and exceptional memory

Warrior   shapeshifters and elevated instinct and senses

Royal   tellers of the future and leaders

Master   excels in one mastery

Malevolent   immortal and do not feel love

Return of the Malevolents

The Levi Sage Chronicles

Kimberly Shirai

Part I

Chapter 1

A blade swipes for my head.

"Duck!"

Doing as the stranger commands, I feel the breeze left by the sword graze my forehead. I dance around my opponent, hopefully like a practiced warrior.

The space around me is black, as far as I can tell. It's as if there's just a teacher, sparring partner, and me in the abyss. I can never recognize faces during my nightly sessions, but from the stance of my opponent and the fierceness of the blows, customized to maximize the swiftness and force for a small body, she's female

Each movement she makes is like a shadow that melts into the darkness. It is like the world was made for her and her body is meant to kill.

She blocks my attempt with ease and parries with a skilled jab to my torso. I shuffle to the side and use my sword to sway the sharp edge away. We back away from each other, both of our chests heaving. I feel a tinge of satisfaction that I'm not the only one exhausted.

Then, the girl readies herself into a fighting stance and I follow suit.

"End it," the instructor says.

I pause, glancing at my instructor. He certainly said it. But not to me.

My combatant charges as I block and strike with as much efficiency and precision I can muster. She gets closer to slicing my skin with each stroke. My defenses weaken, but I hold strong and manage to get a few attacks in, some of them only narrowly missing their target. I smile to myself. Before, I would go down without a chance for offense.

I steal a glance at my instructor. He nods approvingly and my chest wells with pride.

That look costs me.

She slips past my block and punches the hilt of the sword down through my rib cage, until it meets the cloth above my chest.

...

Levi

I jerk up, my chest rising rapidly up in down. The blaring noise of my alarm courses through my ears. I desperately feel for blood and pain, but all I find is the cloth above my chest. I sigh in relief. No hole or sword to be seen. I settle back into the soft mattress and take a couple deep breaths to try to clear my head.

Opening a heavy eyelid, I gaze through my window. The clouds are grey and stormy, about to cry on this rickety old town deep in the California mountains. Generally, I like the rain. It makes me feel fresh when the pure droplets hit my warm skin. Given the chance, I wouldn't complain if I was told to stand in the storm and jump around in puddles to my heart's content.

Groaning, I heave myself off the bed. The house is so silent, I can hear my socks slide across the wooden floor. My father always likes to rent houses with a lot of windows. He says it allows him to see everything he needs to. I never understood what he meant, but I don't press.

My father was born into a rich family and he inherited the money when his father died a few years before I was born. After my mother's soul left this Earth, he began his life of endless travel—me in his suitcase. I can't remember a time when we stayed in a location longer than a year and I don't expect that pattern to change. He's a self-proclaimed researcher, searching for the undefined meaning of life. Again, I don't think too hard about it. My father is a very philosophical man and I know that if I get into a conversation with him over dinner about his work, I would die of boredom.

My stomach rumbles at the thought of a meal. When I turn the corner to the kitchen, I nearly jump out of my skin.

"Good morning Levi," my PhD father greets from the kitchen table. He already has a bagel in one hand and the local newspaper in the other. He narrows his eyes and looks me over.

"Good morning," I grumble back.

I grab the steaming kettle from the stove and pour myself a cup of boiling water. During an excursion to Japan, my father got me some special tea that he says cost arm and a leg. He didn't have to tell me twice to drink it. The taste is a mix of herbs and fruit and its scent calms me after my eventful dreams. Furrowing my brows, I lean against the counter and take a sip. My dreams have only started these past few months and my guess is that it's just because of moving and school stress.

My thoughts fill with frustration. If only he cared more about asking me if *I* wanted to move. Instead of just announcing one day during dinner that we're moving to California, he could've *asked* me if that was what I wanted.

I sip my tea on my way to my room. After a few moments, thoughts about that dream resurface in my mind. It's always the same girl and the same instructor. I can tell that even without seeing their faces. Brushing my teeth, I lean against my sink and ponder the night's events.

They teach me the art of combat, strategy, poisons, and such strange topics of a system that I can never fully remember when I awake. It drives me crazy–not being able to remember what I experienced just moments before. It's like knowing you know something, but you can't reach it.

. . .

Levi

The walk there is cold and wet. Rainwater and slick mud cake the bottom of my trousers while my socks become as soggy as a wet sponge.

I turn the last corner and come across the iron gates of the school. Hawkeye Prep looms in the distance, its tall buildings made of dark red wood that stick out of the side of the mountain like a zit. I scrunch my nose at the sounds of excessive chattering and squealing reach my ears.

Stairs litter the campus, from hall to hall, room to room. Even though I've been here for a few months, I never made the effort to reach out. There's something about being that shadow in the corner of the room that feels comfortable. There isn't as much pain in my heart when I have to leave. I pull my hood over my head and do my best to be quiet and undetectable in the swarm.

A hand yanks my shoulder back. I bring my arm around to make an attempt at twisting my attacker's hand between his shoulder blades. The boy releases me before I have the chance. He smiles a cocky smile and sizes me up.

Faking a calm stature, I look up at him defiantly.

"Hey pipsqueak, you have Mr. Kilver?" It's more a statement than a question.

"Yeah," I reply and scrunch my brows.

"I got a sister in that class and my mom said that she'd buy me a new phone if she didn't get in trouble." His smug grin makes my blood boil. "Her name's Austra." He points a finger at my nose. "Make sure that doesn't happen."

I open my mouth to ask but he turns before I have the chance. I watch as the boy walks away with that same knowing smirk on his face.

"She got expelled from the other school she was at. Nice kid, just a little–strange." He laughs. "I'm sure you'll both get along great."

...

Levi

When the bell rings, I look around for a girl that could pass for his sister. With so many people in my class, it's hard for me to tell if someone's new or not. Giving up, I take a seat without another thought.

"Class! Let's settle down. Hey! I saw that! Put that away." My chemistry teacher, Mr. Kilver, runs a hand through his bright, red hair in distress. "We'll be starting a new lab today everyone! Get to your

6

stations and start reading the instructions. I'm here if you have any questions."

Many of the students let out audible groans. I turn to the person next to me and give a nod in greeting. "Nice to meet you. I'm Levi Sage." The girl looks down at her notebook, her wavey hair falling over her eyes, before nervously taking my hand. "I'm Austra Rabid."

I raise an eyebrow at the sheer luck of her ending up at my table and reply, "I think–I met your brother just a couple minutes ago actually."

Austra laughs and scratches the back of her neck. "Let me guess, he wanted you to make sure nothing weird happens?"

My shrug gives her my answer and she smiles bitterly. "I bet he asked half the class. That little prick."

A grin tugs at my lips. "No big deal. Are you from around here?"

Austra swallows. "I just moved from up North."

I nod thoughtfully and fiddle with the phone in my hand, fighting the urge to turn on the music and put in my earbuds. "I move around a lot for my dad's work. I came in from Arizona about three months ago." I laugh and search for something to fill the silence. "What do your parents do for a living?"

Her left eye twitches a bit, but she answers just as quickly, "They're photographers, so they go off to travel, leaving my brother and I at home usually."

"That's cool," I say. "My dad's pretty boring in comparison. He's a researcher, technically. He makes us travel a lot."

"Why doesn't he just fly out himself?" Austra asks.

I lie. "My dad wants me to see the world with him." I stuff my hands into my pockets and shrug. "Don't get too attached to me," I warn, forcing a smile.

Austra smiles for the first time and says, "Well, we have the present. And we'll see what Fate brings us."

Her attention slides to the redheaded girl in the front row, next to a boy that looks a lot older than fifteen with shoulders twice as wide as mine. "I heard from my neighbor that they're a handful unless you want a broken nose. Is that true?"

I look over to the girls that were swooning over our Chemistry teacher and shrug. "They haven't given me much trouble. Maybe just stay out of their way."

She bites her lip, not meeting my gaze. "The redhead has been staring daggers at me since I entered the classroom."

As if on cue, the girl with red hair turns her head and meets my eyes. They're the stunning color of... gold. In an effort to look closer I squint, but she notices the movement and gives a huff of a laugh. *How have I not noticed her before?* Then her eyes slide to Austra. If a stare could send daggers, Austra would be impaled with twenty.

Austra scrunches her freckled nose. She gives me a look that says, *I told you so.* She bends down to get something out of her backpack and tucks a strand of her brown hair behind her ear, revealing shimmering strands of gold. They wrap around her ear gracefully and drape down almost to her shoulder.

"Wow. That's beautiful," I say, gesturing to her earpiece.

Her hand shoots up to cover it, a soft hint of rose climbing her cheeks. If her eyes could shut the windows to her soul, they would've. "Thanks, it's a tradition from where I come from." Before I can ask a follow-up question, she asks, "Do you want to exchange numbers? Just in case I have any questions on the homework."

I debate questioning her more but decide against it. "Sure."

Chapter 2

Levi

It doesn't take long to locate Austra amongst the crowd. She sits at a deserted table with only a girl next to her as company. As I approach, lunch tray in hand, the girl I don't know looks up with the same eyes as the redhead from homeroom a few hours earlier. A piercing gold. Something about her gaze is harsher though, more mature maybe.

Although the girl seems only about fourteen or fifteen, her posture and the straightness of her shoulders is anything but young. She's stunning, striking. One would have to be blind to not remember her face, even if it might be a tad scary. Maybe she's new like Austra.

Austra looks up a few seconds later and waves me over.

"Hey," I greet and take a seat on the opposite side of the table. "How was class?"

"Good. How about you?"

"Same," I sigh and shove food in my mouth.

I peer around the cafeteria and a handful of wandering eyes stare back at me. I shake my head. At least I'm not the new student this time. It's strange–to sit at a table in the cafeteria with the goal of talking to people. I usually find a tree to sit under in the nearby field, alone.

"Austra, do you mind introducing us?" the girl with shimmering eyes asks, her dark, brown hair glistening of gold from the midday light.

Austra blinks. "Oh! Sorry, um–Levi, this is Skye Fervent."

"Nice to meet you," she says and bows her chin.

The corner of my lip twitches, "Likewise. How'd you two meet?" Come to think of it, I don't remember seeing Skye around school and I feel like she's someone I would remember.

"Poor Austra almost got killed by a few beasts," Skye replies simply while picking at her nails. She peeks at me to gauge my reaction, but seeing nothing particularly interesting, she grins. "I'm just kidding.

A few students were giving her a hard time, so I cleared up the misunderstanding."

Austra just stares at her many golden rings as she twists them over and over again on her fingers.

...

Levi

We engage in small talk for the rest of lunch. Skye's a pleasure to talk to, when she's not glaring at someone who stares at her too long. I ask her questions about her family, which she talks around without giving straight answers. Maybe she just doesn't like talking about her personal life.

Austra spends the time picking at her food and filches whenever there's a loud noise.

We walk together to our next class while Austra tells us about how uneventful Chemistry was. On the contrary, I thought it was one of the more exciting, but I choose not to say anything.

My heart nearly leaps out of my chest when I spot a very robust teen glaring at–not me–Skye. Both her and Austra continue to walk, not giving it a second glance. Looking between Skye and the boy, I ask, "What's with him?"

"He's probably just having a bad day," she shrugs and adjusts the sleaves of her black turtleneck. Her eyes dart to my unsatisfied expression and sighs. "We have bad blood," Skye finishes nonchalantly.

I grab her arm to slow her down. "What?"

She shrugs my hand off and together we stop at what I assume is her locker. "In this area, my family is a fairly well-known name. And it's not remembered fondly." She grabs a textbook and starts down the hall, leaving us to fast walk to catch up to her. "Grudges run high in this community."

She's not new?

"What does your family do? Sell drugs?" I ask, amused.

10

She chuckles at that and shakes her head. "Some lives are more complicated than others, Levi. One day, you'll understand why half of this town hates me."

I open my mouth to press a little harder, but the bell rings. "I have geometry next," I say, heading off in the opposite direction.

"We have that too," Austra blurts and cringes slightly.

I frown again. I would've definitely noticed if Skye was in my Geometry class. Skye doesn't seem to notice my confused glance and walks up to meet my stride.

We make our way through the bustling swarm of teenagers. I take my usually seat and Skye gives those that sit around me a stare sharper than a sword. They turn around promptly, leaving Austra and her open seats. When she sees my mouth open in alarm, she mouths an annoyed, *What?*

Class runs for what seemed like a millennium. Even though we're technically in an accelerated math class, the lessons don't seem like they go any faster. I pass the time doodling little knick-knacks and things that I've seen around town. Some artists love drawing edges and points, but I'd rather depict nature and life.

A gorgeous silver tree manifested in my head and I do my best to portray the gleam with my graphite pencil. My mind drifts off into a dazed state and the vision in my mind intensifies. I can make out almost every leaf as the tree shimmers in a pool of sunlight. I lift a hand to reach out to it, wanting to feel the smooth–

"Levi, would you please tell the class the last step to prove this theorem?"

I jump slightly and look up at Mrs. Sinton. She glares at me over her. *Good job, Levi.* My eyes dart around the room and everyone has their textbooks out, turned to the same page. Skye bites her lip in amusement and leans back in her chair.

"Definition of parallel lines," whispers the person behind me.

What? I fight the urge to turn around and say, "Definition of parallel lines." Sinton seems satisfied and turns back to her desk. The bell rings before I finish my sigh of relief.

I turn around to thank my savior, but whoever it was already left. All that's left is an empty seat.

...

Levi

Although it's technically still summer, the cold air makes its way under my wool coat, sending a shiver down my spine. Clutching my arms around myself, I jog up the driveway to my house.

Even inside, the icy floor seeps through my socks. I settle near the fireplace that my dad must have left on and try to thaw my hands. When I can feel the tips of my fingers again, I tug my folders out of my backpack.

The temperature decreases as the sun sets. I shiver so much, the words on my paper turn shaky. *What in the world?* I get up and turn on the heat and thirty minutes later, my breath still makes clouds in the dense air. The house usually keeps its warmth pretty.

Fed up with the cold, I text my dad that our heater might be broken. I scowl when I don't hear the usual sound that signifies it sent.

The Wi-Fi is down.

Wrapping the blankets around me, I shuffle to the kitchen and check the home phone to see if that's working. The blood leaves my face when I see that the screen's dark. That's not strange. At all.

Then a creak sounds on the porch. I stop dead in my tracks. It wasn't the fire, or there would be sparks, and it wasn't me. It must've been an animal. *Levi, remain calm, it's probably nothing.* I continue up the stairs, trying to keep each step as quiet as possible.

Cold air brushes against my back and the hairs on my arm stand on end.

The thump of my heart pounds in my chest and my instincts tell me to find something sharp. My legs pump up the stairs, as quietly as I can manage, towards the artificial sword in my dad's office. The shadows created by the moon dance in the corners of the room, taunting me. One tug and it breaks off the display. I wrap my fingers around the hilt and the tough leather molds into my palm like clay.

I will my feet to be light as I dash down the steps and lean against the wall next to the hall to listen for any sounds. I risk a peek around the corner and then slam myself right back around.

Tall, cloaked figures glide around my living room, more graceful than anything I have ever seen. My hand shakes in fear, so I grasp the sword harder. Something about them feels wrong–like nature doesn't mean for them to exist. My breaths become sharper as I sense them come closer and closer. The front door is wide open, letting the bitter cold rush into the house.

I clench my jaw to keep my teeth from chattering and get into position. If they come, I will strike. *Levi be brave.* My legs betray me as they knock against each other in fear.

A hand covers my mouth. My eyes widen and I raise my leg to kick when a familiar voice whispers in my ear. "*Stop idiot.* It's Skye, we have to go."

Despite being scared to death, I nod my head. *Why is Skye here?* She lets go of me and gestures to follow her. Her eyes linger on the sword in my hand for a moment, then she soundlessly turns around. Her close fitted black robe makes her blend into the darkness while I stand out like a sore thumb with grey sweatpants and a white t-shirt.

We look at each other in panic when footsteps crash onto the stairs behind us.

We run.

She grabs my forearm and yanks me into the guest bedroom and out through the balcony door.

Something grabs my ankle and I fall onto the wood with a thud, pain shooting up my elbows and knees. My sword makes a blind arc near my foot and a human-like cry roars through the night and the grip on my foot releases. Skye jumps into battle with another one of the creatures, faster than I have ever seen anything move. Her sword glimmers in the moonlight as she brings down one. Another catches her by surprise, sending a thin line of red across her torso. The girl with the gold eyes hisses, grabbing the wound, and delivers a blow through the monster's neck. I scramble to my feet as Skye rushes by, pulling my arm to follow.

Without hesitation, we jump off the balcony.

I yell as the wind whistles past my ears. This part of the house is adjacent to a ravine, which I really had no interest in exploring. I guess fate has another narrative in mind.

I close my eyes as everything becomes silent and brace myself for the end. Maybe I'll fit in better in whatever world I enter next.

Chapter 3

Talons clench around my shoulders and I yelp at the force of deceleration. Bat-like wings spread out above me, maybe ten feet across. The winged thing glances down at me, its eyes so gold they nearly glow.

Skye.

A wave of shock rolls through me. That's it! I'm dreaming. This whole thing is just my imagination. It's like those dreams I have. Maybe this is just a simulation to prepare me for... something.

Or maybe those dreams were to train me for this.

A long black arrow scrapes across the top of her wing. Skye lets out a screech and we plummet a few feet before she regains her balance. Blood drips to the ground far below and I pray that she can hold on for a little longer. To help her a bit, I grab hold of her ankles to loosen the grip she has on me. She looks down at me with grateful eyes filled with pain.

She picks up her pace and swerves, trying to avoid more arrows. I watch from below–helpless–holding on for dear life. After a bit, the arrows fall before they reach us and become less frequent. My house gets smaller in the distance until it completely disappears.

Skye descends into a small clearing on a hill surrounded by evergreens. My feet crash to the ground so hard, they give out from under me. I tumble onto the soft grass, rolling a few times before I lose momentum. The girl–or bat–does the same. Her breaths are short and jagged. I strain to look over in alarm. Blood seeps onto the grass from her shoulder and stomach, staining the ground red.

Slamming my hand into the grass out of pure will power, I get up. My muscles shake from the effort and pain shoots through my legs. I stumble in her direction. My vision blurs and the world around tilts. Shaking my head, I kneel to examine her wounds.

A blackish color trails from both major cuts and the surrounding veins. *That doesn't seem healthy.*

The black keeps trailing farther down her wing. Even though both the wing and veins are black, the poison is darker. It's the black of an endless pit–of the darkest of shadows.

I look around helplessly for anyone or anything. Nothing. Panic seizes my senses as I turn back to the dying creature in front of me. I guess the best thing would be to remove the source of the poison. Flashes of memories tug at my brain and knowledge floods my senses. Letting the memories take over, I tell Skye, "Give me a minute."

I sprint into the woods. Leaves and branches tear at my cheeks and into my already tattered shirt. Nearly crying in relief, I stumble into a shallow stream, not caring about the ice-cold water that soaks my shoes and pants.

Reaching around blindly, a rising lump of fear threatens to break free. Relief tumbles through me as I feel soft moss. I yank it off the rock and put it close to my face. Its roots have a slight glow. Just what I need. I smile in its light before dashing back into the black.

Panting, I fall to my knees next to her in exhaustion. "Hey Skye. I'm going to put this on. It might feel weird and painful for a second, but I think it should get better after a few moments."

She nods her head, eyes shut tight, as if seeing could block the pain from seeping in.

"Okay," I whisper to myself and take a few deep breaths.

She hisses as I apply the plant to her shoulder and jerks when I touch her stomach.

A rustle sounds in a nearby bush and I shoot to my feet. More pats and sounds break the silence and dark, red eyes peer at me through the fold, scrutinizing every move I make.

I slowly grab the sword from where it lay a few feet away and shift its weight in my palms. It's balanced almost perfectly, but a little on the heavy side. It would have to do. Adrenaline pulses through my veins, the only thing keeping me standing.

They slowly ooze out of the brush, gliding like ghosts, their hoods covering their faces and long bird-like claws peeking out beneath the cloth. My eyes dart around me. Seven horrid beings.

The one behind me attacks first. I duck and slice my blade from below, but it cuts air. A kick to my face sends me sprawling on the ground, but I get back up and swing for its neck with all my might, ignoring the blood that flows from my nose. It meets air again and before I can take a breath, I'm pushed into the nearest tree by another.

Groaning, I get onto my knees and raise the blade again. The red-eyed things chuckles. With each breath, I feel a sharp pain along my rib cage. One says, "So this is who the Six Kingdoms has to offer?"

I swipe forward with as much speed as I can muster. I don't inflict damage, but I snag its hood and it falls from its head.

Her face is strangely beautiful, almost human. Her skin is white, nearly grey, and her hair is as dark as the deepest oil. She seems normal, but her hands are not. Long, black talons protrude from the sleeves of her cloak, animal-like.

Momentarily overcome with shock, I reign in my senses and harden my glare.

The creature raises a distorted eyebrow and smiles at my terror. "We found you." And she lunges.

Before I can raise my sword, a flash of brown barrels into the fray. They crash to the ground as one and roll onto the grass. The animal's fur gets soaked in mud and the Malevolent calls out in alarm. The creature makes eye contact with me for a split second and I see a flash of gold.

I look over to Skye in recognition, but she's still down–and the creatures haven't forgotten her. A Malevolent raises his sword, ready to kill.

I jump in front of the strike that would've been her demise. I block the first blow and manage to get an attack in. Red, hot blood leaks from its body and I hit it on the head with the hilt of my sword, knocking it to the ground.

I hear an impact behind me and a thud. Another furry animal attacks a creature, then another, and another. They almost look like... wolves.

Claws dig into my shoulders and I cry out in pain as a burning sensation pools around the wounds. I take the sword in my hand and stab the creature over my head. It lets out a screech and releases. Rolling away, I get up to a fighting stance, my vision slowly darkening at the edges.

Favoring my uninjured ankle and grasping the hilt with both hands, I charge at the monster. It swipes over my head and I duck and slam the blade deep into its gut and twist.

It falls, I with it.

...

Skye

I wake to a warm chest that smells of wet dog and blood. My head shoots up and collides with another.

"Ouch!" Groaning, I rub the area of pain and settle back down with a piercing headache.

"You little–," he hisses. "Lay down and don't move. You'll open your scabs or something," the gruff voice growls.

I fight back a groan. The wolves have found us and I'm not quite sure whether to be grateful or not. An audible snore sounds behind us and I suppress a grin. At least the idiot is still alive.

I gasp as the man carrying me stumbles. Biting my lip, I look down at my abdomen. A new rush of blood leaks through a white bandage.

I glare at my carrier and put my neck back down in exhaustion. Pain curls in my stomach and arm so intensely, all I can focus on is taking deep breaths. I slip in and out of consciousness, darkness constantly tugging at the edges of my vision.

After what seems like hours, each bump feeling like a slap of needles, I will my eyes to open again. A fuzzy outline of long, red hair is all I make out. As if she can feel my eyes, the girl turns to me with a strong scowl. She slows her pace to match the boy who carries me.

"Well, Skye, looks like you owe me your life," the girl with the red hair says. Her voice drips with malice.

"No, Kalica. I owe the Warriors my thanks." I know well that she would've been overjoyed if I had died.

She scoffs and turns her back to me.

...

Skye

"Do you think she'll be okay?" A gruff voice sounds through the quiet room.

Cold fingers press into my wounds and all I can do is tense and hiss. "She needs a Sorcerer or Royal, and quickly. I can't do anything with her. The boy I can try." There's a pause. "Did you contact the people she was sent by?" The ends of her words cracked with age.

"Knowing this young one, she probably did. Their kind are quick thinkers."

I force my eyes open and try to study my surroundings like my father always tells me to.

Even at your weakest, there are always ways to dig yourself a little bit out. Each pebble counts.

A wave of pain courses through my body and I whisper a curse.

"Honey," the elderly voice says, rushing over to my side. I feel a cool towel on my forehead and her calloused hands grip mine. "Squeeze if your friends are coming."

With the remaining energy I have, I do.

"That's good then. I looked at your locket, dear, and called your school, too. Someone should come in a moment with a healer." She releases me and I hear her footsteps echo down the hall.

Heavier footsteps come my way and the same gruff voice from earlier says, "I know Titus, sweetheart. Even if this plan goes through, my people and I will never consider your kind of the same blood." He sends a punch to one of the larger cuts. I yelp and grip my arm, as unwanted tears fall across my face.

I fall back into the fitful darkness until a loud bang sounds at the end of the hall. Multiple steps crash and get louder and louder until a hand grasps mine.

"Skye! Can you hear me?"

Austra.

"Move aside, antelope! Let Aris in."

Spencer?

Austra's hand is ripped from mine and the right of me becomes colder and heavier than before. "Skye," begins the young Sorcerer in greeting, bending onto his knees to be level with me. "I'm going to heal this using the Healing Spell. Spencer's going to provide the energy for you and Austra will provide the energy for Levi. I need to save most of it for Levi and—you know what that means. I'll make sure to use the Elepsing Spell, so you won't feel anything. Okay?"

"And make a movement of some sort to tell us if you brought down a Malevolent. Then Sylas can do the spell for you, so you get your little reward mark," Spencer says.

I try to move, but my eyes won't even flicker. It might have something to do with the poison in the arrow. I know that Hunters generally used a paralyzing poison when they hunt, so maybe the Malevolents used the same thing. The Hunters used it as a form of mercy, but I suspect the Malevolents imagined the opposite.

A moment of silence passes, and Spencer says, "Well, it's Skye we're talking about. Austra, go tell Sylas to do it anyway."

I can almost feel Austra roll her eyes as her footsteps click against the ground. Aris takes a deep breath and soon I feel a soothing sensation of warmth in my chest.

Chapter 4

Levi

Jarring movements shake my body awake, while my mind tells me to sleep despite the roaring of a car engine below me. Groaning, I open my eyes, blinking rapidly at the searing light. My head feels as though it's filled with a gallon of water.

My vision slowly comes into focus and I make out a grey car interior. Austra and Skye are passed out on their seats next to me. Skye's sickly shade of grey and her limbs lay limp. With her lips green, eyelids purple, and breaths shallow, she certainly looks like living death. At the front of the car, there are two people, one with wavy brown hair and the other, bright red.

"He's awake," a familiar voice says, stimulating a pump of adrenaline through my veins. Suddenly, I feel. I feel the sweat dripping from my forehead and the slickness of my hands. I feel the pain in my gut and the tenseness of all of my muscles. I feel the hot blood of the red-eyed creatures dried on my body and the pulse of the bruises, making me wince at the slightest movement.

"Good job, Aris. He's only been out for a few hours," says the driver, looking through the rearview mirror. I fight to raise my head an inch to get a better look of the driver's face.

"Mr. Kilver?" I ask, scrunching my eyebrows.

He nods his head and I can feel him grinning without even seeing it. "Nice to see you alive, Levi."

"Yeah," I mumble, rubbing my eyes. "Me too. Uh, is Skye going to be okay?"

Stretching, Austra nods her head. Her earpiece dangles back and forth. "Aris did enough of the Healing Spell to last her."

I refrain from pinching myself and just stutter, "What?"

Austra plays with a thin, gold chain from around her neck. "That's a question for Aris. Behind you."

I nearly jump out of my skin when I see the boy behind me. He positions himself in the corner of the vehicle, as if curtained by shadows. His black bangs are on the longer side, parted enough for me to see jet black eyes mixed with a flecks of brown.

"Why can't you just tell him about the Six Kingdoms now?" My attention swerves to the boy who approached me just this morning. He gazes through the window with detached interest, his tanned skin glowing in the light. "He'll find out soon enough."

"We should get closer to campus," Mr. Kilver says with a firm voice.

"Six Kingdoms," I mutter under my breath, rolling the words over my tongue. The words stick to my memory, like a puzzle piece. "I think–I think I've heard that before."

Spencer scoffs, "I wouldn't be surprised. They probably used a Recollection Charm on you before or something."

My former chemistry teacher gives him a sharp glare. "Be quiet, Spencer. That's an order."

Spencer rolls his eyes and slouches in his seat. "The things that tried to kill you are called Malevolents. That–at least–you should know."

The red-headed driver clenches his jaw but doesn't say a word.

"Thanks," I say in a bit of a daze. Searching for some level of comfort, I feel around for my phone, but my hands meet empty pockets and I freeze. *There's no way to contact my father. Or help.*

Spencer lets out a long sigh. "Sylas, do you have the reversal potion with you?"

Keeping his eyes on the road, Mr. Kilver–or Sylas–pulls out a small, round flask from his pocket and hands it to Spencer.

"What is that?" I ask, doing my best to keep my voice steady. The liquid is the color of blueberry milk with a bit of a sheen. It moves in an unusual pattern, always flowing forwards and backwards in the same direction as the last.

He ignores me and takes the cork out from the top and chugs the whole thing in one go. I watch him change in a silent horror. From his overall height, to the width of his shoulders, to the broadness of his face, everything just looks... older?

"That's much better," he says with a smug look and shakes out his new limbs. He stops and gives me a disgusted look, "Close your mouth."

I open my mouth repeatedly like a guppy, unable to form words.

"You think that a nineteen-year-old could fit into a high school without getting noticed?" He gives me a pointed look, as if I'm the crazy one.

"Well–"

"Disguises are a wonderful thing." He looks smugly at the empty flask, his eyes now the same color of gold as Skye's.

"Yep. I'm definitely dreaming." I lean back in my seat and close my eyes in an attempt to feel some sense of reality. To my dismay, when I look around the car again, an older, still crabby Spencer looks back at me in exasperation.

"Well on a happier note, we're almost there," exclaims Sylas, turning onto a dirt road. "Levi, look out the window. I find it beautiful every time."

"Finally," groans Spencer. "I've seen enough grape vines for a lifetime."

Tall trees with droopy branches frame the river that runs along the side of the road. To my left is a rocky hillside with ferns and moss and little waterfalls that trickle down the cold, grey rock. Things start to look... sharper. As if a fog has been lifted. The path of the water is so defined, they look like strands, flowing in their respective directions in a silent, beautiful chaos. White flowers decorate the mossy floor, so pure that they look like they glow a soft silver.

I'm entranced. My eyes are glued to the scenery around me and I pinch myself to make sure I'm not dreaming. The others don't seem to care, most of them disinterested or getting a little bit of shuteye. How could they just sleep through this?

It's like magic.

"Oh shoot. I almost forgot. Put on your earmuffs," Sylas says, passing us huge balls of fluff connected by a thick wire. I grab mine skeptically with a raised brow. Scanning my surroundings, there isn't anything that looks unusually threatening, besides some large willow trees and lily pads.

"What are these for?" I ask, my hands still a little shaky.

"We'll tell you later." He waves a hand in a quick dismissal and puts his on, making a slapping sound as he does. The other strange teenagers do the same, leaving me wondering whether or not to follow suit.

"Wait, what about Skye?" I shout. None of them seem to hear me and instead look at me in panic. Austra attempts to lean over and put mine on for me. I pull away when I hear the most beautiful voice.

Everything around me seems to still.

Just ahead is a clearing. A meadow. With green, green grass and light flickering to the ground. Then there are three women that glow with grace and perfection. Their long jet-black hair falls to their hips and crowns and dresses of gold drape to the lucky Earth.

And their voices...

They sing of happiness and sorrow, encompassing stories of false lovers and perfect endings. They give me visions of a field like the one they stand in, but instead it's me resting in its center for hours, maybe even years. I have all the time in the world to listen to the sounds, breath in the pristine air, and gaze into the eyes of nature.

My vision narrows and things start to move again. *I have to go to them.* As I reach for the handle, I feel arms and hands grabbing at my jacket and my hair. All I can see are those women with golden skin and golden dreams. I don't care. I rip away the hands that prevent me from reaching that future and scramble towards the promises.

The van keeps moving, and I barely register the increasing speed and fading voices. My will to leap out of the moving metal on wheels lessens, until it's just a dull throb in my heart.

"What in the world was that?" I breathe, falling back in my seat. My eyes switch from person to person, as if I can just look at their faces and find the answers. Maybe I'm going crazy.

"That was what we call a Siren," Spencer responds, giving his earmuffs back to Sylas, "which is why these contraptions are so important."

"You might have heard of them," Sylas continues, worry lines deepening. "Despite our efforts in keeping magic hidden, some stories do make their way to the light." He turns his shoulders a bit to get a good look at me. "It's okay Levi. Don't look so embarrassed. It happens to the best of us," informs Sylas.

I grit my teeth as my cheeks sting.

"Sirens enchant whoever hears them sing. There are three types, ones who want us as food, ones who want to help us or kill us, or don't care. Those that want to help us, protect the city from outsiders who don't belong here. You have to have special enchanted earmuffs to get by. If an Outsider does find themselves with the Sirens, they contact us. Then we do the Recollection Charm on them and lead them back to the main road."

"Sirens," I say, nodding my head in disbelief.

"You just didn't wear the earmuffs, idiot," mumbles Spencer, picking his nails with an iron knife.

Doing my best to ignore the sharp thing within stabbing distance of me, I ask, "How come Skye didn't get affected?" I gesture to the very sickly-looking girl sprawled just a seat over.

"If you have a strong enough mind and intuition then you don't need the earmuffs," replies Sylas.

"Which you have neither," mutters Spencer.

"Wow," I say, anger slowly rising to replace the fear. "Thanks."

Ignoring the comment, Sylas continues. "Skye has gone through training to learn the art of the mind. It's a very intense and draining process, but it's useful if you go on missions often, like her."

I gaze out the window again. *Spells and sirens.* Things that I only thought existed in books and movies. I shuffle the knowledge around in my brain like a bookshelf to find where each piece fits. These books are like those really tall and intricate ones that just don't fit in with the others that line up perfectly in a row.

The river speeds up a little. Little rocks are sprinkled around the ravine, creating white water that shimmer in the fading sun. The willows are grander and more ancient than before, and some of the tips of the droopy branches skim the top of the water. What alarms me the most are the tiny people either gliding over the stream, sitting on the stones, or playing with the low branches of the willow. Some are even holding small droplets of water that are like clear pearls in the light. The little people are about the height of my pointer finger and wear white, loose clothing that flows like the river they call home. Their hair is the same color as the water and their eyes are like tear drops.

"Those, my friend, are river pixies," Sylas says. "They inhabit all the rivers on Inside lands." Spencer smirks at my pale face, his brown hair bouncing to the drone of the car.

River pixies. That's just wonderful. My thoughts are, again, left sprawling.

A sphere of water comes barreling towards me and crashes into the car window. I fall back, nearly crushing Skye. The remnants of the wad of water drip off the glass, as if there was just a flash rainstorm.

Scooching forward, I press my face on the cold window. River pixies laugh with each other on the damp rocks, pointing their fingers at the car.

"Those water pixies," growls Spencer. "Stop the car."

Sylas shakes his head, "Need me remind you, that would break the law."

Grumbling, Spencer leans back in his chair. "Lila would show them."

"Who's Lila?" I ask, still watching the cocky little river pixies.

"His girlfriend," Austra says with a knowing smile.

"Shut up," mutters Spencer and gives Austra the most venomous stink eye I ever thought possible.

I examine their features, both tanned and with wavy hair. They have the same long eyelashes and soft features, so there's a chance Spencer wasn't lying when he said they were siblings.

We descend into a comfortable silence, the light slowly leaving our surroundings as the tree cover gets thicker and thicker. The others fidget and rustle around, making my nerves rise again.

When it's almost completely dark, the car stops in front of a tall bush. The bush doesn't look like it has a top though… or an end.

"The Wall of Tepidity," Sylas says, grimly. "Levi, whatever you do, *never* leave this car, no matter how terrible the wall is to you." He makes sure I look him in the eye and nod before starting the car again.

I give a look to Austra that's something along the lines of, *What's happening. Please help clarify.*

She winces. "You'll learn more about it in your Six Kingdom's history class."

I decide not to ask more because of the tint of fear behind her honey brown eyes. Whoever these people are, they don't take second chances with security.

All I hear is silence. Noticing the change, I look around yet again. The white blossoms are nowhere to be see and the pixies do not wander here. The willows act like curtains, shielding us from the world we left behind.

"I hate this part," says Spencer, looking visibly paler as we near the wall. For a big burly guy who looks like he could be a world class boxer, he seems unnervingly on edge. I bet that if he could grow wings, he would already be gone.

Aris lets out a sigh from behind, which is perhaps the first sound he's made this car ride. The boy of shadows leans his head forward on my chair and his breaths become short and shaky.

Sylas steps on the gas and the white van goes straight at the bush wall at full speed. I grab at anything I can around me and nearly yelp in surprise. When the tip of the bumper hits the wall, we're enveloped by darkness.

I wake up to a dense mist that blocks my view of anything more than two feet in front of me. I search for Austra, Spencer, Sylas, Skye, or Aris–but it's only me. My gut is heavy, and I yearn for someone to touch. Running my ice-cold fingers over my face and down my neck, I savor the feeling, even though I'm not warm like I should be, and it stings. I bring my hands down and study them. At first, the picture is blurry, like your phone loading a picture with faulty Wi-Fi. Gradually, cuts and scratches mar my palms and dirt is caked under my fingernails. It's as if I crawled myself out of a grave.

A man, with the size and features of a bull, appears before me. He opens his mouth and yells, stretching the thin scar that runs down his cheek. The girl in front of him looks to me with wide, golden eyes. His eyes turn red and his skin turns white and pale.

Skye.

I reach forward, but a car door blocks me.

No. No, this is a trick. It's all in my head, the maze is in my head. The mist is fake and Skye is next to me, unconscious and sick. *Levi, this is not real.*

The view of Skye starts to move away from me as I drift forward in the mist. The van's engine roars loudly in my ears. *Is it over?*

Shutting my eyes tight, I slump to settle into my chair, but I fall. Before I hit the ground behind me, my eyes open and I am again standing in a blanket of fog. *Great.*

In the distance, I see a figure wave to me. Squinting hard, I strain my eyes to see who it is. Austra runs towards me with wild eyes. Her wavy, brown hair is too chaotic to be purposeful and her knees shake so hard, they knock against each other.

A Malevolent jumps on top of her from behind, faster than I can even react. Unprepared, she crumples to the ground and is easily pinned. She screams, and the sound sears into my mind. I turn my back to the cries of pain and helplessly cover my ears with my hands.

Chapter 5

Levi

Cold prickles my arms and I can hear breaths and the warmth to my right. Cautiously, I open my eyes and take in my surroundings.

Sylas has a very determined face, his cheeks a bright red. Austra clings to the bar on the car door for dear life, as white as bone. Spencer has a contorted face that looks as though he might be mad and sad at the same time. Call me sleep deprived, but he looks a little hairier than I remember. Aris just sits behind me, staring at nothing. The emptiness in his face makes me shiver.

"Well Levi, how was your first time through?" Sylas asks with a little tremor to his voice. He attempts a smile and fails miserably.

"Not as bad as I thought it would be. I guess it's beginner's luck," I say with a shrug.

The whole car seems to turn to me. Sylas has to turn back because he's driving, but he keeps glancing at me through the mirror.

"Levi, that isn't what usually happens." Austra studies me carefully, twisting the gold hoops around her wrists. "On my first time, they had to tie me to the car. Once we got to the school, it took them an hour and a half to get me free."

"I turned into a bear," says Spencer, more elsewhere than here. "I think I broke the person's hand that was next to me. Not on purpose. Bears are just... bigger."

"The maze knows your worst fears and will use it to their advantage," Aris says, his tone haunted. It makes me wonder what horrors the wall showed him.

I run through the scenes in my head. "What they showed me was horrible, but I didn't *feel* anything. You know? I just told myself it wasn't real, and I stayed in the car," I tell them honestly.

"You got lucky." Sylas rubs the ring on his finger. "As you grow older and see more things, the maze will know and the experience will worsen."

"Mr. Kilver, how is it a maze?" I ask.

"Levi, you can just call me Sylas. Mr. Kilver isn't my real name."

"Oh yeah." I wince. "Sorry."

"No problem. I get it. And to answer your question, we just enchanted some of the maze so we can ride through it. However, as destined by its creators, the maze must fulfill its duty to torture you mentally and or physically," says Sylas.

We settle into an comfortable silence, each of us deep in thought. I wonder what the others experienced, what their greatest fears are. Maybe this experience can grant me meaningful knowledge about myself. Say everything that I learned so far was true. Say that I'm part of a world I barely understand with red-eyed monsters. Then I would have to do a lot of training and I would never feel truly safe again. You would think that would be one of my greatest fears. Maybe some part of me already accepted that. It's pointless to dread something that I can't stop or change.

What I did see was Austra and Skye getting attacked by those creatures. Something tells me that that may not be the last time something like that happens.

"Hey Levi," says Sylas, having gained back some color in his face. "When we get to the school, I think you'll be rooming with my brother, Elias."

"He looks almost exactly like Sylas," Austra laughs, trying to lighten the mood. "Tall, skinny, has a face peppered with freckles. Green eyes and flaming red hair. You'll know him when you see him."

"He's nice– a little strange–but aren't we all?" Sylas gives me a grin through the mirror.

"Levi," says Austra. "Look!"

A beautiful, bustling town comes into view beyond the willows. The houses and shops are made of wood and stone. The windows shimmer with the last lights of the day. The buildings on the main road are intricate and detailed with a combination of the browns, golds, and greys.

We drive down the main street and my eyes glued to the side of the car the entire time. Through the windows, I see the strangest things. There's pheasants, cats, and very large dogs running around with their owners. Products that glow and smoke are sold at the stores and shops. One building has a fenced area with long reptile-like bodies of different vibrant colors and magnificent wings.

"Are those–?" I begin, pointing to the horned things.

"Yep. Dragons," says Austra, watching them fondly. "At Grantham Willow, you'll need one for class. We'll have to get you one soon."

I nod. *Okay, dragons are normal now.*

An old man walks on the path to my right with a shell on his back like a turtle. Another woman is draped in a long red velvet cloak, her nails long and deadly. Her hands work in strange, jerking motions, a low red mist pouring from her palms and into a shop.

Austra leans in and says, "She's just doing security on her building. It's normal for Sorceresses. They're a very paranoid Kingdom."

Every now and then I see shooting stars fly across the sky. They fly close to the Earth and seem to have a location. They make art in the sunset, decorating the reds, pinks, and oranges splattered across the canvas of dusk.

We follow the main road leading to another cluster of trees. The river, willows, and buildings abandon us. When we get to the foot of a cobblestone path that leads up to a forest, a large stream of glistening water blocks our way.

"Is that a moat?" I ask to nobody in general.

"Yep," Austra says, marveling at the rushing water.

"Wow," I breathe.

Sylas frowns. "We still need to find a way to make it a little more dangerous. It's too... mundane."

My mouth almost falls open. He's got to be joking.

"Well it could give us a few seconds in case of an attack. Those few seconds could be the difference between life and death," says Austra wisely with a tip of her chin.

Sylas clears his throat. "Aris can you do the Mass Charm?"

"I can try," he says. The boy dressed in black starts to mutter under his breath. His fingers twitch, like the lady in red, and Skye drifts out of the car and to where we are standing. She looks very peaceful, as though gravity has no effect on her.

"Ready?" asks Sylas, grabbing hold of a large duffle bag. In his other hand he holds an intricately decorated box with gold symbols and word carvings. Something about it seems old–ancient. Just looking at it, I felt remorse and the pain of loss and sorrow. My fingers twitch, urging me to reach for–

"I always like this part." Spencer smirks and tilts his chin upwards.

I shake my head to get myself out of that daze. *What in the world?*

Everyone takes lockets off from around their necks and dips the round balls of silver into the chilly river. Sylas walks forward and the water parts for him, like Moses and the Red Sea. A little circle surrounds him, the water entirely redirected, and the rest of the group does the same.

"Um... help?" I call, my voice getting higher at the thought of what lies beneath the ripples. It's about 20 feet across and I'm pretty sure that water isn't the only thing in it.

"Oh," chuckles Sylas, rubbing his head. "What did they say in the Six Kingdom's history class about what to do when you don't have your locket? Where is Skye when you need her."

"Apparently unconscious," says Spencer. Austra stomps on his foot with all her might. He doubles over in pain and shoots his sister a death stare, both already on the other side of the river.

"Oh yeah. Here's a knife," says Sylas, throwing it to me. I miraculously catch it without slicing something important off. "Drip your blood in the water. The whole point of the river is to prove that you aren't a Malevolent. No Malevolent would wear these lockets. Your blood will be a good enough proof."

My focus trains on my hand, then to the knife, and then back to my hand. "You sure?"

He laughs a full laugh. "Positive. Oh, and make sure to draw a good amount of blood or it won't work."

I take a deep breath and slice the back of my leg. I read somewhere that slicing your hand isn't the best place because of nerves–or something.

It stings in the open air, but it's nothing compared to what I experienced hours before. Taking a deep breath, I let some of the blood pool in my hand and then drop it in the river. A little circle of dry land within the river appears. With every drop, the larger and larger the circle gets. I wait for it to become big enough for me to step in and then place a foot onto the riverbed. The circle follows me like a shadow as I slosh through the mud of the river floor and to the other side.

We walk down the path and into a forest filled with evergreens and ferns. A weathered cobblestone trail leads the way. We wind through trees, over roots, and around a small mountain.

A massive fort-like building appears behind the trees, grander than anything I've ever seen. It towers over the evergreens with six levels. A huge bay crashes right up to one whole corner of the building with some islands in its very center. The willows graze the surface of the water while water pixies dance. I could have sworn I saw a tail flop out from the surface. On one side of the bank I can see an archery field and stables in the distance. All around the bay, beautiful, white sand beaches and sharp, jagged cliffs make their home.

Another wave of nausea sweeps over me and I collapse for the second time today.

Chapter 6

Levi

"He's awake," gasps a feminine voice.

"Quiet. He probably has a headache." *Sylas?*

Blinking away the sleep from my eyes, I strain to push myself to a sitting position. Everything is dark, except for the one lamp next to my bed, illuminating our faces like a fire pit. I must've slept long enough for the sun to leave for the night.

"How are you feeling, kid?" Sylas kneels at the side of my bed, smelling of mint. My former chemistry teacher pats my shoulder, offering a little comfort.

"What do you think?" I ask pointedly. "Sorry," I pause, wincing at the pain in my side. "I get crabby after I almost die." I pause for a moment and just listen to my breaths. The others watch me, not quite sure how to break the silence.

"All this wasn't a dream, was it?" I ask, pinching the bridge of my nose.

"Sorry," Austra says with a frown.

My mouth dries and I settle back into the pillows. "How long was I out?"

"We got here about an hour ago," replies Sylas.

Not too bad. I laugh in disbelief and study the room around me. Lines of hospital beds fill the hall. "Where am I?"

"You, my friend, are at Grantham Willow. Or at least the Infirmary of Grantham Willow," Sylas announces, a huge grin on his face.

Aris hands me a glass of water. I hesitate before receiving the cup, giving him a small nod in thanks. He tilts his head forward and his eyes don't even soften a fraction.

Austra paces at the foot of my bed. Her frizzy waves from earlier today are unruly, as if she's been tearing her hair out all day. She bites her lip in distress, the worry evident in the creases between her brows.

I take a sip of water and then look Sylas straight in the eye. "Do you all mind answering my questions now?"

"What would you like answered?" Sylas scoots the adjacent hospital bed closer to mine so he can take a seat.

"Can you just start from the beginning?" I've been giving bits and pieces, but nothing to connect them. There's too much missing for me to make a general guess as to what's happening.

"Yes," he sighs. "This may seem like a lot, but I think it's best we just rip off the band aid." He grabs my water glass and takes a sip for himself before starting. "It all started thousands of years ago. It was said that there was a world war. All creatures were being attacked from every angle. Families split apart and friends turned on friends to fight for a stone harder than a diamond, worth more than 15 million dollars per carat with today's money. Seven kingdoms decided that they all had a common goal: to stop the war and protect their territory.

"These kingdoms were the Royals, Sorcerers, Scholars, Warriors, Hunters, Malevolents, and the Unyielders. Today, we call the Unyielders, Masters. These Kingdoms united to form one society. At the time, these people didn't have magic. Without having full control over an area of magic, it made it very hard for these people to defeat the kingdoms around them.

"Years passed and the Kingdoms merged into each other, forming social classes based on the wealth of their Kingdoms and capabilities. To a certain extent, these social classes are still ingrained in many, being the source of much of the discrimination of prejudice in our society today.

"At one time during the war, the King, who was a Royal, realized that we were going to lose this ten-year war. He held a competition to reorganize the social classes. There was already a rebellion simmering in the West, so it was a perfect cover story.

"Each of the social classes held various tests and competitions to decide their Representative. Long story short, the Royal, or the King's son, won. The Malevolent was furious that he didn't get first, which would have granted him the spot as the new king and ruler.

"If he knew the real reason for the competition, he would have been much nicer to his competitors. The truth is, the King wasn't the one running the trials. It was the Fates."

I remember that term used right before I blacked out.

"The Fates," continues Sylas, "are basically the gods and goddesses of our world. They are the masters of, well, fate. They have many gifts, but their most notable is that they can influence fate, or what is to happen. The Fates set up the competition so perfectly that all the Kingdoms revealed their true colors. They wanted the Kingdoms to win the long war, so as the competitors showed their personalities and skills, the Fates decided on what gifts to give each of the individual kingdoms. All from which, the Fates possessed themselves. If you combine each of the gifts of the Kingdoms you would get a Fate.

"The Royals are natural born leaders. The Fates gave them the power to rule, heal, and see into the future. The Sorcerers are masters of deception and always had the heart and soul for magic. They were given the ability to wield magic as well as control one element, unique to themselves. Many refer to them as Elementals. The Scholars always were very knowledgeable. They were rewarded with the ability to make potions. Some are also telepathic, but it's a rare quality and a sign of a hard life. The Warriors were always good fighters and had fast reflexes. The Fates improved those and gave them the gift of being able to change into one animal based on the content of their souls."

So that explains Skye and maybe even the wolves.

39

"Then there are the Hunters, which my brother is. They always had a special connection to animals and nature. They received the gift to manipulate plants and to communicate with animals. Their weapon of choice is almost always a bow and arrow, so the Fates creating a tree whose wood in the form of an arrow can subdue a Malevolent.

"The Masters proved that they will never give up no matter the cost. They were given the trait of determination and the capability to master one thing, depending on their character and soul."

Sylas pauses and the others become as still as ice. "What about the Malevolents?" I ask, wanting to know more about the Kingdom of monsters.

He sighs and leans back in his chair. "Well, they showed that their souls were dark and evil. They were given the curse of never fully dying. Their souls would remain bent and twisted until the end of time. The lockets each of your classmates in this school wear hold all the souls of the Malevolents they subdued. Each contains some of that precious stone that caused all that heartache of war. It keeps them bound and trapped.

"In the Inside lands, weapons only work if they are connected to magic and the good of heart. A person from one of the Six Kingdoms or another creature has to be touching it in order for that weapon to subdue a Malevolent."

If I was able to subdue a Malevolent, then that means I'm part of the Six Kingdoms. But how?

"Wait, is this inherited? Like am I a part of the Six Kingdoms if my dad or mom is?" I think of my father–intelligent grey eyes and always reading a book. Perhaps a Scholar? Given his job as a researcher, it seems like a logical conclusion. Or maybe my mother...

"It's a long story as to why Kingdoms aren't inherited anymore. Now it depends on which qualities you have. Someone could be born to a family filled with Scholars, but in their soul, they may be more deceptive than smart, like a Sorcerer."

Spencer's golden eyes have a devious twinkle. "For example, I'm a Warrior, but Austra's probably going to be a Scholar or something."

I might not even become one. I hear Austra mutter faintly.

I give her a questioning look. "What did you say?"

"What?" she says, startled.

I tilt my head and frown. "Never mind. So, what am I?" There has to be a reason I'm here and why the Malevolents decided to invade *my* house. Unless, it was to get to my father. Speaking of which, he'll be horrified to find me gone with the door wide open.

I fight off a wave of panic and look down at Austra, who stares deeply at my eyes, with an intense focus. I shift, a bit uncomfortable and look to Sylas for an explanation, but Sylas is looking at me with that same intense stare.

"Um, what are you doing?"

Austra doesn't break eye contact with me when she says, "You can generally determine your Kingdom by eye color. Do you have a guess, Sylas?"

"No," says Sylas, with a puzzled look. All the others have the same expression. "Well, that can be expected. How old are you?"

"Fifteen as of late August."

"Well... you see, the Fates decide which gifts to give you around the age of fifteen. It should show up soon," says Sylas, patting me on the shoulder. "If you see your eyes change, let us know."

Austra continues to stare. "Maybe a Sorcerer like Aris. Sorcerer eyes are brown with a splash of color that corresponds to the element they wield. You sort of have brown, but not enough."

"Yeah, too much blue and green." Spencer raises an eyebrow. "Maybe a Water Elemental?"

A Water Elemental. I've always had an affinity for the rain, but I was really scared of the ocean as a kid. I must have a stricken face because Sylas frowns. "I know this must come as a great shock to you."

41

"Yeah," I whisper. "Just one more question. Why can the Malevolents come in other forms? The ones that attacked us didn't have normal hands." I shiver as I remember the claws that gripped my ankles the other day. I don't remember Sylas mentioning anything about shifting as one of their gifts.

Sylas' face becomes very haunted and the mood of the room drops. "They've figured out how to use a crooked type of magic to morph themselves into whatever they want," replies Sylas. "And it's working."

"At least, that's what they think is happening," adds Austra, her voice grave.

"What do you mean?" I ask

"We don't have any proof," argues Spencer.

"We don't have any proof that that's not happening," murmurs a dark voice. We all turn to Aris, who leans back in his chair, almost bored.

I nearly jump out of my skin when Sylas claps his hands together. "Well, I think that's enough for young Levi. All of you, get back to your dorms, it's almost past hours."

"Why'd you have to ruin the fun?" Spencer whines, shaking his head.

"I am teaching a Mastering class, so technically I am a professor. Most of the time, my job is to ruin the fun," he says with a playful wink. "Anyway, go and complete your assignment and settle back into your dorm rooms."

"Yes Professor," salutes Austra, playfully. "Have a nice rest, Levi."

"Wait, Sylas," I say, gabbing his arm. "What about my father. He's going to be worried. Shouldn't we tell him what's going on?"

"Don't worry, Levi. It's been taken care of. Sleep well," Sylas says. "I will be back when you wake up. The spell works better when you sleep soon after it's conjured. Farewell."

I wave them goodbye and my worry isn't lessened at the slightest. What does "*taken care of*" even mean. Despite the fact, I can't help but grin softly as I watch Austra and Spencer through the window. They poke fun at each other as they walk down the path to the school. Aris wordlessly follows them, trailing a safe distance behind.

I let my head fall to the pillow, tenderly, and run my hands down my face. The world I thought I knew, thrown down the hole. There are such things as magic, history other than the Romans and Mongols, and a whole Kingdom of monsters that want to kill people like me. Just hours ago, I was worried about my math test on Thursday.

Thoughts swim in my head until, yet again, I let the darkness swallow me. This time, there are no training sessions in my dreams.

…

Levi

My arm muscles cry as I try to move them from my sides. My whole-body aches and my head pounds. It takes a few minutes before the memories from the night before leak back into my brain. Groaning, I force myself to turn over and stare at the ceiling.

It's dark. I look around for a clock, wondering if I slept through the day. Footsteps sound from down the hall and I spot a tall, slim girl in a white t-shirt and jeans. I struggle to sit up, but she rushes over to stop me. She smells like the sea and has the aura of a warm summer day.

"Good morning, Levi. I think it's best you wait here for a moment. You have a little bit of time before Sylas gets here." She leans me back down and takes a seat next to me, her brown and blue eyes gleaming. "Nice to meet you. I'm Lila."

The name rings a bell. "Spencer's girlfriend?"

She sighs and nods, her brown and blue eyes gleaming in the half light. "As of right now, yes." She purses her lips and a flash of anger comes across her face. As soon as it's there, it's gone. "I'm on shift to watch after you. If you ever want some easy cash, late night shifts at the Infirmary is a good option." She pours a glass of water. I reach for it, but she pauses me with a finger.

"Let me take it." Her hands form a triangle, its tip pointing towards the glass. Soon her fingers start to twitch and I watch, amazed, as a drop of water rises from the glass and floats towards me. I open my mouth and gulp just as a door crashes.

Sylas rushes down to greet me. "How are you feeling?"

"Okay, I guess." I glance at the clock: 11:39. "Did I sleep the entire day?"

He lets out a short laugh and nods his head in confirmation. "The Premier's available to see you now." He comes to my side, swiftly. "Do you think you can walk?" He and Lila help me to my feet.

"I think so," I say, picking at my ripped shirt. Not the best outfit to meet one of the most important people in the school. I wince as my sore leg muscles struggle to support my weight. There are other more pressing thoughts to worry about.

Running a finger along the long white scar along my rib cage, my chest tightens from the memory of the pain. I put on my muddied tennis shoes and do my best to put one foot in front of the other. Sylas grabs my arm to help me regain balance, and I gladly accept the help. It comes back to me slowly: how to walk. Lila waves to us as we leave.

We make our way down a cobblestone path to the main building. It looks like a cross between a fort and a castle. It's in the shape of a rectangle donut with round towers at the corners. Flags poke out here and there with a logo that I can't quite make out. They wave proudly in the slight breeze.

Huge double doors make up the entrance, capable of letting in a dragon. Sylas walks up and whispers a phrase that I can't make out. The doors open slowly. When they're just ajar enough, Sylas and I slip in.

A grand crystal chandelier lights up the room with another large set of double doors on the opposite side leading into a courtyard. Some of those mini balls of light dart around the hall, eliciting a feeling of life and excitement. The ivy found its way inside and makes natural artwork across the stones. There's a lively buzz from the crowd of students that range from my age to about their early twenties. Some walk past us and whisper to each other, eyeing us curiously. My cheeks warm as I feel a little exposed with my half-tattered t-shirt.

"Sylas!" A cloud of curly brown hair runs full speed into Sylas' arms. She has a petite figure with hip length, frizzy hair. From what I can see, she's strikingly beautiful. It seems as though all the people from the Six Kingdoms have that certain glow to them. Even if their features aren't traditionally deemed attractive, the feeling you get around them makes them seem something different.

When they let go of each other, I can see intelligent grey eyes that pop. Her tie matches her eyes that glimmer with joy.

"Claire," exclaims Sylas with the biggest smile I've seen from him. "I'm so sorry I didn't come to visit you yesterday. I fell asleep down at the dragon stables because I couldn't find the energy to walk across campus. How was this place while I was gone?"

Claire purses her lips at the mention of the stables, but it's soon replaced with a dazzling grin. "Less cheerful. Your class misses you," she replies. "I've been doing my best, but since I am not a Master, it's not the same. To be honest, I think I like working in the library better."

"I'm sure you did fine." He pats my shoulder, remembering me next to him. "Let me introduce you to Levi Sage, our newest student at Grantham Willow."

"Oh! Is this the—"

"We really have to go," Sylas cuts. "After I take him to the Premier, I'll meet you at the North Tower. Okay?"

"Um… Sure. I'll be waiting." She scrunches her eyebrows and waves as we rush out of the hall.

45

We scurry to the left and rush past crowds of students dressed in formal attire and different colored ties. The hall is about the size of a one-way road with a series of classrooms on the side that face the courtyard at the center of the school. On the other side, there's huge, rustic windows that take up most of the wall. Ornate carvings decorate the stone, framing the tarnished glass.

When we reach the corner of the large school, my eyes search the wall of ivy. There's no doors. Just a corner overflowing with plants and flowers. But Sylas stops anyway.

"We're here," sighs Sylas and walks right into the vines.

"We're where?"

He steps into the ivy. "The Premier's Office, of course."

Brushing aside the ivy, all I find is the solidity of stones. "Um, where's the door?"

"Right here," he takes off his locket and places it on the stone behind the living curtain of vines. "We're here to see the Premier. This is Sylas Pursue here with Levi Sage. Permission to enter?"

"Permission granted," a voice replies, almost immediately. The stone wall gradually becomes translucent, like it was just a trick of the light.

"Wow," I say.

"When in need of entrances or staircases, look for the ivy," says Sylas and I follow him around a bright spiral staircase that appeared behind the wall. Small windows on the side allow us to see the bay and the... sleeping dragons. I shake my head and wonder if I'll ever get used to this.

We climb until we reach an ancient looking door at least nine feet tall. Sylas turns to me and grips my shoulders. "Before you go in, do your best to accept what you see or hear. It's easier than living in denial." He says it with such conviction it's hard to argue.

After seeing me nod, he huffs, "Okay then." I hold my breath as he knocks on the door twice. It opens without a creak and both of us step into the light.

Out of all the people that I could have guessed would be on the other side of the door, the person standing in front of me, the Premier, is none other than my one and only father.

Chapter 7

I look my father up and down–at his pristine suit jacket and neatly parted brown hair. The same man I saw when I left to go to school yesterday. The same man who missed half my soccer games, back-to-school nights, archery competitions… A wave of emotion rolls over me: betrayal, shock, bitterness–

"Hello Levi," says my dad with a warm smile.

"Hey," I breathe.

Needing space to think, I stride into the circular room. It's a cozy office, the bookshelves covering every wall except for the floor-to-ceiling window behind his desk. Everything's made out of a weathered, brown wood that give the room a sense of comfort. The large window shows the peaceful ocean stretching off into the distance with the crescent moon in the sky.

My father was never the most present parent, always having something to do or some place to be. I've always felt some reassurance thinking that it was just him and me in this world, no roots other than with each other.

I gesture to my surroundings and ask, "Is this where you've been all my childhood? At a school filled with gifted children and a part of a world that's been hidden from me all my life?"

The Premier runs a hand through his brown hair. People say that we don't look very similar, save for the brown hair, pointed jaw, and high cheekbones. My father would tell me my eyes were determined and focused like my mother's.

"All the things I did, I did for a reason. It may not be clear to you now, but one day you'll understand." I can't help but cringe at his words.

Most things in my life right now seem to need time to settle before I can understand. Call me young, but I don't want to wait.

I give him a look of disdain and use the hate to hide the sting.

He frowns at me and says without a trace of remorse, "I kept you from the truth to protect you. Your mother and I thought it was for the best."

My heart pauses at the mention of my *mother*. My dad doesn't talk about her by always avoiding the pressing topic when he can. The only thing I know about her is that she died in a car crash four months after I was born, hit by a drunk driver on the way home from work. I wasn't old enough to remember much, but I can almost picture a beautiful face with sharp grey, eyes and sleek, brown hair.

Grey eyes. What kingdom would that make her? The same as my father's?

"How could you possibly think moving around the world is safer?" All the lies, keeping me from making friends, having a normal childhood...

"Your mother and I had a theory–"

"You did all this because of a theory," I exclaim, my chest heaving.

"Yes, Levi. A theory worth everything." The conviction in his voice startles me. Then the weight of his words sinks into my mind.

"What was the theory?" My voice is deathly calm.

"I–I cannot tell you."

"Why not?" I slam my fist onto his desk, sending books falling from where they stood on its corner. After nearly dying, multiple times I might add, in the last 48 hours, the least he could offer me is the truth.

The Premier grimaces. "We have to wait and see what Kingdom you mature into. Now, Levi, can you please take a seat?" He gestures to a very comfy rustic looking chair in the front of his wooden desk.

I meander to it reluctantly and sink into the soft leather.

"Mr. Pursue, you may leave now. You have done well," says my dad with a look of fondness. I feel a pain in my chest and wonder how many kids my father has helped raise here when he could have been with his own son.

Sylas smiles wide. He glances at me, winks, and dashes out the room to meet his date. What I would do to trade places with the red-haired Master.

My dad makes his way to his desk and sits down gracefully without making a sound. "Now," he says calmly. "What will be your first question?"

I open my mouth to answer but a loud slam of a door cuts me off.

"Premier David! What awful mission did you send my daughter on? She has managed to humiliate her entire family in a matter of hours!" A robust man slams his fist on my father's desk. My dad doesn't even flinch.

At least he didn't fix the books I'd knocked down before he came.

His black hair contrasts with the pale, thin scar that ruins his once handsome face. The gold in his eyes dare you to look away and his dark eyebrows making them seem like dark pits. Skye's eyes are warm, but his are the gold that cuts.

My father merely plays with the silver pen on his desk. "Taking into account that you didn't approach me about this until now suggests that your priorities don't lie with your daughter."

His eyes shoot up and he curtly gestures to me, eyes not leaving the man of nails and anger. "Levi, since my Deuxieme, or second in command, has so decided to barge in, please meet Deuxieme Fervent, Skye's father."

I turn my body a bit and study him more carefully. Skye has his striking eyes and high cheekbones that prove their relation. I do recognize this man, which sends a wave of fury down my spine.

He's the man I saw in the Maze of Tepidity.

"Hello, Deuxieme Fervent. Skye was very valiant the other day," I say with the politest voice I could muster.

All he does is grunt in reply and sprint to the window. I fly out of my chair, thinking he's going to tackle my father. I stop dead when the Deuxieme runs right past my dad and jumps out the open window.

"Whoa!" I run to the door, expecting to see a splash of white in the water. Instead, a hawk darts right past my ear and speeds away. Well–now the vice principal hates me. Not to mention, he can turn into a predatory bird.

My father's eyes focus back on me. As if realizing the situation we were in just moments before, he clears his throat. "I trust Sylas has given you the concise version of our history?"

I nod my head, having lost the will to act on the anger that I feel. Everything's just… numb.

"Have you practiced archery or self-defense since we moved?"

I nod again, recalling the night before that fated day. My dad made sure to set up my targets the day we moved in.

"Well, I hope your athletic history will help you in Grantham Willow. This school will not be like the schools you're used to." He picks a piece of lint from his suit.

"Yeah. I picked that up already."

Ignoring my jab, he continues. "You will have a longer school day–"

I sag in my chair.

"–12 periods. 45 minutes each. 5-minute passing period. You must take The History of the Six Kingdoms, Self Defense, Fighting with Weapons, three electives of your choice, Study of Magical Beings and Plants, Dragon Riding, Survival class, and three or more classes depending on what kingdom you are in. For example, if you are a Scholar, then the extra classes would be potions, History of After Time, History of Before Time, etc." He takes a breath and leans back in his seat, a smug look on his face. "Very fun indeed."

I rub my temples. I had thought the most I would have to worry about was monsters. "Do you think I'll be able to catch up with everyone?"

He waves a hand. "You'll be fine. You will take the Warriors' classes until you mature."

"Why Warriors?" Recalling the harshness in Spencer's stature and Skye's bat form, I'm not particularly keen to join them in a classroom.

The Premier just shrugs, ignoring my hesitance. "They will toughen you up a little. Austra's taking them until she matures too," he pauses his shuffling of papers. "If she matures, I mean. She has until December, so perhaps your presence will spur something in her veins."

"What happens if she doesn't?"

"She'll have to go to the Outside world."

"Oh," I whisper, shifting in my seat.

"It happens from time to time. Look to the Fates to help in this case. Doesn't do well to dwell on such matters."

My breath hitches. I'm in the same situation as Austra. "How do you know if I'm part of one of the Kingdoms?"

He rubs his chin in thought. "Did your eye color change today?"

"Not necessarily," I reply, trying to remember the last time I had the time to study myself in the mirror. My father always made me take the harder classes, so my freshman year felt more like a high schooler's junior year.

"You may think I'm not an attentive father, but I've watched your eyes very closely. They were a brownish hazel when you were born. In the past day they've gotten bluer and greener," he says and crosses his arms with finality. "When the change started, I called Skye, Spencer, Sylas, and Austra to watch over you. The local Werewolves even stepped in, with the help of a Warrior named Kalica."

"Do you know what I could be?" My voice sounds weak, even to me.

"That is something only the Fates can answer," he replies, not too particularly worried, which I guess is a good sign. Again, with the Fates.

"Another question," I state and hold up a finger. "Can you talk about the Fates a bit more?"

"That's a wonderful question," my dad says and adjusts his glasses. "Though we accept any religion here at Grantham Willow, generally the Kingdoms believe that the Fates are our gods and goddesses watching over us and provide gifts to our people. Without that, we could never stand against any other magical creature out there. Though we don't have a church or synagogue, we honor them in our own way by using our gifts to protect and defend the Six Kingdoms."

"How many Fates are there?"

"Seven. One for each Kingdom, each with the decision of who to gift. Though they all possess the powers of the Seven Kingdoms, they only have the ability to give away one. If the Fates pick wrong, then the soul of the person they wrongfully gifted will die. So even the Malevolent Fate, who we call Hardorous, cannot over gift people to fill their population. We have a holiday for each Fate's birthday, so you will learn them soon enough."

"Even the Malevolent Fate?"

"His birthday is unknown to the Six Kingdoms and will never be celebrated within our borders," he says with a hint of darkness to his tone.

Letting out a puff of breath, I lean back in the chair.

"If you need to ask more questions that only I can answer, you may call through here." My father holds out his hand. One of those balls of light fizzes and glows in his palm, yet it doesn't burn him. It like a firecracker that continues to flicker and not burn out.

"These can pass for shooting stars at night but can't be seen in the day. We use them to communicate and watch Lightning TV. You can't watch Lightning TV with this guy, but you can communicate. Just whisper who you want him to fly to with a message. He'll get to that person faster than a text message."

"Thanks," I say with an unintentional bite to my words. I hold my hand over the burst of light to see if it's at least semi warm. "And, uh, I think I lost my phone."

"I'm not surprised. You won't need it anymore anyways." He adjusts his sleeve and looks towards the door. "What are you going to name him?"

"Him?"

"Oh. In your Study of Magical Beings class, you will learn about this guy. They're called Lightning Critters. Here," he passes the ball of lightning to me.

The Lightning Critter is warm to the touch, but not burning. Sensing my surprise, my father says, "They only burn you when they want to. Just–don't irritate him."

"That's comforting," I mumble and pause for a moment to think. "I think I'll name him Sparky." The little creature lets out a brighter spark, as if agreeing with the name. I smile at the light.

"Good choice." My dad pulls out a silver piece of jewelry from a drawer in his desk. "Before I forget, here's your locket. It signifies that you are a member of the Six Kingdoms. It's like a passport of sorts."

I take the necklace, identical to the ones I saw on my friends earlier. There are five bumps. Five bumps for the lives I took or captured, if what Sylas says is true. The essence of the monster that gave me the scar at my side lies inside the metal. I shiver at the thought.

Someone knocks on the door as I put the silver locket around my neck.

"Come in."

Too intrigued, I don't look up. It's cold to the touch and surprisingly very light. A part of me realizes it will get heavier, day by day, as the weight of the souls I subject to endless darkness accumulate in the metal.

"Levi, Spencer will lead you to your dorm." He gets up from where he was seated at his desk and hands Spencer a roll of parchment. I would've missed the transaction if it weren't for the silver seal that caught the light.

"Well, I'll see you sometime soon. Goodbye Levi." A simple dismissal, but there's that tilt to his chin that tells me to be careful. Despite being in such a well-guarded fortress, he gives me that same look that he would always give me before I exited the door to go to school.

Spencer greets me with a roll of his eyes, his hair messier than yesterday. From the looks of it, I don't think he got any sleep.

While walking out the doors, I turn slightly and point a finger at my father. "This isn't over."

He gives a slight nod, resignation evident on his face.

Spencer and I make our way down the stairs and into the main hall again. There are no students to be seen and only the howls of the wind to fill the silence. Out of the corner of my eye, I notice Spencer gloomily looking out the windows on the side of the hall out into the full moon night.

There's a small urge to ask him what's wrong, but frankly I feel the same. Anger courses through my veins vigorously with a bit of sadness that is reflected in Spencer. I wonder if I will ever be able to trust my father again.

"The boy's dorm rooms are always here, on the West Side," I nearly jump, not expecting him to speak. "The girls are on the East Side. Initials and Secondaries on the fourth floor, Junior and Central on the fifth, and Cardinal, Seniors, and Paramounts on the top floor."

"The what?"

"They're grade levels. A lot of it is self-explanatory, like Initials and Secondaries are the first and second year. Just know that the Seniors and Paramounts are the oldest and the Central and Juniors are in the middle."

Both of us gaze out the window to our right, into the water that stretches for miles on end. It seems so peaceful, despite the sounds of the waves pounding at the school that grows louder and louder as we near the corner.

We turn to a corner covered in ivy, behind a slight dent in the wall. Now that Sylas pointed it out, there's little patches of ivy all over the place, leading to separate parts of the school that I have yet to explore.

Mistaking the reason for my confused face, he says, "There are no clear doors in this place, with the exception of some of the classrooms you saw."

Dread fills me as I think about trying to find my way around. "Do you have a map by any chance?"

"No. It goes against security."

We look at the wall of ivy, the space only lit by a single oil lantern. "I have something to do right now, so just do the thing with the locket and go to the first level with a door. Austra and Aris should be there to greet you."

Before stepping away, I ask, "Do you want to talk about it? Whatever's bothering you?"

He rolls his eyes. "I left–on that mission to save your helpless soul–before telling Lila. She's, well. Let's just say, she's not happy." He doesn't even say goodbye before he walks away.

I frown as a sliver of guilt works its way to my chest. They'll work it out.

I do as he instructed and sure enough the wall becomes translucent. Inside is a very wide spiral staircase, one clearly meant for many people going up and down at a time. Ivy works its way up to the ceiling in its curvy designs, following the slope of the railing. A tall window follows me all the way up, showing the grand ocean that glows with water pixies, water lilies, and many other magical creatures unknown to me.

I can't help but think that this all could be a dream. Just yesterday, I was an average teenager going to school, mad about moving around so often. Now I'm a part of a magical kingdom of people with more creatures and stories than I can even fathom.

I remember what Mrs. Pursue told me and turn off onto the fourth floor. Placing my locket on the plain wall, a wooden, fancy double door, nearly 10 feet in height, slowly comes to view. I give the door a good rap and after a few moments it opens slightly, just wide enough for me to go in.

I barely have time to take in the grandness of the corridor before a boy pushes himself from the side of the hall. "So, you're the Premier's son," he snickers.

I fight a groan and turn to the source of the voice. "It sure seems that way." I face a tall boy around my age, radiating arrogance. The sneer plastered on his face and the knife at his hip make me stand a little straighter, wishing I'd asked my father for something to defend myself.

Two of his friends stand up from where they were stationed on the other side of the door. All three are clearly bigger than me, shoulders the size of door frames. My eyes dart around the hall and access my options for a swift exit. The corridor seemed long, but I don't know how it turns, the hiding places. The three boys certainly know more than I do. If I went backwards, out where I came, I would have a head start advantage.

No. I square my shoulders. The first confrontation means everything and I'm not about to have words floating around that I'm the type to run.

"My father is second in command of the USA Six Kingdoms government. That puts him on top of yours," he brags, walking around me. Like a vulture circling its prey.

I stare right into his purple eyes, "Good for you."

"Seems like you got yourself in a bind," he teases, gesturing to my tattered shirt.

"Oh that," I say, a grin tugging at my lips, "I don't think you want to know."

He laughs to himself, but then pries a little more. "And, what Kingdom might have you matured in?" he retorts with a smirk. "What do you think, boys? His eyes look quite normal to me."

I scoff, hiding a bit of shame, "I don't think that's any of your business, either. Can you please let me pass?" His two friends move into the hall, blocking the way to my room. Lovely.

"I too want an answer to my question," he sighs with a wicked grin. Not bad at intimidation, I give him that. But there's no steel in his gaze. Having met enough tormentors at various schools, I know which ones fight back when you swing.

One good thing about my dad is that he didn't lecture me when I came home with a split lip. He would help me patch up, without a word. Then, once he finished, he would ask me to tell him everything that happened, which I would. Each swing and blow that I took, demonstrating with him along the way. Then he'd teach me what to do to block or attack and tell me not to let them get a hit on me next time.

Biting the inside of my cheek, I reply, "As of now, nothing. May I pass now?" Growing more tired by the minute, I tap my foot impatiently. What I would give to just jump into a warm bed and change out of these clothes.

The corners of his mouth bend upward at my statement, as if he could smell my defeat. The features of his face are sharp, the lines filled with mischief and schemes that I hope aren't pointed to me. I thought that I was done with gaining more enemies for the weekend.

"Well, I guess we'll see tomorrow. I'm sure the return of the Premier's long-lost son will be the best story this place has had in ages." I look at him flatly, my knuckles turning white at my sides.

"Shut up Nikolai," someone yells angrily from across the hall.

Austra, Aris, and two other boys I don't recognize come into the hall. Austra looks like she's about to explode.

58

"Well look who it is," says the boy, his grin not leaving his face. "I guess you made friends with the girl who hasn't matured and probably never will, a Sorcerer whose element is useless, and the Hunter that only ever makes his little plants grow. Oh, and not to mention the Darkness Wielder, the epitome of a bad omen." Aris moves to go forward and Austra grabs his arm and gives him a small shake of her head.

Nikolai smirks with satisfaction and turns to me. "Would you like me to continue?"

"Yes, actually," I reply. He raises an eyebrow. I walk to the other side of the dimly lit hall, away from him and towards the group that saved my life a day ago. I make sure to bump the shoulders of his friends on my way though.

"Because maybe you might get to the part where you're just a self-conscious, spoiled boy who will go nowhere in life. It was nice meeting you," I conclude and walk away with a shake of my head.

Chapter 8

Levi

Grantham Willow is a beautiful place. It's easy to tell that centuries of use have worn the white marble in the entrance area and that the gold desks and mirrors that line the halls could probably fund a small nation. It's beyond belief. I can't completely say the same for some of the people it houses. But I won't let them cloud my judgment.

Austra explains that the entrance hall for the boys' dorms splits into two hallways going opposite directions on different sides of the school, one for the Initials, the other for the Secondaries.

While I angrily storm down the hall, I study the plastered walls, painted a warm beige with crown molding rimming the ceiling. Electricity is also a thing here which I'm grateful for. When my dad said that I wouldn't need a phone, I thought I was going completely off the grid. It's slightly comforting knowing that I'll be able to see where I'm walking in the middle of the night.

"Levi, sorry you had to be greeted by Nikolai. He isn't exactly the best example of what Grantham Willow has to offer," says one of the boys that I didn't recognize before.

"Oh! Levi, meet Elias Pursue and Makai Ardent," presents Austra, sheepishly. "They're your roommates for the year."

"I've heard a lot about you," says Elias as he shakes my hand. His piercing emerald eyes are startling against the bright red of his hair.

I give the boy a smile. I'm through with making enemies for the week. From now on, I'll be strictly on a "making friends" agenda not a "making people want to kill me" agenda.

Makai does the same, his hand is cold and firm in mine. He has tanned skin, like Austra's, and black, curly hair. There's a tilt to his smile that makes you wonder if he has something up his sleeve. His eyes are a cloudy brown, not in a way that would suggest a lack of focus. There's just a hint of grey that looks like there's a storm brewing in his iris.

My eyes catch on the plaques, bordered with gold, next to each door that lines the halls. Each with what seems like the names of the occupants, the year, and their kingdom. Little mailboxes stick out from the wall next to the door, all pretty much spread apart, making for good sized rooms.

"There are bathrooms near the center of our hallway and at the end of this one," instructs Austra. Every now and then someone will walk down the hall and give us a questioning glance.

When we pass a few doors after the first bathroom, we reach Room 205. I study the plaque next to our door: Elias Pursue, Kingdom: Hunter; Makai Ardent, Kingdom: Sorcerer; Levi Sage, Kingdom: Unknown.

"Who were those guys back there by the way?" I glance back, half expecting them to come charging down the hall looking for blood.

"Nikolai's from a powerful family in the Royal Kingdom. The power and wealth got to his head," says Aris and sends a pointed look to the boy to his right. Makai jumps and scowls at the Sorcerer. At least I wasn't the only one who hadn't noticed the boy of shadows. Austra just gives Makai an apologetic look. Aris shrugs and leaves, his black cloak flying behind him.

Austra purses her lips in his direction but walks into the room when Elias opens the door for her.

When we go inside, I expect to see the same walls and carpet as the hall, but instead there's only beige stone. A large fireplace makes up for the cold, sending a warm light onto the reddish rug near its base.

Light, flowy material hangs from the bars of the three canopy beds like curtains and the beds themselves are draped with white quilts.

"They took out the walls and rug for Elias' plants," explains Austra.

"How did you manage that?" I ask, wondering how much it would have cost and the logistical aspects of it.

"A while back I went on a mission and the Premier owed me," he replies, nonchalantly. "He just brought in a Sorcerer and it was done." Right. *Magic.* "My plants need nooks and crannies to weave their roots in. Plus, some of my babies need dirt. Dirt and carpet don't mix well."

I look around the room and sure enough, green vines and leaves scatter the room, wrapping themselves around the poles of the canopy beds, decorating the walls, covering the balcony railings outside the glass French doors.

"Is there a place where I can put my Lightning Critter?" I ask and hold out the little guy. I nearly forgot about the creature, but it let out a burst of heat after that small encounter with Nikolai.

"Oh, I keep mine here," Makai says, gesturing to a large, clear glass jar on his nightstand. "You have one too." And sure enough one identical to Makai's on the bed closest to the balcony. "You only need to keep them in during the night. Throughout the day you might want to call on them to send a message."

"It's more humane, too," mutters the Hunter. He walks over to the balcony doors and opens them to let a nice cool breeze seep through from the darkness. "One of the staff members came in and left you clothes and uniforms for school. All you need to remember is that you need a button-down shirt, slacks, and a tie that corresponds to the kingdom you're in," says Elias, petting one of the purple vines to the left of my bed.

"You'll wear a white tie, like me," says Austra with a hint of bitterness.

Letting out a long yawn, I run a hand over the woolen quilt that drapes over the soft silk sheets of my bed.

"I grew some moonlit flowers around the posts. They make beautiful night lights," says Elias proudly. "Some extra comfort never hurts." He walks to his bed to grab some clothes from his dresser. "Well, the plants and I can sense you two have some unfinished business." he says, pointing at Austra and I. "Solve it before I get back because we have a busy day tomorrow." With that he exits the room, Makai at his heels, most likely to get ready for the night.

Austra looks over at me with remorse.

Better to not beat around the bush. "Did you try to befriend me because of your mission," I ask with a voice of stone. The last thing I want is to seem helpless or dependent on her answer. All I want now is the honest truth.

She looks at me with innocent brown eyes and her gaze falls down to her hands, twisting her rings, again. "No. I really enjoyed getting to know you and I'm sure Skye did too."

"Please, promise me that if there's another time my father asks you to do something that involves me, you'll tell me?" I already know the answer before she opens her mouth.

"I'm bound by the blood in my veins to never break a promise to your father when I go on a mission. He makes everyone swear on their life to not lie to him or go against his wishes. It's called the Elven Blood Promise." She looks around us, scanning the balconies around us for open windows or doors. "Fine. I'll find a way to let you know. If I find it necessary."

"You've got some repaying to do. But I trust your word and life is too short to hold grudges." She nods in thanks. I shrug it off and I walk over to my dresser and run my fingers along the carvings painted in silver and the worn, cold metal handles.

"Iron handles keep pixies from getting into your things," Austra says, walking into the room and sitting on Makai's bed.

63

I nod in acknowledgement. On top of the dresser, in a fancy wooden case filled with navy blue velvet, are my white ties. The ties are like any other, ironed to perfection, but with one gold star at the end of the tail.

"What's this for?" I ask, pointing at the pin.

"It shows what year you are at Grantham Willow," replies Austra, her mind off somewhere else.

Turning away, I examine my new belongings for a bit, while Austra takes off her locket and brushes her thumb across the smooth surface tenderly.

"Is it normal to have dots on your locket?" I ask looking at my own. Five dents remind me of that fateful night.

"Very rare. Unless you are really good like my brother or Skye. They have a million. You earn a mark every time you subdue a Malevolent." She breathes out a long exhale. "I wish I just had one," Austra says, glancing out the balcony doors. "The whole school thinks I'm here on borrowed time."

"Why don't you get Spencer to tell them otherwise," I ask, thinking of the intimidating Warrior.

"He isn't as dominant here as your former school. There are bigger, more ruthless people here. He, along with Skye, are very good actors. When they go on a mission, their personalities are totally different depending on their situation. It's easier to feel confident in a place where people don't know you sometimes."

She puts her locket back on. "Skye is so much more... harsh, here. Maybe it's because of her father, but she was unusually nice when we were on that mission. Don't expect her to offer you any more kindness than what you saw during that piece of time."

I gather some clothes to change into. My ripped top is starting to itch. I wonder if I'm a Scholar like my father. My memory is rather good, perhaps even photographic, and school was never extremely hard for me.

Or perhaps I'm a Warrior, like Skye. Then it occurs to me. That day she flew us away from the Malevolents...

"So, Austra? What animal can Skye turn into? I didn't see her clearly." My memory of it is a little foggy because, well, we were being chased after Malevolents.

"You'll get a better look during class when she wakes up. It's amazing," she says while walking to the door. "I have to leave, Levi. It's getting late," she says, checking the golden clock on Elias' desk. "Plus, you look like Grantham Willow's library cat tore you to shreds." I fight the urge to ask her if that has actually happened before.

"Well, I fought a monster and survived. I think I deserve a pass."

...

Levi

"Mate, we have a busy day ahead of us," Elias shouts, waking me from my endless pit of thoughts. He opens the thin, sheer curtains, letting the light blaze around the room. Elias goes outside as I sit up and rub my eyes of sleep. He holds a hand above a planter of sunflowers and helps them turn to the direction of the newly risen sun.

I look to my left where Makai still lays sound asleep and snoring so loud, I wouldn't be surprised if our neighbors could hear him. I see why Elias shouted.

Elias storms over to Makai's bed, lifts the blanket, and yells, "WAKE UP!"

I cover my ears in shock. All Makai does is shift, lift his head, and ask, "Huh?"

"Get up. We're going into town today and I would love to have you come along." Elias turns and leaves to fiddle with his things and Makai falls right back into bed.

65

Elias stands in the center of our balcony with his hands behind his back. His forehead scrunches as he gazes at the sky. "It looks like it's going to rain. You both better wear a jacket," warns Elias.

Waving it off I say, "I like the rain."

Shaking his head, "Still, you should–"

"Yeah don't worry." I walk out to the balcony and stand next to him. "I'll bring something." Closing my eyes, I let the droplets sink into my skin, and smile.

There's a flash in the corner of my eye. A Lighting Critter darts around the room freely, startling a sleepy Makai who just came through the door. The ball of light zips right past my head in greeting and boomerangs right back to me.

It says in my father's voice, "Levi, I left some money in your mailbox for your dragon. Also, for your electives, I recommend first aid and a language. Do what you want, but in my many encounters with death, I found those the most useful. Sincerely, Dad." And the critter exits the room like lightning.

"My dragon?" I look at the others who don't seem alarmed at the slightest.

"I would listen to him," Makai yawns, splitting his messy, brown waves down the middle.

Frowning, I ask, "About what?"

"About the electives. I agree with your dad," Elias says, putting on a black sweatshirt with an intricate emblem on the chest over the heart. "I chose the same and they're pretty useful. Especially the first aid."

"I guess I'll do these then. What languages are there?"

"Well there's werewolf, Valian, and pixie. But most of those speak English pretty well though. Then there's elf and banshee. Trust me, you don't want to do banshee. It involves a lot of screaming."

"Huh. Which one would you recommend?"

"I do werewolf. It's just a lot of howling." Makai wraps a small belt around his waist. A simple, matt knife is sheathed in its holder. "I recommend you do something different though, just in case we're put on a mission together."

"And I do elf," says Elias. "Account for me too."

Nodding my head, I analyze the options. I guess it's between Valian and pixie. I've met the pixies, so it would be useful to be able to speak their language. Then again, Valian seems interesting. "What is a Valian?"

"Vampires," clarifies Elias. "Valian's their proper name. They don't like all the stigma around their Outside land name. There was a time when Valians were one of the most prominent Warriors out there, but now there aren't that many. It's a sad story, really."

"Okay then, I guess I'll do Valian?"

"It would be politically relevant," says Makai with an approving nod. "Whenever I visit the Palace, the government officials are always talking about the Werewolf and Valian conflict. According to his sources, it's getting heated."

He pets one of his Venus flytraps before saying, "We should head to the Capricorn. But send a Lightning Critter to the Premier first on what electives you'll do."

A tinge of anger rises at the mention of my father, but I nod. I walk over to my dresser and lift the jar caging Sparky. The creature darts past my face and around the room, celebrating his freedom, before coming back to hover in front of my nose.

"How do I do this?" I ask no one in particular, looking nervously at the flashing specimen.

"Just say the message as you would in a letter. And make sure to say who you want it to go to," replies Elias, tending to his plants. He holds a wilted flower in his palms. It floods back with life, turning a vibrant red.

"Okay then," I say, and then clear my throat. "Dear Premier Sage, I'll take these electives: First Aid, Valian, and Extra Practice Dueling. Sincerely, Levi Sage." With that, Sparky zooms out of the room through the French doors to wherever my father is at the moment.

The Makai and I get ready for the day and wash up. Elias and growing a sunflower when we come back. "After breakfast, we'll visit Skye and then find Sylas to take us to town to get your dragon, they're a requirement to have at Grantham Willow. I already sent a message to Sylas, letting him know that we'll meet him at around 9," says Elias. "Makai, did you hear about the new protocols? We have to wait until our Junior year before we can go to town on our own."

"Yeah," groans Makai, making sure to untuck his shirt. "I heard there was an attempt to breach the Wall last week." Based on Elias' solemn nod, it's clear that this information isn't just some passing gossip. I wonder just how many conversations Makai has spied on since coming to Grantham Willow.

My blood runs cold. *Malevolents? Trying to get past the Wall?* "You're kidding?"

"Even our defenses aren't impenetrable." Elias takes a deep breath. "Let's go down now."

"Levi, you'll feel like a new person," Makai says, as we head out of the room. I stop at the little mailbox. Tiny white flowers on vines wrap itself around the box, likely Elias' work."I've tried some of the food you eat in the Outside world. It's rather bland. Wait until you try the food the Masters make."

I take out the little envelope and find a wad of money on the inside, each bill a pastel purple.

"Well would you look at that," says Makai, looking over my shoulder.

"What?"

Elias comes over as well. "That's one of the Grantham Willow envelopes."

I study the paper. "What makes it so important?"

Makai points to the silver symbol on the front. "That's their symbol." It's the same symbol on Elias' jacket, but instead this one is an outline in blood red. "If it's on an envelope or object, it marks it as property of this school. If someone touches it, they're jinxed and paralyzed for 60 hours with a beacon that signals the Premier of its location. You do not want to mess with those."

"I mean, what is it of?" I look at the symbol more closely. It seems like a group of different types of weapons arranged as a group.

"It's said to represent all the kingdoms through the different objects," Elias says, his eyes lighting up at the question. "Every couple decades or centuries, a Fate is born on Earth to help defend us against the Malevolents. His Companions, one from each Kingdom, have to earn a certain weapon to be able to defeat the Malevolents. After the Companions succeed in their trials to earn their weapon, they are then considered Representatives. See the bow and seven arrows, those represent the Hunters and Huntresses because that's their weapon of choice."

We start to walk down the hall, but I continue to study the envelope. "The shields are for the Masters because of their well-roundedness and the ability to deflect any obstacle. The severed armor is debatable," Makai says, pointing to the armor for a hand. "Some think it's the Warriors because the fingers are in the shape of claws. The book is for the scholars for obvious reasons. The little glass ball, right there, is for the Royals because of their ability to see the future. The staff is for the Sorcerers because some powerful Sorcerers use them to channel their power. Then the skull on the side," he says gravely, "that's for the Malevolents, representing the death that follows them like a shadow."

"What about the sword in the center?" I ask.

"That's for the Fates. It is said to be the coolest weapon ever created," Makai laughs.

"It seems weird that it would be on an envelope with just money in it. Levi, look through it again," Elias says.

Sure enough, between two of the bills is my schedule.

"Put that in a safe place," warns Elias. "I lost mine on the first day."

He opens the large wooden door with ease and we follow him out the door. Light trickles through the long narrow window. "Hmm," comments Elias, frowning. "Doesn't the wall look a tad bland today?"

He flicks his hand toward the ceiling and the veins of green spread across the stone. With another movement of his wrists, little pastel blue flowers spring up along the vines.

"Close your mouth," chuckles Makai. "You'll get used to things like this soon."

I scoff, schooling my features.

Once we go out the secret entrance, the cold morning air hits me. The wonderful ancient stone walls tower around me, the classrooms vacant. Elias and Makai lead me through one of the large double doors and into the beautiful courtyard. Students hang around the grounds. Some sit on the benches in groups while others race their Lighting Critters around the courtyard. A beautiful cherry tree stands in the middle of it all, full of snow-white flowers.

As we walk by, most of the students stop to watch. They whisper as we pass and I do my best to not cringe at the eyes that follow me.

"The flowers are kept fresh throughout the year by Paramount Hunters. It's considered to be a great honor. Only the people at the top of their class get to do it," Elias says dreamily. "Unless a Scholar can slap the knowledge needed to do that into me, I'm screwed."

"Come on," Makai says, rolling his eyes. "You literally grow moss for fun. Believe in the Fates."

We walk across the large open lawn and through the gigantic wooden doors into the Capricorn. The wonderful smell of eggs and bacon fill my nose, nearly making me drool. I don't think I've had a

70

proper meal in over a day come to think of it. Tables are scattered around the hall with a buffet on the far side of the wall. A stained-glass window makes some of the light entering the room have a tint of red, yellow, and blue.

I grab a plate and stuff as much food on it as I possibly can, even the weirder options that I've never seen before. Figuring I had a rough start to the morning, I picked up a couple chocolates from the dessert table.

I make sure to follow Elias and Makai around closely, so it looks like I know where I'm going. Groups of students crowd around certain desks, most separated by Kingdom. There's a table of Scholars in the corner of the Capricorn, textbooks opened. Another table has a group of growling Warriors, their canines out. Two of them seem like they're going to get into a fight. Elias and Makai don't seem to notice and walk towards Austra, who sits at a table next to a window overlooking the sea.

She puts some berries in her oatmeal before glancing at the paper in my hand. "Good morning Levi." Gesturing to the paper, she asks, "Can I look at your schedule?"

Taking a seat, I hand her the parchment and dig into my breakfast. The purple looking piece of lettuce I picked up is sweet, yet savory. It's nothing like anything I've had before. My eyes widen and Makai smiles at my surprise. He wasn't kidding when he said the food was amazing.

"I have your first class, and all of the last five. Huh, all except your language class actually. I guess your father wanted someone to walk you around." She hands the paper to Makai and Elias.

"I have Self Defense with you," says Elias. "Promise not to laugh when I make an absolute fool of myself. Last Wednesday I almost got a concussion." The Hunter is a tall, lanky kid, nothing like some of the students I see walking around. But his shoulders are toned, probably from endless archery practices.

71

"Only if you promise not to laugh at me. I'm totally out of my element," I say in between bites. Ever since this morning, I've had a weird feeling in my stomach. I haven't gotten nervous for the first day of school since grade school.

"It's a deal then."

"It doesn't seem like we have a class together, Levi," says Makai, shrugging. "I think you'll be fine without my company though." He gives me a wink.

We finish up our breakfast, talking about what will be different and the same. They tease me about trying not to get killed during class. (Apparently, the possibility is there, but it's uncommon.)

When we finish our food, we leave the plates where they are. Austra says that pixies who have committed crimes against the Six Kingdoms pick them up as part of their sentence. It doesn't make me feel any better about my safety in this school though.

Austra and Elias lead me out of the Capricorn, pass the courtyard, and through another double door, cutting through to the outside of the school. To my left is a beautiful vast green field where trees are spread around the carpet of green, each completely unique.

Austra follows my gaze and her face softens. "It's called the Field of the Lost. Every time a student or alumni dies in honor of the school or was influential to the school, a tree grows somewhere in the field." Some part of me wonders how much sorrow follows the bright meadow.

"I think your mother would be somewhere in there," says Elias nonchalantly.

Austra gives Elias a pointed look, but he just lifts an eyebrow and shrugs. "Thought he would like to know."

I give the Hunter a nod in thanks and scan the grove. Next time I see my father, I'll ask him about this place, perhaps get him to take me there.

"Are those... gravestones?" I ask, squinting. Near some trees are plaques, stones, benches, flowers, pictures, and other things I can't quite make out. Some trees are left abandoned, not a marking to tell who to honor, to never be identified by loved ones or remembered.

"In some ways, yes. In the Six Kingdoms we generally cremate the bodies and then pour their ashes where their loved ones think they would want their eternity to lay," answers Elias, his hair like fire in the light.

"How would they know which tree is for who?"

"The time of death would clue them in," Austra says thoughtfully. "But if they were killed during battle, the family can usually feel it when they find the tree. I really don't know how. Gut feeling maybe."

Elias' face darkens as we pass a pair of fiery red maples. "The Premier took my siblings to our parents' tree when we arrived on campus. It just feels right. It's like there's a tether between my heart and the trees." Austra puts a hand on his shoulder.

We continue in the direction of what looks like a stone building. The Infirmary. I grimace at the memory of that place—the dark lonely nights.

We enter through the front door into a front office and the smell of rubbing alcohol fills my nose. A tall lady with black rimmed glasses and a blond ponytail comes in with a friendly smile. Adjusting her collar, she greets, "Good morning. How may I help you today?"

Elias clears his throat. "Good morning Ms. Mendy. We came to visit Skye Fervent."

"I'll show you the way," she says. We follow her into the adjoining room, light flooding around us. I glance up. The whole ceiling is glass. I must've really been out of it to not notice it before.

She leads us past many hospital beds, some filled but most empty. Some students have suspicious burn marks, broken arms, eyepatches, stitches, and other injuries that I would not expect to see in a school. Maybe I should just run away or ask Aris to do the Recollection Charm on me. Maybe it would be easier, just to forget all of this really happened. Maybe a normal life would be less stressful, not having to worry about Malevolents every second of the day.

But then again, I would always question why I feel out of place or that I don't belong. I would always wonder where that missing part of me lies. Maybe finding out the truth is a good thing.

I come out of thought when Ms. Mendy leads us to a bed enclosed with curtains.

"I wonder who ordered those to be put there?" Elias mutters sarcastically, rolling his eyes. Ms. Mendy gives us a side glance, a spark of fear at the thought of the man.

Deuxieme Fervent. More concerned about pride than his daughter.

"Reputation is everything to those high enough in power," sighs Makai. Something in his tone makes me wonder if he's speaking from personal experience.

Ms. Mendy ducks behind the white cloth, us following close behind. Austra covers her mouth in shock, eyes focused on Skye.

Her lips are an alarming shade of green. What type of poison were in those arrows? The white blankets are mountainous and heavy, covering her chin. Even in sleep she looks like she's in pain. Ms. Mendy says something about letting her know if we need anything before giving us some privacy.

I gulp. "I thought Aris did that healing spell."

"Yeah. She should be awake by now," says Makai, scowling. "When you have an inexperienced Sorcerer doing it, it elongates the recovery time."

Austra glances around to make sure Aris isn't here. Not that Aris is hard to forget, he's just good at blending in. "Usually when the spell takes place, energy from both the Sorcerer and the helper are taken. When this one occurred, it only took from her. So, it is as if she received the wound that they healed on you. I think Sylas and Aris wanted to make sure that you got back here safely no matter the cost."

My shoulders slump. If Makai wants to blame someone for this, he should blame me.

Elias pulls out a bouquet of roses seemingly out of thin air and places them in the glass vase next to her bed. "Her favorite flower," sighs Elias. "But only when they have thorns. I made them with thorns just for her."

I ask Elias, "Are you close with Skye?"

"One doesn't get close to Skye," Elias chuckles.

"Why?"

He studies me for a moment, debating whether or not to continue. "There was a mission a while back that really messed with her, as well as her dad. Honestly, I think that after that mission, her father realized how much she means for his station in the politics. After that mission, he trained her harder than ever, molding her into stone. Not that she wasn't pushed hard before that." The Hunter finds something interesting to look at on the ground. "But she's a softy at heart," he adds. Then he mumbles, "I think."

Austra takes a deep breath, checking her watch. "It's nearly 9. We better get going," she says, bowing her head and placing her fist over her mouth. The others do the same. "May the Fates wish you well."

We make our way across the room, towards the entrance. I can't help but look back. A pain keeps nagging me in my gut. Though it isn't entirely my fault, I'm still the reason why this happened in the first place.

I'll make it up to her somehow. "What was that thing with your fist, that you did when we were about to leave Skye?" I ask.

Makai laughs, "It's so weird–finding out what makes us different from the Outside. In the Six Kingdoms we do it to those we want to express thanks to. Generally, it's used in a situation that involves

75

sacrifice, death, or sadness. The balled fist is supposed to symbolize us holding our hopes and wishing the Fates to be amiable."

We walk back to the school entrance hall, me asking the occasional question that springs into my mind. I stop short when I see the entrance hall.

Even though I saw it before, something about its height and detailing takes my breath away. The history radiates off the carved stone with pictures of battles and stories that are to never be forgotten. Students walk across the area, going in their own directions towards whatever adventure they are destined to go on next.

As we walk through, I feel the weight of people speaking in hushed tones around me. Some of them offer me friendly waves and others don't bother to hide their stares. I wonder when the attention will die down. Usually I just have to wait a week or so if it's a small private school. Being the son of the head of the school... it might take a little longer than that.

I do spot a pair of beautiful purple eyes from across the way. She smiles, her beauty nearly like that of the sirens, and waves. I raise a hand, without realizing it, and wave back. The girl giggles, her curled, brown hair bouncing.

"Don't even bother," sneers Makai. "That's Vesta, Nikolai's sister. Just as mean and vain as her brother."

Elias bumps his shoulder, "Speaking from experience, Makai?"

He grunts but doesn't deny it. "She'll turn on you at a moment's notice. The only allegiance she has is to herself. And she's as sour as a lemon."

"I'll take your word," I laugh.

Elias leads us to the middle of the hall. At the center of the tiled medallion, the thousands of little glazed pieces of glass shimmer. Times of centuries past spiral from the center of the emblem, the same seal they described to me earlier. Yes, the medallion is beautiful, but it is also disturbing. The scenes hold my eyes and I watch the progression of a warrior in battle, slain from his horse and buried by what I assume are Malevolents. I shiver at the sight.

Austra checks her watch again, "Should we go find Sylas?"

"Hello mates!" We all turn to the voice. "Ready for a day of shopping?" Sylas smiles widely at us.

We nod in reply and Elias gives Austra a playful push.

"Then let's start walking." We all follow Sylas down the path and into the trees.

Chapter 9

Levi

There are mythical creatures at every turn. Sylas even points out a town of gnomes next to a river of water pixies. They're about a half a foot high with mounds of dirt covered in moss as their homes.

He tells me about their tragic history, centuries of abuse at the hands of the Six Kingdoms and elves. The higher ups signed a treaty with them after they threatened to work with the Malevolents, stating that we can't enter their borders without permission. The little pocket of territory they have in the town of Grantham Willow is demarcated by a line of moss. I almost cross it, not noticing it until I'm just a foot away. Makai snickers and says that if I did step into it, I would've been burned to a crisp.

The stiffness in my stance lessens when we enter town. Austra wraps her arm around mine as we make our way through town. We walk to a little field near the edge of town where dragons of all shapes and sizes munch on fresh meat or sleep in the midday sun. I glance up. Above are scaled creatures flying with their wide, bat-like wings that send shadows across the green.

A man around the age of 40 with a bald head and a long, frizzy, brown beard watches us with eagle eyes as we near. The closer we get, the more clearly I can see his gleaming scars, pale against his muscled, tan arms. The skin on one of his forearms look as though it has been melted, leaving behind a glossy patch of skin.

"I am the Keeper of the Dragons." He bows his head, barely a nod. "It's a little late in the school year, isn't it?" The man studies me, as if trying to figure out how close I am to running in the other direction.

The bone in his right ear, that looks alarming like a dragon tooth, doesn't do much to help me make the brave decision to stay.

Remembering the nights my father and I played poker, I school my features. "I came a little late. Malevolents can be a bit of a pain."

He raises an eyebrow and scans me up and down, probably pondering the chances that a scrawny teenager could walk away from an encounter with a monster. "Let's see which dragon likes you?" He waves his hand towards a black dragon in the far corner of the field, its scales gleaming and horns pointed and poised to kill.

As the dragon approaches, I realize it's not a foot taller than the man six foot tall Keeper of the Dragons. The dragon huffs smoke, but I harden my gaze and stare right into the creature's snake eyes. They don't even soften a fraction.

The man with the bone earing hoists me onto the creature. He teaches me how to ride a dragon, instructing me to grab the long horns and to put my legs above the joints of the wings.

He shouts, "Fly!" And the dragon does.

My body whips back, my adrenaline spiking to my throat. Swallowing a scream, I reinforce my grip on the horns and lean forward, combating the force of the wind. We fly high but remain below the clouds where I can see the town. The people begin to look no bigger than my thumb and the forest becomes vaster than I would ever guess. When I get back, the man shakes his head.

Then for the next dragon, he shakes his head.

And he does the same for the next and next.

...

Levi

On the fifth try, I straddle a dragon that looks like he was forged from a pit of smoke, every inch a beautiful matte color of steel, even the

79

horns. He gleams and soaks in the sun, like an ancient sword that hadn't seen the light of day.

Despite the wind-blown sting of my cheeks and the slight shake of my biceps from gripping the horns so hard, I feel a thrill. I look at Austra, Elias, Makai, and Sylas, their faces masks of surprise and awe. Their lunch that they decided to get after the third dragon lays forgotten on their laps. The Keeper of the Dragons almost smiles before whistling for the dragon to go.

In a blink of an eye, we're off.

After a few runs, I've gotten used to the speed. But this one is faster. I silently thank the bearded man below for not giving me this dragon as my first or I would've fallen right off.

We soar through the sky, wind howling in my ears. His massive wings beat, the air shifting at his command as if he is the master of the skies. I dare look down and see the vastness of the forest beneath. I feel a rising lump of panic, but then I realize that I feel safe on the back of this animal that I barely know. I catch his eyes on me, inquisitive. The sides of my mouth quirk up, as a friendly "hello." The dragon grunts and then plummets head first to the ground.

I howl, holding onto his horns for dear life. My body would've flown off if it weren't for my legs hooked in front of his wings. I let out an "oof" when the dragon of steel pulls back.

"What was that for?" I exclaim to the dragon.

He tilts his head to look at me and I feel him snicker. A jolt of joy and intrigue fires through my veins, but the anger still shines bright.

I'm still seething when we get back to the field.

The man with the brown beard smiles. "I think you have found your new mount."

I don't know what scares me more, the fact that my new mount almost killed me or that I agree with him. There's this link between me and the creature that let me understand him, like there was a small thread of a tether. It was nothing concrete, but there was something.

"Well," I say, turning to the steel colored dragon. "I hope you're ready for a lifetime of near-death experiences."

"He's beautiful." Elias walks over, reaching up to stroke his neck. Elias looks to the Keeper in surprise.

"He's picky," the Keeper of the Dragons, not batting an eye.

I take this opportunity to study this man more. His eyes are brown, not the color of a Hunter like what I would expect of someone who works so closely with animals, and he doesn't seem to have any other magical trait about him.

"What are you?" I ask, forgetting about my manners.

A bit taken aback, he blinks before answering, "I can feel emotions. I'm human for all intents and purposes though."

I nod my head slowly. I guess that would be helpful for someone like him, dealing with creatures who can't communicate using words. I didn't realize there are others in these borders that aren't from the Six Kingdoms.

"The former owners named him Odyssey," suggests the man, turning the attention back to the dragon.

"Then that's what we'll call him," I say, brushing a hand over a spot with a missing scale. "How old is he?"

"He's still young, around 3, so he should grow more." Odyssey's already the size of a small truck, so I'm curious so see how big he would be full size. "But he has seen a lot in his time. I guess since you're the–"

"Levi, I think we better get heading back, it's been a long day," Sylas interjects. "We still have to do some errands."

I look questionably at all of them but they avoid my gaze. The Keeper of the Dragons shrugs and tells us we can take Odyssey after the trading of purple papers. I follow the others away from the dragon stables. Odyssey dragon nudges my back and I nudge him back playfully.

Austra grabs my arm and leads me a little farther ahead. She whispers to me, "Some things are meant not to be read until the right time." Just as quickly, she lets go.

Some things are not to be read until the right time.

The weather is just a dull chill over my skin and the rolling water is a monotonous droll in my ears as my thoughts make circles in my head. With a dragon that blends into the night behind us, we make our way back to the path.

The walk is refreshing, peaceful. I try to forget about the Outside world and just imagine what it would've been like if I only knew *here*. Dragons would just seem like horses and magic would seem like physics. Instead of growing up naive, I would've seen the world with more truths than before. My childhood would've taken place somewhere that I feel like I belong, rather than moving around so often that I was like a butterfly, traveling between flowers but never settling.

When we emerge from the forest, I spread my arms, trying to absorb the open space. Odyssey does the same, spreading his magnificent wings, and knocks Makai into a rose bush.

While Elias and Sylas help the pricked Sorcerer out of the brush, Austra taps me and points to the sky. Together we look up and I lose sense of words.

"Aren't they beautiful?" she breathes. Specks of light dance across the sky, creating constellations and clusters of stars that are chaotic yet peaceful. I could stare at the sky for hours on end, not giving a care for what my father is hiding from me. "Maybe tomorrow when I give you a tour we'll stop here for a look."

"A tour?" I ask, a bit surprised. I thought we saw most of the school already.

"Yep," she says. "There's more to the campus than meets the eye. It was originally built as a fort during the Great War, able to withstand the darkest of magic. They built a multitude of secret passages and hidden doorways that you'll have to get used to. Also, I don't want you getting lost on your first day." Elias rolls his eyes at her pointed look. "Tomorrow should be a free day for you anyways, since you don't start school until Monday."

"I can teach you how to surf," suggests Elias, the sounds of crashing ocean in the distance. "If you take a hike out of the bay, down to the nice stretch of beach, the waves are perfect. Maybe wait until the water gets a little warmer, though. Until then we can play chess. I love chess."

"I'm down for both." Chess, my father taught me when I was young. As for surfing, I spent some time in Southern California a while back. We only stayed through the summer, so I didn't have the chance to ask a friend to teach me before moving. "Wait, how is there a beach? Where are we?"

Sylas shrugs, "We're somewhere between San Francisco and Los Angeles. I'd say a good hour drive south from Santa Barbara."

We approach a field around the side of the school, similar to the one with the Keeper of the Dragons. There are little shelters around the clearing, each with a plaque with the name of the dragon on the top. Dragons meander around the green and I spot some flying over the hills.

We approach one of the stalls where a girl silently attends to a red dragon. The creature snorts in greeting, alerting the girl of our presence.

"Hello Phoebe," says Sylas, giving the short woman a hug.

"Hi Sylas," says Phoebe with a light smile, her green eyes looking at Sylas with admiration. Then her attention settles on the dragon behind my shoulder. "Have you brought a new dragon?"

"Yep. Phoebe, meet Levi, Levi, meet Phoebe. She is the Keeper of the Dragons of Grantham Willow." He grins with pride. I can assume being the Keeper of the Dragons is an earned roll and something to warrant respect, so I bow my head, like I've seen the others do on occasion. "Then this mount, here, is Odyssey."

83

"I see," she says, placing her delicate hands on either of his cheeks. Per Elias' surprise, Odyssey doesn't balk. "The famous Odyssey. I see a life of hardships and glory in your eyes." Phoebe giggles. "You have quite the joker on your hands. He is a very smart talker."

"Tell me about it." I roll my eyes.

"Well Odyssey, let's get you settled." She bids us farewell before leading Odyssey to an empty stall. My eyes follow the dragon, unable to drag them away. His scales seem to absorb the darkness around him, drawing the shadows from their corners.

Sylas looks at the clock tower at the corner of the school and swears. In a rushed explanation about being late to a date with Claire, he darts away. We make our way back to the dorms, our shoulders slumped from the exhaustion of the day.

"Sylas and Phoebe went to Grantham together back in the day," Elias says. "They were a thing at some point and then Sylas met Claire." He shrugs. "They're still great friends though." Based on the longing in Phoebe's eyes, I'm not sure if things are completely in the past.

When we get back to our dorm, I collapse on my bed, almost sliding off before catching myself.

Before I forget, I get up and call Sparky from the balcony like Makai and Elias do with their Lightning Critters. We clean up, Makai conjuring us some sandwiches from the pickup counter in the Capricorn. Apparently, the cooks prepare meals to-go, just in case students are too tired to come down to eat.

Barely speaking a word during our meal, we sit in a circle around the fire and munch, cherishing the warmth. It's a nice feeling, being with people I didn't have to say good-bye to in the near future. For once in my life there's a sense of stability.

Elias tells me about his history with the others. Skye, Austra, Makai, and him have known each other even before coming to Grantham. The government of the Six Kingdoms put them on a few missions together which allowed them to grow close despite the distance between them. After Makai goes to sleep, Elias explains how Makai and Austra knew each other even before the rest of them since they live in the same city.

"What about Aris? Did he just meet you all at the beginning of the year?"

Elias' expression darkens and he looks into the fireplace flames. "There was a trigger by the Sirens about someone who got past them, seemingly unfazed by their songs. Austra and Skye went with a few teachers to help look for the intruder since they were the closest trained students and they were short of staff."

He wraps his jacket around him tighter. "Austra was the one that found him. According to Skye, his face was expressionless and he didn't attack. He only had his sword and the clothes on his back, his face battered and dirty. Austra did her best to clean him up before they came, but he was still a mess. She explained how they took him to the Premier's and for some reason, they let him stay."

He shivers and gets up. "I'm going to sleep."

I stand too, my legs sore from today's adventure. "What's a Darkness Wielder?"

"They wield the shadows and darkness. It's a rare element in Sorcerers and is often associated with evil and bad luck. Some older Sorcerers think it means a cursed life. The Darkness Wielders have great power, but their tails often end in tragedy."

Elias tucks himself in bed and sighs. "From what I've seen, Aris is a good guy. A little quiet and moody at times, but he's good."

I give him a nod and he turns off his lamp. I snuggle under the covers and let my eyes adjust to the darkness. One glance at Elias' side of the room, I can tell he's an archer, his bow and arrow on the floor next to his pillows, a safe reach away in case of an emergency. There's also a pair of ballet shoes poking out of his school bag.

He certainly has the posture of a dancer and that steady grace in his stride. The Hunter could create beautiful lines, drawing on the elegance of how he holds himself. I hope to see him dance one day.

Makai's more of a swordsman and has a highly polished blade lying haphazardly on his desk. He's messy too, clothes scattered about his portion of the room like a storm blew through his dresser. Books and pens lay haphazardly across the sheets, making me question how he sleeps at night.

I don't think it's normal to feel so at home with such a variety of weapons at hand's reach from my roommates, but I could get used to this. I could get used to the easy laughs of Austra, the fun-loving nature of Elias, and the mischievous glint to Makai... maybe even the sharpness of Skye.

However, there's one thing that tugs at my mind when I lay my head on my pillow.

Some things are not to be read until the right time.

Chapter 10

Levi

Austra shows me around the school, telling me about some of the secret hideouts she found in the past couple months. We even go over my schedule to make sure that I know where my classes are, which helps settle my nerves. To some degree.

After lunch, Elias and I take a trip to the archery field to practice. He makes sure to introduce me to a few Hunters and I do my best to remember names. Makai is off causing trouble with some of his friends, according to Elias. Apparently, it isn't uncommon for Makai to make books fly off the walls in the library or to startle a poor cook when their flour explodes in a puff of white.

I see him again later in the night, a satisfied grin on his face. His hair is disheveled with twigs sticking out of his clothes. Elias doesn't comment on it, so I don't either, as we spend the night playing card games until the wee hours of the morning.

Makai tells me about himself, a son of one of the more influential Sorcerers in the Kingdom. Every time he mentions his father, there's a burn in his words, as if the malice could make his father feel pain. He said that he likes causing trouble because it makes him feel free, like the constraints of society can't hold him down like it does for so many others.

He shows me a tattoo he got during last New Year, a band around his bicep, with the circle not closed. Smiling fondly, he explains how it's supposed to symbolize how he's not bound by anything and that the tattoo is simply a mockery towards those who try.

I've met some troublemakers in my time, but never one like Makai. His love for life is impalpable, like experiences rather than books are the answer to his life story.

Elias is a flamboyant specimen, his emotions and reactions seemingly amplified more than the normal person. He grew up in England, but always saw my father as that father figure across the sea. When he told me that part, he looked at me cautiously, unsure how I would take the knowledge. I can see why he would be nervous, wondering how one would react to finding out your father had stepchildren he adopted legally without you knowing.

I nod at the Hunter warmly. To me it's comforting, having adoptive brothers and a sister. Even though a part of me liked things just being me and my father, it fills my heart to imagine us having others to rely on, to depend on. Besides, who am I to complain about my family growing when I'm more concerned about it shrinking.

...

Levi

I wake up at dawn when the sun has not yet shown its light. But for some reason, the urge to sleep has left me. Instead of trying to fall into its arms again, I get up and pull on a hooded jacket.

The ocean's roars reach my ears as I make my way through the school. The double doors of the entrance are closed but the torches on the walls burn bright. Though windows in the hall are worn, I can see the stables and the soft glow from the inside. I smile at the thought of Odyssey finding a way to get used to his new home too.

I continue walking through the entrance hall, which is now vacant, and down the next. Stopping to look through one of the classroom windows, the desks look like any other, with the tabletops connected to the chairs. Windows on the other side of the room allow one to look into the courtyard. I'll probably be looking out of those windows often, wondering what the future holds or drawing the tree in the center of the yard.

I come to a break in the hallway with another pair of large double doors, identical to the ones at the entrance of the Capricorn. However, instead of being large slabs of wood, polished to perfection, these doors are decorated in gold vines and the wood is stained almost black.

Above the massive entrance is a plaque with the words, *Tower of the Lost,* engraved onto the surface.

I turn to walk away and continue on my stroll, but a familiar tug keeps me from going more than a few steps. Curious, I feel that tether, and pull.

It guides me back and my hands find the gold handles, but the doors don't budge. Remembering my locket, I put it up to the Grantham Willow just at eye level. It glows for a second and then something clicks. With great effort, I heave it just wide enough to squeeze through. When I look up, the most astonishing thing greets my eyes.

Picture frames cover almost every spot on the walls, shining in the first light of the day. A spiral staircase goes around and around the sides of the large cylinder room until it reaches the ceiling of glass.

I walk to one of the frames with a painting of a boy, younger than me, with missing teeth, untamed black hair, and shining gold eyes. The words beneath read, "William Everglade, Warrior 3,785 b.f.- 3,778 b.f. He died fighting for his school in the Battle of Grantham Willow."

Doing the quick math, my eyes widen. He was 7 years old, yet he gave his life for this school.

I look at another and another, each having a story of sacrifice, glory, or tragedy. Their death dates are so different that I'm surprised they were able to have a photo or painting of every one of the dead.

"Taking a look at the Tower of the Lost I see."

I swerve around, startled. My father gets up from one of the couches at the back of the tower. His eyes are heavy from sleep, but his face is warm as he studies each of the faces he walks by.

"Your mother is here," he says, his hands folded neatly behind his back.

I follow him with caution. "How did you know I was down here?"

"There's an alarm that goes off when a student leaves the dorms before 5:00 a.m. The Fates gave me a push towards this room, so I followed." He walks to one of the pictures near a large stained-glass window, his eyes fluttering slightly.

My breath catches when I see the same woman in that picture frame my father has carried to all of the places we've been. Her eyes are kind but sharp with intelligence, like she could see right through you. She's striking and young, maybe around her early to mid 20s, a sharp contrast to the natural softness of my father. She has a smirk in her picture, like she's still fighting Malevolents, even in death. Below her picture reads, "Amora Lim Clovis Sage: mother of Levi Sage and wife of David Sage. She died defending her child and others from Malevolents in the Attack of the Fifth Sun."

"Your mother was an amazing woman," says my father. "She was the most intimidating Scholar I've ever encountered in my well-traveled life. There was something about her that made people run away. But of course, being the young and reckless teenager I was, I went after her.

"Because we were both Scholars, we always had classes together. No matter how many questions I answered correctly in class or tests I succeeded on, she always found a way to push me. Even during our combat courses, she would press me to the mat each time. It took until I won a chess match against her for her to finally notice me. Your mother and I were always head to head on the subject.

"Here in the Six Kingdoms, due to the high chance we have of being killed, we often marry and have children earlier than the Outside. There are also more arranged marriages. Luckily, neither of us were spoken for so we got married shortly after graduating Grantham Willow." The glow on his face from the memory vanished, leaving an expression of longing. "She loved you, you know."

"What happened," I ask, my mouth dry.

"I should have seen it coming before it happened." He winces, his face etched with remorse. "On the night of the fifth sun of the new year, the Malevolents forged an attack. No warning, no signal, and no clear motive. Some think that Six Kingdoms rebels let them into our walls to make a statement. Your mother, being the Deuxieme, stayed behind with the younger students to be their last line of defense.

"You were only 6 months old at the time and Skye was born that night. It has always astonished me that one of the fiercest Warriors I've ever met just so happened to be born on one of the most devastating nights in our history." His lips quirk up with a breath of a smile before they fall again.

"The Malevolents knew that we would do something like that—send our young somewhere else, somewhere we thought was safe. They might not know love, but they know that it's a weakness. They sent a force to exactly where they were hiding and Amora was the only one that could fight."

He says, "And she did. She was not the only death, but in that section, she saved many lives." My father laughs a bitter laugh. "I wasn't going to tell you this until you were ready—or maybe until I was ready. But it seems as though the Fates sent me here for a reason."

I can't draw my eyes from the picture of my mother. Part of me wonders what would've happened if she didn't die that night... if my father and her were able to raise me together like they'd planned.

"There has not been another organized Malevolent attack of that magnitude since. But we must be ready." My father pats my shoulder thoughtfully and leaves me there to think, longing for what might have been.

Chapter 11

Levi

"Levi, where in the Six Kingdoms have you *been*?" Elias screeches as I enter the room. The sun has risen and so has the very frazzled looking Hunter. His hair makes it look like little baby antlers are sticking out of his head.

I have to bite my tongue to keep from laughing.

"Well! I was about to send word to your father."

"He was worried sick," Makai grumbles, rubbing the sleep from his eyes. "He even got *me* to wake up for you."

"I went exploring," I say. Seeing the crabby Sorcerer and the shaken Hunter, I hold up my hands in innocence. "Look! I'm in one piece, so stop making such a fuss. I was with my father anyway."

"Never do that again! Do you know what could have happened if you got caught! They can force you to clean the stables... or wash the dishes in the kitchen. Sometimes nightcrawlers get into the halls. You didn't even bring a weapon with you."

"My brain's a pretty powerful weapon."

"Unbelievable."

"Next time let me know," says Makai, grinning. "I can show you some secret passageways, so you *don't* get caught or eaten by nightcrawlers." I open my mouth to make plans with him to go snooping around in the night when I see Elias' red cheeks.

"Not helping," Elias exclaims.

...

Levi

"Hello, Unyielders," shouts someone from across the room, a swarm of cackles following.

Austra shrinks next to me, hiding her face in her hair. Aris slides closer to us, his sneer absolutely murderous.

"Keep your insults to yourself Nikolai," Makai sneers, pressing his fork so hard into the table it leaves marks. "My father would love to know about your use of a term long banned from the Six Kingdoms."

Nikolai scowls. "Wouldn't your parents like to know that you sneak around, spurring up trouble wherever you go. I doubt that will help them with their palace politics."

Met with silence and pursed lips, he shrugs. "Don't worry," Nikolai says and sits next to Elias, "I haven't come to spur up a war."

"I find that hard to believe," mumbles Austra, picking at her food.

"What was that, *Unyielder?*"

She clenches her jaw. "Nothing."

Finding her answer satisfactory, he turns to me. "I came to ask the Premier's son where he's been all this time. Doesn't it seem rather odd that he just suddenly pops up after being missing for *fifteen years–* presumed dead."

This I haven't heard before. Of course, it makes sense that there would be talk around me suddenly coming to school as the son of the most well-known man in the school, but *presumed dead.* Now I understand the whispers.

"What's your problem with using people's actual name?" I counter, avoiding the question. I narrow my eyes at the boy. Based on the reactions of those around us, the term *Unyielders* isn't commonly or fondly used.

"It makes talking to people so much more interesting. A little birdie told me that you haven't matured yet, which I find rather alarming since the Fates usually decide by now whether or not you'll become one of us. Maybe your dad knew, so he sent you away for your childhood. So that you'll be prepared to go back."

I hold down a wince. Cursing myself beforehand, I say, "Do you want to test that theory?"

He stands up and I do the same. Some students passing by stop to look. I keep my eyes on his purple ones. I'm taller than him, but not by much. His shoulders are broader, probably from months of training when I had none. It doesn't take a genius to guess who would win the fight of skill.

Knowing Nikolai, he'll want the first punch.

And he does.

Seeing it coming, I have enough time to dodge, feeling the breeze of his fist passing my cheek. He was banking on a first blow victory, so he becomes off balance from the force. I grab his arm and twist it behind his back, recalling my years of self-defense classes.

He lets out a yelp of surprise and pain. "Don't ever insult my friends again," I hiss. I push him away, disgusted, and release his arm. He stumbles and runs away like a coward. His friends follow him, dashing out of the room, giving me evil looks as they run. I wipe my forehead, not quite believing I walked away without a broken jaw.

When I sit down again, I take a much-needed bite of my breakfast. Sensing the tension in the air, I look up to my friends and then around me. About a dozen people just watch. I chew and swallow.

"What!"

My classmates start talking and socializing again, like someone unpaused the scene.

"Levi," Makai exclaims, a smile spreads on his face. "What in the Six Kingdoms was that! Do you realize how much trouble we could stir up? I thought you would just be dead weight, but I could use you."

95

"Mate," says Elias, his hands gripping the table so hard, moss starts growing across the table. "That was brilliant. Quick, but efficient. Austra, did you see his face?"

"Yes Elias, I saw his face," mutters Austra, still frowning at her oatmeal.

"Then what's wrong?" I ask, leaning forward.

She sighs, letting her spoon fall, "Next time he comes at you, he won't underestimate you. He's one of the best fighters in the school." She takes a pause before saying, "He's also a Dueler."

Tilting my head, I ask, "What's a Dueler?"

Elias grins, "In the Six Kingdoms, all the schools have a Dueling team. Two students from each Kingdom are selected based on how good they are at their gift and fighting. He's one of the favorites to be selected for next year's team."

"And Skye's a favorite too," adds Makai, taking a bite of his apple. "You can't join in your Initial year. Sadly. So we have to wait and see."

"If you're on the team, you're like a Fate. Duelers are the pride and joy of the school. No amount of inherited glory you have as the son of the Premier will help you against that." Austra picks up her plate and takes it to the drop off area.

When she's far enough away, I ask, "What does *Unyielder* mean?"

Elias purses his lips and says, "Well, the Six Kingdoms used to be a very rigid caste system and the Masters, then called the *Unyielders,* were at the bottom. After the Throne Trials the caste systems were no more, but some prejudice remains. The changing of their name to *Masters* was meant to mean an ending of an era of oppression. The use of the term is like saying they still believe the Masters to be lowly or view the targeted person as inferior."

Before the first bell chimes, Makai hands me a map of the school. I thought maps were against protocol. Seeing my raised eyebrow, he shrugs. "My plans need visuals sometimes."

"Thanks." Taking the parchment, I examine the paper.

"Do you think you're set?" Austra asks in slightly better spirits than before, though her shoulders are still slumped.

"Sure," I grumble, stuffing the paper in my pocket. "Let's see if I can survive the day."

"Well, there's nobody trying to kill you here," Elias says, patting me on the back.

I take a deep breath as I hear the first rings across the courtyard. "I hope it stays that way."

Chapter 12

Levi

"Won't the grass be wet?" I stare down at Austra who sat down with the other students. Considering the dampness of the air, the grass should still be wet from the morning dew.

"We have spells for that, remember. A simple one at that."

She tugs me down. As she said, it's perfectly dry.

I hear the bell sound again in the distance as a misty breeze sends a chill down my spine. At the sound, the last of my classmates trickle into the Field of Love, a majority of them wearing either gold or brown ties.

"The students wearing brown are Sorcerers and the students wearing gold are Warriors. Oh! We also have some Masters in here. They're the ones in either light or dark blue. The ones with dark blue have specialized. You know how they can master any gift that the Fates chose for them, right? The ones in the light blue haven't discovered theirs yet."

Most of the Warriors sit with near perfect posture, as if expecting an attack to come at any moment. A lot of them eye me wearily, probably assessing my capabilities. Barely 5 minutes into the day and I can feel potential danger mere feet away.

Aris comes up to us, his chin lowered and black coat waving behind him. Our classmates give him hesitant glances. Austra waves him over and offers a warm smile. Aris gives a small grin back before taking a seat.

"Happy Monday everybody!" I look up and see Phoebe, her long black hair now in one braid trailing down her back. "Miss Holly is out today visiting her sister in Scotland, so I'll be taking her place for now. You can call me Ms. Everglade."

Everglade.

"Today we are going to study why trees grow on this particular part of the campus whenever someone dies."

She paces in front of us, gazing out into the grove. "You all know the stories by now. This school was founded after a great war against the Malevolents. The final confrontation was the Battle of Grantham Willow. It had the most casualties recorded in a battle in our long history. The surviving Hunters and Huntresses grew a tree for everyone lost. Some say that when someone dies on campus, their loss triggers something in the Hunters and Huntresses around them, leading to the growth of the tree. So why only here? Through the study of a particular text, it is hypothesized that the Sorcerers and the Hunters/Huntresses worked together on a spell that will grow a tree every time someone dies on or for this land."

A Sorcerer with short black hair raises her hand.

"Yes, Melonie?"

"Which ancient text was it?"

The Huntress smiles. "The Story of Grantham Willow."

Several gasps echo through the room.

Austra raises his hand.

"Yes, Austra."

"If it was that particular text, why isn't it considered fact?"

"Some hard-core historians don't believe in the accuracy of the book. In Grantham Willow we have no doubt about it since we believe in the integrity of our founders. Although, recently some predictions made in the book have come to light, allowing us to assume that its contents are valid."

I scrunch my brows in confusion and raise my hand.

"Levi?"

Clearing my throat, I ask, "What is the Story of Grantham Willow?"

I hear a low snicker in the corner of the group and grimace.

"The Story of Grantham Willow is the document that tells the start of Grantham Willow through the eyes of the first queen of the Six Kingdoms. You are required to read it in your Paramount year or your last year here at the school. Not before or after."

"Why?"

"It reveals the truth about our history. People can give you a synopsis, but not in high detail. Even if you did manage to find someone willing to tell you its contents, they are bound by the Elven Blood Promise not to speak a word and would die before muttering the first words. It is to remind us of where we came from and how our Kingdoms were born as one. It reminds us to not take things for granted and to not lose sight of what is important."

We continue the rest of the class learning how trees grow to match the personality of deceased and the underground tunnels that used to be used to tend to the roots. Austra tells me about how the most prestigious school in the country has something like this for their grove, inspired by ours.

Phoebe gives us our homework assignment just as the bell rings.

...

Levi

Dragon Riding is the class that I look forward to the most. Even though I barely know Odyssey, I've missed him over the last couple days. I came by on Sunday to give him a slap of beef from the Capricorn, but I didn't stay more than ten minutes.

"Having a busy day, Ms. Everglade?" Austra comes over to the exhausted looking Huntress, sweat clinging to her forehead in the midday sun.

"Yes. Very. I'm not fully worn out yet, but I'm sure it will settle in soon," she replies, glaring at the heat. "There's been some ruckus at the palace, so some of the professors have been coming and going. Do you know if Makai knows anything about it?"

Austra looks at me, but I shake my head. "Nothing out of the ordinary. He would've said something," she says.

Austra and I wave good-bye to Phoebe and Austra leads me to see her mount. "This is Zafira," she says, introducing me to an elegant, green dragon with a long neck and thin horns.

"Nice to meet you, Zafira," I say and lower my head in greeting.

The dragon bows back in acknowledgement.

We both set our book bags down on a bench just in front of our dragons' stalls. Austra tries her best to teach me how to ride a dragon, hoping to make my first class as smooth as possible. Together we saddle them up, using a wrap of leather so that we don't get "scale burns."

Ms. Everglade blows her whistle, signaling us to bring our dragons into a line at the edge of the field. "Hello everybody," she yells. "This new guy here is Levi! Levi?"

I wince, my cheeks stinging. "Yes?"

"How are you on a dragon?"

"Not too bad," I say, not quite knowing what would be considered "good" or "bad." Austra gives me a reassuring look.

"Okay then, everyone, today we will be racing around the school. Whoever makes it to this willow tree and grabs the flag around its trunk wins this potion that I got from Mrs. Winchester. She said something about it being able to make your steps silent and your voice unheard. If you use it and get caught, you never got it from me!" Once each and every one of us nods, she continues. "Good. Approach the starting line."

I haul myself onto Odyssey, not as gracefully as I would like. I hear a familiar snicker from behind. Seems as though Nikolai and his friends deal with shame and embarrassment quickly.

"Ready?" Austra asks from atop Zafira.

"I don't know." Flying around for the first time with Odyssey was thrilling, but I wasn't trying to steer him in a certain way. I just let him do his thing. Austra said that dragons can feel your emotions, so you just have to convey to them in a solid way where you want them to go. Of course, I just nodded my head and tried to make sense of it, but now I'm not too sure.

"Hello, Levi."

I let out a subtle groan. "Hi Nikolai."

"Ready to lose?"

"Never," I say, mustering a smirk. Let him think that I know what I'm doing. I'm the mysterious son of the Premier who came back from the dead. I bet I could make people believe anything if I tried.

"I'm going to win. Get ready to eat mud," Nikolai spats, his dragon growling at Odyssey. My dragon just looks away, bored, which just infuriates the dragon even more.

"Oh, and one more thing! Don't fly," instructs Phoebe. "Felix is out practicing his flames and I don't want to deal with singed students, dragons, and/or birds today." She puts her whistle near her mouth and smiles giddily. "Ready. Set. Go!"

And we're off. Odyssey charges ahead on his four legs, his wings propelling him farther with each step. I never realized how fast dragons could run, having only imagined them in the air. My smile from the rush of the speed fades when I see Nikolai out of the corner of my eyes going higher and higher.

"Didn't you hear her?" I yell over the wind. The rest of the class is a few lengths behind, too preoccupied with keeping their dragons on course to pay attention to us.

He regards me curiously. "You must be someone who likes to play by the rules." I catch a mischievous glint in his eyes, but then he then descends back down. I let out a sigh of relief as we reach the Infirmary. Halfway there. The Royal stays at my side, his teeth clenched with determination. The others remain a good five lengths away.

Just him and I. Bring it on.

I wipe my forehead just as we pass by the Magical Practice Building. Almost there. The bay comes right up to the corner of the school, two cliffs branching out like wings. Do we just jump over it? Luckily, as we approach the cliff, I see that the water is at low tide. Where water would usually be there is just white sand. Still, are they trying to kill us?

"Odyssey," I yell, leaning close to his ear. "Get over this cliff safely and I'll get you some steak from the Capricorn. I don't want to die today so... please."

He grunts in reply, leaving me unsure of whether that was an affirmative grunt or not. My life lies within the hands of a temperamental dragon. Or in his claws, I guess. Three strides from the jump, I close my eyes and hold my breath, praying to the Fates for mercy. I prepare for a harsh jolt, but it doesn't come.

I risk opening an eye. To my surprise, we ride forward on the hard, wonderful ground on the other side of the cliff. Hooting in joy, I lean forward on Odyssey and make the final sprint to the tree. We race across the cobblestone path that leads to the Entrance Hall and back toward the stables. The willow tree with the red cloth finally comes into view.

"Over my dead body," roars Nikolai. He steers his mustard colored dragon right into Odyssey's side. I tumble off Odyssey and crash into the muddy grass.

When the world finally rights itself, I raise my throbbing head just enough to see a blurry picture of Nikolai waving the red flag in victory. Hissing, I inspect my skinned elbows, covered in mud and blood.

A wet nose nuzzles my arm. Odyssey stares down at me, a trace of worry in his eyes. "I'm fine," I say, nudging his head away. "It's okay. We'll beat him next time. Mark my words." The dragon gives a grunt in reply, agreeing with me.

"Nikolai, what in the name of the Seven Kingdoms was that?" I hear Makai yell. I scrunch my brows in confusion. He doesn't have this class. Maybe he was ditching class when he saw.

Makai runs across the field, straight at the victorious Nikolai.

"Mr. Ardent! Watch your language," Ms. Everglade calls from the willow tree.

I can assume the term *Seven Kingdoms* isn't the most polite term. Based on the look on Phoebe's face, I wouldn't put it past her to throw him in the dungeons.

"But, Ms. Everglade," calls Austra, breathless, jumping off Zafira. "Nikolai knocked Levi off his mount!"

"Shut up, Unyielder," spits Nikolai.

The Royal doesn't so much as turn his head before Makai sends a fist to his jaw.

Nikolai falls to the ground with a thud, too stunned to slow his fall.

"Mr. Ardent," exclaims Ms. Everglade, her face pale. "Premier's office. Immediately. You boys," she points to two of Nikolai's friends, "take Mr. Goldfinder to the Infirmary. Take his stuff with you." When Nikolai and Makai are on the move, in their separate directions, Ms. Everglade turns back to Austra. "Ms. Rabid, are you sure that Nikolai pushed Levi off his dragon?"

Austra nods, still in shock. Her eyes dart from her teacher to the brown-haired boy stomping away.

"Well class," says Ms. Everglade, exasperated. "Did he?"

Some give some humble nods, probably scared of what Nikolai would do if he found out they snitched on him. If today was any indication on what it means to get Nikolai to hate you, then I don't blame them.

Ms. Everglade sighs and rubs her forehead. "Well, I have two potions, one I was going to use for the other class. Considering how this class went, we're not going to do this for a while."

She holds the two flasks in from of Austr and I. Austra takes it, not quite formulating words. "Are–Are you sure?"

Phoebe just sighs. "It's deserved." I grasp mine and stuff it in my pocket, the scrapes on my elbows stinging.

She offers to put Odyssey and Zafira back into their stalls for us and we make sure to thank her many times before leaving. Austra and I walk away from the stables in silence. After a few minutes she grabs a perfume bottle from her bag.

"Do I really smell that bad?" I ask, trying not to laugh.

"I think you just rolled around in dragon manure," she teases. "But no, not really. Spray some of this potion on. It will make any stain disappear. Take this too." She hands me something that looks like a lotion bottle. "It's an ointment to help your elbows heal faster."

I do as she says and watch in astonishment as they do just that. The mud on my new clothes slowly fades from view and is replaced with the subtle smell of jasmine. My skid marks knit themselves together before we make it to our next class.

Chapter 13

Austra

Levi went to take a nap after the day was done. I don't blame him. My first day, I went to my room and didn't come out until the next morning. Skye literally had to drag me out to go to class.

Elias and I leave the library, where we were doing our homework, to go meet Makai. He sent us a Lightning Critter letting us know that he was finally released from the Premier's Office. By the time I get to the corner of ivy, I have my whole lecture planned out about why it's not good to punch people we don't like. However, with one look at his face, it flies away in the wind.

He tells us that his father called the Premier as soon as he heard about what he did from Nikolai's father. I've never liked the infamous Mr. Ardent who's too preoccupied with his position in government to care about his son. The Sorcerer mumbles something about his father threatening to disown him, wincing as the words come out.

Taking his arm, I lead him to a comfy chair in the library and grab a cup of tea from one of the library pixies.

Makai and I have known each other for as long as I can remember because our parents were both in the government. We didn't really get close until my brother passed last summer. My brother, Kal, was older than both Spencer and me. He was prepared to take on my father's role as Governor. He was the best fighter of us too. We were told that the Malevolent jumped him in a surprise attack and stabbed a knife through his heart.

Shortly after the incident, Spencer denounced his claim to our family name, and I had to step up for the role. It was the worst possible time for me to leave my family to go to school, but they said it would be best for me to get my education and worry about my new responsibilities when summer comes. I have to admit, Makai was the only one I could talk to these things about nowadays.

Elias leaves just before the sunset to help with the Hunt. At the beginning of the week, Hunters and Huntresses go out to hunt the game used for the meals. They head into the Forest of Deception to track deer, rabbits, turkeys, you name it. The fruits, vegetables, cows, goats, and chickens are already tended to daily by all of the Hunters.

While writing an essay for one of my classes, Levi sends me a Lightning Critter asking me where we are. It takes Levi a while to get here, even with Makai's map. Aris comes shortly after, saying he was doing some extra training after school. My lips spread into a tired smile as he takes a seat next to me. We sit in a humble silence while working on our homework, though there's a subtle tenseness in the air.

Aris rubs Makai the wrong way, which I think is due to the fact that Aris is much better at snooping around than he is. Makai finds it insulting that the boy would rather sit in a corner and sulk than utilize those skills for trickery.

When I see Aris patrolling the room, it's like a warm blanket during the cold of winter. It's a feeling that I get with Skye, instead of the chaotic nature of the other three boys. Maybe it's because I was the one to find Aris that fateful day with his eyes filled with uncertainty and fear. The boy I saw wasn't a Wielder of Darkness, but rather someone who didn't know where to go.

When the clock strikes eleven, I find myself missing Skye. The Head Librarian comes over to shoo us out of the study room behind the layers of bookshelves. Taking one glance back at the pack of boys walking in the opposite direction, I stride to the girls' dorms, alone.

...

Austra

After hours of staring up at the ceiling, I slide out of bed. Stuffing my shoes onto my feet, I debate the ethics of my plans. It's against the rules, but there's something I need to get done before I can function properly again. Anything would be better than waiting for sleep that won't come while thoughts attack me from every angle. They remind me of my status as an Unyeilder and add to the pounding ache in my heart.

My tennis shoes tap on the cold stone of the empty halls. Worrying that a Warrior will hear the subtle sound, I take out the potion in my pocket from Ms. Everglade. A small piece of paper tied to the round glass bottle with twine reads:

To the beholder who wants nothing he does to be heard, drink all. To the beholder who wants nothing he does to be heard but for those he wishes to be heard, drink half. To the beholder who wants nothing but to walk in silence, drink a fourth. The sound will mend, after the second hour ends.

"Please work," I whisper to myself.

Tipping the bottle back, I drink half, just in case I need to use it again later. Checking my watch, I make note of the time. Before heading out into the night, my fingers reach for the knife at my side. Night crawlers usually come out around 3:00 a.m., so I should be alright.

Before I can second guess myself, I run down the hall towards the only person who understands.

…

Austra

The cold night air stings my lungs and numbs my ears. The water in the bay is vicious and crashes against the rocks. Fog hovers so close to the ground, my line of sight only goes as far as five feet in front of me. Spray flies into the air, spreading the scent of the ocean.

By the time I make it to the Infirmary, my clothes are damp and cling to my body. Willing silence into my movements, I slowly turn the handle of the entrance. It's unlocked. Whoever's shift this is, they really suck at their job or perhaps the Fates did this as a favor. The lights are out and walking through the Infirmary without crashing into someone's bed is harder than I expected. Relying on my choppy memory, my hands finally grasp the sterilized curtain that towers around Skye.

Sitting down soundlessly on her bed, every rational thought in my mind screams that this is a useless venture into the night. I reach under the covers to grasp my friend's cold hand and I silence the doubt. Those thoughts can haunt me later.

"Hello Skye," I say and look around the curtain to see if anyone wakes from their beds. Nothing. Only darkness greets me, clinging to the edges of the room. "I guess I better start by saying that I miss you, a lot. I know you would wave off such thoughts as trivial, but I can't help it."

Laying my head on the covers next to her, I breathe in the soft smell of vanilla. Squeezing her hand harder, I say, "I don't know if I can go through with these plans. There's too much at stake and I don't know if I have the heart. Makai doesn't know, but for a split second I thought his father told him today—about the arranged marriage. Before, there was no doubt in my mind that I needed to do this. Now, I'm not so sure."

A breeze brushes my shoulder and I clench my jaw to keep from screaming. Levi kneels at the side of Skye's bed, his expression filled with amusement.

Hitting him on the arm, I hiss, "What are you doing here?" Feeling a bit out of place lying next to Skye, I slide off the bed to crouch next to Levi.

"I should ask the same," he whispers.

"I'm talking to Skye, privately," I add, giving him a hard glare. Then I lean on the bed, defeated. "Please don't tell anyone–about Makai."

"Of course." He doesn't press or ask questions. He just glances around at all the sleeping patients and then at the unconscious Skye. "You took the potion, didn't you?"

"Yes," I say, rolling my eyes. "I did." Noticing his tired face, I ask, "Couldn't sleep?"

He nods thoughtfully. "I didn't visit today–and I felt that I should. Elias gave me the go ahead to come as long as I brought her a rose." He places the flower in the glass vase, already filled with fresh water, as if Ms. Mendy was expecting us to come.

"Keep talking to Skye. I'll join in." He shifts his position to match mine, elbows resting on the neatly tucked blankets. "It's like we're talking to a grave," he mutters. I just stare at him, blinking in surprise. "If we're doing confessions, then I'll go first."

He rests his chin and gives me a look that asks, *I won't tell if you don't tell*. Taking the hint to keep this event to myself, I bob my chin slightly for him to continue. The son of the Premier gives me a grateful look and begins. "I learned how my mother died yesterday. I know it's normal to feel a bit shaken after finding out something like that, but that's the problem. I don't *feel* as much as I think I should."

My mind flashes to my brother at the mention of *death*. "I do not feel a loss," Levi continues. "I see the pain in my father's eyes and yet I can't say I have the same look in mine. Where those feelings should be is just emptiness. Something isn't right and I don't know what it is."

His tone turns contemplative rather than bitter. "It's the same thing with this new world. When I found out that there was this other side of the world that has magic, monsters, and dragons–I didn't find it extremely strange. It's like I knew about it already. I know that sounds a little delusional, but that's as close to the truth as I can get. Maybe this world is a part of me and something within me just knows."

The soft moonlight illuminates his face, showing a look that might just be acceptance. I can't imagine what could be going on in his head. In some ways, he's taking it better than I expected him to. "I hope that didn't sound as cheesy as I thought it sounded." He laughs to himself, running a hand through his tousled hair.

Levi and I sit together in silence, listening to the shallow breathing of our friend. A few days ago, his life was so simple. There was no over looming threat of Nikolai or any of the others. He didn't have to worry about being murdered by a Malevolent... Now someone he barely knows lays on a hospital bed in front of him, recovering from being shot by poisoned arrows trying to save him.

"Well, we better go. This potion isn't going to last long," I whisper and rise. Levi does the same. Bringing a first to my mouth, I bow my head. My chest warms when Levi does the same. "Good night, Skye. We'll see you again." With that, I walk back to the school, Levi by my side. He keeps silent, noting my unwillingness to talk about... my dilemma.

We say our good-byes in the Entrance Hall and head our separate ways. I start to hear my steps halfway back and when I turn the doorknob to get in my dorm, the squeak sounds in full glory. I sneak into bed, doing my best not to wake Vesta from her slumber. The brunette Royal doesn't so much as stir. Settling into my sheets, a feeling of peace lays over me, a weight lifted off my chest. Saying it to someone out loud, even if she isn't conscious, helped.

This time, sleep takes me gladly.

Chapter 14

Austra

Levi seems to have gotten the hang of things, relatively. There was one instance where Odyssey decided to singe the tail of Nikolai's dragon and there was this whole debacle about who would pay the medical expenses that the Premier had to settle.

He seems to have gotten to know some of his classmates, waving at people in the halls every now and then. Back in the Outside world, he seemed closed off. The smile on his face and his knack for starting conversations shows progress. Levi's easy to get along with and easy on the eyes, which is always a popular combination. My gut fills with envy each time, wishing my peers would feel the same about me.

"Elias!" Our group stops in the middle of the courtyard.

"Aspyn?" Elias jogs toward a girl, a black cat closely trailing behind her. Her nose ring glistens in the light and her short figure is almost consumed by her large, grey hoodie.

"Where were you?" The blond puts her hands on her hips, her green eyes harsh with annoyance.

"Just hanging out. Why?" Elias asks, his face twisted in confusion.

"We were supposed to work on our project," she says, an edge to her voice. "Remember?" The Hunter's hair is cropped short, at a light angle, strands of red peeking out from underneath. It's a bold choice, considering it's the color of the Malevolents.

Elias thinks for a moment, tapping his chin. Then his eyes widen. "Aspyn, I'm so sorry. I totally forgot."

"Well, let's go work on it!"

She grabs his hand and together they run toward the library.

Levi nears my side as we watch them race across the courtyard green. "What's the cat?"

Makai answers for me, "They're called Fate Animals. All Hunters have them. Their souls are connected through life and death."

Levi nods in acknowledgement before him and I start walking to our next class. Makai waves us a quick farewell before heading in the other direction, likely skipping his next class again.

Aspyn has taken a liking to us ever since her and Elias started on their project. Elias and she get along great, both lively enough to make a room feel alight with conversation. I don't question it. Being an Initial, friend groups are still flexible based on the gossip Elias was telling me. Some of the seemingly strongest of bonds are on the verge of breaking. The latest news is the rift between Vesta and Nikolai Goldfinder, the Royal twins. It's the civil war of the gossiping community and from the looks of it, it'll be a while before there's a truce.

Vesta's been quiet, spending less time out of our dormroom. There's that tug of guilt every time I see her return from the bathroom with her eyes puffy and I hate myself for not trying to help. But if I did, there's not a doubt in my mind that she'll just shoot an insult back at me.

When I enter my First Aid class, all threads of thought sever. I stop dead in the doorway and Levi's breath catches.

Skye. Skye's awake. Walking around and well. She does look a little frail, but she's standing.

"You're back," exclaims Levi, his face spreading into a huge smile.

She finds us in the rush of students, her golden eyes locking with ours. The side of her lips tilt up, her only sign of emotion. We rush towards her anyway. Some of our classmates give her surprised glances as they pass, likely going on to spread the word that the Duexieme's daughter has returned. When they stare too long, she looks right in their direction with a hard glare. They look away just as quickly and quicken their pace away.

"Austra," she says and frowns. "Still haven't matured?"

I look down at the ground, biting down the sting. "Not yet." Skye doesn't walk around questions when she has them. There are times where it's appreciated, but there are others when it's not

Folding her arms across her chest, she says in hushed tones, "My father will bully the Premier into letting you go before the next full moon."

"Don't worry about it, Skye," I say, furrowing my brows. I don't want to have this conversation with someone who just woke up from a comma.

Sensing my discomfort, Levi drops his bag onto the floor with a thud. "Good to see you again." I silently thank him for changing the topic. "How are you feeling?" Those who don't know him wouldn't hear the hint of remorse in his tone.

She leans against the table, contemplating her answer. Skye looks thin, a bit pale, and in no shape to take on a Malevolent. Before she has a chance to answer, she stiffens, feeling a shift in the room.

"Daughter, I see you're awake." Her father comes up behind her. She doesn't so much as turn.

"Yes, I am," she says calmly, her words are laced with venom. She takes the seat next to Levi, opening her notes to the first clean page. A dismissal.

The Deuxieme huffs and leaves.

The class goes as planned, however, everything about Skye is on edge. Her posture is rigid, and her eyes are as sharp as a blade. That conversation with her father went too smoothly and she knows it. There will be punishment for getting injured and bedridden.

The answer to my worry comes when we make it to Self Defense. The Deuxieme finds us sitting together in the crowd of students. There's a dark flint to his eye, which sends a chill down my spine.

"Today we have special entertainment. My daughter shall Duel Levi Sage," he calls over the Practice Hall.

I widen my eyes. You *have* to be kidding me. Not to discredit Levi, but he's a little rustier than the others. Skye's face is creased with worry. We can tell the Deuxieme is not kidding. My senses are doused in dread as Skye and Levi make their way to the center of the room. She wears a black jacket with a high collar, making her seem tall and elegant against the ragged, scrappy Levi. Her hair is up with strands of stray hair frame her face. She examines Levi with a face of concentration, debating her first move.

Levi doesn't seem fazed, as if he was expecting a move like this from her father.

"Begin," the Deuxieme commands.

Skye mouths, "I'm sorry." She ducks low, swinging a leg out to trip Levi. He steps aside easily, right into a blow to the gut that knocks the air out of him. Coughing, he staggers back, out of reach. He throws a punch for Skye's cheek. She ducks in the nick of time and counters with a blow to his ankles again, this time taking him to the ground. Skye pins him, pressing Levi into the mats. With a face made of stone, she stands to face her father, Levi in her grasp, and blows a stray hair from her forehead.

He nods, "Good."

She releases him before the word finishes.

Deuxieme Fervent strides toward my humiliated friend and leans in to whisper in his ear. Being in the first row, I'm close enough to hear. "Now you know what it feels like to lose," he says in a low voice. "Get used to it because this won't be the last time."

...

Levi

115

"I mean, you could have done worse," says Elias, patting me on the shoulder.

"Thanks," I say dryly, pressing a damp cloth to my busted lip. My cheeks burn with embarrassment.

"Most people who get paired with Skye are out with the first blow," adds Austra, concern written on her face.

We moved on to shooting practice by the time I got back from the Infirmary. Austra's arrows are an acceptable distance from the bullseye, but nothing close to the precision Elias has with his aim. I had thought I was pretty good at archery, but he's another level. We had a friendly competition when we went to the archery range the other day. He blew me out of the park, and I lost a few purple bills as a result.

"That makes me feel so much better," I grumble.

Tossing the towel over my shoulder, I shoot my arrows at the board to dispel my anger, each one of them hitting their mark. Deuxieme Fervent yells at the class to put everything away, so I head to the storage area at the end of the field. Feeling sorry for myself, I chuck my bow onto its holder.

"I really am sorry."

Knowing who it is, I continue on my walk towards the bleachers with a bit more force in my step. "It's nothing."

"To you it's not nothing," she says, following me at my heels. The bell shrills, igniting my annoyance even more.

"No, really," I ground out. "Don't apologize."

"Just know that I held back."

I turn to face her. "Don't you have a class to go to?" I ask, irritated.

She crosses her arms and grins smugly. "See. You do care."

I roll my eyes, but she talks again, refusing to back down. "My father likes to make a fool of people and a lot of the time, the silent blame lands on me. As Fate would have it, to answer your question, I have the same class as you this period."

She seems satisfied when I allow her to walk by my side. We go through the bustling halls in silence, a part of me frustrated that she's right.

...

Skye

I hate to admit it, but Levi's actually pretty good at Valian. He says a lady that looked after him when he was young taught him a little bit of Russian, which is similar to Valian. But, still.

During class, we learn about the history of my people. I've already read the stories a million times, but it's interesting to hear the tale told from an actual Valian's point of view. Yes, Ms. Valcov is a Valian. The only one, other than me, in this school.

I like her. Like the Premier, she doesn't follow my father's orders out of fear. Not that I would admit it out loud, but I find it comforting that if I told her a something personal, she wouldn't run to my father. I'm glad that she's found peace in herself, after what happened to her son, Zander. Her narrative could've ended in tragedy, however in instances like that, we choose our fate.

"Please turn to page 165 in your textbooks. We're learning about The Tale of How the Valian Fell," she begins, sorrow heavy in her words. Every member of the Six Kingdoms knows the premise of the story, leading to a blanket of disgrace over the Valian population.

"Before the uprising, the Fates believed Valians to be wise and valiant, trusting them with strong gifts. They could fly for miles because of their large wings and they could see in the darkest places. And they did, for a number of years. Jealous, a group of Warriors popularized the idea that Valians were too superior to be tied to the Six Kingdoms. This group of Warriors were Werewolves.

"A large number of Valians caught on to this false propaganda. What started as a plan to incite treason, grew. Even though the Werewolf troublemakers disassociated themselves from the movement, it still persisted. About ten years later, Valians united under one clan and separated from the Six Kingdoms. They built the Empire from the ground up and made Valian the official language. They were wonderful leaders with less flaws than one would expect. Many people thought this was going to be the birth of a new kingdom. Brewing under their noses was Six Kingdoms. They ragged war against us–them, I mean. Valians were major leaders within the Six Kingdom army, which angered the government.

"That is also how a lot of the horrible stories about *vampires* were started. That we prey on mortals for their blood, are deathly pale, and cold-hearted. Sadly, these rumors cannot be taken back.

"Anyway, during the war, we lost all of our wonderful castles and towns. Our culture was ripped away from us. A Warrior was king of the Six Kingdoms at the time, named King Titus Morbid. And luck may have it, he was a Werewolf. He showed no mercy and our numbers drastically fell. When we lost over half of our numbers, the Valians raised the flag of surrender. The King took our request for surrender. Instead of putting the remaining Valians in prison, King Titus Morbid executed every Valian that he could find."

I lower my chin in respect.

"Mad with the Werewolves, the Fates made them slaves to the full moon. They are forever cursed to become beasts when they see the light of the night. They also lost the ability to lie. The king was assassinated by members of his personal."

She took a breath. "Around five hundred years after the end of the war, the first vampires in centuries started popping up again. Rarely, but they came about. I was one of the first, along with my brother.

The Kingdoms, knowing the wrongs that they have done in the past, bought books and made special classes just like this one, to convey our stories and cultures, so history doesn't repeat itself."

She looks directly at me when she says, "Remember the fallen Valian."

The bell rings knocking all of my classmates back into reality. Even then, many of the students don't rise from their seats. All except me. I shoulder my bag and crash through the door.

...

Levi

Austra and I sit on the side of the class and do our homework while the Warriors warm up. The sky is cloudy, forcing the use of electric lights in the window heavy room. The gloomy weather isn't too uncommon near the ocean, nonetheless, it dampens the mood.

When Mr. Tranipuso gives the call to morph, I watch Skye intently. She notices my stare, but turns away quickly, ignoring me.

It starts with her arms. They elongate three times their length and become thinner and the skin around the bony arms and legs turn into a black leather like texture. Her face shrinks and scrunches, and her hair recedes into her head. At first, she looks like a crow, but there's no feathers and claws stick out at the end of her wings and feet. She looks like a bat... well, not really. It's much bigger, more human-like than a normal bat.

Austra leans over and whispers into my ear, "*That's* a Valian."

All I manage to rasp out is, "Wow."

Her sharp claws and teeth are like streaks in the air as she swarms her opponent. When she finally pulls away, little scratch marks scatter the brown bear's fur. Austra tells me that in the Six Kingdoms, they learn to not mind the little injuries. After enough practice, they're practically painless. Warriors generally have a high pain tolerance and heal quicker than the other Kingdoms.

I'm not worrying about whether or not the bear will be okay, physically. The bear looks downright terrified, his legs shaking slightly. When they train with weapons, they're charmed so they don't inflict damage if it's a significant wound. When training in their morphed forms, there's no real way to prevent serious injuring if they're not careful.

After some painful looking seconds, she transitions back. She asks Mr. Tranipuso, "Can I half morph?"

"What does half-morph mean?" I ask Austra.

She looks up from her textbook. "When they only morph into some parts of their animal form."

"Why would they want to do that?"

She gestures to Skye, "It takes a lot of energy to morph into larger animals. She's probably still weak and healing."

"I'm sorry Ms. Fervent," says Mr. Tranipuso. "Mr. Lee needs to practice both. And I don't know if he knows how to fight half morphed yet."

"I'll practice with her," yells someone across the room. The heads of all the students in the room turn to a boy with golden hair and golden eyes. He has wider shoulders than most and a crooked but charming grin on his face.

The look on Skye's face is one of pure loathing.

"Are you sure, Mr. Grave?" Mr. Tranipuso asks, glancing between them. No questions about whether he's cutting class or contemplation of turning the Warrior away. There's something that almost looks like fear on the teacher's face.

"Very," the older boy says, not a doubt in his tone.

The teacher doesn't seem to know what to do for a few moments, debating if he would rather feel Mr. Grave's wrath or Skye's.

He decides to nod his head. "Then I won't stop you."

Mr. Grave and the brown bear switch places. I don't know what I'm more alarmed by: the fact that Mr. Tranipuso let the boy join our class out of the blue or the fact that the boy doesn't look the least bit scared of Skye.

The disgust in Skye's eyes grows exponentially as he nears, as if being close to him repulses her. The boy only half-morphs, so I can't quite tell what animal he can turn into. His hair grows out and his canines and claws elongate. Skye only has her long wings spread wide, angled back like a bird. Her two fangs lengthened and her eyes promise a swift end.

"Is that a—"

"Yep," Austra says. "A Wolf Shifter. The Outside World calls them Werewolves."

They fight like a dance. Each stroke is a product of long hours paid to the practice room. The boy looks maybe a year or two older than us and the skill in his movement shows that time.

People stop to watch. A few students peek through the various windows. Skye is composed and each movement is meaningful and clean despite her muscles being weak from disuse. His style is rabid. But not messy. There's snarls and claws; his fight is for dominance.

After seemingly endless minutes of nonstop movement, they pause, both of them gasping for breath. Many of our classmates stare at the two, open mouthed, as if witnessing history. It's quite a sight. It's rare to watch Skye fighting someone who can actually meet her level.

It's silent, save for the ragged breaths of the two Warriors.

The next thing I know, claws and fangs flash. Something catches and I hear a crack. The boy falls to the ground, out cold, and blood drips onto the mat.

"What in the Six Kingdoms was that?" We all look at Mr. Tranipuso, his face as red as a beat. "You are not allowed to knock out classmates in this class. Only temporary pinning or slight dizziness. You should know better! Mr. Sage, Ms. Rabid, get over here. Carry Mr.

121

Grave to the Infirmary. Make sure this does not happen again, Ms. Fervent, or I will tell your father."

Austra and I get up to do as we are told. We strain at the weight, dragging the boy of pure muscle through the door. She glares at the limp boy with so much fire and contempt, I wonder what else went down in that fight.

Chapter 15

Levi

Nerves kindle in my stomach as I walk to my father's office, the halls my only companions.

During the course of the past week, I was contacted by my father's Lightning Critter with instructions to come see him. I haven't really seen my father in a while. I mean, he talks to the school during dinners about upcoming events and such, but the last time we talked face to face was when I nearly got sued by Nikolai's dad because of Odyssey's temperamental nature.

Just thinking about seeing my father again makes my blood boil. There is that loss of trust and I don't know if that will ever be regained. I let myself in without knocking as a silent protest. My father stands looking through his office window into the distance. He's as polished as ever with an immaculate suit and tie.

"Good evening," he greets, turning around to reveal a warm smile.

I take a seat with more gusto than necessary and give him a hard glare. "What do you want?" Noting the concern in my father's eyes, my worry deepens: *Could there be any updates about Malevolents? Or was there something else...*

"Today is November 20th," he begins, coming around to his desk. "In two weeks, Ms. Rabid will either be considered a part of our kingdoms or be sent away to attend a school in the Outside world."

"I know," I say, irritation rising. "She's my friend.".

"I want you to know that I have no way to get her more time. A few people have been doing everything in their power to find a reason to get the Court to make me step down. If I extend her time, they might use that against me." He leans back in his chair, the lines on his face deepening. "My hands are tied."

"Try harder," I say, grinding my teeth.

"I will. Trust me." I scoff at that. "Just support Austra through this time," he says. "She is pure of heart and the Six Kingdoms would accept her gladly if the Fates wish it. I brought you here so that you can try some methods to help her mature into a Kingdom."

I nod my head, willing him to go along. He places a small book on the desk just as a loud crash makes both my dad and I jump.

I whirl around in the direction of the door, reaching for the dagger in my belt. Having recently earned the silver blade in one of my classes, I have full intentions to put it to use if need be. My hand lowers when the Secretary, a plump, white haired woman, scurries into the room.

"An urgent message from the General," she exclaims, fanning her reddening face. "Malevolents have been spotted!"

The Premier grabs the note and immediately rips open the red wax seal. His eyes scan the letter, the blood draining from his face. Without looking up, he says, "You may go Levi and take the book. I think that I've told you all that I wanted to."

I shake my head, snatch the book, and charge out of the room, anger sizzling in my veins. *Of course, he has business to attend to. Of course, he doesn't tell me about what's happening with the Malevolents.* I pretend to walk out of the room and tuck myself behind the door, receding into the shadows.

"You may leave too. Thank you." I press myself harder against the wall as the Secretary hustles past, a hand on her forehead in distress.

"General Callus," begins my father. "Yes, I'm alone. Explain the urgency of this message. Malevolents always try to get through the walls so what's so different this time around?" I hear my father talk to the miniature sun.

124

The Lightning Critter speaks back, "Premier Sage. Based reports from the local water pixies, there have been sightings of Malevolents traveling through their waters. The Malevolents have found a way to morph themselves again, but this time using the blood of Selkies," says a man with a deep voice. A shiver runs down my spine. Why would they need blood?

I remember the mention of Selkies in one of my classes. They're Warriors that diverged from the Six Kingdoms in the Battle of Hightide. Seal shifters. I guess school really does come in handy sometimes.

A stretch of silence follows the message. After a couple of seconds, I start to worry that he heard me. Then my father asks, "What are their numbers? Are they heading to Grantham Willow?"

The General replies, "There are about two dozen, if not more. It does not appear that they have a set path. They go from one direction to the other. At first, we thought they wanted to go to Grantham Willow, but now they're closer to Grim Dawn. We're unsure. Be cautious. Lord Prophetic has a feeling and his intuition is usually right, as you know."

Peeking through the space between the door and the wall, I watch my father slump onto his desk, running a hand through his hair. This is bad. Really, really, bad. I hurry down the stairs and back to my dorm room, my mind numb. A few classmates wave at me and I give them convincing smiles to hide my dread as I jog down the halls.

I crash through my dorm room and sag against the closed door. "That was quick," greets Elias, reading a magazine on his bed. He flexes and points his toes, probably an exercise for ballet.

"Yeah," I reply. Remembering the thin walls, I lower my voice before saying, "There's something I need to tell you all. Now."

I give them a brief overview, the mood in the room darkening. Makai's expression turns grave and he grips his sword for comfort. Elias suggests we send a Lightning Critter to Skye. She responds within seconds, telling our group to meet her at the foot of the girl's dorm.

Austra, Aspyn, and Skye are waiting for us when we arrive. "Come with me," is all Skye says. She leads us through the halls, none of us muttering a word. She stops at a patch of ivy in a sharp gap in the wall and places her locket between the vines. The surface of the metal is filled with about a dozen small indentations. Thinking of all of the souls locked that necklace sends a shiver down my spine.

A moment after the locket is tucked back inside Skye's turtleneck sweater, the stone of the wall starts to disappear. She walks through the small opening first, the rest of us following like little ducklings.

The area that we duck into is so small, we have to crouch to fit in. A ladder climbs up the opposite wall. It looks old and worn, but solid.

"Just to warn you," cautions Skye, glancing over her shoulder, "the ladder leads all the way up to the sixth floor. If you fall to your death–it's not my fault."

"Thanks, Fervent," says Makai. Harsh shadows and light make his smirk look absolutely devious.

She ignores the sarcastic tone and begins to climb. Even with the warning, each of us follow. The rungs of the ladder grow monotonous as we climb two, three, five stories. My hands begin to go raw and burn from the metal rails. The rungs are smooth, as if they were used hundreds of times before.

"How much farther?" Aspyn asks, her arms trembling slightly.

"As far as it takes," Skye says, five lengths in front of us and barely breaking a sweat.

Makai rolls his eyes, a bead of salted water falling down his temple. Elias doesn't look any less tired than Makai. I have to admit, my shoulders burn, my palms beginning to dampen.

Skye reaches the end and crawls to the landing, the rest of us catching up slowly. Aspyn rolls on her back in exhaustion. Elias just wiggles onto the flat and doesn't move, his face in the ground. Austra manages to stand and I do the same, Makai following as the last one on the landing. Aris just rises and walks over to sit in the corner, his eyes observing the small room for any signs of danger. Skye looks down at us, disappointed.

"You all need to get in better shape," she says. I can already see the thoughts working in her mind. My guess is that we'll have a new workout routine by morning.

"Duly noted," Elias grounds out, short of breath.

"Wow," says Aspyn in awe, still laying on the red rug of the landing. "Aren't the stars beautiful?"

We all gaze up, even Skye. Her expression softens slightly at the sight. I heard about the Astronomy tower and the translucent ceilings. This room must be directly underneath that part of the school.

I let them rest a few moments before telling them what I overheard from my father's conversation. As I give them the debrief, they huddle around me, their eyes etched with worry and dread. Aris' face somehow manages to look even more covered in shadows.

"Why do the Malevolents have the blood of Selkies?" I ask.

"It's the same thing with the Malevolent that attacked you that had claws," Austra says, twisting her bracelets around her wrist.

Skye leans her head back onto the wall, resting. "I was doing some research in the library the other day about something called Blood for Blood Magic. The book I found only had a paragraph on it, but essentially, if done correctly, the use of the blood of a magically gifted creature can give the wielder their gifts for a few years. But the being that gives the blood must die."

"What," I exclaim with disbelief. "So, they can just insert their blood into their body and suddenly have the gifts that each of the kingdoms have?"

"Well, not really," she says. "After it wears off, instead of living… they'll be existing for all eternity, unable to be at peace. Once started, there's no going back. It's like death… but not. Their souls are rejected by the Gates to the Afterworld."

"That's horrible," I say. "Why would they do that?"

"It gives them power. Hate makes everyone go mad at some point," says Makai. "Think about it, the Six Kingdoms have made their lives a living hell through Ninety-nine Wars. We don't give them the opportunity to exist. They're at a constant state of hunt and kill. Their life's existence is dedicated towards killing us. The last war is predicted to occur in the next century, so they might be preparing to rise again."

"The Selkie blood gives them the ability to breathe and travel through water," I say, connecting the dots.

Skye nods sadly. "From what you've said, it seems like the General thinks it's just a possibility that the Malevolents come here. I don't think that we should worry about it too much."

Aspyn's gaze falls to her lap. "What if it's true?" Her cat snuggles into her leg, letting out a deafening purr. I raise an eyebrow, wondering how the feline made it up to the landing.

"We're at Grantham Willow," Austra says, looking on the positive side. "We have one of the best teaching staffs in the world and some highly trained students."

"I mean, we have a Skye... and they don't, so...," Elias says with a wide smile.

Skye rolls her eyes but doesn't say anything.

"I'll pray to the Fates that you're right," Aris mutters, a piece of black hair just covering his eyes.

Chapter 16

Levi

Life goes on. Even if monsters threaten to terrorize schools.

It has been about two weeks since the meeting with my dad. We haven't heard anything about Malevolents in the daily newsletter. Apparently, Aspyn and Elias are in the newsletter club, so it's mandatory for us to read each day's issue... unless we want to feel their wrath. Usually they get word from their connections in the government pretty fast when there's something juicy to tell. Today there reports of an ongoing investigation over rebel sympathizers and spies.

"Who are the rebels?" I ask as I read the article before class starts.

Austra leans against one of the classroom desks, her mind off somewhere far away. "The rebels were founded on the ideology that the territories of the Six Kingdoms should have more of a say in government. Basically, anti-monarchy. The United States has states, we have territories."

"They were founded around the time of the American Revolution," Austra finishes, adjusting her tie. "During that period, there were a lot of revolutions and uprisings, which didn't exclude the Six Kingdoms. They staged one that failed, though they never fully disappeared."

I nod and adjust my wetsuit collar. Our project for the day is to practice saving people from drowning. Austra and I are debating the probability of getting hypothermia when Deuxieme Fervent arrives, a short, plump man following not too far behind. Skye and another boy, who I recognize as maybe a grade older than us, enter the room and go to stand by Duexieme Fervent's side.

The Duexieme has a way of sucking the air out the room in a suffocating way. When he sees Austra and I, he tips his chin up and gives us cross between a sneer and grimace. I give a full-fledged scowl back.

"My daughter and Mr. Lark will look after you all when you practice so that you don't die, along with Mr. Prophetic." The old man with round glasses waves shyly at us. I sit up a little straighter. I remember his name from the conversation I overheard in my father's office. "Now, if you'll excuse me." My shoulders relax when he leaves.

Skye and the other boy walk toward us, our classmates stepping away from them like a disease. The boy next to her gives his classmates a raised eyebrow, but Skye keeps her eyes neutral.

Her cheeks and undereye have filled in since she's women up. Skye's complexion has also become less pale and her hair more vibrant. Makai and she have been training every day after to school together to try to build up her muscles again. Every time, she talks and smiles a bit more, like restoring her skills makes her feel more like herself again.

"Hey Skye," I greet. I look at my classmates out of the corner of my eyes. A good amount of them look back. "How do you feel about watching us freeze to death?" I tease. "Maybe I'll push you in the water too."

Austra sighs but grins sadly at us. She sniffles, her eyes red and puffy. Today is December 9th. One more day until Austra has to leave for the Outside world. Elias and I helped her pack her things in her Grantham Willow duffle bags. Though I hated every second of it, I don't know what else to do to help her. I've tried everything in that little book my father gave me. We've tried drinking ginger shots, a whole roasted garlic, and even had Skye drop her from 100 feet in the air and catch her just before she hit the ground.

Even Makai and Aspyn helped look through other texts in the library for advice. Makai is more quiet than usual, having stopped his nightly adventures and excursions. I think he knows it bothers Austra when he actively goes out to get in trouble. Maybe that peace of mind is his gift to Austra to help her feel better.

Skye raises her eyebrow and purses her lips, hiding a smile. "Better not drown because I might let you," she says with some playfulness. "This is Wesley," she says.

Wesley gives us a kind grin and a nod, his silver hair stark against his deep skin. I bow my chin, offering him a friendly grin despite the constant storm of thoughts in my mind.

The school newsletter said that a Malevolent Warning was sent to Trinity Dale Academy in the south. I guess the General's crew pinpointed the target, which eased me to some extent. Some of the teachers and older students went over to help defend against attack, so the past week has gone by fairly slowly without their company. The Deuxieme has been running the school since my father went to help Trinity Dale.

Thinking of it, I would much rather jump into freezing salt water than fight Malevolents. Ms. Mendy, our teacher for this class, is out to aid Trinity Dale in case an attack does come, so I guess we have Mr. Prophetic as a substitute, making me grateful that Skye and Everest are helping with the class.

Mr. Prophetic clears his throat to get our attention. "We must go down the cliff now, children," he says adjusting his collar. His cheeks are stained pink and his forehead is damp. My classmates chatter over his announcement but follow his instructions.

In wetsuits, ready to be frozen to death, we make the cold trek down to the beach. Skye and Everest are in their school uniforms, making me question whether or not they're expecting to actually do some saving today.

The salt wind bites at our faces, making me wince at the sting in my eyes. If I wasn't fully awake from the morning, I am now. We go over to the cliff and hike down the rocky path to the beach. Two students help the sub down the rocks as he shakes his head and mutters under his breath. Austra and I give each other uneasy looks, the deafening sound of the waves crashing against the rocks numbing our ears.

"Skye. Austra," I call through the wind, forcing a smile through chattering teeth. "If we die today, I just want you both to know that you're pretty okay for human beings."

"You aren't going to die," Skye says, not bothering to look at us.

"From now on I'm going to call you Sunshine. How's that?"

She shakes her head and gazes up at the grey sky. "Shut up."

"Okay... Sunshine."

"Ugh!"

"Do they always do this?" Wesley asks Austra, who looks about to turn into an icicle.

"Sadly, yes," she replies, her voice shaking.

We slide our shoes off when we reach the white, sandy beach and put them where the waves won't reach. The sand is damp, even this far away from the shore. The waves are monstrous today, brushing piles of seaweed almost to the cliff itself. As we near, my toes start to freeze.

Everest shivers and starts to morph into a large water bird. Not wasting another second, he launches into the air to stretch his wings.

"It's a Little Blue Heron," Skye says, as he does one pass around the edge of the water.

"I can see that," I say, gesturing to the little, blue bird.

"No, I meant that's the name of the bird," she says.

"Oh," I say, my eyes not leaving him. "That's kind of unoriginal, isn't it?"

She ignores me and beings to morph into her Valian form. First, her arms and legs turn into black, leathery wings and claws. Then, her ears and canines elongate, making her look stunningly, terrifying. She jumps off the sand to meet Everest, the force of her wings sending a blanket of sand into my face. Both Everest and Skye weave through the grey sky, creatures of deep blue and tar black.

Austra and I eye the waves ahead uncertainly.

"Want to run into it? Get it over with?" I suggest, shrugging my shoulders.

She nods quickly. "Fine by me."

"Okay. On the count of three. One. Two. Three." We both charge into the small waves, water splashing into my eyes. I take a sharp intake of breath as my body becomes stiff, submerged in the water.

"I–I didn't think it would be this cold," I say, hip deep into the freezing water.

Austra doesn't reply, trying to rub her palms against her arms for warmth. Clouds of breath fill the air between us. We both shake uncontrollably, our lips paling. We keep swimming farther in, knowing that if we don't get past the waves while they're small, we might get caught under a bigger one. I don't feel like gulping a mouthful of saltwater today.

A huge gust of wind almost knocks me over completely and sprays water into my eyes. As I catch myself, I see a glimpse of a black shadow fly over my head.

"Skye! Now you're definitely going to get thrown into the water."

She looks over just a smidge and smirks, her sharp, white fangs showing.

I wade farther into the bay until I have to swim to keep my head afloat but can reach the bottom if I tried. Water pixies make the bottom glow through the surface and tease me by tickling my feet. I stop myself from kicking them away, remembering Spencer's girlfriend, Lila. When we said good-bye to the students leaving for Trinity Dale to protect the school, she told us that she would keep an eye on us through the water pixies. Apparently, they like to gossip a lot.

A hand pushes my head under the water. A wave of panic rippling down my veins. I kick my attacker and start to scratch at its hands. When I come up, I cough up salt water and gasp in the freezing air.

"Getting used to the ocean, Premier Junior," says a voice I recognize as one of Nikolai's followers.

"Hello Ryker," I grumble looking up at a boy with messy, shoulder length black hair. He towers over me by over a foot and his thick eyebrows make his eyes look like pits.

"Premier Junior, call me Giant," he chuckles, ruffling my soaked hair. His hazel eyes are unnerving, nearly all brown. Having one of Nikolai's friends so near me makes me want to shiver.

"Maybe if I call you by your real name, then you might start calling me by my real name," I say, a bite to my tone. "Second of all, I'm not my father."

"But you are. You're all the same," he growls.

A sharp whistle pierces the air. We turn our heads toward the beach where Mr. Prophetic gives us the signal to begin our exercises. I feel Giant's stare on my back even after he swims away. Austra and I pair up and begin practicing what to do if someone's drowning. When Austra tries to save me, I try to make it as hard as possible. I kick and swing my arms, making it as realistic as possible. I'm doing her a favor, training her for the hardest of cases.

The next whistle signals for us return to shore and get ready for our next class. I thank the Fates and start swimming back. Austra and I are pretty far out, so most of the class makes it back to shore before we're halfway back. My peers chase each other around the beach, trying to throw the seaweed on each other.

I burst out laughing, almost choking on sea water, when Evie, a petite girl with purple hair, trips Giant into the water as he was chasing someone. When Giant comes up spouting water like a whale, he charges up the beach and launches her into the deep end of the bay. When she resurfaces, she spits a mouthful of water at him.

The pixies tickle my feet again when I look up at the top of the cliff, where Wesley waves at us. Austra and I wave back.

A scream echoes off the walls of the cliff. I look over smiling, expecting to see Giant throwing someone else into the bay. But instead, I see Evie's face struck with pure terror.

Her finger points towards us.

No–behind us.

Turning around, I scan the bobbing waves. I count my breaths, my heart beating in my chest so loud, it's all I hear. Time starts again when I see the tops of heads. My blood goes cold.

Their eyes are red.

"GO," I shout across the bay, willing my voice to carry. The students on the beach dash up the path and stairs, scrambling towards the school. Austra and I race for our lives. The water pixies leave our sides immediately. Maybe their pestering wasn't to play, but to warn us. Never has the shore looked so far away. When I catch a breath, over the water I see Mr. Prophetic rush into the water, helping students out of the current. The salt makes my eyes hurt and my lungs burn. I stumble onto the wet sand. The cold bites at my heels.

Out of the corner of my eye, I watch as a Malevolent grabs Mr. Prophetic. It takes him under the water. I stand frozen, counting my heartbeats. He does not rise again.

Austra stumbles into the stand. I turn around in a daze and practically lift her onto her feet and keep running. Together, we crash up the path, towards the stone steps of the cliff. The cuts into the rock are smooth in some areas and rough in others. Too rushed to care, the bottoms of my feet scratch on the surface and my hand gets impaled with dozens of splinters as I tug on the rickety railing.

Shadows pass over us. In the mass of screams, Skye and Wesley fly down to help fish the remaining students out of the water. When the last of the students are on land, I let out a breath. But my relief is short lived. None of the hundreds of students at Grantham Willow are safe.

It dawns on me that all of our trained personnel are at Trinity. Realizing the same thing, Wesley and Skye start to attack the Malevolents. But that's only two against what looks like over one hundred.

Austra and I make it up the cliff, stopping to rest on the grass for a few moments with our classmates. Evie is hyperventilating and Grant tries to calm her down. I crawl over to the edge to look at what's happening below. Skye swoops down and picks at the Malevolents with her pointed claws. Wesley can't do much except peck at them. The red eyed monsters are almost to shore, too many of them for the two Warriors to keep back. As Wesley goes down for another peck, the Malevolent grabs his leg and pulls him down into the water. Austra slames her hand over her mouth to stifle a scream. Skye goes dives towards the chaos and uses her leather wing to knock the monster down. She goes underwater for what seems like an eternity but comes up with a limp and wet bird. Skye makes a beeline for us and drops Wesley at our feet.

He slowly morphs back into the Wesley we first met.

"Austra," I exclaim, rushing over to his side. I press my ear to his chest. "He's not breathing."

"Move over, Levi," says Giant as he pushes me away. He does CPR, trying to get air into his lungs. My classmates crowd around, waiting for the Warrior to breathe again.

Austra scoots closer and lifts her hand over Wesley.

I scrunch my brows in confusion. "What are you doing?"

"Giant, stop for a moment," she says, her attention fixed on the fallen Warrior. Giant does what she says, his gold eyes lifting to meet ours with panic. Austra moves his hand up above his head and then drops it right before it reaches Wesley's mouth.

He lurches up coughing up water. We all jump back in shock. Evie stabilizes Wesley once he stops coughing.

Knocked out of my own panic, I shout at the group. "Someone! Alert the rest of the school. They have to start blockading *now*."

Just like that, things start moving again. All except Austra, who just examines her hand in wonder.

"You did it," I exclaim, giving her a pat on the back. "Great timing." After a moment of peace, I remember Wesley, whose lips have turned an alarming shade of blue. "We have to move him. Giant and Austra, get Wesley to the Capricorn. Evie you go with them. I'll go to the South Bell Tower and signal the alarm."

"Let me go with you," Evie says, jaw set. "It's not like I can do much to help with Wesley now."

I nod my head and wipe sweet from my brow. "Help me knock on the doors and shout the warning."

"Keep an eye out for Aris," Austra says, coming back to reality. "I didn't see him around school today."

"I will," I breathe. With that, Evie and I start sprinting toward the bell. Evie follows close behind. For a tiny thing, she's fast. When we crash into the halls, we don't bother to be quiet. We yell and bang on the doors. Some teachers stand in the hall, wondering what the commotion is about.

"Malevolents!" I shout again to the teachers. At first, they seem shocked and narrow their eyes at me, questioning whether or not I'm telling the truth.

"This better not be a joke, Mr. Sage," calls Ms. Valcov from across the hall.

I look over my shoulder and say, "Honestly Ms. Valcov, I wish it was." A shadow passes over her face in realization and she orders her students to follow her to the Capricorn.

"Evie," I say, breathing hard. "Make sure all of the rooms are notified and that their students are led to the Capricorn. Some of the subs might not know what to do. I can make it to the Bell Tower myself."

She looks at me with worried purple eyes, but her gaze is unwavering. She bows her head, her fist to her mouth. I do the same in farewell.

I make a note to myself that not all Royals are like Nikolai.

I sprint down the hall ignoring the burn in my legs.

When I finally reach the South Tower, I climb into the patch of ivy and place my locket on the stone. As soon as the wall is gone, I run with all my might up the spiral staircase. Each step, I wonder whether each of my friends are okay. Hopefully Makai isn't off wandering the forest and Aris isn't found by a Malevolent if he is in one of his secret hiding places around campus.

I pound through the door and into the round circular landing. The huge bell hangs from the ceiling nearly, touching the stone floor beneath. On a hook in the corner, I unravel the rough rope and scramble closer to the bell to get better leverage.

Using my whole body, I swing the bell.

...

Skye

One.
Two.
Three.
And the fourth bell rings.

I have knowledge of many different cultures around the world, having seen and traveled to many places. Before my parents went to Grantham Willow to teach, they lived in Japan, where four is the number

138

of bad luck. My father still makes sure to never use the number four, no matter how many times he says that superstitions are fake.

It's the number of death.

Help will come. The bell will ring in all of the schools in the Six Kingdoms. The bells in each school are charmed to only be rung manually if the ringer believes the school is in peril and will notify the Six Kingdoms about the location of the threat. I pray to the Fates to let them come in time.

I bat my wings, facing my body towards the onslaught. The wind that I make keeps them back, but there are too many and they keep creeping closer and closer. I look up to the South Tower, barely visible above the cliff. There's a flash of metal and a glimpse of brown hair through the windows.

I screech as a sharp pain on my forearm erupts. Cursing, I propel myself above the cliff and collapse onto the grass. I crash into the grass, sand embedding itself into my back.

"Skye!"

Pounding feet near me, but all I can manage to do is hold my arm and close my eyes tight, trying to will away the pain. Some time in my pain, I morphed back into my human form. White dots scatter across my vision as I stay, kneeling in the muddy grass. I only look up when they reach me.

"Skye," gasps Aspyn. She falls to the ground to look at me clearly. "We were just going to the Capricorn. Can you get up?"

I wince but nod, taking a few deep breaths to steady my thoughts. Aspyn and Elias grab my shoulders to help me. I shake them off, frustrated with myself. I can't believe I got distracted so easily. Pressing my hand on the wound to stem the flow of the blood, I hiss. One glimpse at it makes my toes curl.

"That looks nasty," says Elias, gulping.

"Well aren't you observant," I say sarcastically, picking at the torn skin. A Malevolent must've jumped out of the water. At least the gash isn't as deep as the arrow wound earlier this year.

"Let me take a look at that." I look into Evie's purple eyes and nod my head. Royals are known for their healing skills, so I let her examine it. She looks through the torn fabric of my jacket. "I can heal it. But you need to take off the jacket if I want to get it cleanly. You've heard the horror stories of healing the skin over foreign objects, right?"

I nod my head and shrug off my jacket, wincing slightly. Evie places her hand over my wound as soon as I peel the fabric off the blood. My skin starts to feel warm and then hot, the sensation spreading across the surface of the skin and then deeper. I had a Royal heal me once on my first mission. Although Sorcerers can heal too, Royals are needed for the more severe cases because their magic doesn't need to take from another's energy.

When Evie pulls her hand away, all that is left is a small pale line stained an irritated red.

Out of the corner of my eye, I see a group of Warriors push the emergency boulder to block the only stairway to the beach. It isn't much, but at least it'll give us a couple extra seconds which can mean everything.

"We need to go to the South Tower," I announce, nodding a thanks to the Royal. "I saw something. I think Levi's in trouble."

"You know," says Aspyn, blowing a strand of blue hair out of her face, "I am honestly not surprised."

"I can fly two up with me. Evie, we'll meet you back at the Capricorn. You're going to need to rest for a bit. Same with your classmates over there. Aspyn and Elias, come with me," I say.

Aspyn gives me a worried look. "But your wing–"

"Is fine. Go!" I morph back into my Valian form and lift my wing tentatively. It's tender, but I can fly.

Before anyone can argue with me, I launch myself into the air. There's just a dull ache in the muscle below the scar, as if I had done a workout the day before. Evie is one healer that I will always want on my side.

I make a swooping turn and go back in the direction of the group. Aspyn closes her eyes tight and holds her arm up, knowing what I'm going to do. Elias puts up his hand, his mouth open to protest, but I grip them with my claws and pull them up into the air.

Aspyn lets out a squeal and looks at the ground in terror.

Elias laughs, trying to hide his own fear. "Oh Fates! Why did I decide to be friends with you lot."

...

Levi

I dodge another knife, ducking behind a pillar.

The Malevolent pounces with lightning speed. I dodge the initial blow, water spraying at my ankles. I use the huge bell as cover and I run around it, hoping that the water from the rain will make the stones slippery enough for the Malevolent to trip.

This Malevolent looks more human than the ones I saw months ago. His face is pale, but there's nothing else that would tell me he's evil other than his eyes. There's just a wildness to him, his fighting stance more feral than what we learn at Grantham Willow.

Not having any weapons and a school of defenseless student beneath, I know that I can't escape or fight back. My job is to keep the Malevolent from reaching anyone else, meaning that I have to play a game of chase until someone notices the commotion and helps.

When I pass the balcony window for the fifth time, my knees almost buckle from relief as I see a familiar group flying towards the tower.

Panting, I say to the Malevolent, "You may have gotten into my home base, but I will *end* you."

The Malevolent just growls, the red of his irises promising death. I grin back, darting behind the balcony. He runs after me, throwing knives. I try to dodge by running side to side. For the first time, I send a prayer to the Fates for his knives to miss their mark.

Faintly, I hear Skye say, "I got this."

The next time we come around the tower, the Malevolent collides with a huge, leathery wing. I skid to a stop, my breath heavy in my lungs. Elias takes a Death Arrow from his quiver and stabs the Malevolent in the center of his chest.

I collapse into a sitting position, shivering from the cold of my wetsuit. My feet are ice from the cold of the stone. To bring sound to the silence, I ask, "I know this is a shot in the dark, but does anyone have an extra pair of shoes? Or socks?"

Elias gives me a breath of a grin. "Sorry. I sort of forgot that part in the *hours* I had to pack."

"Doesn't hurt asking," I say, holding up my hands in surrender. I lean my head back on the stone wall, gulping in air.

"Come on guys," Skye says from the window, her body facing away from us. "I don't think the Malevolents will let a boulder stop them."

I stumble to my feet and run to the edge of the balcony to get a better look at the beach. Malevolents climb up the sides of the cliff like ants, most still on the sand.

Ignoring the rain that runs down my face, I close my eyes and listen to the thunder crackle through the air. As the energy fires, I feel it in my veins, igniting my nerves and bringing warmth to my fingers.

Aspyn bangs her fist on the stone railing and lets out a cry of frustration. "I hate them so much."

Elias rubs her on the back as she lets her tears fall. "You and I both." He looks out into the distance, grimly. We don't stand a chance against that many full grown Malevolents without our strongest students and faculty.

"Why can't they just leave us alone?" The Huntress cries, her cat snuggling against her shins.

"They have coal burning in their hearts," says Skye. "They are following what they were bred to do. They've never known love or kindness, and I am sorry for them. The Fates don't make that many mistakes, but by banishing Hardorous, they've doomed us." Her normal turtleneck jacket is gone, revealing a long, jagged scar that runs from her chin to beneath her shirt.

Noticing my stare, she runs her hand along her neck. "That doesn't excuse their actions."

I nod my head and look back out to the bay. Some older students in their fourth or fifth year have gathered around the edge of the cliff, waiting for the Malevolents to reach the top. The teachers that are present stand in the frontlines, their weapons at the ready. I even spot Ms. Valcov in her Valian form, heading the army of scared teenagers.

"We need to go help them," I say to the others.

Skye agrees, her expression darkening. "I'll take you and Elias down. Aspyn, go down to the Capricorn and get Levi a sword. Quickly."

Chapter 17

Levi

Elias is focused for once in his life and doesn't notice Aspyn and Austra coming towards us. Aspyn hands me a sword along the same measurements I usually use and I whisper a thanks, too nervous to offer a proper reply.

"The Malevolents haven't breached the cliff yet?" Aspyn asks, her voice trembling. Her normally light, wavy hair, lays plastered to the sides of her face from the rain.

"They will soon. Let's get closer to the front," Skye says, looking over her shoulder.

"I thought you were with Wesley," I say to Austra, testing the weight of the sword in my grasp.

"Giant and the other Royals took care of him. I slipped out before they could close the doors. They're not allowing Initials, Secondaries, or Juniors fight," she says. Water drips down her face, making it shine when the lightning illuminates the sky.

"Well," says Skye, getting our attention again, "too bad for them. Let's go." She leads us through the crowd of people to get near the front line.

The thunder crackles nearby. I count the time between the next lightning and thunder: two seconds. A few minutes ago, the count was four. The storm is nearing.

The five of us line up two paces away from the ledge. The waves crash up–more vicious than minutes before–taunting us. My mind drifts to the water pixies and their help, maybe this is their way of helping us, attacking the Malevolents in the only way they can.

Austra sees the waves and tries to help, straining to bring the sea closer to the cliff and wash away the Malevolents. Her fingers are twitching, her hands following the movements of the water. The Malevolents stick to the cliff like glue.

"Are you okay?" Elias asks Aspyn, who looks as though she might be sick.

"No," she replies with a quivering voice.

Skye doesn't even glance over, her focus trained on the nearing Malevolents. Part of me wonders if she's scared. Surprisingly, my nerves have calmed as I let the rain run over my clothes, not feeling an ounce of chill. Squaring my shoulders, I harden my gaze. I might not have spent much time at this school, but I'll protect it with all I have.

Spotting Phoebe, I stiffen. *Please don't notice us. Please don't notice us. Please don't notice us.* She comes and does a double take. "What in the Six Kingdoms are you kids doing here?"

"Isn't it obvious?" Skye gives the Keeper of the Dragons a hard look. They're nearly the same height, their eyes level.

"You kids shouldn't be here," she says with her hands on her hips, not backing down.

"Come on Phoebe," Elias pleads.

"You know your brother will kill us both if you die," she says. I can't help but notice the shrill tone of her voice.

"Don't you think my father would approve?" Skye sends the professor a pointed look.

"If I am going to be straight with you, no. No matter how heartless you think he is, I can tell he does care about you. Even though you're more skilled than the majority of the people on the field, you can still die," Phoebe snaps back, leaving Skye speechless.

She opens her mouth to say more but is slammed to the ground. She claws at the grass looking for a hand hold as something pulls her off the ledge. We jump out to help, grabbing for her. Aspyn, Austra, and Elias scramble ahead to hold her in place while Skye and I go to the

Malevolent at her heels. Skye's hand morphs into a claw and she slashes at the creature until it lets go and falls onto the beach.

All along the rock cliffs, the Malevolents climb over. One grabs Elias from behind and his face fills with panic. Phoebe stabs a Death Arrow through its shoulder in a blink of an eye and kicks the creature off the cliff.

More Malevolents continue to spill over and swarm my classmates and friends. The students scramble around, some panicked and some calm. The teachers are a bit more composed and organized, making me wonder if they've ever fought in a battle before.

Phoebe roars at the Hunters to shoot. But the students are mixes in with the Malevolents, so there are next to no clear shots that they can take. Students and teachers desperately try to hold the line, buying time for the help to arrive.

Skye takes a sword from a fallen Malevolent. The obsidian weapon arcs through the air, taking down Malevolent after the Malevolent. I watch in awe as one of the greatest Warriors in Grantham Willow charges into battle, however unconventional it is. Fire, wind, ice, and water burst across the field and cries of pain fill my ears.

Elias, Aspyn, and Austra fight a Malevolent as one. Both of the Hunters have resorted to knives since they can't use their bows. To my dismay, the Malevolent grabs Austra when she tumbles in the mud, holding her in a position that would spell death for both of them if Elias or Aspyn attacked.

My knees wobble when the Malevolent tumbles off the cliff, revealing an astonished Makai with a bloodied sword in his hands. He hugs Austra, who cries into his shoulder. His face is a mirror of disbelief.

Horror and dread fill my soul, weighing me down to where I stand in the mud.

Then something else awakes inside of me. The rain pounds at my feet as I crash to my knees. The thunder booms into my ears, into me.

There's electricity and ringing in my hands, my ears, everywhere. There's a crack and I grasp the surge of energy with all my being and aim it towards the damp sand below.

I see a flash of bright light and shield my eyes.

My ears ring and every muscle feels sore and heavy. Curling into myself, I will energy back into my body and slowly come back to my senses. My muscles twitch and my vision blurs.

Then there's only darkness.

Chapter 18

Levi

Hands grasp my arms and shake me back into reality. The ringing stops. My friends look down at me, some with concern and others with happiness.

Elias is the first to speak, "What in the Six Kingdoms was that?"

I blink. "I–what?" I ask, groggily. "What happened?"

Austra's eyes light up. "You wielded lightning to attack the beach below. You must have electrocuted them."

"I thought some got up the cliff," I say, rubbing my head.

"You were out for a bit. We took care of them," Skye says, blood coating her arms and face. There's a hint of fatigue in her stance, leaning against the sword for support.

"Ah," I hiss, squeezing my eyes shut. Gasping in pain, something burns the skin of my forearm, searing a mark into me.

"What's happening," Austra cries, gripping her arm.

Skye yanks me over and uses her knife to cut back the wet suit. I watch as a line, about an inch long, tattoos itself into my skin. When I think the pain has ceased, another diagonal line with a small circle on its top crawls across my skin, intersecting with the existing line.

"What in the Six Kingdoms," I grasp, gingerly touching my arm. "Why–What is it?" I ask and scoot over to Austra's side, not minding the mud coating my wetsuit. Sure enough, the same symbol is branded on her.

Elias just looks at us in daze and Aspyn stares at the burn marks with a look almost like dread.

"Should we go to the Infirmary?" Austra asks, looking up to Skye for an answer.

"Ms. Mendy is at Trinity. If this is what I think it is, we don't want many people to see this," Skye says with a grim look on her face. "We need to wait for Levi's father. Cover that up. I'm going to help tend to the wounded."

Royals of all ages are scattered across the field, healing the students that are still on the ground. Electricity crackles in my veins as some students are wheeled or carried away.

After a few minutes of rest, I try to rise with the help of Elias and Aspyn. Makai lets Austra lean on his arm and we walk towards the first aid camp that they set up. The pain in my forearm has dulled, but Austra has a few bruises on her neck that we want to check out.

"Guys," calls Aspyn from where she stands at the edge of the cliff. "I see them."

I jog over to her, through the maze of subdued Malevolents. Off into the distance, a herd of dragons fly towards us. They hold banners of all colors, not just of Grantham Willow. *Other schools have come to help.* My dad is the first to land.

He jumps off his dragon with so much energy, you could mistake him for a young twenty-year-old. I raise my hand to wave and he wraps me in a strangle of a hug. I stay there for a moment, stunned at my father's affection. I pop my head over his shoulder and take a much-needed breath.

"Hey, Dad? I have to breathe."

He lets go almost immediately and straightens his glasses. "Of course. Are you okay? Were there any casualties?"

"Only Mr. Prophetic, I think. And yeah... about that," I say and pull the cloth of my sweater away from my arm. Students bustle by us, some running towards the Capricorn and others dropping off their dragons in the stables.

His eyes widen and I gasp as he grasps my forearm hard and examines it closely. His eyes darken with something between sadness and acceptance. Glancing at the students around us, he says, "You better come to my office."

Stopping him from dashing into the school, I say, "Austra has the same mark."

My father's eyes shoot towards the newly matured. "Ms. Rabid, come here," he says. Austra does as told and holds out her arm to my father. He places the two markings next to each other and looks at them closely.

"What is it?" I ask.

Instead of answering my question, he counters with a question of his own. "Did any of you mature into a kingdom today?"

"Both of us did." In another situation, I would've told him with a feeling of pride and relief. The relief is still there, however something within my gut tells me that I just signed a contract to a difficult destiny.

"When did this symbol appear?" he asks, not bothering to ask me what I matured into. No "congratulations" or looks of joy. His frown only deepens.

"It happened just now," I answer for the both of us. Austra seems a little out of it.

"Which one of you matured first?"

"Austra did."

"The symbol burned into their flesh after Levi matured," cuts in Skye. I hardly noticed her listening in.

My father asks, "Are both of you in the same kingdom?"

"Yes," I reply. "Why does it matter?"

"The two of you have to come with me. *Now*. Ms. Fervent, go to your father and tell him to do a headcount and address the school. Use the code word, B.O.X. While you're at it, take my dragon to the stables."

Skye nods and sprints off with the dragon in tow, making sure to avoid the Sorcerers. They do the spell on the Malevolents to put their souls in their slayer's lockets, their fingers twitching and their lips muttering silent words.

It looks like the spirits of a whole graveyard have come to life with their bodies disappearing like the walls behind ivy. I feel my locket open from around my neck and watch dents form on the metal as dozens of souls are pulling until the necklace. The locket grows colder and heavier with each one.

Some enter my friends' lockets and one even enters Austra's. If anyone would have asked me what I would have predicted Austra's reaction to be after subduing her first Malevolent, I would've said cries of happiness. In reality, all she does is stare at the ground, following my father and I into the school.

I examine the new grooves in the metal of my locket.

Fifteen. I sent fifteen Malevolents to endless sleep. A wave of guilt hits me, but then I remember what happened to Mr. Prophetic–what almost happened to Wesley. These creatures have no heart. They can never feel regret even if they wanted to. So why should I?

"How did I subdue them? I didn't have physical contact with them," I ask.

"Your lightning," rasps Austra, speaking for the first time. She clears her throat. "The sand was wet and water transfers electricity well. The electricity was yours." Her face turns from one of shock to one of worry. "Premier Sage? How do we know that there aren't more Malevolents coming?"

"They already got what they wanted," he says as though it's obvious.

"What do you mean?" Austra asks, confused.

"Ms. Rabid, the General sent Mr. Prophetic to the school as protection, not expecting the Malevolents to come here. I'm assuming Ms. Fervent has informed you about Blood for Blood Magic. They took the best fortune teller in the Six Kingdoms and if they use his blood, they'll be able to see our next moves. *That* is why the Malevolents attacked us today."

...

Levi

"Do you remember the talk we had about your mother in the beginning of the school year?"

I give him a look and say, "Yes." Like I would forget that night.

Austra and I sit on my father's nice leather seats. We both still have our wetsuits on and luckily, the secretary got us some towels. Even then, Austra and I probably look like a sad lot.

The rain outside has slowed to a light drizzle and the thunder has completely stopped. I smile, thinking about my liking for bad weather growing up. Maybe my blood always knew.

"Well," my father says, running a hand over his face, "I told you that the reason why we kept you away from the Six Kingdoms was based on a theory."

I nod my head. I can't say I wasn't curious about it all this time, but there wasn't really anything I could do. Especially since everyone who could tell me was under an oath. One day, Skye got so tired of me bugging her about it that she pulled out a book that told about the specifics of the oath they took. Sure enough, if they broke it, they would die. That didn't help my curiosity. What could be so important that my father would make teenagers swear their lives away?

"You also recall that the Six Kingdoms started out as seven, correct? The seventh, the Malevolents, branched out after receiving their curse and swore revenge on the Six Kingdoms. Their Fate, Hardorous, was also banned from the circle of the other six Fates. The remaining six, noticing their mistake upon giving Malevolents the curse of never being able to love or die, let one of their own, a Fate, be born into a family of

152

the Six Kingdoms to protect us all. It happens about every two hundred to three hundred years, with few exceptions. The latest one was during World War II. The prophecy states that one hundred wars will take place before the judgement is decided. The Malevolents will rise after each war and the one hundredth war will either spell their demise or ours." He taps his fingers on his desk, the only sound in the room.

"This Fate is given six companions from each of the Six Kingdoms to help him or her on their journey."

"What are you getting at?" I ask, my voice steady despite the nerves.

My father runs a hand through his hair. "Your mother and I thought that you were the Earthen Born Fate."

My eyes widen. "You can't be serious."

"I wish I wasn't," he says, a look of grief on his face. "If there was a way that I could make it so my only son could have a safe life, then I would. Levi, the life of an Earthen Born Fate has almost always led to tragedy, which is why the Malevolents have been able to rise again and again."

He looks at the worn picture on his desk. "Your mother and I did our calculations and research. You had an uncanny way of attracting Malevolents as an infant. When we would travel to the palace or around the Six Kingdoms, we would almost always be attacked. To a certain degree, it's normal. However, this was too much to be a coincidence. Our suspicions were confirmed in the Battle of the Fifth Moon." My skin prickles at the mention the night Skye was born. "The Malevolents didn't come to make a statement or because of the rebels… they came for you."

Looking me in the eye, he says, "That's why I couldn't keep you at Grantham Willow. We needed to keep you moving so you were harder to track."

"Why didn't you at least tell me about the Six Kingdoms?" I look at him, a little betrayed. The weight of being a Fate hasn't sunken in yet, just the feeling of lost time. Time that I could've spent here or somewhere, training.

"We didn't want you to feel disappointed if you weren't the Fate. Also, we didn't want you to go out and actively hunt Malevolents for what they did to your mother. There were too many loose variables," he says, still confident in his decision.

"Fates have gifts from all of the Kingdoms," breathes Austra, her hand over her mouth. "L–Levi... Oh my goodness."

"The burns on your arms prove it," the Premier replies, sitting back in his chair.

"But–can't it be Austra? She has the same thing," I say, thunder rumbling through my chest.

"I've done the research and the marks start to appear once all of the chosen companions have matured into a kingdom. Sorry Ms. Rabid, but that counts you out as the Earthen Born Fate."

"That means I'm..." She looks up at my father, the color leaving her face. "Oh my."

The Premier just nods at the realization. "A Companion of the Earthen Born Fate, destined to earn your weapon and fight by his side. Assuming you both live long enough to make it to battle."

"What do we do?" Austra looks like she's about to puke. I can't say that I feel any better.

"As history foretold, the Fates will assign you tasks that will test to see if you deserve the weapon. When the weapon decides, you will be presented with the weapon, which is necessary to defeat the Malevolents. Contrary to popular beliefs, the Fates don't control or know everything. The Companions' weapons are a force of their own and they do not care if you win this war or if you never prove yourself worthy. Levi will do the best that he can to protect you throughout the trials. For now, you are tied to each other by the Mark of the Fates."

He lets us sit for a few moments to sort out our thoughts. "What is it?" I ask, studying the mark.

"It kind of looks like a map," Austra says, doing the same.

"Good guess, Ms. Rabid. But, not quite. Does it remind you of a particular school logo?"

"Oh. Oh!" It's a part of the Grantham Willow logo.

"Yes. The straight vertical line is the sword, representing the Fates. The diagonal one with a circle at its tip is the staff, representing the Sorcerer. The rest of the objects have not appeared yet for the other companions have not been chosen by the Fates."

"I still don't believe it," I say, shaking my head.

"Soon you will," my father says in a matter-of-fact way. "It will become quite evident."

"We're the 100th," Austra says in disbelief. "We decide the final fate of the Malevolents and Six Kingdoms."

Of *course,* we are. Out of *all* the other Earthen Born Fates I could be, I just so happen to be the one that decides whether or not the other ones fought in vain or not. I can barely keep myself alive, let alone the entire Six Kingdoms. My stomach starts to turn. *I decide their Fate.*

"That's quite right Ms. Rabid. Even the Fates don't have a role in our end. This final fate of the wars is left to work itself out without their influence." The Premier bends under his desk and opens his drawer and pulls out a very intricate looking box, stained black with gold engravings. Austra looks at the box in horror. The box radiates a thick air, like it isn't from this world. I stop myself from running out of the room when I hear it whisper.

They're inaudible and muffled sounds. That doesn't make it any less creepy though.

Recognition dawns on me. This was the box Sylas brought with him when I first came onto campus. I didn't hear the whispers then and I was right next to him for a few moments. Maybe I was distracted–or maybe something's different this time.

"One of the uses of this box is to determine that the person who claims they are a Fate is actually a Fate. If you could imagine, many

155

people have tried to pass for a Fate before. This ensures their authenticity."

No, actually. I don't understand why someone would voluntarily want to have this type of responsibility. Deciding it best to keep the thought to myself, I ask, "What do I have to do?"

"Place your hand on the box and will it to open."

Expecting some elaborate process, I ask, "That's it?"

"Have you ever heard of Pandora's box?"

"Yeah. The one that held all of man's horrors," I say, recalling my English class back in the Outside lands.

"Something like that," he says, wincing. "That's what it's like to put it short. You'll be fine. I've just read that it might take a bit of time for the images to stop coming."

I take a deep breath, trying to block out what my dad said. I make a mental note to never ask my dad for a pep talk. "Here goes nothing,"

Closing my eyes tight, I place my hand on the ice cold box, bracing myself.

"Ha! I'm not a Fate then. Sorry Dad, I guess you're–"

I gasp and lurch forward in my seat, as if yanked by invisible hands. A sharp pain goes through my head and images flash through my brain. I pinch my eyes shut, not wanting to see.

The school lays in pieces before me, the bodies of my friends scattered on the grounds, beaten and battered. The visions don't give them faces, but I know what they mean to me. The sky is grey, like it was today. Instead of just clouds, smoke pollutes the air from the fires that threaten to burn down my home. Malevolents begin to surround me, crawling out of the corners of the rubble. Fear does not reach my system, just ice-cold rage. Anger so potent, it burns my soul. I don't know what to do with it, so I lash out, throwing all I have at them.

I hear a click. The pain is gone and with it, the vision is too.

All I feel is the cold of the desk on my forehead and a pat on my back, "Now we know for sure."

Still breathing hard, I try to sit up. Austra looks just about to pass out. Fatigue hits me too, but I glance into the now opened box. A large book lies within, binded with black leather. I reach over the sides and drag the book into my grasp, trying to avoid touching the actual box again. The book is warm, like it's alive.

Flipping to the first page, I'm surprised to find it blank. I turn to the next one. Blank. Flipping through all of them, every one of them is blank. Nothing. All of that work for nothing.

My father must have noticed my confusion. "The book will be your line of communication with the Fates. I'll have it dropped off at your room tonight. Just write in it and the Fates should answer."

Closing the book, I whisper, "What's next?"

He pauses for a moment before answering. "Only the Fates can answer that. I don't want the whole school knowing that you're the Earthen Born Fate yet. Once the world knows, the Six Kingdoms must prepare for war. I will notify the King right away, of course. You should ask the book if you're the 100th Fate, just to make sure. For now, we must mourn the loss of a faithful teacher," the Premier says.

"How can you be so calm about this?" I ask him.

He says. "I do not wish this upon my son. But I will do what I can to bear at least some of the weight by keeping myself together in the case you need my help."

Giving both Austra and I one more reassuring pat, he says, "Now, we must go to the Capricorn so we're accounted for."

...

Levi

157

"Some things are not to be read until the right time." I roll the words over my tongue, not quite understanding. It's what Austra said to me on the day we got my dragon. "How was that supposed to be a hint?"

"The Story of Grantham Willow," she says simply. "The book that all Paramounts read before leaving this school? It's the story of the Alliance for the Ages and the Great Trials, when the Seven Kingdoms were still seven. Even though the students are under oath not to talk about it, everyone knows that it's the tale of how this all started. I thought it would at least put you in the direction of the One Hundred Wars."

We fall into silence as bustling halls and entrance to the Capricorn comes into view. People are crying and others are rushing around, carrying supplies and medicines. Students and faculty from other schools do their best to help, offering aid when they can.

As soon as we enter the Capricorn, Spencer crashes into his sister and engulfs her in a hug. He grumbles something about how scared she made him.

"Don't ever do that again," he says, his voice breaking. "Mom can't take another heartbreak. You're lucky I didn't send her a Lightning Critter, or she might've had a heart attack." *Another heartbreak?*

"I know," she says, wiping away a tear. "That didn't stop *you* from going."

Austra was appalled to find him gone a few days ago. He didn't tell her that he was going to leave for Trinity Dale. She specifically asked him about it when she heard the call for all Seniors and Paramounts to go protect the school. The Warrior said no but left anyway. Aris offered her one of his rare hugs and she stayed there, sobbing, for a good five minutes before getting up to eat food.

"Pipsqueak! Did you get a tattoo? Mom's going to kill you," laughs Spencer, dodging the subject.

"No, I didn't get a *tattoo*. Uhm, it's just sharpie. But I did mature into a kingdom," she says, her smile bright.

Spencer's eyes widened even more. "That's great! Did you turn out to be a Scholar after all?"

"Nope! Sorcerer," she says, her face lighting up.

"What element?"

"I'm pretty sure it's water."

He hugs her again, spinning her around. "My little sister can drown people! That'll teach all those snobby Royals to not mess with you!"

"Spencer! Not all Royals are bad," scolds Lila. She comes up behind him and wacks him on the head.

"Sorry babe. You know who I'm referring to," he says, giving Austra a wink. "Looks like we have a fair share of Water Elementals in our family." Lila blushes at being called a part of his family.

I smile to myself and walk nearer to the front of the Capricorn. Knowing Elias and Skye, they would want to know what's going on. My father rushes gracefully up onto the stage and whispers something to the circle. They begin to talk amongst themselves with looks of disbelief.

Honestly, am I the only person that didn't know my father's genius theory? By the way, how do you react to finding out that you're destined to fight in a war you didn't start but must help end. In a way, it's a burden that all of the Six Kingdoms have to shoulder. I just have to be more involved in it than most.

When I approach Skye and Elias who are talking with Sylas and Claire, their discussion turns into uncomfortable silence. Crossing my arms, I stare at the ground, not knowing what to say.

"He told you. Didn't he?" Skye asks.

There's no point in denying it, so I nod.

"Levi," I lift my chin to Sylas' piercing blue eyes, "I know what you have learned is very… disturbing. However, you were chosen out of every other member of the Six Kingdoms. The Fates didn't make this choice lightly."

Sylas looks to Claire, whose lips are pursed. Turning back to me, he says, "I know the Fates have made mistakes over their long history, but none of the Earthen Born Fates have failed yet. Some have died, yes. But they didn't lose their wars."

"Attention everyone!"

The whole school becomes unnervingly quiet to listen to the Premier as he stands at the head of the Capricorn, the stained-glass windows framing his sides like wings. The sun decides to shine on us, the colored light of the glass reflecting on our faces.

"This has been the first Malevolent attack on the school in fifteen years. I know you all are probably very confused, scared, and a little rattled, but rest assured that we have all our forces back on campus and they are not leaving." His shoulders sink slightly. "We have suffered one loss so far as our headcount reveals."

"I am sure that they will not come back again today. I believe they have already gotten what they wanted from us. At the moment, I want each and every one of you, save for the Healers, to go back to your dorms, clean up, and rest for the day. School is canceled for the rest of the week." No one cheers. Only grave faces stare back at my father. "However, I must call upon you tonight so we can properly say farewell to Mr. Prophetic."

He pauses a moment, gathering his thoughts. "I want all of you to be aware that our world is changing. When we do resume our normal school schedule, I expect all of you to put more effort into your training and take what you learn to heart. On your various adventures and journeys, you will use the skills you learned here, and you will thank your teachers and peers when it comes time to use them."

He straightens his shoulders and brushes some dust off his suit. "That is all for now. Go to your dorms. Meet us down at the beach when the clock strikes eight." The Premier scans each and every tear stained, bruised, and horror filled face.

He touches his fist to his lips and says, "I will see you all again."

...

Levi

The whole school, some reluctantly, climb down to the place it all happened. A few Hunters confirm that a new tree growing in the Field of the Lost, extinguishing the hope that there could be an attempt at a rescue mission for Mr. Prophetic. We gather on the beach, each of us holding a ball of fire, given to us by Fire Elementals.

If you knew the person very well then you could write something about the deceased and burn the paper in the flame. They say that the Gates to the Afterworld are guarded by the Judges and the light from the flames notify them that there's a new soul waiting to enter. Burning the message in the fire is to send the words to the place where all things go to rest, so that the dead may read it.

I didn't know that much about Mr. Prophetic, so I wrote a short note about his sacrifice. Nothing too extensive. I mentioned what I saw in his last moments and his act of bravery and kindness.

I asked around after my father's speech to find out who that girl he saved was. I startled to find that it was Vesta Goldfinder. Throughout the evening, she was crying so hard I thought she was going to fall apart. Now she just watches her letter turn to ash in the flame, her jaw set and eyes flickering with grief.

In our own time, we set the flames on the water and leave them to float into the bay. They mimic the stars in the night sky, to make the ocean on this earth the sky's equal.

Next to me, Skye speaks for the first time in hours. "It's a beautiful thing: fire and water. Two things so different coming together, just for a few moments, to honor the dead."

Part II

Chapter 19

Levi

The moonlight flowers give a soft glow to the room. It seems like a normal day in the life of Levi Sage, except for a few vital details.

I slowly get out of my bed, trying not to wake my roommates. Makai's snores drown out the creak of my mattress. Elias is a trained Hunter, taught to recognize the smallest of sounds. I tiptoe over to the glass globe that holds my Lightning Critter.

Silently, I pick him up along with the haunting, black book. When we came back from Mr. Prophetic's funeral, we found the book lying ominously on my desk. The three of us spent a half an hour discussing whether or not to try speaking to the Fates.

Elias knew about my father's theory but didn't quite connect the dots that I'm the Earthen Born Fate. Makai only knew the stories of the One Hundred Wars and nothing about the theory. At first, he thought that it was really cool that he knew the next Earthen Born Fate, until he realized that would mean Austra and I have a high chance of dying before our time.

He became silent after that.

We decided to leave talking to the Fates for another time. A few hours later, I'm overturning that decision.

With Sparky lighting the way, I creep out onto the balcony. There's just enough room for me to sit, the rest of the terrace filled with various plants. Placing the Lightning Critter to my right, I open the book, the old binding crackling. My fingers run along the yellow pages, wondering how many Earthen Born Fates have had their destinies read within this leather.

A faint sound of writing emerges from the page, leaving black ink in its wake. My heart stops at the words. In a neat cursive writing, it says:

100 including you

Speechless, I stare at the page. Closing my eyes tight, I breath in quickly, the dread rising in my throat. It's confirmed. This will be the One Hundredth War. Something snaps in place and I feel calm again, as if the Fates themselves told me to get it together.

I check the balcony door to see if it's fully closed and open my mouth to speak. "Hello Fates... Are you sure that I'm the person you're supposed to be talking to?"

Yes. We are sure of it.

Well. That's great. When is Austra's first trial?

They will start when the moment presents itself. When it comes, you will know. For now, we must tell you about your fate.

Any hints?

Your challenge as the one hundredth Earthen Born Fate will be more urgent than the others before you. You and your companions must rise to the challenge. As an Earthen Born Fate, you will have gifts from all of the Kingdoms. As an Earthen Born Fate Companion, Austra Rabid will represent the Sorcerers and will be gifted as such.

However, the Malevolents have broken some fundamental rules of our terms of war. We will determine the fate of their decision soon enough. You will pay the cost.

Even more of a cost than having to make sure the Six Kingdoms doesn't implode... When will my variety of gifts show up? Also, who are my other Companions?

Your gifts will come when your Companions do. You will meet them when the time comes.

So, what is the gift that I gained from the Sorcerers?

You have the power to control storms. Read books about the Storm Wielders that have come before you.

Anything else that you think I should keep in mind while I try to save the world?

You must not tell anyone about what you learn from these books unless you have their full and absolute trust.

Why?

People aren't meant to be secret keepers.

I continue to ask the book questions and each time they are answered. Each time I turn the page, the writing disappears, as if they never existed.

When the sun starts to appear over the horizon, I go back to bed. A small amount of sleep is better than none. Even Sparky's light starts to dull. Sometimes I forget that even Lightning Critters need to rest.

Playing with electricity between my fingers, I watch the light flickering off the balcony railings. I lean close to my Lightning Critter. "I guess we have more in common than I thought."

Chapter 20

Levi

Everyone is concerned about Austra and how she's dealing with everything. It's common knowledge among the Six Kingdoms that the Earthen Born Fate is revered and featured as the all-powerful savior of the Kingdoms. Frankly, I don't feel all-powerful.

Along with giving Austra and I books to read about the Hundred Wars, Skye came up with the genius idea of doing extra practices after school. Thinking about it, it's actually a good suggestion, given that I'm just above average in combat and Austra needs to improve to stand against a Malevolent. Skye said that Makai would train me, and Aris would train Austra.

I didn't know was that Aris was good at combat. Like, *really* good. Skye told me about how she tested him out herself, after hearing from her father that Aris could be one of the only people in the school that could match her. Elias was there to watch, and he said that their duel, using charmed swords to not inflict death, lasted over thirty minutes and only ended when Skye swung out and from sheer luck managed to pass her weapon through a vital artery in his neck. If she struck a millisecond later, who knows who would've won.

"Levi? Uh... Levi!"

"W–What? Sorry." I rub my eyes. "I was just thinking."

"It's fine," replies Skye as we eat our breakfast on the cliff where all this *stuff* started.

The others are off watching Aris and Austra have their first session, which I couldn't find the stomach to watch. Skye offered to come with me and suggested that we go eat our breakfast where the stares and whispers can't reach.

I go back to picking at my oatmeal.

Skye bows down to get a good look at my eyes, her gold ones sparkling in the light.

"Are you okay?" she whispers so only I can hear. Around here, people have to be careful about pixies. They like to gossip.

"Yeah. I'm fine."

She raises an arched eyebrow. "You're a horrible liar."

I lift my head to look right at her this time. "Really, don't worry about it."

She shakes her head and rolls her eyes. "Idiot."

"What are you calling me an idiot for?" I say defensively.

"Because you just are, Levi Sage." Her look hardens and she turns fully to me. "Do you want to know why?"

Groaning slightly, I lean back. "Fire away."

"Because you don't realize that we all care about you. Just know that if you need to vent to someone other than your pillow, you can talk to me. Okay?" She fiddles with her sleeve and mutters, "I know I keep critiquing you every chance I get, and that's because that's all I know how to do. I'm not good at that comforting kind of talk, but I can listen well."

I look down again and nod my head slightly. She notices and lets out a small smile. Satisfied, she gazes out into the sea and sips her boiling hot green tea.

"Can I ask you where you got that scar?"

Her expression becomes cold again. "No."

"Then should I demand the answer?"

"No."

"Why don't you want to tell me?"

"Because," she says, looking for the right words. "It's not a story people want to hear."

"Let me decide that for myself," I say. "You can't feel my feelings for me."

"Why are you so stubborn?" she mutters. After a few moments, she sighs. "Fine. I'll tell you."

This time I give her a smug grin, which she just scowls at.

"You know how sometimes information about the Six Kingdoms gets out into the Outside world? Well, the Six Kingdoms government sends out a team of people to deal with it. To be asked is a great honor and is not taken lightly.

"I was part of a team with Austra, Elias, and Titus to go get a book that had information about Valians, information that the Outside World doesn't know about. Our missions was to steal it, and destroy it."

I lean in, intrigued. "Titus is the guy you punched earlier in the year, right?"

"That's the one," she says, a bitter bite to her words.

"All of our parents are well known in the Six Kingdom government, so they decided that we were fit to go on a low-profile mission that required young children. Of course, Elias' situation was a little different, being something like an adoptive son of your father. It's complicated. We were all about 12 around then."

My heart stings a little at the "adoptive father" part. I've never really thought of it that way. Elias being a kind of stepbrother. Some part of me feels jealous that he was able to spend time with my somewhat absent father, but at the same time, I'm glad Elias and his brother and sister were able to have a father figure, back then.

I swallow and ask, "What do you mean 'back then'?"

She takes a deep breath and looks out into the ocean. "I don't know. They used to be closer when Elias was a little kid running around the halls of Grantham Willow. The same goes for Sylas too. Both of them spent their summers at Grantham even though they went abroad for school. As Elias got older though, the Premier and the brothers grew

169

apart, more separate. The Premier got closer to you and Elias got closer to his brother. Sylas and Elias are a package deal now."

I nod thoughtfully and she takes that as a sign to continue with the story.

"We all planned and organized the mission until we thought nothing could go wrong. It was a quick heist, nothing too complicated. It should've just been an in-and-out mission."

Her brows scrunch together as she says, "Titus was captured by a Malevolent during our journey to where the book was located. The place the book was kept was enchanted so cars and planes couldn't go through, so we had to walk and visit Six Kingdom inns along the way. The people keeping the book found Titus, then tortured him until they got the information they wanted."

I purse my lips and study my hands. Titus is about a year older than us, so he was thirteen years old then. *Thirteen.*

"He told them *my* location," she said, her cheeks flushing. "Out of everyone's location at the time of the heist, he told them mine." She huffs a chuckle and bites her lip. "He said it was because he thought I could handle their ambush, but I have my suspicions. Titus and I got along the least. Out of all the people, to him, I was the most expendable."

Her eyes are dry, but there's something other than anger in her eyes. "The next morning, I woke up with a scar from my chin and down my chest that will follow me for the rest of my life."

"I'm sorry," I say. I would have been traumatized for life if something like that happened to me. But I'm not Skye Fervent.

"Remember this, Levi. We all make mistakes. The Earthen Born Fate will definitely make a lot of those and most of the time, we get scars from them. Wear yours proudly, for they remind you of what you can do better. You will need these reminders in order for you to succeed." I suppress the urge to ask her why she doesn't show her scar.

My lips tug into a smirk, "I know. Unlike you, Skye, not everyone can succeed all the time."

She punches my arm softly and chuckles softly. We settle into a comfortable silence, both lost in thought. She wrings her hands, making me wonder what could be going on in her head.

Deciding not to press for more information she might not want to give, I ask, "Are you staying here for New Years?"

"Yeah," she answers with a slight smile. "It's my favorite time of year. There's a party in the Capricorn, if you want to go to that."

I nod thoughtfully, fond of the thought of seeing the Capricorn decorated and filled with joyous students. "I'll check it out."

She nods in agreement and takes another sip of tea.

I smile, thinking about what the others are doing. Elias is probably laughing at Austra's attempts at getting a hit on Aris, while Makai stares at the Shadow Wielder, daring him to hurt Austra and get his butt whipped.

"Skye? Can I ask you a question?"

"You just did, Levi."

"No, I mean a more serious question."

She sets down her navy-blue mug turns her focus to me. "Fire away."

I take a deep breath and look out into the ocean. "What do you think will happen if we *do* fail? Will everyone be ruled by Malevolents? Or will everyone in the Six Kingdoms cease to exist?"

She takes a moment to ponder her answer. "Those are a lot of questions that I do not know the answer to. All I can tell you is, if you do happen to fail, which I really hope doesn't happen, I will kill you myself."

"You make me feel *so* much better." I lay down on the grass, closing my eyes to shut out the world.

I hear her do the same. "I know that may or may not help, but get it into your mind that I will do my best to aid you in whatever way possible, okay?"

I nod, a small bit of warmth spreading across my chest.

"Good. Also, I want you to at least have *some* fun. I don't want you to be a complete downer for the rest of your childhood."

I smirk to myself. "Did you just make a joke, Skye?"

"Shut up, Levi."

Chapter 21

Levi

Makai grins at me from across the field.

"Was this really necessary?" I exclaim and gesture to the endless waves of grass around us. "My storms aren't that, you know, huge."

He chuckles softly and starts to walk towards me. "I have a feeling that you're just underestimating yourself. For goodness sakes, you're the Earthen Born Fate. Who knows what you could do."

The Sorcerer chews on a grass as he studies me up and down. His tie is tied around his head, the ends flying along with the wind. "Now, I don't know too much about Storm Wielders, but as an Air Welder, I can give you some pointers. I'd like to think they aren't that different."

Aris scoffs from where he meditates a few feet away.

"Keep meditating, Dark Vader," shouts Makai.

Elias bends down and attempts to hide his laugh.

"Can we start, please?" I stare up at the beading sun. "I'm going to melt."

"Well, here Earthen Born Fate, let me help you." He balls his hands into one first and swings his arms towards me. A huge gust of air knocks me off the ground and I fly through the air for a few seconds before landing on my back a few feet away.

I wheeze to catch my breath. Between gasps, I grit my teeth and yell, "What in the Six Kingdoms was that for?"

"Get up Fate. Hit me back. You can't let the seven Fates think you're the disappointment in the family, can you?"

I wince as I push myself to my feet and wipe my forehead with my shirt. I close my eyes and try to visualize that space in my gut where I got the power.

Another gust of air flings me to the side, my shoulder erupting in pain as I crash to the ground. "Would you stop doing that," I hiss and stand, grabbing my throbbing arm. "I need to think."

"No," Makai says. "You don't." He moves the wind to nudge me back, making me stumble. "When Malevolents attack you, you can't afford to simply close your eyes and *think*. You use that *anger*, that *panic,* but most importantly, *control.*"

He sends another attack, but I lock my knees in place and kneel to stop myself from falling over. I fling up and arm towards the sky, not really having any intention.

Rain begins to fall and thunder crackles. Elias curses and looks up from the tree he was attempting to grow. Aris just continues to meditate, his expression as serene as before.

"Thanks, Sage," Makai laughs, the greys of his eyes becoming more prominent. "The rain is *so* deadly. Malevolents will *cower* at your feet."

"Makai," I hiss. "*I need time.*"

"We don't have time, Sage. We have now and we may not have a future if Malevolents infest the world. Get it together."

I scowl and send a haphazard hand towards him, wind flowing from above me and towards the direction of my swing. The grass rustles violently towards Makai and he sidesteps easily.

"Too slow," he says, that smirk on his face growing again.

I send another attack and another, the power like caffeine in my system times twenty. My hands start to shake slightly, and all Makai does is stand soundly on his feet, dodging each blow.

"With wind, you have to gather it from right in front of your opponent, otherwise they'll see it a mile away, quite literally in your case. Remember you can't conjure your element though. It has to be present around you. Find a strand of wind, feel it, and capture it. Try again, but this time pull from the air closer to me."

I do as he says raise my hands to feel the currents of wind around us and shoot forward my hand to capture the strand of air, this time with purpose. Makai tries to avoid the blow, but I catch his shoulder, sending him twirling through the mud and falling on his behind.

He smiles widely. "Not bad, Sage. Do that again and this time I'll counter."

I smile back and nod.

Together we send arcs of wind and air across the grass. My brown hair whips around my face and Makai's tie gets ripped away. I roll through the mud to avoid an attack, covering myself with it.

Makai doesn't look any better.

I try to send a swarm of spinning wind towards him, resembling a mini tornado. It catches his shirt and sucks him in and into the mud. I release the tether of power to the tornado and it disappears.

Makai rises and spits dirt into the grass. He runs towards me and I run towards him.

I crash into something–hard, falling to the ground. I grab my nose and roll through the mud in pain.

"What in the Six Kingdoms," exclaims Elias. He kneels next to me and inspects my face. Aris does the same, checking my nose.

"It's not broken," he says, resting a hand on my forehead. "I should be able to heal it. I would let the bleeding subside and see if you're okay with just letting it heal on its own."

I nod and wince at the movement. Warm hands pick me up and lay me down on something dry. I open my eyes once I can think again. Some fresh, young leaves cover the sun, their vibrantly green leaves flashing in the light. This must be the tree Elias was growing.

"Sorry, Sage. That was a dirty trick I pulled," Makai says sheepishly.

I furrow my brows and wince as Aris presses his shirt on my nose. "What'd you do?"

"A wall of air. I made you run into a wall of air."

I smile and cringe again. *Ouch.* "Nice one."

"Yeah," he says and rubs his neck. "I'm not used to combat training. It's not something Air Wielders practice often."

"Why?"

Aris gets up abruptly and goes to meditate again. Elias sits on the other side of the tree, listening in. Makai rubs his neck and sits down next time me on the bed of moss Elias probably grew.

"Air Wielders usually don't fight. We're more on the healing side of things. We can suffocate people, yeah, but that's more useful for torturing and stuff. It's not something you see in Duels for example. It's not considered an honorable way to kill someone." He adjusts his sitting position and looks away. "I don't know, it's like a stereotype in the Six Kingdoms, I guess. In our history, Wind Wielders were looked down upon. Even today, some of that still remains."

I ponder that for a moment. Like the Outside world, the Six Kingdoms has their fair share of prejudice and discrimination. It just shows itself in different ways. I say, "If it's any consolation, I think it's pretty cool."

The corners of his mouth turn up. "I know." Glancing down at me, he says, "Someone once told me that even if my skills aren't suited for the frontlines, I can make a difference in other ways."

"Like walls of air?"

He laughs. "Yes, walls of air."

Chapter 22

Levi

Austra and I crash into the tall, wooden door just as the Bell Tower sounds.

Our teacher glares daggers at us. "Ms. Rabid, Mr. Sage! Why are you late?"

"Well," I begin, "there was a banana, a lot of paper, and my clumsy friend here–"

"Sorry, Mr. Topography, we'll be on time next time," grumbles Austra, eyes set on the floor as we find our seats. All the chairs are taken except for two that just so happen to *not* be next to each other. I groan and sit in the one closest to me. A girl with two blonde pigtails and thick glasses that make her eyes look like a fly's, sits next to me.

She shoots out her hand with a toothy smile, "Hi! My name is Miranda. You're Levi Sage, right? The son of the Premier? Oh, and I can't believe you're a Storm Wielder! I mean like, oh my Fate!" She basically screams it in my ear while shaking my hand wildly. I nod my head up and down as she goes on, trying to signal to her with my eyes to stop.

My heart leaps out of my chest when Mr. Topography shouts, "Mr. Sage! What did I tell you! If I hear another *word*, I'll give you detention!" I rip my hand out from Miranda's grasp and bury my face in my book.

Miranda keeps pestering me all period. She doesn't seem to mind when I ignore her questions. Maybe it's because she's just talking too fast to notice I'm not replying.

Between questions, I manage to make a miniature tornado on my desk, which makes papers fly across the classroom. And right after I get it all cleaned up, Austra finally gets a grip on her element and sends all the papers and more sprawling on the ground, swept by a small gush of water. Mr. Topography seems about to explode before he gives detention to both of us at the end of the period.

"This your first detention?"

Austra nods in a sort of daze. Her skin is pale and puffy, as though she's about to cry.

The bell rings and Austra and I make our way up to the secret meetup place. After a heated argument, Elias and Aspyn settled on a codename for the room so that we don't have to keep referring to it as, "the room." They decided on Gemini, since it's near the astronomy tower and they figured it would be a good name to call the place we might do some plotting and scheming in. I always feel like Geminis get a bad reputation for being two faced.

"I wouldn't put too much into it," I say, pushing down the bustling hall. "Sometimes teachers can have bad days too."

She just shrugs and looks at her shoes.

"Why are you so down about it?" I ask, patting her on the back. "I think Mr. Topography had a bad day. Plus, he's probably frustrated that someone else didn't get the job of being my Sorcerer Companion." I wink.

"Maybe the Fates made a mistake," she whispers. "There are so many people in our classes that are better than me. So many water Elementals that can conjure a whole lake of water, whereas I can barely summon a cup full. And when I do, I can't even control it. What am I supposed to do when Malevolents come knocking? You must think I'm useless."

I look at her incredulously. "How could you think that?"

She shrugs and takes a shaky breath. "It's pretty obvious all the teachers hate me isn't it?"

"That's not true!"

"Can you tell me one Sorcerer teacher who wasn't frustrated, upset, or angry with me today?"

I scrunch my eyebrows, taking a second to think about it.

She widens her blue and brown eyes in emphasis, "See!"

"Austra!"

"Well? Wouldn't you like to have someone who actually knows what they're doing?"

I shrug in exaggeration. "I don't know! I would have liked to!"

Austra's eyes flash with hurt until they harden as she turns around and stomps off. I look around the hall, most of the students have filled out, but those who haven't glance over at the commotion. Shaking my head to get rid of the thoughts of gossip, I run after her and grab her by the shoulder, making her turn around. "You didn't let me finish!"

"What's there left to say Levi! I'm useless!" Tears stream down her face.

"No, you're not! I said I would like someone who knew what to do! Name one person who knows how to do what we have to do! There's literally no one. With that said, I'd rather have a friend than someone that knows exactly what to do. I know that some of these teachers are jealous, but that's only one of the things that we will have to brave through, okay?"

She faces me with defiance, but then looks down and nods her head.

I put my hands on my hips. "If we're going to survive this, then we have to do this together."

She nods back, but there's doubt in her eyes.

I put my hands on my hips, frustrated. "Then I need you to at least try. Try to have a little faith in yourself. If you don't believe in yourself, then you're losing the fight before you even start."

...

179

Austra

I wonder if it's cowardly to be scared of Aris. He's a mysterious boy who hides in the shadows that no one really knows much about. He's just a shadow in the corner. Some people around school have started to call him that. The Shadow.

After resting in Gemini for a bit, eating chocolate candies and working on schoolwork, Aris sends me a Lightning Critter, calling me to a clearing near the cliff. It's chilly, so I made sure to pack a hoodie in my bag.

Despite the rough start to the day, I can't help but hope that this practice session with Aris isn't as hard as I think it to be. After Levi told me to be brave, it triggered something. Maybe he's right. I've just spent so long, dreading the future, wondering if I'm good enough. If I don't believe in myself, then why should the Six Kingdoms have faith in their futures.

My breath catches when I see Aris sitting at the edge of the cliff... meditating.

Not knowing whether to tell him I'm here or not, I wordlessly walk up to his side, breathing in the sea mist from below. The fog hovers close to the water and I wonder what lurks behind the curtain of grey.

"Sit," Aris whispers against the wind. His face is as calm as I've ever seen it, content to sit and listen to the sounds of the bay until nightfall. I like this Aris. The other Aris is constantly on alert, wondering what's going to attack next. Even now, come to think of it, he's on high alert. However, there's a certain peace to it that makes all the difference.

I do as he says and sit. Crossing my legs like him, I close my eyes. It was never in my training to meditate, but I've seen others do it from time to time. I've doubted whether or not it helps with focus. Spencer would say that it's a waste of time and argue that training is more effective. For the sake of not getting yelled at by Aris, I do my best to look the part, relaxing my shoulders, letting the feeling of numbness spread through my body from the cold.

"Stop thinking," Aris says in the silence. "Just... feel. Feel the wind on your cheeks, the chill of the sea, the life under your body— everything."

Letting out a long breath, I try my best. Thoughts of being the Companion of the Earthen Born Fate creep into my mind like unwanted monsters. I let them flow out of my mind like water in a river.

We sit like that, for what seemed like hours or minutes. It's hard to tell. Sometimes, I listen to Aris' breath or mine. Other times, I listen to the soft waves below or the singing of birds. There's the chatter of the forest pixies behind and the water pixies below.

I open my eyes when I hear Aris get up beside me. Aris is in his stealth mode. On a normal day, I wouldn't have noticed.

"Come," he says, his dark eyes reflecting the coming night. "You brought your sword, I assume?"

Nodding my head, I pull out Pia, the sword gifted to me when I turned fourteen. The sword absorbs the light of the sun as well as the moon, turning gold or silver depending on which one is in the sky.

Noticing Aris' eyes on the blade, I say, "It was given to me by my mother, common amongst the higher status families in the Hawaii territories."

"That's one special sword for someone who doesn't know how to use it," Aris says, swinging his around artfully.

Taking the jab, I shrug. He isn't wrong. If someone said that to me right after I matured, then I would've hid and cried. But, no. Not now. "That's what you're for," I say, not backing down. "I know that I can't beat a Malevolent with the skills I have now. Teach me so that I do not fail."

"First lesson," he says, pointing the blade at my neck. "Don't fight not to fail. Fight to win."

"Noted," I say, tying my long wavy hair out of my face. After a few stretches, I get into my ready position which Aris mirrors, a smirk spreading on his face.

He lunges and uses an attack that I'm familiar with. Spencer used to teach me the common ones back in Hawai'i on our days off. I swat the sword away easily, spinning back around to face him. Before I can blink, he lunges again, quicker than I can react.

Falling on my butt, I look up to a sword between my eyes.

Scowling, I bat it away. "Again."

And we do it again. And again. And again. Each time I fall, I dig my sword into the ground as a crutch and rise. There will be far greater opponents that I will face, and they won't hesitate to kill.

An hour in, I'm bruised, dirty, and cold, whereas Aris doesn't look fatigued at all. As he waits for me to get up, his gaze is fixed on the moon, bright in the sky, a quiet sort of amazement on his face.

Such a strange boy.

Shaking my head, I say, "Again."

"Why are you doing this?" He doesn't move from where he studies the sky. "Fighting the Malevolents, I mean. When they just keep coming back." Aris asks, not in a mocking way, but in sorrow.

Wiping the sweat off my brow, I say, "I don't know."

"No, I'm asking you why. Why are you doing this? What for?"

I gulp. "My family and friends. For those I love."

Chuckling, he says, "Love hurts. Why fight for it?" There's an emptiness in his eyes, an emptiness that I don't understand and maybe never will.

Taken aback by the question, I reply, "Nothing comes without a price, even love. I will try to fight for the love I have in my family and my friends. At the end of the day, that's the part of love that matters."

"Then let's train, Austra," he says, my name rolling off his tongue like oil. "Let's train so that you can fight for that love, so that one day we may all understand."

...

Skye

"I hate snow," sighs Elias, looking out the Capricorn window. Normally, it doesn't snow in this part of California, but earlier Levi might've been practicing snowstorms with Makai.

I lift my book closer to my face where I sit comfortably on the wooden bench of our table. "I love the snow and the night. It matches the characteristics of my heart."

The redhead does an elaborate sigh and flings himself down next to me. "Always such a downer, Skye. Why are you like this?"

I give him a hint of a smile and ask, "How's dance going?"

Elias doesn't talk much with the others about his hobby and he does a good job at hiding it. However, not much gets past my eyes and I see his ballet shoes peeking out of his bag every now and then.

Truth is, I find it admirable that Elias is doing what he loves to do. Although it's tragic that his parents passed away, he doesn't have them holding him back from pursuing that passion. It's taboo in the Six Kingdoms to invest so much time into an art form if you aren't a Master. When I first asked him about it, he told me that at his boarding school, they were really into the arts. Considering that his brother is a Master, they let him do ballet, thinking that he was also going to be one too.

Elias was devastated when he matured as a Hunter and thought about quitting. I guess that he got so good that his teacher, who knows the dance teacher here at Grantham, asked for Elias to be let into the class. The rest is history.

Elias' face lights up. "Fabulous! We're working on the casting for Swan Lake. They're very hierarchical here, so I won't be a lead. But, when it comes time, I would *love* for you to come."

It's more like they're overlooking Elias because of his Kingdom.
Sighing, I turn a page in my book. "Perhaps I could spare the time."

Elias shoves my shoulder and I let out a grin before checking my wristwatch. "We should get going. The Team Challenge will be starting soon."

Last month's Duel was canceled because of the attacks, but as always, they will resume. Duels are when two representatives from each kingdom from each school participate in trials to compete against each other. Those kingdoms that win get to represent their school in the Final Duel. This Final Duel will be especially uninteresting. I heard my father talking about how it's just a race to see who can find the 200-dollar gift card for the school library in the snow first.

Florence Wildflower isn't a very big school or proficient in the Dueling area. The only Kingdom they managed to get on their team for the Final Duel are the Masters. It should be a relatively quick win for Grantham.

Elias and I grab our big fluffy winter jackets and go to the South Bell Tower. As punishment for their Sorcerer mishaps, Levi and Austra have to sit with Mr. Topography on the Astronomy Tower and remain silent during the entire thing. Horrible idea for punishment, but I guess it's good enough.

I know the Duel is about to begin once the crowd below starts to erupt. Our band plays its traditional school anthem and Lightning Critters shoot across the darkened sky. The big jumbo projectors illuminate all of the action.

But something feels off. I run to the railing of the balcony and look over at the Duelers. There's that feeling that I get when things are out of place, like an instinct.

"What's wrong?" I shoot my gaze to Elias, who looks at me with a playful concern.

Fear edges on my voice. "Have you seen Makai?"

He laughs. "He'll show up."

"Maybe," I mumble and follow him to the bench.

I hear a bang and leap up, drawing my knife.

"Whoa," exclaims Aris, holding up his hands. "I didn't know you startled so easily."

I snarl at his dark smirk and sit back down on the bench. Scanning my surroundings, I make sure that Levi and Austra are okay and that the Premier is where he's supposed to be. *What could be wrong?*

A piercing yell ignites my adrenaline, making my hair stand on end.

This time it's Elias who leaps up from his seat. "What in the Six Kingdoms was that?"

I shift into my Valian form and launch in the direction of the sound. The crowd around me shifts from happiness to confusion, all searching for the source of the scream.

Relying on my sensitive hearing, I fly towards the Astronomy Tower. Landing swiftly, I scan through the darkness.

"Skye," exclaims a voice I know all too well. "What's going on?" I avert my eyes to none other than Levi Sage.

"Didn't you hear the screams?" I ask him and look at Makai who's visible to my eyes but not theirs.

He cocks his head to the side and says, "I think everybody is screaming at the top of their lungs right now."

"Ms. Fervent!" I roll my eyes and face Mr. Topography. "What in the Six Kingdoms are you doing here! Your classmates should have already told you that they are being punished, correct?"

I take a deep breath. "Mr. Topography, I am here to inform these two about important Premier information. Unless you want me to inform my father about you delaying us, I would suggest leaving us alone."

He narrows his eyes at me, but I give him a look that leaves most of my classmates cowering in fear. He grunts, adjusts his glasses, and walks off toward the other teachers.

"So," says Levi suspiciously, "what is this official business that you have to tell us about?"

"Skye? I think I hear something, too," Austra says and strains her eyes to look into the distance.

Fates, why couldn't Levi have gotten his Warrior senses sooner. It's a weakness.

I dart towards the other side of the balcony and whistle to the spotlight directors below me. "*HEY! EVIE, GIANT! WE NEED LIGHT ON THE OTHER SIDE OF THE BUILDING. SHOOT IT THROUGH THE WINDOWS.*"

Evie rushes to the lever and pulls, the lights illuminating the darkness. In the distance, held suspended by invisible hands, is a boy. Makai Ardent lets out a terrified shout for help and my knees begin to shake. No warnings from the Book of Mysteries. No warning of what was to come.

Dread falls on the three of us like a bucket of cold water.

Chapter 23

Austra

All the teachers and students surge forward, and I just stand there frozen like stone. Then it dawns on my, *this must be my first test.*

"Austra?" Someone nudges my shoulder, but I don't take notice. The person nudges me again, this time with more force than before. "Austra. Come on!"

I finally turn my head when Levi begins dragging me towards the crowd. He hisses something about *Fates* and *unreliability* as we push through the crowd. There's a streak of darkness from the corner of my eye that I recognize as a large bat. Skye. A boom sounds and a low, scratchy voice rings through my bones. "NO! Only the companion of the Earthen Born Fate is allowed to save this boy." This unknown voice lets out a dark chuckle that makes the person next to me whimper in fear.

I probably would have too, but the shock numbs me.

"What do you expect her to do? She's a Water Elemental," Levi yells fearlessly out into the void.

"Ah! Young Levi Sage. Apologies for the abruptness of this trial. Among us there were some… deliberations that took a bit of time to settle." The feminine voice laughs again. Levi's rage can be felt radiating from his skin. He scowls into the night sky–at the voice. Thunder crackles behind us. I admire his boldness.

"You have more guts than Earthen Born Fates often do," she chuckles.

Whispers erupt around us. So much for keeping this Fate business a secret. Lightning Critters start to shoot out of the school,

187

spreading the news far and wide. An Earthen Born Fate is alive and there will be war.

"Just you wait," Levi shoots under his breath, but the voice hears.

"Oh, I'll wait to see what *you* can do, Fate. For now, I want to test your friend here. I take it that you liked your first test."

"What do you mean?" Levi demands.

I could almost see the owner of that voice grin. "We used the Malevolent attack on your school as the first trial. I see that your Companion has displayed her water element. Now, I want to see another."

A shiver runs down my back. I flick a lock of brown hair from my face and walk up so I can be seen in my full scope by the voice. "Who are you?"

"I am Zarha," the voice booms, sending a chill through my body. "I rule the gifts that reside in your blood, Austra Rabid." Gasps ripple across the stone of the school and I see someone faint out of the corner of my eye. Levi is utterly pale in the bright spotlight, realizing who he was talking to so harshly.

The Fate of the Sorcerers.

"What do I have to do?" I try to hide the shake of my words, feeling the attention of the school weighing on my shoulders.

"You have to save him," the Fate replies simply. I can almost see the grin behind the words.

"How do you expect me to do that?" I counter weakly.

"You tell me. Use the special element that earned you a place next to your Fate. Or should I say *multiple*, which your poor Fate will have to pay for."

Murmurs flood the space around us. I puff out my chest to seem worthy of the responsibility, stopping the doubt that threatens to creep in. *People don't get more than one element. That's not possible.*

Skye landed sometime during the speech and made her way to stand next to Levi, her face grave. We all know that everything comes with a price and with something as big as this, there will be a mighty price to pay. Maybe this is what they meant by what Levi showed me in the creepy book about breaking the terms of war. There has never been a Companion of the Fate that had more than one gift. Scratch that, there has never been *anyone* gifted more than one gift.

Levi has the same recognition on his face. He shakes his head at me as if to say, "Don't worry about it now. We have to save Makai."

Skye comes up to my side and whispers, "She wants you to use wind. The only way that you can get to her safely is through the air. She's too far away from the bay, fire wouldn't do anything, and the ground is too far below to rise."

"She's right," Zarha booms. Skye scowls. "She's brighter than most Warriors."

I dig deep into my being, gathering all the magic I can find to wield and produce air. I try summoning a breeze, but the air remains stagnant around me, bringing a swell of panic.

"You can do it," whispers Levi.

"Yeah," I hear Aris say from behind me. He's panting hard, probably from running from one corner of the campus to the other. "Focus on all your training. Remember what your teachers taught you."

"No," cuts in Levi.

Aris looks to him in confusion and so do I.

"What do you mean?" I ask, frowning at him.

He shakes his head. "None of the textbooks and instructions ever helped us, right?"

I nod, recalling all the embarrassing moments over the past couple weeks.

"One thing that I've noticed is that there's a place inside of us that holds the power. Instead of feeling the power through the element, feel it in yourself. Try doing the opposite of what the books tell you."

"What do you mean?"

189

"Um." He tries to grasp a way to explain it. Then he snaps his fingers. "What did you feel when you released your powers?"

I shrug. "I don't know. I remember a type of crack. Then there was this place where the power resides in me that I pulled on."

"Maybe try reaching for that spot. It might take something else to get that crack though... I'll leave that to you to figure out." He backs off, along with the other students in the area, to let me do my own thing. Elias looks too shocked to speak, which is a first. Aris looks around for potential danger, offering a level of protection while I focus. Despite the danger and how close Makai is to death, I feel a sense of comfort.

I close my eyes to think. *What makes me feel the place of my power?* Maybe it rises when I feel intense emotion. I've never been the best at hiding my feelings since my face usually tells all. However, there are secrets that I keep, and guilt and sadness that come with it. One surrounds loss and the other surrounds the lack of control.

I think back to the times I've cried myself to sleep, my heart betraying my responsibilities, so quiet that even Skye can't hear me. I think about the times I felt like I would fall apart and the times I felt like I would never mature into a Kingdom. When I felt the fear of disappointing my mother. I love her dearly, but I don't think she realized how hard she was pushing me or how hard I was pushing myself to mature into a kingdom.

I tried everything. The people around me tried everything. I've had my bag hung from the top floor balcony and a pie smacked in face, for heaven's sake. The memories warm my heart. Then I remember when Nikolai left that banana on the ground for me to slip on. I never told Levi who I saw peeking around the corner and laughing with all his friends. I remember the time Wesley laid limp in front of me. I was angry at the Malevolents and all that they have done to me and my family. But I was also angry with the Fates for giving my brother his Fate.

I remember the day I got the call at school that my older brother was killed by a Malevolent. It happened almost a year to this date–the day my life changed forever. The day I first lost control with my emotions and completely broke down in front of my friends, classmates, and teacher. I remember the time he held me when I scraped my knee or when my favorite toy broke. He was more of a father figure than my biological father will ever be.

What I felt that day changed the way I looked at everything. Instead of making me stronger, I became weaker.

My teacher escorted me out of school and held me until I was able to walk to her car. She drove me to the hospital with my mother, who couldn't drive herself.

I vow to myself that I will hold myself together this time. I will protect my friends until my last breath. I will do my very best to make sure that the Malevolents won't win this time. They will *not* take me like they did my brother.

Something rises in my gut. Instead of a sob, it's something bigger, greater. Screams sound around me as I run towards the back of the tower and ready myself for a sprint. Pumping my legs as fast as they can go, I launch off the railing and into the open air.

A crack rumbles through my veins.

Instead of falling to the ground, I use the air to support my weight. The wind carries me a hundred feet from the school. No, five hundred feet to Makai. The wind howls against my ears and my hair is ripped from the tie that kept it together. Makai lays, floating in thin air, oblivious to the word around him. I catch him just as he's about to fall to the hard floor beneath. I grunt at the weight.

Shifting around in the air, I see an object hurtling toward me. I dodge the rock as it glazes my shoulder, leaving a scrape behind. I scan the forest floor for my attacker, but nothing but brush and shadows. I hiss in pain, but when the next rock comes, I'm ready.

The air morphs to my will and swerves us around the rocks and arrows that are aimed to kill. A rock almost crashes through my skull from behind, but I duck just in time. I reach a pause in the flying objects, using the moment to let out a sigh of relief.

Then I hear a deafening crack. A tree falls to block my view of the school, but I'm going too fast to get out of the way. I shield Makai with my body and hurtle straight through the branches and leaves. Twigs leave scratches all over me and leaves lodge themselves in my hair and clothes. When we reach the other side, I push out all of my remaining strength in one last thrust to send us crashing to the deck.

There's a pop in my arm and I cry out in pain. Makai, who tumbles out of my arms, groans softly. Arms engulf me just as quickly, trying to see if I'm okay. Dark spots litter my vision and I blink at the sudden light. Raising my neck slightly, I look over to Makai who also has people crowding around him. Ms. Mendy pushes through the crowd to help. In the chaos, someone pulls off a note from Makai's wrist.

I grab my shoulder and push my way towards her. Elias holds onto me as I stumble towards Makai. "What's in it?" I ground out, limping over.

Levi snatches the note from Aris and reads, "You are the pawns."

Chapter 24

Levi

One look at Austra and you would assume she's dressed as a mummy. Bandages wrap her arms, legs, torso, face, you name it. Luckily, her cuts and bruises are shallow, and should heal quickly given Ms. Mendy placed some herbs to help the soreness. She already closed the wounds, so there was just the matter of making sure they didn't have any bacteria or poison in them.

Makai is mostly unscathed, save for a few scratches, so Skye took him to his room hours ago.

"Levi, you should go to sleep." Skye squeezes my shoulder in comfort. I don't look up. The moonlight shines on the milky skin of her hand and when I finally move my eyes to meet hers, they pierce through me like starlight. I feel a pain in my gut and tear from the gaze back to the sleeping girl in front of me.

"Do you think I should have told my father about everything?"

She looks at me intently. "You knew there was a chance Austra might've had more than one gift?"

I nod my head and bury my face in my hands. "I told Austra right after I found out. The Malevolents told me not to tell a soul. But, if I told him, he could have helped prepare Austra for this. Maybe he would've known what the Fates were going to do to make the playing ground even for this final war." When I went up to my father's office after the trial, he just seemed more hurt than angry that I communicated with the Fates without updating him. "I messed up," I whisper to no one in particular and bury my hands in my hair.

Skye drags over a chair to sit next to me. The clock on the wall reads just past 2:00 a.m. Even the most restless sleepers have made their way to bed. "No, you didn't. This was as much Austra's test as yours."

I give her a curious side glance. "In what way?"

She takes a sip of her ginger tea and says, "Figure it out yourself."

On that happy note, she gets up from her chair and walks out the Infirmary and back to her dorm room, or wherever she decides to go after this. Even as the son of the Premier, most of the staff make me follow the rules.

I rub the black leather book in my hands. No warnings, nothing.

The latest page says, *"The Malevolents were woven into the fate of this test. Be on the lookout."*

That was fifteen minutes after Austra's shoulder popped.

...

Austra

"Again," commands Aris.

I gulp and glance down at the black sword that was pointed at my neck just moments before.

When Skye first brought up the idea of Aris helping me with my combat skills, I thought that it would be maybe once a week. But, no. This Sorcerer decided that it would be smart to make me do a session every day, except for Sundays, for two hours before dinner. To make matters worse, Aris didn't let me pick up a sword again until I had two weeks of muscle building. He said that our teachers aren't doing enough to strengthen our core before teaching us the basics. In my opinion, the Grantham Willow teachers are great, I think Aris just has absurdly high standards.

Picking up my own sword that was flicked away with one smooth motion, I get into my ready position. Grinning, he circles me, taunting me.

"Why do you do this?" I ask, sweat trickling down my temple. "It's like playing with your food."

"It's so much more entertaining," he drawls, teasing me again.

"I don't agree," I say.

"Pity," he says and attacks.

Side stepping, I swing my arm around, hoping to elbow him in the back. He anticipates my counter, grabbing my shoulder, and shoves me away. I roll and hold up my sword again, expecting another attack. He stands where he was, watching me intently.

"Where did you learn this?" I ask. The techniques he uses aren't from around here. I've watched enough Warriors in class to notice.

Shrugging, he says, "My father taught me."

I paused at that. He's never said a word about his family before. The Premier spent enough time interrogating him to realize that he would never talk about them—or where he came from. I've tried to pry for weeks, but he would always dance around the topic. But yet, here we are.

I press further. "Was your father a Sorcerer like you?"

He smiles to himself, but it's a grim smile. "No."

"A Warrior then?"

"So many questions," he says, stalking closer to me. It's not in an intimidating way. Rather, it's as if he's trying to figure out why I want to know.

I hold my ground, but do not strike. "I'm just curious," I say, stiffening as he nears.

He gets so close; I can smell the faintest hint of salt and ginger. Being near him is like sitting near a fire pit. At a safe distance, it's nice and comforting, but when you get too close, you fear getting burned.

There's so little I know about the Shadow Wielder. It seems as though every facet of his life is hidden by darkness, never to see the light. However, the Premier saw something in this boy and allowed him to stay. Curiosity may be my downfall, but I want to find out what lies beneath the shadows.

I feel his breath on my cheek. I don't dare move. Closing my eyes, I take in a shaky inhale.

"Don't press," he says, rasping. Aris pulls away and turns his back to me, leaving me flustered. Not a threat, more like a warning.

"Get ready," he says, cleaning his blade. "I'll meet you at the foot of your dorm. I believe there's a celebration in the Capricorn."

...

Austra

After putting on a pastel purple dress, I run down the stairs. It's slim fitting and not too frilly. It's just mature enough for someone my age but not too young either. After one of Vesta's shopping sprees, she tossed me the dress, saying something about how it looked good with my eyes. Now that my eyes are hazel, I don't know if what she said still stands. Despite the fact, I choose to believe that it does.

I hold my breath, wondering if Aris was just playing me. But sure enough, he's there, fixing the cuff of his suit. There's a dark kind of aura to him, his voice and stature too old for someone so young. Vesta, the beauty queen herself, mentioned that he was easy on the eyes when he first arrived. I heard that she even made a move. Aris is just one on a very short list of people who've turned her down. I didn't think anything of it then, but now that I take a good look at him, he's not *not* easy on the eyes.

When he hears me come down the stairs, he lifts his eyes and pauses. Blushing, I hurry down the last steps and grab his arm. Surprisingly, he doesn't pull away.

"You clean up nice," I say, remembering his sweaty figure just an hour ago. Even then he looked devilishly good, but I won't feed his ego that much.

Smirking, he says, "I know."

Mouth open, I smack his arm. He just chuckles and together we walk towards the Capricorn. There have been a few precious times where I've made him make that sound. The boy rarely smiles at anything, but everytime he shows a form of emotion that's geared towards the light, it's a mini victory.

Lightning Critters dance across the sky and moonlight flowers illuminate the halls. New Year's is so beautiful. Sometimes, I wonder if the Fates tug at the fabrics of our world to give us that little bit of beauty to lead us into the New Year.

"What are you thinking?" I turn my head to find him staring at me intently.

I press my lips together, not realizing that I was smiling. "Nothing. Just that it's beautiful out today."

He grunts and looks around, as if seeing it for the first time. "Where I come from, there isn't much light." Something like regret flashes across his face, but it's gone as quickly as it came.

I scrunch my brows in frustration. After almost half a year, me being one of his closest friends, he still refuses to tell me his past. "Why don't you talk about it? Your past, I mean? If you ever need to talk to anyone–"

He shrugs my arm off and walks in front of me. "What's wrong? What did I say?" I match his face and make him turn to me. "One thing I've learned over the past few weeks is that it does no good holding in your emotions."

He continues to stride forward, his face a mask of what it was before. "There are some things that shouldn't be spoken."

"That's what I used to think," I say, trying to look into his eyes. "I'm starting to realize that maybe it's better to just let it out."

He shakes his head and mutters, "I sincerely doubt that." He thinks to himself for a second and grits out, "I *can't* tell you."

I nod my head thoughtfully, debating my next steps. Clenching my jaw, I realize, I *trust* this Sorcerer. "My brother was killed by a Malevolent when I was thirteen." Something like actual pain flashes across his face and he looks away. "Sometimes hardships don't make you stronger. I felt weak, like the world was mocking me. It started to get better when I told Skye about my feelings. Sometimes the best thing to do is face your fears. *Please* tell me."

I can see the gears turn in his head. My heart drops when he pulls his arm away. "I don't rely on others to help shoulder my pain."

He leaves me standing in the cold, darkness threatening to close in.

...

Levi

The cakes are decorated to the brim with roses, the salads are stuffed with more fruits and vegetables than I even knew exist, and the duck has a honey glaze that shines in the light of the chandelier. Everyone gathers in the Capricorn for New Year's Eve. All the teachers laugh with their coworkers and the students play games with each other. The Capricorn is filled to the brim with music and laughter. Some families spend the New Year at the school. What I've noticed about the Six Kingdoms is that everyone seems to know everyone, creating this huge, tight community.

Of course, with all the liveliness and dancing, Skye's slouching in a secluded corner, observing the dancefloor. She doesn't so much as glance at me when I sit down next to her.

"What do you want?" Skye asks dryly.

"Having a bad day?"

She doesn't reply, but I follow her eyes to where her father's talking to a rather gruff looking family. Based on how they look so admirably at the arrogant Werewolf, they're Titus' family.

"Your fangs are out."

Both Skye and I snap our heads to a girl with blonde pigtails. We didn't hear her coming, which says something, considering how good Skye's hearing is.

"Hey Miranda," I say, secretly hoping she sees a leprechaun and runs in the other direction.

"Oh Levi," she says, fanning her pink cheeks. "Can you *please* sign this for me." She holds up a napkin. "My sister has been begging me all month."

Her hands shoot out to reveal a huge picture of my face. "Um…"

"Please, please, please, please, please!"

"Okay, okay," I say to get her to stop talking. Half of the room is already staring at us and don't want Titus, Nikolai, or–

"Oh dear," says a sly voice. "Looks like someone got an unfortunate crush on Levi Sage. Though, I can't imagine why."

"What do you want, Vesta?" Skye says, looking lazily at the pretty brunette. She wears a long, silky, cream colored gown that compliments her violet eyes.

In another world, I think Skye and Vesta would make a good pair. Both of them have that same glare and bite to their words.

"Nothing much. I'm just going to take Miranda away from the ungrateful Fate," Vesta says, while pointing her perfectly manicured nail at me.

"Come on, Vesta," I say, sipping my sparkling drink. "Lighten up! It's New Years. Celebrate! Or at least let us celebrate in peace."

She scoffs, grabs Miranda's arm, and saunters off to the other side of the room, her perfectly curled hair bouncing behind her. People watch as she passes, mesmerized. Don't get me wrong, she is gorgeous, but she doesn't have the personality to match.

"What was that about?" I laugh. Skye just stares grimly in their direction.

"I don't know," she replies simply.

"Hey," Austra says, and sulks over to our table. Her gaze is lowered, and her shoulders are slumped. Last I checked, Aris and Austra usually have their sessions around now. After the first session, Aris exiled others from watching in, saying that it interrupts her focus. Something tells me that there are other reasons he would want to be alone with my Sorcerer friend.

I smile at the sight of her. "What happened to you?"

"Nothing," she mutters. "Don't worry. For once I'm not upset about Fate stuff. Just... let me be sad for a few moments."

"Alright," I say, leaning back in my seat. Scanning the room, I catch Aris' eye, who looks just about to murder something. I take it that it's a good sign Aris didn't go off into the castle to find a secluded secret cabinet to hide in for the rest of the night.

"The New Year is almost here!" Aspyn jumps over to us, dragging Elias along with her. They look extremely warm from dancing, but neither of them one bit tired.

We all jog outside to the courtyard where the South Clock Tower is lit up with more Lightning Critters than I've ever seen in one place. They make the clock tower sparkle as the second hand gets closer and closer to the twelve.

The night is chilly, and the ground is covered in white, but we begin to count. At "one", everyone shouts and sings until their voices are hoarse and dances until their legs give out. One thing the Six Kingdoms does better than the Outside world is party. The older students, above the age of sixteen get to go to the Magical Practice building to dance the night away, leaving the rest of us to drink our punch and hang out with the adults.

In the Six Kingdoms, due to the high probability of being killed by Malevolents, people are considered legal adults once they turn sixteen and are allowed to drink. Something I've learned to appreciate about the Six Kingdoms is that they focus on the now rather than the future.

When I was in the Outside world, people always stressed about getting high grades and going to college, about what is to come. Here, there isn't a guarantee that you will get to go to school after your main schooling. Mostly only Scholars end up going to University with the rest going either into the Six Kingdoms' Army, working at a school, working in the government, running their family business, etc. School doesn't do grades like the Outside schools, instead the teachers just make sure that their students know the material so that they don't die when they exit the gates. The motivation to work comes with that thought in mind.

I dance with my friends, doing what the Six Kingdoms know what to do: enjoying the present. All of us have learned the hard way that the Fates can only pull strings in our lives and don't control it. They're like puppet masters, however, at the end of the day, we can choose our own destiny. Yes, we feel the strings that tug us down various paths, but there is the option to ignore it and follow your own.

In my life, I will laugh, and I will cry. But, tonight, I choose to live.

...

Skye

Vesta stumbles into our room half past one, her lipstick smudged and hair messily put up into a bun.

When I come back late from practicing or a late-night fly around campus, she doesn't ask me questions. Whenever she comes back disheveled, I don't pry. Austra just sleeps through both of our nightly outings.

"I don't trust that girl," she whispers.

I open my eyes just slightly. She knew I wasn't sleeping.

"Who?"

"The girl with the pigtails."

"Miranda?"

"Yes her," she says, a little in distress.

"Why is that?"

"I have a feeling."

"You–"

"*Skye Fervent*," she hisses. "I live in a world of politics. I know you do too, but your father he kept you mostly out of it. My parents did everything they could to ensure I was at *every* ball, *every* dinner with the King, *every* political scandal. Do you know how many times I've been betrothed, sold off to the person with the highest rank?"

She breathes hard and I can see the reflection of tears in the light of the moon. "I know things. I know when someone lies to me or when they're scheming about something. *Keep an eye on that girl.*"

Chapter 25

Austra

"GET UP!"

Groggily, I peel my eyes open and groan. "What?"

Then I hear Vesta say in a daze, "Do you smell smoke?"

I sit up and bump heads with Skye. "Sorry!"

She grabs her forehead and hisses, "Get up, Austra! This is your next test!" Practically tossing me out of bed, she runs over to my weapons and straps them on me with precise fingers, knowing exactly where each strap and buckle goes.

Vesta stumbles to the wooden door and grasps the handle. She cries in pain and gazes down at her bright red palm. "Do you know another way?" She looks over at us with pleading eyes. In any other scenario I would've relished her expression, but instead I feel the exact same fear. We might die today.

Skye shakes her head. The balcony door leads out into the courtyard, which won't do us any good since we'll just suffocate in the smoke. Then, there's the matter of helping those in the corridor get out.

After a moment, she morphs into her Valian form and rams her shoulder into the door. It bursts open, the broken wood feeding the flame. "Come on," she roars, pulling Vesta through the door. Seeing me rooted where I am, Skye yells again, "Come on, Austra!"

I stride to meet her side and give her a look of pure flame. "Let me go first. This is my responsibility."

Skye clenches her jaw and for the first time, I see indecisiveness in her eyes. "I need to keep you alive. That's *my* job," she says in a hurt and torn voice, looking between me and the hall consumed by flame.

"This is *my* test."

I muster all my fear and anger and force the fire away, calling upon the power within me. A crack sounds through my ears.

I feel the flames recede, making a tunnel for us to pass. We run as fast as we can, passing by empty rooms. When we get farther down the hall where the flames haven't burned, some of the remaining students run past us. Many have folds of fabric covering their noses and others stay behind to use their gifts to slow the fire. At the very end of the corridor, I find a door fully engulfed by flames. I run through the licks of fire, completely immune to the heat, as if they are just warm water.

"Watch out," I warn over the crackling of burning wood. Shutting my eyes, I hold up a hand and feel the fire surge around the frame. Remembering what Aris taught me about controlling my power, I will the temperature to surge. When I close my fist, the door crumples to ash.

Two roommates rush out the room, hacking so much, my lungs hurt in sympathy. I sprint out after them and listen for any more cries for help in the area. A few other Fire and Air Elementals do the same, doing their best to hold back the flame for their classmates to run by.

I hear a crack to my left as a chunk of the ceiling falls to the floor. "Let's go!" I snap my head around to see Skye and Vesta already at the end of the hall, waving for me to follow.

As I go through the hall, I think back to the tales my mother told me when I was younger about the adventures of various Sorcerers. Going way back into my memories, I try to remember the Tale of the Broken Heart and the town that discarded the only Air Wielder in a town of Warriors. They called him useless until the town was burned by their enemies. The Air Elemental saved the people by suffocating the fire.

Air! Sometimes it isn't the best idea to fight fire with fire. I call upon the feelings that I distinctly felt on that day of the second test. Not the fear, not the panic, but the feeling of the power itself. Levi told me a while back, on the day that we went into town, that our powers stem from the power itself, gifted to us in its purest form.

The flames at my sides slowly shrink and turn into black ash as I run after Skye and Vesta. Vesta hisses when a bit of debris falls onto her shoulder, leaving behind a dark welt. Instead of crying or fussing about the pain, she looks up at me with anger in her eyes and yells, "Are you done saving people now?"

I give a firm nod and the three of us sprint down the hall to the tall staircase. All the ivy that used to line the railings are burned, now either ash or crumbly, shriveled sticks. The marble, normally cold in the winter, is now boiling, melting the rubber soles of my shoes.

We leap onto the ground floor and run outside of the school near the jagged cliff. The walls have vines of fire, searing so hot and fast that only dust is left behind when they leave. The flames roar into my ears, but I stuff them out with a flick of a finger. We turn a corner and see the open air in the distance. So close. We sprint to the opening, a wall of flames threatening our exit. I tear the curtain of fire away and together we crash onto the melted snow.

Most of the school made it to the emergency roundup location. Once a month, we have a fire drill, like a normal non-magical school. A lot of the students thought it was stupid, because obviously, we're a *magical* school. *This* isn't supposed to happen.

We crawl further into the safe zone and I raise my arms to do my best to put out the remaining fires that I see. I close my eyes and pray that my powers are enough. I push all the energy that I've been saving in my body and shoot it out to eliminate the hungry flames, suffocating them with air or pulling the energy of the fire back into me.

The snow seeps through my pajama pants and shoes. It shocks me to imagine something so cold could exist next to something so hot. I raise my gaze up into the sky as water droplets begin to fall from the sky, like the tears that fall from many of my classmates' eyes. The sky is cloudy today, but rain wasn't predicted in the forecast.

Levi.

Too tired to move, I lay in the cold snow and soak in every drop of rain that sizzles onto my skin. Evidence of the flames are still visible in the school.

"Levi," shouts Skye into the mass of people. "Elias!"

My arms strain to pull me up, but I get my head high enough to look through the crowd. *Where's Aris?* I don't want the last memory he has of me to be one of anger.

"HEADCOUNT EVERYBODY."

Premier Sage tries to gather all the students into a small group in his white, fluffy slippers and floppy night hat. He then locks eyes with someone across the clearing and pushes his way to reach a male student. Skye lets out a sigh of relief when she recognizes Levi.

"Oh Levi, my dear boy," he whispers into Levi's soot-filled hair.

I almost sag in relief when Aspyn and Aris finally emerge from the crowd, covered in ash and soot. "Hey," Aspyn smiles, even though streaks of wet skin reveal the path of tears. Aris' expression is as cold as always, but I can't hide the relief I feel.

Aris offers no slant of a smile to ease my mind. Instead he strides up to me, black eyes ablaze and his hair sticking to his face because of the rain. He goes down to his knees to get a better look at me. "What was that," he asks with a deathly calm voice.

I shake my head trying to scan the building for any more breakouts of flame. "I–I don't know," I swallow away the dryness in my throat. "My second test?"

His eyes don't leave mine. "You think?"

I shrug sheepishly.

He nods his head slowly and starts to turn. Just before walking away, he glances back at me. With a sigh, he leaves me in the snow.

Chapter 26

Levi

For the remainder of the week, we all help clean up. I wield the weather to give us some light and warmth in the middle of January. The sun tickles my skin as I lift up another roll of carpet to get levitated up to Level 3.

I mean, the aftermath isn't as bad as I thought it would be. I think the most damage was done to the students. Many of them decided to either take a small break from school or leave the campus entirely because Austra and I go here. It's a little insulting considering the fact that if we didn't exist, they would all be dead. They're not the ones that this whole thing was designed to traumatize.

The roll of carpet is lighter in my arms than I would have expected as I carry it over to Austra, who's overseeing the Mass Spell station.

If there was a spell that could just magically clean everything up, that would be my life calling. It will be a beautiful day when some ingenious Sorcerer finds the code to that spell.

"Hey," I greet Austra.

She gives me a sad smile while rubbing her mittened hands together for warmth. "Hey," she breathes.

I glance at the sky and squint into the sun. "I did my best to make the weather warmer, but I don't want to mess with the natural cycle of the temperature and the seasons."

"It's not that." She glances around the field for probably the one hundredth time today. "Have you seen Aris?"

I swivel my head and my eyes fall on a very fiery looking Skye who's barking orders to a group of older Warriors. Even the Seniors and Paramounts follow her word, knowing that it's a *really* bad idea to go against Skye... on anything.

"Nope," I say, patting her shoulder. "Why do you think he got so angry the other day?"

She shrugs. "We had a bit of a falling out."

"Do you want to talk about it?"

"It's okay. He's just touchy. That's all."

"The offer still stands," I say, dipping my chin in farewell. Bidding her farewell, I drop the maroon colored rug on the pile of furniture and walk back to my pile of decor and furniture.

The teachers were given the chance to go through the torched rooms in search of surviving belongings, so of course the magical book survived. Some of our clothes lived, but many students already went out to town to restock. All of our Grantham Willow ties and clothing items survived, so most people are representing our school on the daily.

Since the whole school is mostly made of stone and reinforced with charms and enchantments that keep it structurally stable, the repairs are mostly on the decor. All we really have to do is clean everything out and refill it with things to make it livable and functional again. We're also lucky that only about one side of the school was affected. The place needed a good renovation anyways.

We never found where the fire started originally, let alone who the person was who lit it. We do know the general idea, though.

When my father found the book clean and crisp despite being in a burning oven, the Fates said that the Malevolents started the fire, no doubt intending for the search for them to be another task. It wasn't a big surprise, but it still angered a couple of choice classmates of mine. Nikolai has been stirring up trouble after hearing the rumor that this school isn't safe anymore. Him and Vesta were one of the first to pack their bags and move to the Alexandra Dominique after a brief vacation to the palace. Apparently their "cousin that's in line for the royal throne" attends.

I'm glad they're gone, but I have to admit, they left a lonely hole where my mind is always subconsciously preparing for a mental blow to my ego. About two thirds of the students remain on campus with some parents that volunteered to help. Even some of the teachers left.

My father wasn't happy with the amount of his faculty that decided to transfer. Once they sent out their notices, he ripped them to shreds and threw them into the dragon scat. After that, he fired the living daylights out of them and gave them all a lecture that will remain in the minds of their grandchildren.

I asked him if that might have been a bit harsh, but he just straightened his suit and said that it was part of the job description to protect Grantham Willow with their lives. It's sort of like the army in that way. It's disgraceful to leave the school that you have made a home in because in the end, the teachers are the first line of protection for the students.

At the end of the day, I'm doing this for them and their future even more than mine. I will do everything in my power so that the Malevolents do not rise.

Elias groans as he passes me. His red hair is sticking in all directions and his freckled face is covered in dirt.

I step back in surprise. "What happened?"

"I died! That's what happened!" He slumps onto an antique looking chair that I was about to pick up. "It's tiring looking for animals! All of them got scared off by the smoke and now we have to hunt for them every day because of the stupid shipping company not wanting to drive all the way out here anymore! Who knew one little fire could scare away so many things!"

"Don't worry about it. Soon this will blow over and we'll have a wonderful feast made by our new Master Cooks." The Cooking Masters also quit. I liked their chicken noodle soup and hot chocolate, too.

Elias nearly falls out of his chair as Skye comes up from behind him. I haven't seen much of the Warrior as of late since she's always off doing something for the rebuilding. The first night we shared a fire and slept in the same area. Since then, everyone has been doing their own thing, working to rebuild our home.

"You almost scared me senseless," he gasps. She just looks at him with a sort of question in her eyes.

"Be more prepared next time," she says, crossing her arms. Pieces of wet hair fall over her face at the movement.

"Don't get your wings in a twist. I just caught your dinner." The Hunter lays his neck back on the couch. "What've you been doing all day?"

"Getting the Warriors in line," she says, tucking her hair behind her ear. "They're incredibly unmotivated. A lot of people are *extremely* unmotivated." She gives him a pointed look, eyeing the couch he lays on. To Skye, anything less than working 24/7 is considered unmotivated.

Elias rolls his eyes and then studies Skye's appearance. "How'd you find a shower?" None of us have been able to use a normal bathroom or shower in days.

She sighs at the question. "My father's room has plumbing and wasn't touched by the fire. Now, if you would excuse me, I've lost my taste for taking a break." With that she turns on her heels and leaves us in the dust.

"And she says I'm unmotivated," scoffs Elias, watching her stride in the opposite direction. "I've smelt like dirt and animals for the past week."

"To give it straight to you Elias, if she was in one of her bad moods, you wouldn't be able to feel the side of your face right now."

The Hunter nods in acknowledgement before getting up to get back to work. "See you later, Levi. Have fun lifting heavy things."

"Good luck on your hunt for non-existent animals."

"You really are a joy, Levi. Aren't you?"

I give him a smirk. "I do my best."

Chapter 27

Austra

Aris leans over to look into Elias' bag. "Can I have one?"

Elias shoves the fried potatoes into his lap, "Knock yourself out." Austra examines the chips like a foreign object.

I refocus my eyes on the page and resume reading. Skye assigned some new readings for me. Everything is mostly about the heroics of it all. Lucky for me, they at least give me an outline on the different tests all the Sorcerers had. Since the Book of Mysteries hasn't been telling us anything useful for the past couple weeks, we have to start fending for ourselves.

Levi comes around the table and peaks over the page. "Did you find anything yet?"

"No."

He pulls out one of the old, wooden chairs and takes a seat next to me. He glances around, studying the intricate carvings of the bookshelves and the stories told on the stained-glass windows. Tapping his fingers on the table, Levi sighs. "How about now?"

"Levi! If you want to find something faster, then you read a book yourself." Levi makes a mocking noise that's supposed to replicate what I just said, which by the way, sounds nothing like me, and goes looking through the shelves for another book. Even Elias and Aspyn stopped talking about the announcement of the arranged marriage between the Sorceress daughter of the Governor of Quebec and the Warrior heir to Paris.

A bang sounds on the other side of the bookshelf. We all look up in alarm. Shooting from my seat, I swerve around the side of the aisle to face a small, grey-eyed Scholar.

…

Austra

"Hermia! What are you doing here?"

Skye looks down at the young girl in confusion. The Scholar has a darker complexion with black hair that contrasts with her lighter eyes. She looks too young to be a student, but the name tag on her collared top says she's a library aide.

Levi widens his eyes in surprise. "You know her?"

Skye replies, "Of course. She's the librarian's daughter."

Levi makes a big "oh" with his mouth and settles into the background to listen. I've heard about the three daughters of the Librarian. Though I don't spend as much time here as some, I've met Claire and briefly talked to Courtney. Claire's a sweetheart and Courtney's someone you don't want to mess with. Strangely, I haven't heard much about the third daughter.

I bend lower to come in eye contact with the young Scholar. "Hello, Mia. How are you today?"

It's Mia who looks at me in annoyance. "You do realize I'm a Scholar, correct? You have no need to talk to me as though I am three."

I take a couple steps back in defeat, smiling at the small but mighty girl. Her eyes dart around the room, observing each and every one of us. I can tell that Aris notices because he shifts in his corner uncomfortably. He's used to being the most detail oriented in the room.

"Yeah, Austra," chuckles Elias. "Give her some respect."

I give him a stink eye and then turn back around to face the tiny smart aleck. "Well then Mia, what were you doing listening in on our conversations?"

She looks around the room and says nonchalantly, "I wasn't listening in on anything." I raise an eyebrow.

Skye gives the girl one of her glares–the one that makes children run away. The look that she gives Hermia tells me that she doesn't believe her one bit. "If that's the case, then we better get going." The others and I play along and start to gather our things.

After a few moments, Hermia taps her foot in indecision. "Actually," the Scholar says, "I couldn't help but catch something you were mentioning earlier. About the possibility that you might need the assistance of a Scholar in your search for helpful information on the matter you are researching."

Levi narrows his eyes. "How long *were* you listening to us?" I wonder the same and debate whether or not this Scholar will use this information against us. Scholars can be too smart for their own good sometimes.

"Long enough to know that you need to investigate another area of the library to find your answer," she says.

Skye scowls at the Scholar but nods her head. "What are we looking for?"

"Answers," Hermia replies simply. "I'll lead the way."

"Thanks," I say, offering a soft smile.

"You're welcome." With that, she promptly turns around and walks in the opposite direction. We all look at each other, pondering the benefits of entrusting our secrets to this unknown. Sighing, Skye nods and together we rush up in unison to catch up with her. Hermia doesn't waste her time, so we have to jog after her, even with her shorter legs and stature. We venture upstairs, around corners, and through arches of books until we reach a large, slick, wooden door. The engravings are like that of the box that held the Book of Mysteries, sending a shiver down my spine. The black paint of the door seems to entrance with the gold ivy carvings trailing up the sides.

"What's in there?" I ask in wonder. Levi looks at the door with a hard gaze, as if he's expecting a monster to come out behind the door. For all we know, there could be.

"We don't know," Hermia says with the same sort of curiosity as me. Her finger is poised on her chin. "We've tried to open it using various methods, but the intent of the door has been clear from the moment I first laid eyes on it."

"We? Why didn't my father show us this?" Levi asks, anger lacing with his voice.

"He doesn't know," whispers Mia. "This room is secret to only the Earthen born Fates, their Companions, and the Librarians of Grantham Willow."

Levi tilts his head like a dog, "But you're not a Librarian."

Skye rolls her eyes, but tells him, "Librarians are like a monarchy here. It's matriarchal though, so it passes from mother to daughter. They're the keepers of the knowledge of the school, with most of the schools in the Six Kingdoms having knowledge that is meant to be held until the Fates decide to release it. I guess the Fates decided that we need to know about their secrets now."

"In theory," replies Hermia. "It changes if the family dies off or the family is not worthy to continue serving the school. It also skips the daughter if she gets married to someone not of Librarian blood, hence why Claire is no longer eligible to become the next Head Librarian of Grantham Willow. Second in line was my sister, Courtney, now first in line." She sends a side glance to the redhead. "Your brother caused quite a fuss in my family, Elias." The Hunter shrugs, faking ignorance. "My mother read the stars and thought you should know now. She sent me to see if you were worthy."

"Well," Skye questions, "are we deemed worthy?"

"Isn't the answer obvious?" She sighs, raising an eyebrow.

I decide to cut in, impatient. "Hey? Can you open the room now?"

Mia instantly turns her cool, marble eyes to me. "There is no door I can open for you. You should know that from the books and stories that you have come across. There is no door that a descendent of a Librarian can open for the Fates and their Companions that they can or cannot do for themselves."

Aspyn asks, "Do you mean that literally, or metaphorically?"

"That answer varies depending on the situation," she says.

"Well, if you can't open the door for us, can you at least tell us how?" I ask her, trying to be as polite as possible.

She nods, "As you wish, my Lady."

Frowning, I say, "Lady?"

"The correct way of addressing a Companion of the Fate is Lady. You're given the same weight as a member of the Council of the Six Kingdoms once you turn sixteen. The Earthen Born Fate is given the same weight at the King or Queen. You all need to read more ancient texts," she says, disappointed at our knowledge. "Anyways, based on my studies, the only way you can open the door is by proving that you are a Companion or a Fate."

I take a deep breath of frustration. "How do we do that?"

"That, I can't answer," Mia states, looking at the door with worry.

"Well then," I say in exasperation, turning to my friends, "any ideas?"

Elias and Aspyn look at each other and shake their heads. Skye and Aris remain silent, more confused and lost than ever.

"Wait," mutters Levi, "I think I know what to do." He walks over to the door and studies the engravings once more. Then he takes a deep breath and places his hand on the black wood, just like he did for the box that held the Book of Mysteries.

I hold my breath and watch the door in anticipation. There's a satisfying click as the door cracks open.

"Austra, would you like to do the honors?" Levi smiles and gestures to the long, pitch dark hallway.

"Sure," I say. My heartbeat quickens as I lead the pack into the darkened corridor. Though the sun is still shining outside, all light leaves a couple steps into the corridor, leaving us in complete darkness. I take my box of matches from my pocket and strike it. Reaching inside me, I grasp a kernel of that power and take the ball of flame into my palm. The walls of the corridor turn from stone to something that resembles the remnants of an old-style castle.

When the hall opens, I stop to consider my surroundings. Aspyn grunts, crashing into my back. From the sound of it, she wasn't the only one.

"Austra?" I hear Levi ask somewhere behind me. "Why'd we stop?"

"Would you look at that," gasps Elias not far behind me. "I think I found the switch!"

Skye's voice cuts through the air. "Wait!"

Gas lamps sputter to life around us. I shield my eyes, blinking and waiting for them to adjust. Slowly, I look around the square room with floor to ceiling bookshelves, filled head to toe with dusty, old, textbook-style literature. Hermia looks like she's in heaven and Elias and Levi look at it with dread.

Wooden chairs, desks, and tables stained a dark brown, scatter the layout of the room, making it look more rustic and ancient than what I thought possible. A grand wood-burning fireplace with a magnificent mantle finish everything off.

"Wow," breaths Skye as she studies the intricacy of the carvings on one of the seven desks. She picks up a feathered quill. "How old is this place?"

Elias jumps onto one of the red velvet couches in the center of the room, catapulting a plume of dust into the air.

"According to the books that I have studied, this was the common room for the seven Representatives in the Alliance of the Ages," informs Mia over Elias' hacking. She examines one of the crackling paintings hanging on the wall.

Levi shouts from the top of one of the bookshelf ladders, "The what of the what?"

"The Alliance of the Ages," Elias calls back in between coughs.

"I know that," he yells back. "But what is it?"

"It's the story of how the Seven Kingdoms became Six. There were Seven united kingdoms fighting the War for the Riches. So naturally, they fought over who would rule them as a whole, so each kingdom elected a Representative and they fought for the crown," I call back.

"Hunger Games style?"

"No. More complicated than that."

He sighs. "Of course, it was."

"I guess this is where they prepared and rested in between tests." I scan the room in wonder. "The stories *are* true." Every child in the Six Kingdoms is told an assortment of stories, the Alliance for the Ages being the most renowned. Some believe it to be just a myth, but I guess this is the proof.

Skye observes the dark, stained desks. "There's one for each of the representatives.

"This one has *Scholar* carved into the name tag," she says, running her hand along the blanket of grey fluff. "This one says *Unyielder*." The former name for the Masters, when the Six Kingdoms were even more prejudiced than they are now. Or should I say Seven Kingdoms.

"And this one says *Sorcerer*," says Aris. He gives me one of his crooked smiles, "I believe that one belongs to you."

Walking up to him stiffly, I give him a glare before sitting on the plush embroidered silk pillow..

"Here's the Hunters. And here's the… oh dear." Elias says where he is, rooted to the spot. He stares at the desk in horror.

"What?" I ask, getting up from my chair. Or the chair of the first Sorcerer of the Six Kingdoms. Curious, I walk over to where Elias stands and place a hand on his shoulder to steady him. He's shaking.

I gasp and back away when I see the word carved into the plaque: *Malevolent.*

…

Austra

"What were you expecting?" Skye scolds us as she stalks across the room. "This is where *all* of the representatives spent their spare time. That includes the Malevolent."

"It's still creepy though," mutters Elias, his green eyes fearful. "Just think, the first Malevolent was in this very room. The events that made the Malevolents who they are happened in this room."

Mia perks up at that. "Technically he wasn't the first Malevolent–"

"Yeah, we know. He was just the one that caused the creation of the Malevolent Kingdom we have today," finishes Levi. "Since I don't have a Malevolent Companion, I guess the desk is mine." He reluctantly pats the chair and gives us an awkward smile.

"Yeah, I guess so," mutters Aspyn, running a finger over the dusty desk. Elias doesn't try to hide the disgusted look on his face.

"Well," I sigh, "we better get started on what we came here to do in the first place."

Levi starts to meander away and offers us a salute. "I'll start looking."

Skye frowns at him with a helpless look on her face. "I better go make sure he doesn't do something stupid." With that she jogs off to help him.

"I will help them as well." The librarian's daughter stumbles gracefully in their direction. With a *humph* she straightens her sweater and dusts off her skirt before skipping over to where Skye and Levi went.

Elias and I split off from Aris and Aspyn to look for books. Every ten seconds, I glance over at Aris. We haven't spoken about that night or the day the school burned, and I don't think he's inclined to start a conversation. At first, I was fuming to Skye about how I should just go up to him and ask him what his problem is. She just shrugged and continued to sharpen her knives. Then I realized, watching her sharpen her knives, that I still need to be trained and prepare for the next trial. Dealing with this complicated boy should be the least of my worries, so I sent him a Lightning Critter asking to resume our lessons. He sent one back six hours later agreeing and that we were to start immediately after the school was put back together. Which was earlier today.

It didn't go as bad as I thought it would be. He didn't talk, save for the few times he needed to correct me on something or give me a command. I'd like to think that I've been getting better, so his instructions have gotten sparse and his need to get close to me to teach me skills have lessened.

The lesson was just an endless symphony of metal on metal, sword against sword. It's astonishing how good Aris is at such a young age. He has always seemed older to me though. Maybe he was forced to mature earlier than the rest of us, but something about his soul feels like it could be one hundred years old. At some point, I even asked him, "How old are you?"

Backing off for a few moments, he said, "Sixteen."

We clashed swords again, but this time my mind was spinning. Students begin class at Grantham Willow the year they turn fifteen. My birthday was a few weeks ago when everyone was too occupied with worrying about the Fates to celebrate it. It wasn't a big deal really; I had almost forgotten until Makai reminded me. "Why did you come in as an Initial then?"

Wiping a brow, he replied, "Premier Sage spent so long interrogating me that I think he gave up at the end and just put me in as an Initial."

I smile at the fatigue in his stance. Most of the time he gives a death blow within five minutes and then I black out for a bit because of the charm on our swords, which gives both him and me a break.

After narrowly blocking a blow, Aris backed away again. Grinning, he said, "My turn for a question." His eyes flicked to my earpiece and I covered itself consciously. "Who are you arranged to marry?"

That stopped me in my tracks. I wouldn't be surprised if my heart missed a beat. "How did you know?" It's an ancient tradition in the Six Kingdoms territory where I'm from to wear an earpiece when you have a commitment to someone or something. I like to think that my earpiece symbolizes my commitment to my family rather than the boy.

"How'd you know what this means?" I asked again between breaths. It's not a known thing. Skye and Levi know. Skye knows because she just knows things and Levi knows because he walked in on me that night I went to visit Skye. Although I don't think Levi knows the whole story.

Panting, he says, "You told me where you're from, so I looked it up. I found a book that talked about."

Remembering one of our first training sessions, I nod my head. In truth, I didn't want to tell him. My parent's agreement made it so that I didn't have to marry Makai until I graduated, which at Grantham Willow won't be until I'm about twenty. That means I have five years to go about my life not tied to someone. I just want to spend those years without thinking about it.

I went in for an attack to hopefully catch him off guard. He blocked the blow and swung the blade around to try to catch my neck. I saw it coming. Ducking, I slid around his side, hoping to bring him down with a kick to the knee. He moved, but his image blurred, making me miss. Blinking my eyes a few times, I looked behind me and then I saw black.

When I woke up, Aris said that Skye sent a Lightning Critter asking us to meet at the library. After we freshened up, we did as we were told.

...

Austra

Skye traces all of the plaques on each desk, the gears in her head turning. She murmurs, "We're thinking about what will happen in the future. But we're not thinking about *how*." Skye fishes out a dusty block of chalk, finds an old chalk board, and starts to draw. "Remember the day of the second test? When Austra had to save Makai?" she states plainly. "The Fates said that the Malevolents were involved, we assumed the Malevolents threw the rocks. When the Premier and my father investigated, they looked for breaching in security, specifically for Malevolent intruders. Nothing was found."

She draws a stick figure flying through the air, mimicking what I did that night a couple weeks ago, with little colored dots representing the stones. Malevolents are scattered around the base of the board, an approximation of where they would've had to be to throw the rocks at me.

"Your drawings are to *die* for," gushes Elias, clapping his hands with exaggeration.

Skye scowls at him. "Try explaining how rocks end up hitting Austra. The above average Warrior couldn't even throw that high. It would also take a whole lot of Malevolents to cut down a tree that size."

She's met with silence. Elias frowns and his face pales. "Whoever threw those rocks weren't Malevolents. Were they?"

Skye gets a black eraser and makes all the Malevolent figures disappear from the board and draws one in the shadows. "We're saying that whoever instigated that trial was a Sorcerer."

Chapter 28

Levi

"Are you sure?" I ask.

"What else could it be Levi?" Skye says with a look that resembles helplessness.

I fight to make my face neutral. "Do you have a hunch as to who it might be?"

"I wish," sighs Austra, her face scrunched up in worry.

"How do we know it's not an ogre?" Aris asks. His forehead is creased which is the most emotion I've seen on his face in a while.

"An Air Elemental could lift the stones and knock down the tree. Whatever carried Makai into the air could've been an Elemental. Direct meddling by the Fates in our world isn't their style, which makes it seem unlikely that they held Makai in the air. They just pull at souls and manipulate events to shape the present to what they want it to be," states Skye with a hard tone. "I wish I were wrong."

"How do we know there's only one?" Aspyn's pale skin becomes chalky. "I–I mean, couldn't there be more?"

"We have to take into account that the Sorcerer would have to have been persuaded by the utmost evil to join them," Skye replies grimly. "We are taught from the moment we are born to hate Malevolents. Call it brainwashing or propaganda, but that's how many people's brains are wired. How many people do you know who would side with the Malevolents?"

I think about Nikolai and Vesta, then maybe Titus. In the end, I know they wouldn't be that stupid. They may be total nightmares at times, but to imagine them standing with a Malevolent sends chills up my spine. "That's a good point."

"I haven't heard much about the rebels recently," mutters Skye. "There's a chance that they were just rallying their forces to rise against us when we're the weakest. Although, because Levi is the Earthen Born Fate, it clears up the idea that the rebels have associated with the Malevolents. I don't see another way the Malevolents could've gotten a Sorcerer on their side."

"You never know," Elias says. "My brother was talking about how they're raising anti-monarchy sentiment around the Kingdom. With the King getting old, I wouldn't be surprised that they're rising again and using the Malevolents as a tool or the other way around."

I lean back in the dusty couch, breathing in the old must. There are so many things that I don't know about this world. Sometimes I wonder if my father's decision to keep me away from this world was a mistake. I feel as though there are things, like this, that I would've known if not for being in the Outside world. It makes me wonder what else I don't know.

Sensing the swirl of emotions in the room, Elias lets out a very exaggerated looking yawn. "I think we should all call it a night. We need time to absorb all of the new info. My brain hurts."

"I agree," says Mia, looking very desolate.

Getting up from the couch, I hold out a hand to Skye. "Let's go to bed." Looking drained, she takes it and lets me help her up.

We file out of the room to find that the library is pitch black and undoubtedly empty. Even the most persistent Scholars left for their dorms. All of us do our best to sneak out of the library. We're about an hour past curfew.

"I think we made good progress today," smiles a triumphant Austra, despite the dreary news. I can tell that she's just trying to lighten the mood, considering the very solemn Skye. The others go to the dorms the other way, giving Skye, Austra, and I some space.

I laugh back, "To be truthful, I think we opened more questions than we closed." I let out a very satisfying yawn. "I just–"

"Wha–?" I slam the palm of my hand onto Austra's mouth. She looks at me with wide eyes, but I press us against a wall. "Be quiet," I tell them. "I think I heard something."

After a few moments, sure enough, the muffled sound of voices grows louder. Their footsteps echo through the hall, my heartbeat quickening. We hold our breath as the two people come around the corner. I risk a glimpse. My mouth falls open.

It's Deuxieme Fervent and my father, the Premier.

...

Austra

I muffle a sound of surprise as I watch two of the most important people in the school come into view. Their faces are illuminated by the soft glow of the torch lights and they whisper despite the empty halls. Levi and I look at each other in alarm.

I mouth to him, *What are we going to do?*

He shrugs in distress. *I don't know*, he mouths back.

Skye gives him a look that says, *You're the one that got us into this mess. Fix it.*

After a moment of thinking, his face lights up with realization. He holds up a finger and starts to dig in his pocket. Waiting for whatever genius plan he has; I listen in on the two heads of the school.

"What are we going to do about this, David?" A gruff voice, which I can only assume is Deuxieme Fervent, asks the Premier.

"I'm not quite sure. Are you sure your guards didn't see anyone pass?" I hear the Premier reply.

"My guards are the best in the country. Do not doubt them."

"The Scholars and Sorcerers are saying that the fire was started using Polrais, since it makes the fire burn quicker and hotter. The only place you can get that here is in some of the tunnels near the bay. Even then, you would have to go underwater and be lucky enough to pry it off the walls without getting hit by a wave," Levi's father says.

"We got lucky," the Deuxieme says. "Normally the substance burns up when used, but they found some near the Bell Tower."

I turn my attention back to Levi as he pulls out a round flask, half empty. I read the piece of paper tied to the neck. It's the potion we both got on the day of the dragon races.

"To the beholder that wants nothing he does to be heard, drink all.

To the beholder that wants nothing he does to be heard but for those he wishes to be heard, drink half.

To the beholder that wants nothing but to walk in silence drink a fourth.

The spell will end, after the second hour ends."

Drink half. I jump back in surprise as the words vibrate through my head.

What was that? I say right back in my head. Levi's just as surprised as me, both of us wide-eyed and shocked.

Did you–? The Earthen Born Fate asks in my head.

What the–

Whatever. We'll figure this out later. Drink a quarter of this, he shoves the glass into my hand. I take a good swig of the potion and wince at the sour taste. *Can you suffocate the fire?*

I nod, still freaked out by his new gift. Pulling from that same energy as before, I feel for all of the flames in the area. As my fist closes, I feel the fire sputter out.

We hear some startled yelps as the Deuxieme and Premier work to find the torch. Skye and Levi take the rest of the potion and together we sprint down the hall. The potion does its work. Even as my feet pound on the floor, I hear nothing. Levi swerves off to go to his dorms and Skye leads us through a secret passageway that opens a few rooms down from the opening to the girl's dorm. We crash through the door and Vesta bolts upright as we charge into the room.

"What in the Six Kingdoms happened to you guys?" The Royal gasps, glancing at our sweat covered figures. Even in sleep, her hair is in a perfect braid and tendrils frame her perfect face.

"We fell asleep in the library," Skye says and starts preparing for bed as if nothing happened.

I do the same, but I can't quite seem to shake off the shock about talking to Levi in my head. It didn't even feel like I was in his head; it was like he was in mine. After reading book after book, I haven't heard of something like this happening to the Earthen Born Fate. There are cases of Scholars who can read people's minds. Then again, very few. Maybe Levi manifested the gift from the Scholars.

Hey.

I bang my knee on the dresser. Kneeling over in pain, Vesta looks over from her bed. "What's *wrong* with you people today?"

Rolling my eyes, I say in my mind, *Levi?*

You bet, he says. *What do you think this is?*

Hmm. Maybe it's a way for you to communicate with your Companions. Perhaps your Scholar Companion will have it too.

He's silent for a moment. Thinking he fell asleep, I start to get in bed. I'll deal with everything in the morning. Even though it's before midnight, which is early for most teens, my body needs the rest.

I guess you're right, Levi says. *Don't worry, I won't like... go in your head unless I need to. I can only tell you things and hear you when you say something back. So it's not like I can see what you're seeing. It's strange. Maybe overtime it'll get more detailed.*

Yeah, I say.

I don't even hear the subtle snoring from Vesta's bed before I'm consumed by sleep.

...

Levi

Even though every school has been on high alert since the Malevolent attack on Grantham Willow, the Duels have resumed. To the Six Kingdoms, the Duels are what make the world go around. Even though the Earthen Born Fate has been sent to the Inside world to fight in an eminent war that will determine the fate of millions of people, the Duels must continue. Of course there was a fuss after the second trial in the government, wondering whether or not everyone should shelter in place until the war comes, but the government just waved it off and said that if the Fates wanted us to stay in our homes then they would've done something specifically to warn us.

To put my life into perspective, I'm more worried about how my best friend is doing playing games against Malevolents rather than who's currently leading the West Coast Dueling League.

So yeah, I haven't been completely up to date. From what I have heard from Elias, our school is currently tied for first with Grim Dawn. I didn't have the energy to go to the other Duels, being either occupied with classes or sessions with Skye. The Dueling championships are coming up and Elias is going nuts. The same goes for pretty much everyone else in the school. There's a healthy buzz, which is promising, considering the stress of the fire.

The Duel will decide who gets to go to the United States' territory championships. According to Elias, it's usually a tossup between Grim and Grantham as to who gets to go to the championships, but Alexandra Dominique always winds up going to the World

Championships. Therefore, most exciting Duel for us is the West Coast League finals.

Makai came back from the palace, specifically for the Duels. Over the last couple weeks, I have to say that I've missed the guy. Hours after he got back to campus and unpacked, he and Elias went down to watch the Duel. The rest of us stayed in the hidden room in the Library doing as much reading as we can. Makai's face was hilarious when he first saw it, making us all laugh at his surprise. To be honest, we all probably had the same look on our faces when we first saw the room.

Hermia told us that the room was called the Representatives' Room during the Trials, so we figured that that was ominous enough for us to use it.

Hermia almost falls off her chair when a loud *boom* sounds from the door. She scurries over to open the door and Elias runs down the hall looking a mix of horrified and elated.

His face is flushed under his face paint with the school colors of Grantham Willow, red, black, and white. Red to represent that we all bleed the same color. Black to represent the Malevolent heart. And white for the heart of the Six Kingdoms. The way he painted it makes him look like a very inventive peace sign.

Skye frowns in his direction. "What's the matter?"

After catching his breath, he rasps, "I'm going to be an uncle."

We descend into a stunned silence. Hermia grabs his arm and says, "Excuse me? You mean to say that my sister is pregnant?"

"Yeah," he says, not quite believing it. "I didn't even know they were trying."

"Six Kingdoms," exclaims Austra, a smile spread across her face. She sets down the Book of Mysteries that I let her borrow. "That's great!"

As if snapped out of the thought of becoming an uncle, Elias' face lights up, "Also, Grantham won!"

Elias grabs me by the shoulders and shakes me. "They're going to the United States Championships!"

We erupt in cheers and give each other celebratory hugs and high fives. Hermia and Elias run out of the room to see their siblings. The rest of us follow close behind, starting to hear the sounds of celebration the closer we get to the courtyard.

Chapter 29

Levi

"Levi? Do you really think that much chocolate is good for you?" Skye looks at the cake in disgust.

"Yes, Skye. I do," I shoot right back and to prove the point, stuff the sugar in my mouth. Ever since we started our training sessions, she's been bugging me about my diet. I figure that I won't have a good metabolism for the rest of my life, so I should put it to use.

We sit at our normal spot near the window facing the bay. The snow is finally starting to melt, and the trees have started to come alive again. Valentine's Day is coming up soon and all the halls are decorated in pink, red, and white decorations with all sorts of glitter and hearts. When all the decor appeared one day, Skye nearly gagged, and Aris looked just about to disappear in the shadows. Elias and Austra seemed to be in exceptionally high spirits that day.

To my delight, the effects of Valentine's Day are not only in the festivities but also in the people around the school. Once again, every corner I turn, there's eyes that follow. Skye said that it's because I'm officially the most eligible bachelor in the Six Kingdoms because I'm a Fate. It's a little uncomfortable to think about, but it kind of makes sense.

"I don't understand how you're the Earthen Born Fate," Skye sighs. "I imagined someone who glowed with power, knew how to beat me in a fight with two blows, ate his vegetables…"

"I'm sorry for being such a *disappointment*, Skye," I say, pointing my fork at her. "However, considering how many people keep expecting me to ask them to the dance coming up, despite being too young to go, I'd say that in their minds I am quite the Fate. I'm going to focus on positive energy. Even then, my heart belongs to only one thing," I say. "Chocolate. Let me eat in peace."

"Fine Levi, fine," says Skye, rolling her eyes. "Do what you want." She gets up from her seat and goes off, probably to do some training.

Elias and Makai sit on either side of me. "I had the weirdest dream last night," mutters Makai. "I was back at the palace, but I was my father. I ordered a bunch of people around to do by bidding and get me food. It was amazing."

Elias laughs. "I've been trying to get Sylas to let me use the Dream Teas so we can influence each other's dreams. Levi, you've experienced it. How real is it?"

I nearly choke on my cake. "What?"

"You know? The Dream Teas. Your father made you drink some everyday so the Duexieme and Skye could enter your dreams and teach you stuff about the Six Kingdoms." Elias' face falls when he sees my shock. "Oh my Fates. I'm so sorry, Levi. I thought they told you."

...

Austra

Valentine's Day weighs heavy on the minds of teens in the Six Kingdoms. It's not unusual for people in the Six Kingdoms to find their soulmates in school because most people get married in their twenties.

The Fates, being the master of fate, have us all tied to a soulmate. We just call them our Partners. It isn't like love at first sight, where someone just knows that that person is the love of their life the moment they see them. It's more gradual and it requires both people involved to recognize their feelings for each other, which makes things hard.

If someone's Partner dies, then there's sometimes a Second-Chance Partner. They're rare and they only come if the person is willing to move on. Personally, I haven't heard of any so far, but it does happen from time to time, more with those who lose their Partners young.

Levi storms across the lawn at us, his eyes blazing. "Did you and your father sneak in my dreams at night?"

"Oh Levi–," I say, reaching out to grab his arm. He backs away, his cheeks tinging red.

Skye crosses her arms, thinking for a moment before answering. "Yes, Levi. We did. And it ended up saving your life and mine."

Skye and Levi turn their attention to the other side of the courtyard. Skye's face contorts in confusion, mind off of Levi. My heart drops when I see Makai storming across the lawn, straight at me. The wind starts to blow when Skye and I share a look. Even Levi stops talking.

The Air Elemental grounds out, "Is it true?"

Pursing my lips, I ask, "What do you mean?" There's no way he would know what I know we're betrothed. Unless his father told him, there's no way.

"Is there a marriage alliance between us?"

I open my mouth and close it. Looking over to Skye in panic, she's just as shocked as I am. Even Levi's a little taken aback. "How did you know?"

Makai's face falls and he runs a hand over his face. "Don't you think that you should've told me? I mean, you know how I value my freedom and hate that courtly crap. To be tied to you would mean a lifetime of that. Did you just expect me to go along with it when the time came?"

Taking a shaky breath, I say, "No, of course not. I just wanted to go on like normal. We've known each other since we were kids. It would make things weird and there's nothing I can do about it."

"Of course, there's things you could do!" he exclaims. Some of our classmates turn to watch. "You could've said no! You could've told

234

them that you didn't want this. That *both* of us don't want this." His voice falters at the end.

"I don't have a choice," I say, hating how desperate my voice sounds. "There's no way that I can be elected to follow my father as the Territory Governor without a sound alliance. We have a duty to our people. You know that you won't be elected to govern your father's city because of how notorious you are and that I won't because my brother died. You're a Wind Elemental and I'm the Earthen Born Fate's Companion. Separate, we're a liability. Together, there's more of a foundation."

"Being an Air Elemental is not a liability."

My face crumples. "That's not what I meant."

Waiting for his reply is painful. My heart hurts and my soul hurts. Everything just hurts. "You could've told me," he whispers, the same pain in his words.

"I should've," I said. "I was selfish. I just wanted to pretend I didn't have to do it for a little longer"

The anger leaves his face and all that's left is the look of betrayal. Shaking his head and muttering, he starts to walk away. A loose string tugs at my conscience. "Who told you?"

Chuckling a dark chuckle, he sneers, "Levi."

No.

I thought it was his father or mine, but no. *Levi?*

Levi looks completely appalled; his mouth wide open. I don't sense a lie in Makai's voice. Skye looks at me and I can see it in her eyes. *He's telling the truth.*

I turn and stride out of the courtyard, not able to take it anymore. The cool weekday morning mocks me as I jog through the Entrance Hall and towards the edge of school to sit on the cliff. The saltwater makes my skin and hair sticky and the sand scrapes against my legs.

How could he? I trusted him. There has to be a mistake. There's a growing lump in my throat and I rake my hands through my dampening hair in distress.

Levi does have a tendency to be a little clueless during highly social conversations involving a lot of emotions, but I thought that it would be implied to not tell Makai. Maybe he took it upon himself to tell Makai because he thought he should know. Or maybe he suspected that it could be used as a trial against me. A large drop of water falls from the sky and lands on my forehead. The slush of footsteps through the mud and sand get louder and louder.

When it stops, I look up to Levi whose hair is damp from the slight drizzle. "Go away, Levi," I tell him, willing poison into my words, and get up, my sweats and shirt already getting heavy from the rain. Rain due to Levi no doubt.

"Wait!" he calls as I jog away.

I keep my pace and let him catch up, wanting to see the regret on his face. There is none. Just the eyes of someone who looks betrayed himself. "I thought you trusted me," he says.

"I *did* trust you," I say, pausing.

"No. If you did trust me, you would've believed me," he raises his voice and a thunder claps in the distance. "If you trusted me, then you wouldn't believe a word Makai said. I'm the Earthen Born Fate and you're my Companion and I would not do *anything* to jeopardize our mission."

"Who else could have told him? He even said it was you," I scoff. He just looks at me with pure fury.

"I don't know who told him, which makes everything even more concerning," he says.

"Makai's story is more realistic. How would some random person know? How can I believe a word you say when it doesn't even make sense?"

236

"You didn't even stay to hear my half of the story," he growls, running a hand through his hair.

"What is there to tell, Levi?"

"What's that supposed to mean," he grits. Again, a roll of thunder sounds in the distance, but I hold my ground.

"You lost my trust in you, Levi. I lost Makai's trust. I don't even know if I can trust Skye, Austra, Elias... How are we supposed to defeat the Malevolents if I don't know if I can even trust the people who are supposed to help me?" Something rips open inside me. I grasp it in a rush of anger and hear the ground shake. Slamming my hand on the ground, I grip the grass, feeling the soil dig into my fingernails. I feel the energy that connects me, and the earth and I tug. "Just go away!"

A wall of earth rises to divide the space between me and Levi. The wall, though impressive, is not very tall. I see his face as he nods his head in acceptance and leaves. A crowd builds up around the walls, wondering what the commotion is about. My classmates are easy to ignore, but the thunder and lightning that rumbles through the school follows me.

I don't care that I just made an enemy of someone that I am supposed to help. All I worry about now is that I can't rely on others to help me.

...

Unknown

"How is she?" asks the Commander. His handsome young face is deceiving, hiding the evil and malevolence within.

"Distraught and hurt," I reply and snicker. "She seems to have distanced herself from the Earthen Born Fate."

"You have done well, child," he chuckles. "Make sure they do not make amends. Austra is one who is not mentally strong, you see? Or physically, for the matter. I am so very curious why the Fates have decided to select her, of all the Sorcerers in this wretched world. Even if I picked someone at random, it would have been much better than her."

I laugh right along with him, the sound raspy and haunting. It would be stupid not to, unless I want my head hanging on his wall. Throughout my short life, I've seen children younger than me die and tortured at his hands. He claims it's to establish an example and insight obedience.

I dare to look up at his red eyes, fueled by all the blood that he has split. Even though he is still a boy, his stature demands respect. When he left the Six Kingdoms to come here, he was beaten and used for months. Most would die within the first week, but he lived and fought through the ashes of what used to be his life and constructed himself a position here.

All Malevolents knew him as the son of two teachers at the most prestigious school for our enemies in the world. Now they know him as Zander, the Commander of the Heartless Army.

Chapter 30

Levi

"Did you do it?"

"No! Of course not," I exclaim. Skye looks at me through the moonlight of the small window in Gemini.

After a bit, she nods her head. "I believe you."

"Well, at least someone does." I throw up my hands in exasperation. "You would think they would have more faith in me than Austra." Elias and Aspyn went with Austra, and both Makai and Aris disappeared. Skye, thank goodness, came with me.

I'm pretty sure I didn't tell anyone anything. I would have been absolutely crazy if I did. Of course, I remember that night we went to see Skye, but I didn't think much of it. I hadn't even thought about it much since.

"I thought it was out of character for you. The problem is, I don't think Makai lied. I think he legitimately believes that you told him about Austra." Skye scrunches her brows in thought.

"Maybe someone told Makai, saying that I was the one who the information came from. Although, the only people who know are you and me, which greatly narrows down our choices," I say, laying back on a fluffy blanket. I soak in the comfort, wishing I could just be consumed by the feeling. The last thing we needed was for something like this to happen. Knowing the Fates, this is probably a test in its own right. "Do you think this is just a misunderstanding? Maybe Makai's father told him, and Makai just wanted to create a rift between us out of spite."

Skye shakes her head. "I saw his eyes. They didn't flicker. He definitely told the truth."

"Are there any charms or things that can be used to trick someone, make them think something's true when they really aren't?"

She thinks for a moment and then says, "The Recollection Spell does something similar. After you wipe someone's memory, you can tell them what to believe happened during that time. It's a difficult spell to specialize and execute properly. We mentioned before that we might be dealing with a Sorcerer. Maybe they got closer to us than we realized."

We sit in silence for a moment, thinking.

Skye opens her mouth. "About the dream thing–"

"Don't worry about it," I say, holding up a hand. "You were given orders and you didn't even know who I was. I've lost enough friends today."

...

Austra

"Austra? Don't you think you're being a little harsh?"

I look up at Elias who gazes at me a little fearfully. I'm not done ranting yet. There's a lot more in my system. "No! I was supposed to trust him, Elias! And now, I am never going to be able to walk out in public again!" I flop down on my bed. Most of the girls have gotten used to Elias trotting down the halls. From what I understand, Aspyn and Elias have found a real past time gossiping and hanging out together.

"Come on," groans Elias as he drags me up into a sitting position. "Don't be such a drama queen. The future of the whole Six Kingdoms is on your shoulders. Actually, scratch that, the whole world is on Levi and your shoulders."

I bite my lip. "How am I supposed to work with him now?"

He exclaims, "Who's to say he did tell Makai? For all we know the Sorcerer that you're all so certain is aiding the Malevolents could've done it. Maybe the Sorcerer spied on you and figured it out!"

"Who knows anymore," I sigh. My throat starts to close and I try to take some calming breaths.

"Who cares if Makai knows? You're only fifteen! You have your whole life ahead of you. When we grow old, I bet you we'll all laugh about this," he says, dangling off Skye's bed. He really does find a way to make himself at home wherever he is. "Plus, he's one of your best friends. Why would he do that? If he did, it was probably unintentional."

"Are you saying that for me or you?"

"What do you mean?"

"If I fail, not only do I die, but you'll be living in a world governed by Malevolents."

"How could you think that?" Elias gets up into a sitting position to look at me more carefully. Aspyn said that she was getting a headache and left Elias and I alone. Now I wish we had her company. "Yes, I want you to succeed. I was friends with you long before all of this Fate nonsense. I was friends with you before you matured into a Kingdom."

I wince at the truth in his voice. But then the doubt edges into my mind. How can I be sure anything he says is true? I look at him hesitantly. "Go away," I whisper.

"*What?*"

"Go *away.*"

Elias just stares at me for a few moments, not believing what he heard. His hands ball into fists and leaves the room, another blow to my soul.

I slump down onto my bed and look at the ceiling. Everyone's upset at me and it's mostly my fault. Levi started it, but Elias and Makai are on me. I supposed I should feel anger or frustration, but those feelings left me when Elias left the room. Now, all that's left is loneliness.

"Keep it down would you," someone yells through the wall. "We're trying to do homework!"

I run a hand over my face. "Apologies."

"What!"

"Sorry! Okay?"

"Whatever. Just stop slamming doors," the girl yells back.

"That wasn't me," I say, groaning into my pillow.

"I don't care!"

After that, there's silence. Never have I felt this–alone. Not even being the only person who hasn't matured in this school could compare. I spend the rest of the night thinking about my words and decisions.

Skye doesn't come back to our room.

Chapter 31

Levi

Elias joined the *"Austra's going through a mid-Companion trial crisis"* phase group that's just going to lay back until she feels better. All of this happened only about two weeks ago. Frankly, it feels like months. Elias and Skye have gotten Lightning Critters from their friends across the Six Kingdoms, wondering if it's really true that the Earthen Born Fate and the Companion aren't on good terms. Apparently, the information spread through word of mouth to the Six Kingdoms Magazine and the main channels of Lightning T.V.

I can tell that both of them refrain from telling me their opinions. That we should just straighten things up for the sake of the Six Kingdoms. I've done my best to avoid the school newsletter and the updates my Lightening Critter tries to bring me every day. If Vesta and Nikolai were here, I bet the rumors wouldn't have stopped until the day I die, which might be sooner than I would like because of Austra's foolishness.

During the nights, Elias and I just sleep in Gemini because the thought of Makai gives me a headache. All the supplies that we hauled up there actually came in handy. Aspyn would have liked that we did something useful for once. She stuck with Austra, which is good considering that Austra will, at least, have someone there for her.

Skye suggested that we ask the Book of Mysteries if this is a trial, but the Book of Mysteries has been more of a mystery than I would like it to be. It has said nothing the past couple weeks. Absolutely nothing. Skye said that the Fates' silence probably means yes, considering that if it is a trial, it would kind of defeat the purpose.

I have to stop them. The Malevolents. If I have to do it alone… I will. Or I will die trying.

"Mr. Sage! Mr. Sage!"

I roll my eyes and then turn around with a smile. "Yes, Miss?"

My father's secretary comes scurrying down the hall through the crowds of people. Some of the older kids look at me and snicker. Usually when the secretary comes for you, it means the Premier wants to "talk.".

"Premier Sage would like you in his office."

Closing my eyes for a moment, I ask, "Can't it wait? I'm sort of–"

"No. He said it's urgent."

I take a deep breath. "Lead the way." *What does my father want now?* We walk past the students in the hall. Their voices sound throughout the school, the bustling of the passing period making our walk across the school filled with bumps and turns. I bypass Skye and she gives me a questioning look that says: *What in the Six Kingdoms did you do this time?* I give her a shrug and hurry up to catch up to the secretary. For a short and plump lady, she sure can walk fast. When we get to the corner, she takes out her locket, which I notice is bare, and holds it up to the wall. We walk through the invisible barrier and bolt up the stairs.

"Go to your father. I'll be in my office," says the secretary, breathless. She holds up her locket and enters a room through the wall of ivy.

My heart starts to beat when I think about whether there was a Malevolent attack or that the rebels staged a coup in the government. Come to think of it, I think I would be one of the first people notified if there was a situation like that. My father hasn't said much about the politics of it all and I haven't seen much publicity relating to me being the Earthen Born Fate. Common sense says that I would be relatively high in the pecking order of the palace.

I knock on the office door and wait no longer than a second for my father to say, "Come in."

I enter the room as quietly as I can and close the door behind me. Mentally, I prepare myself for the worst. "Why did you call?"

"Take a seat, Levi," the Premier says gesturing to the leather seat in front of me. My heart drops as I get a weird sense of déjà vu from the first day I came here, which seems like a millennium ago. I sink into the plush cushioning and glance out the window behind him. Spring is coming and the trees in the distant small islands in the bay are blossoming. It's quite beautiful, but there's still the grey overlay of a light drizzle.

"Levi?"

"Huh?"

"Have you been getting enough sleep recently?" My father looks at me closely, assessing my messy brown hair and thrown together outfit. Looking down, my tie is crooked, the brown piece of fabric at a diagonal on my chest.

"Don't worry about it. I'm fine. What did you want to talk about?" Rubbing my eyes, I focus my attention on the Premier.

My father leans back in his chair, making me wonder how much sleep *he's* been getting and asks, "It has come to my attention that you and Austra are not on speaking terms."

Frowning, I debate whether to tell him the whole truth or nothing at all. Also, how in the Six Kingdoms did this information get to him? "Well…"

"Why?"

"Come on, Dad. I mean, we were bound to have a fall out, right?" I try to laugh to lighten the mood, but he just gives me a flat stare, not amused.

"May I ask what happened?"

"Uhh, well, it's really stupid," I mutter. Running through it in my head, the situation is stupid. Is an arranged marriage between teenagers in a world where arranged marriages are common really a reason not to talk to each other? No. Absolutely not. But, is that the current predicament? Yes.

"Then why are you mad at each other?"

"It's more about the loss of trust because of the event rather than the event itself," I say, trying to reason it out. More to myself than to my father. What I said is true. I'm really not upset about what actually happened and I'm sure Austra's over the fact that Makai now knows. I think that what's mainly keeping us all on different islands is the loss of faith in each other.

"I see… But you need to make amends."

"Excuse me?"

Seeing that I'm at a loss for words, my father continues. "The Malevolents are going to take it as a weakness and use this to attack. If the school gossip traveled up to me, then there's a good chance it's made it to the Malevolents."

I think to myself for a second. "It's more complicated than that. Some wounds take time to close before you can start using the limb again."

"Levi, sometimes you need to clean the wound first before it can heal. Not to mention, you're one of the most stubborn people I know. Austra's very driven by what other people think of her and doesn't hold onto things very long. My guess is that she's waiting for you to make the first move to amend things."

We spend a minute or two in silence. When my father and I used to have conversations and talk about things less serious than the fate of the world, I would ask him deep questions. I would ask him about why he chose the career he chose, his greatest regret, what it feels like to fall in love… Maybe it's because I was more disillusioned with the world than a normal kid, but I liked asking those questions because I wondered why some of them were so hard to answer. I was naive and I liked to see the gears turning in my father's brain and he would pause before

246

answering. Despite my eager waiting as a ten or nine-year-old, he would be patient with himself. He said that giving a good answer is better than a rushed answer. Now, it's my turn to answer a hard question.

"I'll talk to her," I say, biting my lip as the nerves already start building. There are so many ways the first conversation could go. A good amount of those scenarios, I don't like.

The Premier looks at me in bewilderment. "Yes. That would be great. You go do that." He practically shoves me out the door and gives me a late slip to hand to the teacher when I get back. I have a hunch he thought that conversation was going to be a lot harder than it was. If only I could ensure the conversation with Austra will go just as smoothly.

My next class is Self Defense at the Practice Hall. The halls are empty except for a few of the students that are sulking in the halls, probably cutting class. They give me slight waves as I walk by and I do the same.

When I pass him my late pass, Deuxieme Fervent grunts, then nods for me to join the group. The problem is, everyone is paired up. Just as I open my mouth to ask what to do, someone else enters the room.

"Sorry Deuxieme." Austra pauses when she sees me. Noticing her hesitance, she continues, "I thought you wanted to see me in your office?"

"I was testing your intelligence. You failed."

"But you said–"

"I know what I said! Now use your brain. Get going. I believe you have to partner up with Mr. Sage." The Deuxieme walks away from my side and over to critique someone's form. There's a sliver of dark delight in his eyes, as if he's watching a fly get caught in a Venus flytrap.

Austra rolls her eyes, but together we roll out a few mats onto the floor. Both of us know the drill since we do it so often with our extra sessions with Skye and Aris. As if on instinct, I get into my set position and she does the same. "I think they want us to get along again," I tell her.

"Oh really?" She throws a punch to the side of my face. I duck and balance myself again. It was a messy attempt, but it was quick and accurate. She doesn't put all of her bodyweight into the punch, not giving me that easy opening. "What makes you think that I'm ready to do that?"

"What makes you think that I am either?" I duck low and try to trip her, but she anticipates my move and dodges. When I rise, she sends a jab to my side. Grunting, I grab her leg and tug forward, so she falls to the ground. She begins to get up, but I push her back down. "That doesn't mean we can't act like it," I say next to her ear.

She bolts up and attempts to send a full forced punch to my jaw. Dodging, I back away, giving us both time to catch our breath. "I meant that we can pretend to be friendly."

Wiping the sweat from her brow, she asks, "Why would we do that?"

"So that David doesn't bug me and the Malevolents don't find us vulnerable. My father said that they might view this as a weakness. For all we know, the Fates could be testing us," I say, keeping my gaze hard.

She looks at me warily, but I can tell she's thinking about it. "Fine." My Companion shoves a finger in my chest. "That doesn't mean I forgive you." Then, she holds out her hand for a shake.

Chuckling, I grip it firmly. "Same with me. Deal?"

"Deal."

Before she can let go, I twist her arm behind her back. She lets out a yelp in surprise when I kick her knees forward, forcing her to fall to the ground. Her eyes ignite with anger. "What in the Six Kingdoms was that?"

"Deal's still on. Just wanted to do that," I state simply, walking over to get a drink of water.

"Classic Levi."

"You would know," I say, dipping my chin.

"Yeah. I guess I would," she says, the corners of her lips turning up. It's not quite a grin, but I can tell it's her attempt at amends, even if it's just for show.

"Don't think so highly of yourself."

She scoffs. "Whatever."

Chapter 32

Skye

I sit reading a book on the red velvet couch in the middle of the ancient library, only lit by a small candle. Mia, because she's so small, sleeps on one of the bookshelves. Elias and Levi said that they didn't want to be surrounded by books when they sleep, so they went back to Gemini a while ago. Austra and Aspyn make sure to stagger their time in the room so that they don't have to spend more time with the others as possible. Every now and then I'll see Aris make an appearance, like a neighborhood cat that doesn't have much real interest in passing events.

Setting down my latest book, I go up to the large window at the end of the room. The night is clear, and the full moon illuminates the dense woods. My fingers scape against the worn lock on a pane of glass and click it open.

Analyzing the opening, I calculate when I would have to jump and morph to make it through. Taking a deep breath, I run. My feet absorb the power of the carpet with each silent stride as I propel myself through the window. I morph seamlessly, keeping my wings close to my body. Once through, I fall. The wind whistles in my ears and I welcome the death that's so near. My body feels a thud when pulled up, extending my wings.

In all of the horror stories that I've read about my kind, we're depicted as soul sucking night walkers. Most Valians I've come in contact with don't usually roam the night and instead prefer the day. However, the ability to see during the night certainly makes the option of becoming nocturnal more inviting. Every now and then, I like to take advantage of that gift.

I savor the cool air flowing over my skin and soak in the sounds of the night. Sounds of rustling make my ears perk up, alert. Normally, the night creatures don't make much noise. If they do, it isn't constant. My eye catches a light as luminous as the glow of a candle near the Magical Practice Building.

Strange.

I dip lower to get a better look. Something exits the forest and treks into the clearing, near the structure. Not wanting the creature to see a large bat stalking it, I land and hide behind a golden valorberry bush. They are said to give you valor–as the name suggests–and some of the students like to eat them before a Duel or test.

The creature is dressed in all black. I study how it walks, its stature. From the looks of it, it seems human. My attention drifts to its shadow, cast by the moon.

The moon.

I shoot up into the sky but I'm too late. A clawed hand grasps my foot and tugs hard to the ground. I roll as gracefully as I'm trained to do and morph into my transition state, only my arms remaining as wings. What I find as my attacker is worse than what I thought. I look into the red eyes of the thing I assumed would be a Wolf Shifter this time of month.

I was wrong.

The body is nothing like I have witnessed before. The nostrils are squished inward with the ears long and pointed to the back of the skull. The body of a man, yet not a man with the structure more like a dog on its hind legs. Its skin is pale and milky in the white glow of the moon. The hands and feet have elongated claws that look like kitchen knives.

I am not a coward. However, I know when I see someone, or something, I can't beat. I do what I've done a couple times in my life.

I run. It chases me and I sprint as fast as I can. I don't want to try and morph since I don't know whether I will be pulled down again and if that lost time will cost me. I dash through low branches, scratchy underbrush, even the kindleform plant in hopes of it poisoning the creature. Worse comes to worse, it'll leave some scars. That *thing* might not know that.

Turning fully back into my human form, I run with all my might through the woods, away from Grantham Willow. I don't want it getting into the school because of me. The bushes and bramble cut at my skin and the roots threaten to trip me. A sharp pain erupts in my heel and I tumble forward, scraping my elbows and knees as I fall. Breathing hard, I push myself up and dart away, letting the creature send a slash through the grass where I was a second before.

The creature is fast and with my injured ankle, the amount of time I'll be able to run is quickly dwindling. It's now or never. Summoning all the valor in my being, I swing my wings behind me. The creature dodges with magnificent speed and continues its pursuit. It attempts again and I swerve to the side, but I'm not ready for the next blow. It cuts through my shoulder. I ignore the pain, it isn't deep. Warm blood slides down my arms and with rage, I tighten my muscles in my working wing and start slashing as quick and as random as I can manage. When I make contact, I don't give a second thought and continue to hack my way.

I am hit with what feels like a solid stone wall and am hurled into a tree.

From the speed, it takes me a few moments to stop rolling. The world is patchy, and I try to blink it off, but I am slow to lift my head. When I do, I see the creature walking slowly towards me. My blood left red marks on his nails and its unhuman legs and body.

Come on, Skye. You won't go down like this. This is not your fate.

I gulp down the burning in my palms and stand.

My arms have morphed back in my tumble, so I reach into my back pocket to grab my sword. One of the Sorcerer teachers helped me spell my pockets so it could fit. I slide it out and face the Malevolent.

The characters on my mother's sword say, *Winning wouldn't be worth anything if there wasn't a cost to losing.*

I hold the sword with my one arm, the other arm too damaged to do any good. I swing, but it avoids the metal easily.

It *smiles* at me.

When it slashes, I duck as well. The adrenaline pushes down the pain, giving me a shot at survival. A low howl sounds off in the distance. Oh no. That's the last thing I need right now. I focus back on my opponent. If I have to fight more than this *thing,* I might not make it.

I rush to get the job done but the creature is too fast. All the cuts I've made before are not affecting it, clotting quickly. My moves go for the vital organs near the stomach and neck. The skills that my father taught me are fresh in my mind as I force it to bend to my will. I use a maneuver over my shoulder that catches it off guard and I slide around its side. It snarls and whips a sloppy hand towards me. It trips over a tall root with the kick I land on its side and it falls flat on its back. I raise my arm quickly for the kill.

A streak of black lands on my victim and rolls him into the underbrush. Pushing through the thorny hubble flower bush, I follow the snarls and crashing.

A large wolf and a creature battle to the death in a field, the full moon shining across their faces. The Malevolent is weak and within a few minutes, the wolf has the upper hand. One wrong move later, the thing lies motionless on the ground and the wolf stands over it, panting.

The wolf turns around, meeting his familiar golden eyes with mine.

Titus.

"That was my kill," I exclaim, stomping over. "I had him."

The wolf cocks his head and gives me a look that says, *Are you sure about that?*

"I do not need saving!" Pulling my hair out, I wince at the cuts on my arms. My body starts to itch from the various plants I tore through, making my cry out in frustration.

His brow furrows in worry, but he doesn't make a move to go towards me. He knows better.

"Stupid dog!" I mutter angrily and pace back and forth, trying to calm my nerves. Once my heart rate is relatively back to normal, I turn to face him again. From the looks of it, he found a nice rabbit to gnaw on. "You did get the kill and might've saved my life. That doesn't mean I forgive you, though." The wolf knows that I'm not just talking about the creature.

He gives me a growl, but I turn to face the subdued Malevolent and begin reciting the words that will send the souls to its bearer. The body starts to fade and the soul travels to the locket around Titus' neck.

I hear a sharp rustle and ready my sword again. Into the clearing comes Levi, the Premier, and Deuxieme. My father looks about to explode and the Premier just looks a bit pale.

"I felt something," says a very pale and shaken Levi.

I bite my lip to keep in my frustration. My father won't let this go without punishment. What if I wasn't able to kill it? What if Titus wasn't there? In the end, I know that if the Fates pulled at Levi then it could've gone very badly. It worries me to think that I'm somehow intertwined with the fate they have for Levi to the point where they need me alive. I shake my head. That's something to worry about later.

"Thank you," I tell him and then turn to the Premier and Deuxieme. Anger sizzles through my senses. "*What was that.*"

The Scholar Premier thinks to himself but my father immediately answers. "They're Punishment Dogs, used by the elves mostly. They sent some to help with… school security."

"Well, it seems to me like it's doing the opposite," I snap.

254

"Skye, respect," my father scolds.

"I almost *died* just now," I exclaim. "And I want to know why! Why were there Punishment Dogs at a *school?*"

"She deserves to know," Levi says, his brows furrowed in determination. He turns to his father. "And I do too! You haven't given me the full story from the moment I got here. You've either been lying to me or keeping information from me for my entire life. For Fate's sake, what I'm doing holds the futures of every single person in the Six Kingdoms."

"Levi, I–"

"Tell me," Levi says, deathly calm. My heart skips when I see his eyes flash red. "*Now.*"

The Premier looks conflicted, his eyes widened a fraction, but nods slowly. "There have been Malevolent sightings regularly, more frequently than usual. Some nearby schools have been bulking up their security and the Six Kingdoms military is working on protecting us around our borders. There have been some instances of Blood for Blood Magic with selkies as well." He frowns, the years of decision making falling as a shadow across his face. "I didn't want to worry you more than you already are."

Levi takes a moment and I notice his fists at his sides are balled tight. "Tell me *every* update you get. I don't *care* about my stress. *Tell me.*"

"I ask the same," the Premier says. "My reports say that you have the ability to read minds and you failed to inform me."

I look over sharply at Levi who doesn't even glance over. I clench my jaw. How did this just fail to be mentioned in our daily conversations. If he expects me to help protect him, *I* need to know these things.

His eyes go aflame. "You have people monitoring me?" He laughs bitterly. "You didn't tell me you were *drugging* me with Dream

255

Tea so people could influence my dreams. *You do not get to say that to me!"*

The Premier purses his lips. "Fine then," he grits out.

I look between the son and father, who sound like anything but.

"Ms. Fervent will teach you about the art of the mind, who I've heard is knowledgeable in the area. Unfortunately, all the teachers I had contacted for you have either been killed or don't want to be connected to the most wanted teen alive."

"We have something else to tell you," I say. Levi meets my eyes and gives a small nod, so I continue. "We think that a Sorcerer is working with the Malevolents. Based on how rocks were thrown at Austra and Makai on that first trial and the tree that fell, a Wind Elemental could do damage like that but not a Malevolents. It's not with their skill set."

The Premier pales but nods his head. "It was a possibility we were considering, but you're right. We'll keep an eye on it and update you."

Titus turns to walk back into the woods, his eyes not meeting mine again.

"Mr. Sage," the Premier says, his voice as cold as I've ever heard it, "please take Ms. Fervent to the Infirmary. I'll talk to you both again soon."

Chapter 33

Levi

"And you failed to tell me this?" Skye hisses, her eyes murderous.

Avoiding her glare, I explain. "Sorry! My mind was too busy worrying about Austra and the Malevolents." Even to me it sounds like a wimpy excuse for not telling them earlier. "I've been busy. I think it has something to do with the next Earthen Born Fate Companion." Hermia looks just about to faint.

"Can you see what people are thinking?" Hermia leans forward on her chair.

"Maybe. I haven't really tried."

"You haven't tried!" Skye leans back on the couch, astounded. "How long ago did you find out?"

"Like a week or two, maybe," I say, sheepishly.

"A week or two," exclaims Skye. "Levi, you know how valuable this could be? Power over the mind is one of the most dangerous and useful gifts someone could have."

"Really?" I don't like the tone of her voice.

"Yes. But it always comes with a price," Hermia says, deep in thought.

"As I've heard," I mutter. It seems like all I'm doing is paying prices nowadays.

"Everything comes with a price, Levi," Skye says. "Everything has to be in a balance with each other. That's why we are so worried about this cycle of Malevolents and Earthen Born Fates. You and Austra have been gifted these unprecedented abilities, but we have yet to see the price that you will pay."

"How do you know that this ability will have a price?" I ask. "As you've mentioned, other people have had it. Why can't it just be like a normal gift from the Fates?"

Hermia says, "In all the books I've read, I only recall a few times a Fate had this ability and they all had quite gruesome endings." The Scholar cringes at the memory. "Both of your gifts are only given to those who really need it. They gave you this ability knowing the cost it might have."

"Well, if I'm burdened with this ability, I bet a thousand water pixies that they want me to use it," I say, definitively.

"Then we better start practicing." Skye orders, "Tell me what I'm thinking. I'll make it simple at first."

She closes her eyes and I follow.

I try to reach deep into my mind and wade through the darkness. Then, there's a small light, like a candle a hundred feet away. There's a warm feeling to the light, like if I get to the other side there will be something beautiful. As I get closer, a throbbing pain comes into my chest. I push forward, but something prevents me from entering. I scramble to get closer, but then all I see is black.

...

Skye

"Levi. Levi! Get up!"

"I don't think he can hear you," Mia tells me.

"I've figured." I tug on the leather tie of my hair in distress. "What happened?"

"I would be more concerned about whether students outside this room heard us. We've yet to test how soundproof this place is and that was a pretty audacious scream," Mia says, her brows furrowing.

"Austra charmed the room," I say, waving her off. "I'm more concerned about the passed out Earthen Born Fate at my feet. I don't know what happened!" My father had me train in Japan for a summer about the mind-reading. There's a population of people in Japan who are Scholars and have this exact gift. Though I don't, my father wanted me to know how to seal my mind and win in a fight of the minds.

"Maybe you subconsciously keep your mind closed off," Elias suggests.

"Maybe," I whisper, glancing at Levi with concern.

"We'll try again tomorrow," states Mia, yawning. A rise of annoyance threatens to claw at me at the lack of concern on the herface. "I'm going off to bed."

"You sleep here," I insist.

Ignoring my comment, she says, "I recommend you get some sleep too. It doesn't do well to dwell on things you can't control," she says, a bite to her tone. "If my theory is correct, Levi should be up by morning. Get some sleep, Skye. I'll look after him."

The knot in my chest loosens a bit. "Thank you," I grumble. Rubbing a sore spot on my neck, I ground out, "Goodnight."

...

Skye

I stop before my door of my dorm room and sniff. There's a scent, vaguely familiar with a tinge of rose and sugar. My hand grips my knife as I creak open the door. I sigh in relief when I see a brunette girl with a huge collection of large suitcases.

"Vesta?"

She whips her head around, startled. "Skye?"

Too shocked to hide my surprise, I ask, "Why are you here?"

"Isn't it obvious?" she scoffs and turns back to her dresser. "I came back."

"I thought you and your brother moved in with your cousin," I say, closing the door behind me. I can't say I missed the Royal, but her absence was noticeable.

"Well... He thought it was best if we went back. You see, Alexandra Dominique is filled with spoiled brats and snakes." *The irony.* "Plus, he wanted me to keep an eye on *you*," she continues, pointing a disgusted finger at me.

I lean back on my bed frame and cross my arms. "And why would that be?"

"He said you're in trouble."

I cock my head at that. "In what way?"

"Why should I tell you?" Vesta huffs, lifting her chin.

"Fine," I sigh, too tired to fight back.

She frowns, disappointed at my easy surrender. "Alright then." She goes back to unpacking all her things. After a few moments of silence, she groans. "Fine! I'll tell you. He said something about family lineage. Would you happen to know what that might be?"

"I'm related to a lot of important people," I say, deadpan. She throws up her hands in frustration.

"Now I remember!" She places her hands on her hips and says, "He said that the owl is sick and to be ready–whatever that means. Do you know what he's talking about?"

The owl. The owl. It couldn't be–

"I have no idea," I say, keeping a steady voice. So she can't see my face, I turn to my own dresser and snatch my toothbrush.

"If you ever *do* find out what it means, let me know because it's a whole bunch of gibberish to me." She continues unpacking her first suitcase, each designer clothing item at a time.

Muttering something about going to the restroom, I stumble into the hall.

The owl. No. It can't be.

I jog down the marble tile swiftly and around an abandoned part of the hallway. Moving a planter box aside, I crawl into the small dark opening behind it. It's not a secret passageway, but it's a good hiding spot.

Crouching into a ball, I look into the darkness.

My mind travels to the owl. If he is sick, then I don't have much time.

...

Levi

"Skye? Are you okay?" I ask, still groggy from sleep. Memories of last night come seeping back as I watch Skye pace back and forth in the Representatives' Room. The memories of, you know, Skye overriding me with pain. Well, I can still feel the aftereffects even now, a pounding pain at my temples.

"I'm just tired, that's all," she says and settles herself on the couch next to me. Her long, brown hair is down, unlike its usual ponytail. Something about it being left to fall over her shoulders makes her look softer, more like a teenager rather than a girl trained to kill monsters. "Don't worry about me. What happened last night?"

I cringe. I can't just say, "Well, touching you is a pain," or, "Do you always feel that?" Why *did* I feel pain in the first place? I don't even think *she* would be able to answer that. "Uh… well, I don't really know. Maybe I just did something wrong," I suggest. "Why don't I try Elias again to see if the same thing happens?"

Elias shrugs, his curly red hair looking like flames in the sun. Locks stick to his forehead. My guess is that they had another morning dance practice to get ready for their performance. "Sure. Why not? Just leave the private stuff to me, got it?"

"Yeah, don't worry. Close your eyes," I instruct, shaking the last bit of sleep off. The impending possibility of being knocked back asleep has the same effect as a shot of espresso. Luckily, today's a weekend, so I would only be missing some study hours that I could make up for tomorrow.

"Think of something simple to start out with," suggests Skye.

Elias frowns. "Like what?"

"I'm not going to tell you," Skye grumbles. "That's the whole point."

"Okay," says Elias, smiling to himself. "I'm thinking of a unicorn."

"Don't say it out loud! I meant, think it in your head," she says, messaging her temples. For the first time since coming to Grantham Willow, Skye looks nervous. Even when preparing for battle on the edge of the cliff and facing a Malevolent head on, one on one, she did not cower in fear.

"Oh," Elias says, lying limp on the couch. "Sorry. Practice was hard today. I'm a little out of it."

"Rest, Elias," commands Mia. "Do it on me." Squaring her shoulders, she faces me with her misty, grey eyes. She sends a sharp glance to Skye, "You're not the only one trained with the art of the mind. I come from a long line of Librarians, it's part of our training."

Skye scoffs and settles back into the couch. Getting up, I motion for Hermia to sit with me on the floor. If either of us collapses, we won't have far to fall. "Close your eyes," I tell her.

She does.

"Your opponents won't have their eyes closed all the time, Levi," Hermia tells me.

"We'll get there soon," Skye says, which is what I assume is an attempt at reassuring me. "Usually it is easier for the subject to think of something when they don't have any distractions from their surroundings."

"Are you doubting my ability to think, Warrior?" Hermia raises her eyebrow, but keeps her eyes closed. Scholars are very sensitive about others' perception of their intelligence. Skye knows that. What's with her today?

Closing my eyelids, I become surrounded by darkness again, this time the darkness that I want. The world is black, and I swim through it like water. Then I see the light. This time, it's grey like the color of her eyes, not gold like Skye's. When I reach for it, I don't feel immense pain.

"I see a parrot," I say, keeping my eyes closed.

"What color?" asks Skye.

Scrunching my forehead, I strain to make the image more detailed. In my mind, it focuses, and I start to see color, texture, and then each individual feather. "Red and blue," I say with certainty.

Skye hums, her voice somewhere distant. "Is he correct?"

"Yes," replies Mia.

"Now think of something more complicated like words."

Clenching my teeth, I go through her mind and reach towards the light. It's a bit easier than last time since I know what to expect. As I work towards conjuring the picture in my head, the image isn't clearing like it did last time.

"Don't try to make out a picture," Skye says with the same precision as usual. "Just think. Don't use imagery."

Wincing, I ask, "How do I do that?"

"Bring the thought to you."

"Um…" That doesn't really help.

"Just do it."

"Fine," I grumble and try to open my mind to the light and let it flow through. The thought comes to me just as naturally as my own. "Clovis." My mother's maiden name. Hermia must've done her research on me.

"Yes."

And we go on like this until lunch. Then after lunch, we continue. We continue for the next week until I can master how to read full conversations. It's like learning a new skill. The more practice I get, the easier it is to read people. Soon, it's just like poking through a hole in a wall. But, when the walls are up, it takes more force and the more breaks I have to take in between reading.

Austra even let me practice on her. It's simple, but the reading of minds has a certain etiquette. Skye said that people don't usually let people read their mind unless they have a certain level of trust.

I don't know if our mind reading practice was any indication of her trust in me, but I'll take it as progress.

After a bit, we decide to take a break. Skye assigned me a book to read about mind reading etiquette and goes off to look out the large window. In the middle of one of the books Skye assigned to me, she sighs loudly. We turn to look, even Aris raises his eyes from his book.

She doesn't even turn to see if we're paying attention when she says, "The King is sick."

"What!" Elias looks just as shocked and for the first time in a while, he's quiet. There isn't much that Elias can't make light of or talk about in general. Seeing Hermia not quite know what to do to bring logic to the situation is equally unnerving. There's something else in their faces other than surprise and sadness. Dread.

Austra covers her mouth with her hand and whispers, "I'm so sorry, Skye."

Where Skye and the King close?

Aris has a mask of neutrality, but Aspyn looks just as taken aback as Austra.

"I just found out last night," Skye sighs, wrapping her arms around herself. "I don't think I'm supposed to know. My friend Everhett told Vesta about it in code. Just... keep it to yourselves for now."

"Why aren't they telling the rest of the Six Kingdoms?" Elias, shaking his head in disbelief. "When this gets out–"

"My guess is that the Six Kingdoms government doesn't want the Malevolents to take it as the work of Hardorous and raise morale. Although it is against the terms of war to initiate the final battle before the Fates mandate it, they are not forbidden to strike Flare Barrer," she says. Turning to me, she says, "It's the name of the center of the Six Kingdoms and the home of the King and Queen."

"The current king is a Warrior, right?" I ask. I remember one of my classmates talking about him.

"Yeah," Elias replies. Laughing to himself, he says, "He can morph into an owl. Who would have thought? An owl won the Throne's Trials."

Seeing my confusion, Skye clarifies, "Descendants from the original set of representatives for the crown when the Six Kingdoms were first formed are given the chance to compete for the crown when the King or Queen dies. They're chosen by the Fates, like your Companions. One from each Kingdom."

"Ms. Fervent is part of the royal family," Mia says, frowning at the Warrior. "From what I've gathered, you may earn a spot in those trials."

"My grandfather's the King," Skye says, ringing out water from her hair. She looks at me, studying my reaction. "My father's technically a prince but will likely not inherit the crown. The Fates choose those young in age so that they can rule for as long as possible. As much as I detest the cruelty of my grandfather, he has soft edges where my father does not." She turns back to the widow and studies the peach colored clouds. I have no doubt that she's wishing she was flying through them now, not a care in the world. "It saddens me to see him near the end of his road."

My body stiffens. It has never occurred to me that all the fear and admiration from our classmates was due to another reason than how notorious her father is. Based on what the Premier made it out to be, both of our fathers gained high positions in a highly regarded school at a young age. I don't know the reason for why my father got it early, but the training that Skye's father must've gotten would've made up for the age.

"I guess I have some important friends in high places," I say. Hiding my shock, I get up to place a comforting hand on her shoulder. "You'll get through this."

Skye doesn't look at my, but she dips her chin slightly.

Hermia gets up, dusting off her pants. Although we've been in here many times since we found it, there's some lingering must that will remain for a while. "I'm going to get my eight hours of sleep. I recommend you both do the same. You'll need it." She gives us meaningful looks so that she knows we heard. I honestly don't think I'll be able to sleep at all tonight. "Have a good night." Elias and I watch her exit the room.

"I don't understand some of the things she says," mutters Elias. "She makes me feel really stupid sometimes."

I let my hand drop from Skye's shoulder. "Same. There's so much about the Six Kingdoms that I don't know about until one of you tells me. It'll be a while before I start to feel like everything is normal."

Elias sighs, shrinking deeper into the cushions. "I've lived in the Six Kingdoms my whole life and everything *still* doesn't feel normal. I'm afraid you'll be waiting a long time for things to feel like that."

Chapter 34

Austra

My soul feels heavy every time I think about Aris. He's just so... hard to read. My feelings are sporadic, and I don't know what they mean half the time. For a time, I thought I had feelings for him, but if he leaves when I'm in need of help the most–I don't know if I want that in a partner.

When I'm with him, there's something though. There are unspoken words between us, and I don't know if they should be spoken.

"It's time to go to dinner," Levi says. He looks at me with his brown hair flying in all directions and his hazel eyes of nearly every color.

I groan and cover my head with some fluffy blankets Hermia brought into the Representatives' Room. What I would do right now to just take a nap.

Aris walks by, his hands in his pockets and immaculate posture. I cover my hair with my hoodie and sink into my covers. I probably look like a sewer rat, whereas Aris always seems to look impeccable. "I found a passageway that opens near the Capricorn. It starts in one of the upper bookshelves." He wraps his hands behind his back and studies us. "Care to try it?"

Levi nods his head and says, "Sure."

I've never liked passageways, or at least the ones that are smaller. I remember talking to Aris about it once. He looks at me in question, perhaps remembering the encounter, when he sees me behind Levi. Waving a hand, I ignore the concern. This is a fear I just need to conquer.

Skye crawls into the bookshelf and pushes some books out of the way. There's an opening in the wall just big enough for Aris to squeeze through, who's the tallest of us. Levi and I start to crawl into the little opening. Inside, the walls are stone, like the tunnel was chiseled out of the building blocks of the school itself.

"None of the square footage in this school is wasted," Skye says. Looking at her surroundings in awe, she says, "I wonder what type of origin story this had."

The ground is dusty and cold. I try to see what's ahead, but all I can make out is a pit of black. The further and further I go, the narrower and narrower the tunnel feels. The floor of the passage is rough, same as the wall, but bugs crawl along the edges. A shiver runs down my spine.

"Ouch!" I rub my forehead and look for what I hit it on. The passage's ceiling took a dip.

"You good?" Levi asks, his voice laced with concern.

"I'm fine," I say with an unintentional snap.

We crawl along and soon the walls scrape my sides. I'm a little on the smaller side, so I wonder how Aris is doing. His shoulders are wider from his training.

I look around me, only to find darkness. Then I stop and feel around and my breathes come quicker. Up, down, side, everything's stone. Covering my face with my hands, I lay on my back trying to take deep breaths. What if I run out of air? What if I'm squeezed to death? A hump of stone digs into my back and all the body does is conjure beads of sweat that run down the sides of my face.

I feel a squeeze at my shoulder. "Hey," asks Levi with a tinge of worry to his voice, "are you okay?"

It takes effort to shake my head. All he can probably do is lay on his stomach or he'll touch the top. He can't drag me out.

"Did you hurt anything? Maybe you got hurt from hitting your head."

I just shake my head. I pull my arms as close to my sides as possible to save space.

"Are you claustrophobic?"

I pause for a second and then nod my head. I still have that feeling of panic as I stay stationary in my position. Soon my breaths come out in pants and I squeeze my eyes shut in hopes of opening them to the light.

"Here," begins Levi. He shifts a little bit and I feel a hard thing on the crown of my head. "Just even your breathing." I hear his voice closely. He's probably lying as I am now, head to head.

I try to do as he says, but then I feel that feeling again and my heart beats starts to rise. This can't be happening. I have to be stronger than this. What happens when I face a Malevolent? I need to be able to deal with stuff like this.

As if he read my mind, for all I know he might've, he says, "Don't blame yourself. Everyone has fears and they're not something to be ashamed of. Just listen to my breathing. Close your eyes."

I close my eyes. Levi breaths, accentuating each inhale and exhale. I listen and follow the steady beat. Only thinking about my breaths. When we're breathing in unison, he starts to shift. "Are you ready?" he asks.

I nod my head. Levi turns around. How is he able to do that in such a small area? I feel my surroundings again and find the walls about an arm's length away. Before I can question more, I decide to push it out of my mind and focus on getting out of here.

A bead of light in the distance grows bigger and bigger, forming an outline of a square. I hear some of my classmates talking and rushing by. It must be near the dinner rush. We usually avoid it by getting to the Capricorn a tad early, but I guess I ruined those plans.

Skye stops just before the opening. She pushes slightly on the board that blocks me from my fresh air. She ducks when two students walk by but then looks out again. When the coast is clear, we scramble out quickly, trying to act as normal as possible when a new herd of students run past.

Florin Kim, who I know from Dragon Riding class, looks at me with a raised eyebrow. "Austra, are you okay? Did you run a mile or something?"

"No, Florin," Levi says sarcastically. "We just went through a secret passageway across the school and she's claustrophobic."

My eyes widen in shock. What in the Six Kingdoms is he *thinking*? When I look back to Florin and he just rolls his eyes with a grin and waves at us as he walks away with his friends. Levi and I just make a beeline to the food.

We all pause our conversations and questions until we gather at our table.

"I don't get it," says Levi, munching on some greens. "You never got claustrophobic when we went through other passageways."

"That's probably because I didn't have to crawl through them. I actively avoid the smaller ones if I can," I say, blushing with shame.

"How about Gemini?"

"It's not that small, Levi," I say and take a bite of my sandwich. "Just drop it, okay? I'll be fine."

"It's not fine," Levi says with force. "Everything can be used against you. This is just adding onto that already long list. I should know these things."

"The list isn't that long," I grumble, trying to close my eyes. I've calmed down a bit, but my adrenaline is still pumping.

"Exactly, Austra. I don't care what your fears are, just that we know them so we can be prepared." Turning to me on the bench, he says, "Every weakness you have is my weakness. I'm the one that's responsible for keeping both myself and you alive, not to mention entire Six Kingdoms."

There's something in his eyes that I never noticed before: fear. When we first matured and found out about everything, he seemed so

270

calm about it, which made me feel self-conscious about how I didn't know what I was doing. It never occurred to me that he also feels that pressure.

We sit there for what seems like eternity in silence. I can't read his mind, but I can assume that he's thinking the same as me. Is one fight worth the fate of so many? Is this fight making the probability of failure higher?

The silence, the peaceful silence, is answer enough.

...

Skye

"What's the matter?"

She's been quiet since her and Levi's conversation, both of the deep in thought. I take the pause as a good thing. The others watch them like they're two bulls that could go at each other at any moment. Something about Austra's expression though tells me she's not thinking about Levi. There's regret in it–sadness.

Austra jolts at my voice, her spoon clanging. "Uh, I've been thinking about Makai and how he found out about him and me being betrothed. Yes, I did give Levi a hint about it once, but it wasn't enough for him to figure it out. Then there's you, but you're not the type to get involved with stuff like that. The only reason I doubted Levi was because he has a big mouth sometimes."

She takes a breath, eating another spoonful of her soap. Swallowing, she mutters, "The other day, I asked Evie about how Makai's doing, since they both hang around the Circle of Myths."

The Circle of Myths. They're practically famous around school, a group of five Centrals, each extremely powerful. Not only from a Grantham Willow standpoint but compared to the entire Six Kingdoms. It's considered a privilege to be at their table or to be with them in the halls. I've never bothered myself with the social hierarchy of the school, but something about them makes you think that they're fated to stand with each other, in life and in death.

"Evie said that Makai acts strange when approached about the topic, defensive. I thought it was normal and that's probably how he's coping. She said that he doesn't talk about how he found out. He just keeps saying that Levi told him, like he was told to say that's what happened."

It dawns on me then. Locking my jaw, I say, "You think that someone used the Recollection spell on Makai."

Chapter 35

Skye

Sometimes I feel like the most intelligent person in the room, noticing things that others fail to. Only recently have I met someone just as attentive as me, Aris. Even then, not much catches me completely off guard.

But this... this changes things.

If someone used the Recollection Charm on Makai, then this rift created between Levi and Austra was planned to weaken them. It also means that the traitor was able to get close enough to Makai and into the school itself.

"How would they know about Austra and Makai?" Aspyn looks between us frantically, as if realizing the same thing as me. We're no longer safe.

"They might've overheard us in the Infirmary," Austra says to Levi. Noticing our confused faces, she clarifies, "We went to visit Skye one night when she was still recovering, and Levi first came to Grantham Willow. I mentioned something about how I didn't know what to do and debating on whether or not I should tell Makai. A patient might've overheard."

My heart clenches at the thought that she came to me, of all people, to talk about her love life. I guess I do have experience with her type of situation, but I don't know if my advice would be any good. I offer Austra a small smile in thanks. "Hermia, do you know how to restore someone's memory?"

Hermia nods, taking off her reading glasses. "It's complicated and we'll need a Sorcerer. Do either of you have experience?" The Scholar looks between Aris and Austra expectantly.

Aris nods his head slowly, making us look at him in disbelief. Sorcerers aren't taught that type of magic until their later years since it's considered more dangerous and skill based. I've accepted that Aris will just remain a boy of mysteries. As long as it helps us, I'll be content.

Not batting an eye, Hermia says, "Good. Meet me after school today and we'll start collecting ingredients."

After a few moments of uneasy silence, Elias brings up his upcoming performance and when to start buying tickets. The others break into friendly conversation, probably just as eager as me to think about something other than the fate of the world. I, meanwhile, rest my brain before I take my History of the Six Kingdoms test.

Hoping to do some last-minute studying, I take out my textbook and go over the famous people and dates for this lesson. One man by the name of Nori Watanabe was an Earthen born Fate Sorcerer Companion during World War 2, the 99th War. She was known as one of the bravest Earthen Born Fate Companions to exist since her trials were the hardest recorded with the added pressure of her country, the United States, being at war with Japan. Although the Outside world countries are separate from the Six Kingdoms, the political turmoil tends to blend with that of the Six Kingdoms.

I remember one tale my father used to tell me when I was young. Nori almost lost a trial during the bombing of Pearl Harbor. Her house caught on fire and she ran inside to try and save her family, but she knew it was useless.

She had hope that the Six Kingdoms would become better and that the world would find peace. She knew that the only way anyone would live past this decade is if she lived. She ran from that house, just far enough away so that when the tank of gas in her garage caught fire, she survived.

It is up to the Fates whether or not Austra will have to make a decision like that.

...

Austra

It takes more time than Hermia expected to brew the potion to clear Makai's mind. All Aris can do is the reversal spell. Sometimes there's a lingering block on the victim's mind afterwards, which is where Hermia's potion comes in.

Hermia's frizzy brown hair is pulled back behind her head, a few strands sticking in all directions. She has a look of determination as she stirs the mixture in the bowl, her small arms straining to turn the liquid. It's smaller than I thought it would be, but I guess Makai won't need much.

Aspyn's cat monitors the room, sniffing the air. The black feline is sweet with those she likes, but she'll attack if need be. Trust me, I've seen her hunt Felix Silverwit's guinea pig fight before. The poor Scholar thought his pet was going to become dinner. Even the vicious, fluffy library cat decides to sleep on the opposite side of the library from Sydney.

Skye has a class now, but there isn't time to waste. She agreed that it would be best if we did it without her. Levi's out getting Makai with Elias. We found out that only Levi and my lockets work on the door to the Representatives' Room, so one of us has to be with the group to go to the Representatives' Room.

"Hey? How's the potion coming along?" Hermia doesn't react to my touch or voice and just leans in closer to her work. I walk around to the other side of the desk so I can see her face more clearly. The potion is a dark brown, bubbling with heat, despite the absence of a burner.

"We always mess up at this part," Hermia grits out, continuing to mix. "Aris, when I tell you to, do the spell."

Aris and I glance at each other for a moment, his black eyes meeting my hazel ones. After I matured, they started to show the mist of wind, the blue of water, the brown of the earth, and the crackling yellow and orange of fire.

I look away swiftly, my cheeks stinging. He doesn't seem to get embarrassed when I catch him staring and just continues to study me even after I look away.

"Now!"

Closing my eyes tight, I feel a rush of air and then–nothing. Peeking in their direction, my shoulders sag at their smug grins. "Finally," grumbles Hermia, satisfaction settling on her face. Checking her watch, she declares, "They should be here any time now."

I pour both her and I a glass of water from the table.

"Why are we here?" I nearly choke on my water. *Makai.*

"You wouldn't believe me if I told you," Levi chuckles, a hand on his shoulder as they come into view. I forget how to breathe.

How Levi somehow convinced him to come, I have no idea. Last time I checked, they were also on bad terms.

Makai's smirk leaves his face when he sees me, his face contorting in anger. "What's *she* doing here?"

It's Elias' turn to laugh, patting him on the back. "C'mon, Makai. We're only passing through. Look, Hermia made us something to drink." He takes one of the cups that I gave her and another I didn't see before. Aris winks.

Elias hands Makai the new cup and drinks it readily. Shrugging, Makai does the same. His face scrunches in disgust and bursts, "What in the Six Kingdoms is that?" Looking around at us, he slurs, "Why does everything look swirly?"

Elias guides him onto the couch, making sure he doesn't fall off. "No problem, Makai. Just rest for a moment and then we'll be on our way."

Makai nods, raising his eyebrow as Aris approaches, the shadows wrapping around him like wings. "Why is Aris coming over?" If Aris wasn't my friend, I would've been afraid too.

The Sorcerer just smirks and raises his hands, fingers twitching. He mutters something under his breath, something I can't hear. Makai's head droops to the side and comes back, his eyes rolling.

Aris' jaw clenches, straining from effort. "What do you remember? Did someone use the Recollection Charm on you?"

Makai's eyes open, hazed over. "Nothing. Someone came from behind and whispered something in my ear. That's all."

"Did Levi tell you that Austra's betrothed?"

"No."

I lift my hand to my mouth and turn to Levi to apologize. He smiles softly and says in my head, *Don't worry about it.* I'd guessed what Makai would say, but the confirmation makes it that much more real. Nodding my head in thanks, I listen to whatever comes out of Makai's mouth next.

"Who told you?" Aris grounds out, his fingers straining.

"I don't know," Makai says, still in daze. "I didn't see who it was."

Aris holds on for a few more moments, whispering more words I can't make out.

He releases, slouching into the nearest chair, drained. Makai falls back into the couch, breathing hard, sweat dripping down his temples. Hermia hands him her water as he raises his gaze to mine. Bracing an arm on the table, Aris gasps, "You were right."

...

Skye

After my last class, I dart out of the room, not bothering to say good-bye to my teacher. Ducking behind a corner, I use my locket to get into a secret passageway to the library. The Premier and the Deuxieme have eyes everywhere and I would much rather have them not question me on why I was running full speed through the halls.

I pop out near the tunnel that we used the other day. Since I don't have my locket, that's the only way in if I don't want to risk breaking Aris' focus if he's doing the spell. I slide through, ignoring the bugs and the spider webs.

My Valian hearing catches Makai's drunken voice. They must've just started the plan.

Willing silence into my movements, I slink out of the passage and stay on the ledge, not risking climbing down the ladder. I watch carefully as Aris approaches Makai who mutters ancient words.

My muscles freeze. It doesn't sound right. Alarm shoots through my nerves. If he fails, then we would have to go through this all over again. I listen closer.

The temperature around me drops.

He's not doing the reversal charm... he's doing the Recollection Charm.

I watch in horror as Makai repeats exactly what Aris tells him to, word for word. What startles me most is that Aris does the reversal spell at the very end, after knowing that Makai doesn't know who did the spell on him.

Aris.

The Darkness Wielder is the traitor.

...

Levi

278

When Makai comes back around, all is chaos. It's as if he just realized that Austra and him are betrothed for the first time. I can't help but feel horrible for Austra, who looks as pale as death. I watch in pride as she holds strong this time, taking the verbal blows.

"Makai," she says, trying to calm him down, "you have to understand that I needed time to process too. I've known since the beginning of the year and it's barely past winter. Call me a coward, but I wanted just a little longer without this nail in our friendship."

Makai runs a hand through his curly, brown hair, looking as disheveled as we all feel. "You should have told me sooner," he whispers, all the force drawn out of him.

Austra walks closer like she would approaching a wild bear. "I know," she sighs. "I know."

The rest of us wander around aimlessly, trying to seem like we're minding our own business. All except for Aris, who looks close to pouncing on Makai. Darkness seems to hug us all a little closer.

Hermia comes trotting in with cups of tea and hands one to Austra and Makai as they sit together to work things out. I'm just glad that he didn't storm away, never to be seen again. This is already going better than the last time.

Skye comes up behind me and tugs on my sleeve. I jump, not hearing her approach. She signals me with her finger to follow her out of the Representative's Room, the others are too occupied listening in on Austra and Makai's conversation to notice. She leads me around rows and rows of books, far deeper than most students go. The titles get older and older and the pages become more yellow and faded the longer we walk.

She pulls me into a study room, charmed to be soundproof in case students want to use it for a group project. After she closes the door, I ask, "What's wrong? I thought you had a test."

The golden eyed Warrior nods slowly. If Skye's this unsteady, then what she has to tell me has to be a whole different level of bad. I grip the chair so hard, lines get pressed into my skin when she says, "I think I know who the traitor is... Aris." She takes a shaky breath. "It's Aris."

Aris? No. The boy who everyone thought had a dark history and was trying to find the light. The redemption story of the school. The stars were aligned, almost too perfectly, for him to be seen as evil–seen as someone to fear.

Slumping into a seat, I rub my eyes. "Why?"

She explains what she saw in the Representatives' Room, the words he whispered that signed his guilt. Skye does not falter, her voice steady again. The only sign of hurt is in the tenseness of her lips and the shame in her eyes. "Austra's not going to take this well," she says softly.

Remembering the lingering stares and the glimpses I've gotten of their practice sessions; I bow my head. "We can't keep it from her. I'll call her over." Closing my eyes, I reach out with my mind, searching for her.

Entering the light, I say, *Come to the study room near the back. Make sure no one's following you.* I project an image of our walk to the room.

I raise my head to meet Skye, whose lips press into a line. She takes a seat next to me, so close I can feel her warmth and smell the vanilla in her hair. Maybe my Warrior gifts are starting to come in. Skye said that maturing for her was more gradual, the heightened senses the first to come.

Austra opens the door, shaking both Skye and I out of our bottomless thoughts. "What's up? Did something happen?"

Skye and I look at each other for a split second before she begins. I watch as Austra's face falls, the light slowly leaving her eyes with each word Skye mutters. She leans on the door, using it to keep her standing.

280

When she finishes, we both look at Austra with concern. Part of me expected her to cry, but what I see is worse. Her eyes are empty.

Chapter 36

Levi

"What in the Seven Kingdoms?" Elias explodes, tearing out his red hair. "What does *trust* mean anymore! I need to punch a pillow."

"I have something even better. There's a beanbag chair over there," I say, pointing to the corner of the room. Austra conjured it the other day, figuring we would spend more time here since the Representatives' Room has the passageway that compromises its security.

Skye, Austra, and Elias have a history that I may never understand, but both Austra and Skye seemed insistent that it was alright to tell Elias. Out of caution, even Elias agreed that it's best not to involve Aspyn, not knowing much about her background either. He was opposed to that at first, but eventually just resolved to shouting and externalizing his pain.

Telling Hermia was almost a given, her birthright almost guaranteeing her silence. The Librarians have been faithful for centuries and the Fates wouldn't be cruel enough to make her a traitor... I hope.

Elias crawls across Gemini and starts punching with all his might. "That little dragon manure."

"I can't believe it," Austra says under her breath, in a little daze.

"It might not be him," defends Hermia.

"But it could be?"

"Y–Yes."

"What in the Seven Kingdoms," Skye curses, strangling her book.

"Everyone!" I exclaim. "This isn't going to help us. For all we know, it could be any Sorcerer. Maybe something will come up that will lead us in another direction."

Austra doesn't even move from where she lays on the sleeping bag. "Aris is the most logical choice. Singing sirens. He had me."

"Austra," I sigh. "What'd I just say?"

"But Levi, it doesn't matter if it's him or not. I'm supposed to be on the lookout for this stuff. I *shouldn't* have been surprised." She pauses, looking down at her hands. "I thought there was a person underneath those shadows. I guess I was wrong"

"Don't be so hard on yourself," Skye sighs, patting her shoulder. That's about as much comfort I've seen Skye give anyone. "He surprised *me*, for goodness sake. I'm the third pair of eyes. I should've caught onto this earlier too."

Trying to offer a little bit of support of his own, Elias places a hand on the Warrior's shoulder.

"Don't touch me."

"Okay."

"It's just that," Skye sighs, "when I feel like things aren't under my control, I remember all the people that I can rely trust. It helps me narrow my look out circumference. It's a tactic one of my War Strategies teachers taught me this summer. The funny thing is, Aris was one of the names I would say. Stupid!"

She lays down, covering her face with a pillow.

"Let's just worry about this later," suggests Austra, cocooning herself in blankets. "I think we should just take a moment to think." With that she makes her fluffy cold weather jacket into a pillow and snuggles up.

"Then when do you think we should talk about it?" I counter, a little agitated, but not agitated enough to turn down the chance of stealing her blanket and using it myself.

"Jerk. It's cold," she shoots and fights for it back.

Skye gets up from her sleeping bag and sighs. "Levi, will you please stop making it so cold? You know it's not good to let your feelings use your power."

"Thanks, Skye. Maybe we can work on that during detention," I say with a slight snap, falling back onto a mattress signed by one of the Grim Dawn Duelers. It's a long story that involves an Elias with too much caffeine and a conjured alpaca.

"Just calm yourself and control your emotions. Don't let them leak into your power," she says and settles back into silence.

We lay there listening to Elias' monotonous beating on the beanbag chair and the May drizzles pattering on the roof. Through a small window, I watch the thick clouds, light peeking through the cracks.

I jerk up at the sound of a crackle. Skye's already crouching, her eyes trained on the small window. A Lightning Critter nudges it open and darts towards Elias, who just looks about to pass out.

"What do you want," he wails.

"Hey Elias." Sylas' voice sounds through the ball of light.

Collapsing onto the mattress next to me, he sighs, "What do you need?"

"Sorry to bother you, but Claire seems to have a craving for a Brown Yellow-Bellied Goose. Can you find one for me? I'll pluck it and everything, but I have to watch some students for detention."

"Ughhhhhhhhh."

"Come on! Please? I'll never hear the end of it if she doesn't get it. I'll pay for your food the next time we go to town."

"Ughhhhhhhhh."

"I'll owe you a favor?"

"I don't know…"

"Please? I'll get you some seeds the next time I see a vendor. I know you like sunflowers." The poor Master sounds desperate. Hermia tries to hide her laugh at the Hunter's distress.

284

After contemplating a few moments, Elias says, "Okay."

"Thank the Fates!"

"Don't forget! I like the big sunflowers. The ones that are pure yellow. Bye."

"Bye."

The Lightning Critter zooms away and Elias rolls over to scream into the cushions. "Wow," I say in awe. "You really know how to barter."

"Tell me about it. I once got him to pay $69.99 for a red urchin from the bottom of the bay when I just paid a water pixie a dime to get one for me," he laughs, getting up. "Claire's craving the weirdest things. See you in a bit."

"See you later, bud."

Letting out a huff, I get up and take out some homework and Skye does the same. Hermia excuses herself, saying that she's going to have a movie night with Claire.

Reading the contemplative look on her face, I ask, "What do you have to say? You have that feeling."

"I have a feeling?"

"You know what I mean. You have that *aura*–or something– when you want to say something."

She looks down at her textbook and then back at me. "Here." She turns the books around and points to a paragraph next to a gruesome picture of a battle scene. "Read it, out loud."

I take the book from her and she scoots next to me, hovering over my shoulder.

I lower my chin and read. "In the folktales of the Six Kingdoms, a collateral or payment is required in deals with the Fates. Fates don't give when they don't receive. When the Fates lack in kindness, they make up for in equality."

From the side of my eye, I who looks at me like I died.

"What's this supposed to mean?" A tinge of fear coats my words.

She shifts in her seat. "You know how Earthen Born Fates are given gifts from each of the Six Kingdoms, correct?"

"Yeah."

"Well, you have been given the gift of manipulating storms which has never been given to any Earthen Born Fate before."

"I thought there were some–"

"There haven't. The school library has the most accurate set of stories in existence. Only listen to those books from now on. You were given the ability to read minds, which is a gift given to some Scholars and was never given to a Fate. Austra is not supposed to be able to control more than one element. Companions wield exceptionally powerful elements, but never all of the four major ones."

I shake my head and frown. "What are you getting at?"

She looks up at the stars and before facing me again. "I just want you to be warned. For when it does happen."

"The price," I say. The room becomes cold again. "You have a hunch. Don't you?"

"Just answer me this question," she says. "Since the beginning of the year, have your feelings towards your father changed?" Her eyes search my face, reading to find bluff.

"I don't know," I admit. "When I first came, I was mad at him for a long time. A part of me still hangs on to that anger, that feeling of being deceived. In truth, our relationship has never been like the other kids around me. He's been gone from a lot of my childhood, coming here," I say, referring to the school of magic and fate around me. "I barely see him nowadays. When I do, to me he's more the Premier than my father."

I see her jaw clench, her brain working. "If you had to make a choice between saving your father or Austra, who would you choose?"

"Austra," I say, frowning, "I have millions of people depending on me and I know my father would understand. That's not a question."

"If you had to choose between your own life and your father, who would you choose?"

Swallowing, I say, "Myself. Same reasoning."

Her posture remains true, but something in her falls. She would make those same choices if she were in my position. "I'm not sure what I think, so I won't burden you with it now."

She grabs the books back and stuffs it into her bag. "Let's just say, I think the reason the Premier didn't show you this world until now wasn't just because he thought you were the Earthen Born Fate."

"Where are you going?" I ask, not done questioning her.

"I have a private archery lesson," she says with just her head peeking out above the landing. Noticing my unease, she says, "Don't worry about it too much. When the moment is right, you'll know. Things like this are best left to the Fates to decide the right time."

"Okay," I reply solemnly.

"I'll see you tomorrow." She gives me a good solid nod and disappears through the opening in the ground.

...

Skye

After school, Levi and I drag ourselves to the Representatives' Room, hoping to get a nap in before starting on Valian homework. He and I do extra practice together since knowing multiple languages when he enters politics one day.

He opens the black and gold door. I grab Levi's shoulder when I hear soft, feminine sobs.

"What?"

"Shhh." I hold a finger to my lips. "Someone's crying."

"Well, I'll start to cry if I can't go lay down in the next five minutes," he hisses. He gets grumpy when he's tired.

"Go lay on the couch then." He gives me a stink eye. "Over there," I say, annoyance gripping my tone. I also get grumpy when I'm tired.

He stalks over to the worn-down sofa and falls face first onto the cushions, not even bothering to get his whole body onto the furniture.

I roll my eyes. Lazy idiot.

Straitening my shirt, I walk into the Representatives' Room. It can't be anyone particularly dangerous, considering only a few people know the Representatives' Room exists, let alone would feel comfortable crying in there.

Not wanting to startle whoever it is, I walk through the hall to the room in darkness. When I emerge, I blink at the light from the window and strain my ears to find the location of the whimpers.

I lift my chin to one of the higher bookshelves, a puff of dark brown hair peeking out of the books.

"Hermia?"

The sniffling stops. "Go away! I'm fine."

Stalking closer, I cross my arms. "No, you're not." The Scholar and I have never particularly seen eye to eye, but that doesn't mean I want her to suffer. It's a mutual, peaceful dislike for each other. "Do you want to talk about it?"

Warrior and Scholars generally don't have the best relationship because of some political turmoil that happened a while ago, which is echoed between my dad and her parents. Also, they're just opposites of each other in so many ways. A good amount of Scholars view Warriors as weak minded, whereas some Warriors view Scholars as physically weak. That's false, but the prejudice remains, even unintentionally. That's something I hope to change one day. For now, I'll go throughout my life doing by best to recognize these prejudices and live a life aware of the biases.

"No," grumbles Hermia.

Figuring that this might take a while, I sit on one of the wooden chairs and let out an audible sigh. "I'm not leaving until you tell me."

I'm met with silence. Both of us are too stubborn to back down, so I get out some of my homework to work on while I wait. The Scholar has a commendable resolve and doesn't speak until the ninth minute passes.

"Okay fine," Hermia snaps. "I'll tell you if you promise to leave me alone for the rest of the day."

"Deal," I say, a smug grin spreading on my face. "Tell me what's eating at you."

She pauses for a moment and then motions for me to come up to her bookshelf. Eyeing the tall ladder and considering the amount of energy I have left after the school day, I weigh the pros and cons. Finding the rewards appealing, I start to climb. When I haul myself up, I look around her little space. It's decorated with posters of various book characters and famous scholars, the walls lined with various books, probably some of her favorites. I smile at the moonlight flowers that illuminate the small space.

Hermia's maybe a year or two younger than me. With her nose pink and her face puffy, I'm reminded that she might not even be a teenager yet. Instead of the arrogant, overconfident Scholar I first met when we were merely toddlers, she's huddled in her blankets with tears rolling down her face.

She wipes her nose and looks at me warily.

"Well, go ahead now," I say, wincing at my words. I'm not so good at–soothing people.

That flash of defiance comes back to her eyes. I guess that's a good sign. "My sister, Courtney, is being a pain. I mean, she's always a pain, but now more than ever."

A tear escapes and she wipes it away bitterly. I wait for her to continue. *Patience*, my Royal friend Everhett said, *is the key towards making people feel better. Patience.*

"Ever since Claire married Elias, my family's been a bit of a mess. At first, I was happy because Courtney's the smartest of us, the most skilled and the logical best choice to be the future Head Librarian. I can't throw a punch to save my life and she's one of the best Duelers in the Six Kingdoms. Then, Courtney started to get nasty. Every single thing that I did, she critiqued, saying that I needed to do better or improve. It's like she's better than me, like I'm never enough."

The Scholar stares at her palms, sucking in a deep, shaky breath. "I'm just so tired about feeling crappy about myself, all the time. Claire's always been the larger than life and the joy of the family. Courtney's the pride of my parents, always getting straight A's and winning Duel after Duel. Then there's me, the third child–the disappointment."

I bite the side of my cheek, my own eyes stinging.

When she finishes, I wait until she makes eye contact with me. My heart stings a little at the hope I see–the hope that I won't be like her sister and criticize her for crying. It's the same look I gave my father growing up, when he would make me train until dawn.

I tell her what I wished my father told me. "Don't be ashamed of who you are. There is so much in you that people won't be able to see, even if you let it out. What matters isn't what others think, but what you think."

I lift her chin, ignoring the salted tears drying on my fingers. "The moment I stopped caring what others thought of me, was the first time I was able to fly. Live life the way you want to live it."

Chapter 37

Levi

You know how most people have an alarm clock? Well… I have an Elias.

"GET UP, YOU LAZY BEANS!" I jolt up from my warm, comfortable bed and watch Elias with blurry eyes, running around the dorm room like a maniac. He's dressed head to toe with Grantham Willow merchandise, complete with brown wings for our owl mascot. I didn't even know that they had Grantham Willow knee length socks. "Today's the Final Duel!"

"Yeah, Elias! I hope we beat them to shreds," our neighbor yells through the wall.

"Yes!" Elias yells right back, dancing across the rug.

Makai grumbles and pulls the blanket over his head. Not giving him an extra minute of sleep, Elias jumps on his bed and pulls the blankets off.

After Makai's spell was broken, things between us got a little better. It's hard to blame someone for something they did under the influence of magic. Elias and I agreed that it was okay to move back into the dorm and back to our own beds.

"Hey, Makai," I say tentatively, not wanting him to suddenly wake up and punch me in the face. Trust me, it has happened before and I suffered a week with a nasty bruise on my left cheek bone. I thought I looked pretty hard core, but Skye said I looked like someone beat me up in Self Defense class.

He grumbles and tries to bat me away. "You better get up before Elias dumps a bucket of water on you."

He mumbles something again and curls up in a ball. Shrugging, I walk over to my dresser to find my clothes for the day. Most of school is canceled because we're going on a big field trip to the school that Grantham's dueling. Our way of travel will be by dragon, which just screams a sore back and butt.

I gather my shower bag before walking down the hall. The white marble illuminates the bathroom, reflecting the early morning sun. It's grand, but the sinks are always wet, so I never have a good place to put my stuff.

The mint fills my nose as I brush my teeth. I almost choke when Nikolai enters the room, the smug grin on his face widening when he sees me. He puts his bag right next to mine and starts to brush his teeth. He pays ignores me, but it's clear he knows who's next to him.

When the Royal finishes flossing his last tooth, he turns to me and says, "Just so you know, I'm not the undercover Malevolent."

I nearly gag on my toothpaste. "What?" How could he know?

He raises an eyebrow and his violet eyes look a little confused. "Why wouldn't you suspect me?"

"Why would I?" Honestly, I've thought about it before, but never very seriously. Plus, since he's so high in the pecking order of the palace, people must keep close tabs on the boy. There were also interferences by the traitor while he was gone, cutting him from the suspect list.

"I think you know, Levi," Nikolai grumbles. "My dad somehow found out that I'm not your favorite person in the world. With the question going around the higher ups about a possible traitor, he didn't like the idea of me being a suspect."

My breath goes back to normal. My father probably told the king about a possible rat.

"While I was there–," he pauses, shaking his head. "Man, it's a mess."

"Really?" I ask, unable to contain my curiosity.

"Yeah! The government's falling apart," he says, looking at me like it's obvious. "The people of the Six Kingdoms are freaking out and the economy is down. It was just leaked a month ago that the King has a weird virus and the Royal healers and Medicine Masters don't know how to cure him. To top it all off, the King doesn't want the Royals to sacrifice a life for his."

Skye mentioned something about how a Royal can save someone from death by giving their own life, but it's not considered honorable. They also give up the chance of going to the Afterworld if it's done out of vain or selfishness, both the Royal and the person saved. The King must think that his life isn't imperative to continue much longer.

"How do you know this?" I cut in. I've seen *nothing* in the school newspapers and my father didn't mention those things when we last spoke.

"You don't know how protected Grantham Willow is. Have you ever wondered why there are absolutely no reporters craning their necks to take a picture of the one and only Earthen Born Fate?"

It never really occurred to me that I'm famous in that sense, or that people in the Six Kingdoms care about that stuff. The Outside world is so media driven, I guess it's not surprising that the Six Kingdoms is too.

"Then again, how do *you* know this?" I ask, my eyes narrowing. "Even if your dad is up in the ranks, they wouldn't openly tell you this knowing you might tell me."

"I–I spied on them." Seeing my questioning look, he narrows his eyes. "It's not what you think. I may be good at spying, but I would never do it for the Malevolents. These are rough times, Levi. The more we turn on each other the closer we get to losing." I nod at the truth in his words. Placing both hands on the wet sink, he says, "Skye's in for a treat when the King dies and so is my cousin. The same goes for you." He starts to pack his things, the anger evident in the force of his movements.

"Why should I believe you?" I study the Royal, just as pristine as his stunning twin. There's a certain edge to him that wasn't there before the fire. Maybe he did see some things at the palace that are worthy to note.

He doesn't even snapback. "Just remember what I told you. Okay?" With that he turns and leaves me to mull over my thoughts in the morning glow.

Chapter 38

Levi

The wind bites at my face and small drops of rain dampen my clothes as we ride towards the cliff on our dragons. We were told to all meet at the edge of the cliff near the water's edge. Makai, Elias, and I stand at the front of the pack near Spencer and Lila.

The steps of Skye's gold dragon sound behind us, coming to our side. She gives a small smile and strokes his glittering scales. Austra, Aspyn and Aris follow closely behind. No matter how positive we are that Aris is working with the Malevolents, we can't risk him knowing.

Skye and I talked to my father about Aris. We figured that it would be best if the teachers were alert. Better safe than sorry.

The Premier looked just as we were, slightly pale the entire day. I remember someone mentioning that he felt a tug from the Fates the day he showed up at Grantham Willow. Why would the Fates urge my father to take in Aris if he was allied with the Malevolents?

Austra and I share determined stares when the Premier's booming voice sounds over the crashing waves. "Attention students! Today we are to witness the Dueling Finals." He is cut off by an explosion of applause and cheers.

"I expect you all to be on your best behavior. The Initials shall go first and then the Paramounts, so be ready. Oh! One final thing. Duelers... show them what Grantham Willow is made of." The Premier's devious grin brings a smile to my face and the students around the Duelers give them pats on the back and words of encouragement.

As the cheers rise, so does Phoebe's arm and we listen close for the whistle to sound. I give my friends one last fleeting glance before the whistle blows and I send my dragon through darkness.

Images and scenes flash by me before I can recognize my surroundings. It's like looking out the window when a plane's about to take off. Maybe a little faster than that even. I tighten my grip on Odyssey's horns and lean forward to whisper, "Okay, just like we practiced. We're just going to go a bit farther than the Astronomy Tower. Take me to Alexandra Dominique."

I already told him the destination before we started going the speed of sound, but it's a precaution so they don't get caught up in the thrill and go to the wrong place, even though Odyssey has an elephant's memory. He never forgets when I do something unjust to him. Like the time I accidentally forgot to feed him because *I was unconscious in the Infirmary*. Or the time I had Elias feed him and all he gave him was a bucket full of carrots because apparently that's what his dragon likes. Odyssey, on the other hand, would rather have deer and maybe a raccoon or two.

After a couple minutes, my eyes get used to the rapid speed and wind, letting me make out figures of my classmates around me. We shoot through the sky, all of us just streaks to the world below.

Soon the vision of my surroundings becomes less and less of a blur and dies into one last scene, a field with hundreds of teenagers laughing, singing, and dancing. The woman, who I assume is the Premier of Alexandra Dominique, sits on a long stage with the rest of her staff. I can spot her long, red hair and cunning piercing green eyes from my altitude

Odyssey descends and the nearby students make a clearing. He slams into the ground, sending a boom through the field–likely wanting to show off–ten yards from the woman with hair of fire. The huge mansion of a school towers over us, grander and more elegant than Grantham Willow could ever be.

"Humf!" Elias lands by my side and gives me a goofy grin.

Skye, Austra, Aris, and Aspyn follow, all a few seconds in between each other. Aris and Aspyn go off to the stables, saying that they missed breakfast and wanted to look for food. Skye's eyes don't leave Aris' back until he's out of sight.

All of us have ruffled hair, except for Skye who manages to look put together every second of the day.

"Do you see Makai anywhere?" I ask, but Elias just shakes his head. "We left at the same time."

"Maybe he just wants to be fashionably late," says a snarky, feminine voice. I can tell who it is by the smell of the perfume from here. It's a nice scent, but it sours as the person comes into view. "Makai has a knack for drawing attention to himself." She gives Skye a sly look, the violet of her irises reflecting the light. "Much like someone else I know."

"What do you want, Vesta?" Skye rolls her eyes, the annoyance rippling off of her.

She smiles sweetly and with a flip of her brown hair, she replies, "Nothing. I have no interest in you. I'm just looking for my cousin." She makes a show of craning her neck. "I'm sure you'll meet him soon." With that she guides her white dragon away, her friends following suit.

"She irks me," grumbles Hermia. "I think she's just jealous of you, Skye."

Grumbling, Skye gets off her mount and walks towards the stables. Some of the Alexandra Dominique students stop their games to watch the Warrior pass. Most of the students here are well connected in the government, so I wouldn't be surprised if the news about the king spread here already.

Makai comes up just as she leaves and looks at us confused. "What'd I miss?"

"Don't worry about it," I say.

"Hermia?" Elias says with a hint of surprise. "What are you doing here?"

The Scholar adjusts her bag as she slides off her dragon. "My family wanted to watch Courtney compete. It's only logical that I tag along." The glare of the sun reflects off her glasses, but her grey eyes still shine through. "Not to mention all the stupid decisions that you'd make without me."

"What's Vesta jealous about?" I ask, scrunching my forehead, bringing the conversation back to Skye. I've always thought that Vesta's a pain just to be a pain.

Elias just gives me a look that says, *Are you kidding me?* "Levi," Elias says with a look of pity, "is there something wrong with your eyes or ears?"

"What? No," I say incredulously. "Why would you think that?"

He shakes his head. "First of all, Skye is gorgeous, which Vesta wishes she could be. Secondly, I don't know if you know this, but Skye's already engaged. And she's engaged to one of the most eligible bachelors in the Six Kingdoms."

My blink is answer enough. With Austra betrothed, I shouldn't be surprised to find out another one of my friends is also destined to marry someone specific. It's just that–I thought that Skye would tell me. Based on the way Elias phrased it, it probably isn't a secret. I just miss a lot of valuable information by only being with them for a half a year.

"Wow," the Hunter runs a hand through his hair in disbelief. "I'm surprised she hasn't told you."

Hermia whacks him on the back of the head. "Elias," she hisses, "that was Skye's secret to tell."

"Well, it's not much of a secret. It's pretty much open news about their alliance, it's all the newspapers were able to talk about for a while. Skye herself doesn't mention it much–or at all."

"It's a royalty thing," explains Austra, studying my face. "Skye's pretty high up in the rankings of the Six Kingdoms as well as the Valians."

"Skye's mother was well respected amongst Valians, not to mention her being the granddaughter of the king. Because of this, her hand in marriage is very valuable. It was set when she was thirteen," Hermia says.

"Thirteen," I stress, rubbing my temples.

"It's not uncommon for someone of her status. The Valian Council has arranged a treaty with the Werewolves. It won't hold unless there's a blood bond between a Valian and a Werewolf. And before you ask, a blood bond is when they marry and have kids."

"What?"

"Oh, calm down. Skye knows what she's getting into. She was reluctant at first and she did plead for a reconsideration, especially when she found out who her betrothed is. But there's no other Werewolf influential enough in her age range." Austra cringes at the memory. "The Six Kingdoms did allow her to back out if she were to become Queen–or if she found someone willingly to marry her that is of higher rank than her betrothed."

"Who's the guy?" I ask, getting off Odyssey. My legs feel like jelly, so I wait for my muscles to settle before moving again.

"Titus," Elias says, the name rolls like gravel.

I pause at that. Taking a breath, I say, "Well, I can't say that I wasn't surprised. She has a duty to the Six Kingdoms and the Valians." Over the course of the year, I've learned about the history of the Valians and their relationship with the Werewolves. If they'd finally found out a way to end their cold war, then that's a good thing.

Glancing back at the others, I raise an eyebrow. "What's the matter?" Slowly Elias pulls his hands away from his eyes and Austra looks mildly surprised.

"I thought you were going to take this a lot worse," Elias admits, frowning, "and do something with lightning and stuff."

I shrug in response. "It explains some things. Like why she hates him so much."

Elias laughs, "Trust me, that isn't the only reason."

Phoebe checks our names off the list at the stables, which I might add is the grandest dragon home I've ever seen. The warm glow of the sun lights the golden dirt and the stalls are spacious, made of light willow wood. The smell of roses and vanilla fill my nose from the vases next to the stalls.

Plain pixies in green dresses made of grass and crowns of mini daisies flutter around feeding, washing, and grooming the dragons like royalty. We spot Skye at the end of the aisle and make a beeline over.

She brushes her dragon's back and glances over her shoulder ever so slightly when we put our dragons in their temporary stalls. "You all should keep a lookout. Since this is such a public event, it gives the Malevolents a platform to publicize their prowess."

"Isn't this the most protected school in the world?" Elias gives his dragon a carrot he found in one of the golden drawers. "I mean, that's the only reason the Premier let us come in the first place."

"Still," Skye murmurs. Hermia walks around and starts to braid Skye's hair. I raise an eyebrow and Skye just waves me off. I didn't realize they were such on good terms.

"Why isn't ours the most protected?" I ask curiously. "Not to sound pretentious, but I think the safety of the Earthen Born Fate and his Companions would be high priority."

"There was debate on taking you here instead of Grantham," says Elias. "I remember Sylas talking about how the Premier was set on you coming to Grantham instead."

Skye nods, making Mia slap her arm at the movement. "The sons and daughters of great political figures in the Six Kingdoms go here because they're high targets. Grantham is focused on protecting mainly you and Austra whereas Alexandra Dominique is prepared to defend the entire school. Not to say that some students are more imperative to protect, but imagine, the assassination of one of the kids here could start a war between territories."

"Levi, will you please tame that hair of yours?" Hermia scowls. "You're going to meet some of the most influential teenagers in the world. If you befriend them, they might be able to help you down the road and Grantham Willow is going to need it."

Glaring at her, I pat a few standing strands so they're closer to my head. When Mia looks satisfied, I ask, "What do you mean? About Grantham Willow."

"My parents were talking, your father is in all this trouble on whether he is qualified enough to be the Premier while you're trying to save this world," she sighs, finishing off Skye's braid.

My eyes widen. "You're saying they want to fire my dad because they don't think he can handle me?"

"Or protect you," she points out, finishing off Skye's braid. "They think you're too close to him emotionally."

I groan and run my hand through my hair.

"Levi! Come here." Skye lunges forward and grabs my arm, pulling me over.

"Hey! Don't touch the hair!"

"Hold still," she wrestles to smooth my hair down and then examines my face and smudges something off. Flinching away, she finally lets up only to straighten my collar. "There," she says, grinning at her work. "Don't even think about fiddling with your hair again."

I grumble something about personal space as we head out of the stables. Stares and snickers from our classmates follow. "See! Look what you did," I exclaim.

Skye rolls her eyes and tugs on my jacket. "Get ready, we're about to meet one of the most important figures in the Six Kingdoms. Premier Citrus is closely related to the former King. She is also an advisor to the current King and will help supervise the next succession of the throne."

"Great. It's just too much to ask that the Premier of Alexandra Dominique be a regular lady who has my best interest in mind and

301

doesn't have a say in the employment of my father." I close my mouth as we near.

My father shakes Premier Citrus' hand with a polite smile. "It's nice to see you again, Premier Sage," she says in a soft voice that screams wealth and maturity. Not to mention, she stands three feet off the ground on a stage, allowing her to look down on all of us.

"Same to you, Premier Citrus. It has been too long," he replies. My father grabs my shoulder and guides me over to the stage. "As you well know, this is my son, Levi, and his very exceptional friends. Austra, here, is the Sorcerer Companion."

The Premier bends down from where she stands on the platform to get a better look at us. Despite having tightly curled hair, she still manages to make it look perfect. Premier Citrus has eyes the color of moss in the sunlight. A gold type of jewelry drapes over her forehead like a metal veil, but not in the form of a net, rather in the design of curls and delicate sweeps of color. It's like metal lace. A precious stone hangs from each ear, so shiny it's to the point of blinding.

She's a rather attractive lady with only a few wrinkles to give away her age. An aura of warmth wraps the air around us, but her eyes stare daggers.

"I am pleased to finally meet you," she smiles, the warmth not meeting her eyes. "You've caused quite the stir. And here I was thinking that Amora's line didn't continue." She knew my mother then. The Premier of Alexandra tilts her head and examines at the mark on my forearm. "Do you mind if I have a look?"

"No," I say immediately. "Knock yourself out." I wince.

Good job, Levi. You just told one of the most important people in the world to knock herself out.

I hold out my arm and she turns it over to study the marks closely. "That doesn't give us much does it?" She sighs and pats my shoulder before setting it down.

She gets up gracefully. "Anyways, I hope you enjoy your stay here. The bags you sent will be waiting in your rooms." She gestures to the open double doors made of vintage glass and bronze. "One of my students will show you the way."

"Thank you," Skye says with a nod of her head. The Premier gives her an icy stare and stiffly bows her chin back. Skye narrows her eyes and leads us away towards the school.

"Complicated relationship?" I ask once we're out of earshot.

"Yes," she breathes. "She's on the Wolf Shifter's side."

"I heard that her ex was a Valian," Elias snickers.

The doubt in Skye's eyes tell me otherwise.

The large, intricately carved gold doors are open, greeting us as we walk in. A lot of our classmates have started looking around and introducing themselves to the students of the other school. Skye told me that good civil manners are expected, despite the tension of the Duel. Since we're on their campus, we have to be extra polite.

Skye leads us into the large entrance hall with her chin held high. Whispers scatter the room; some I catch are about me–others are about Skye. Ignoring them, she walks straight in the direction of a tall boy with light brown hair, on the longer side, and dark indigo eyes. His posture is immaculate and there's not one piece of lint on his white button-down shirt. There's a slight cut on his forehead–probably from training–that interrupts the perfection of his face. He grins a grin that any girl would melt over. "Welcome, Skye. Long time no see."

All Skye does is say deadpan, "Hello, Everhett."

Then the Royal does the last thing any sane person would do: he hugs Skye. The *really* weird thing is, she hugs him back.

After pulling apart, she lets out the hint of a smile. "This is Everhett Goldenrise. His father is an advisor to the King."

Elias steps forward and squints at him. "You look familiar."

"I wouldn't be surprised," Skye says. "He's Nikolai and Vesta's cousin."

Chapter 39

Skye

I've known Everhett since I was born, practically.

Both of our fathers are well acquainted and in return, we spent a lot of time together. Since school started for him, I haven't seen him as often as I did before and we grew apart. To this day, those younger memories glow in my mind. Before going to a secondary school, like Grantham Willow and Trinity Dale, some members of the Six Kingdoms get personalized tutors that teach the basics of mathematics, science, etc. There are a few boarding schools around the world as well, offering protection for those who need it or don't have guardians to watch over them.

Everhett's a special case, since he's the son of a high official. Both the rebels and the Malevolents want him dead. He usually stayed at either Grantham Willow or Alexandra Dominique. For a period of time, we took classes and spent our spare time training together.

Everhett tells my friends this, but they're as stiff as a redwood. I have to give them a confirming nod to validate his words.

"What grade are you?" Levi looks him up and down. Everhett has always been a lady's man, being tall and handsome, not to mention his family background. Though, he's practically a brother to me, having grown up together. He's one of the only people that has never looked at my father or me in fear.

"I'm a Junior," he replies. "My third year here. I'm assuming all of you are Initials?" Their nods give him the answer. If he notices their suspicion, he doesn't show it.

"Well, I'll lead the boys to their dorm rooms," he tells us, then looks around the bustling hall. "Rosemary!"

"Yes?" A petite girl with rosy hair comes pushing through the crowd. Something I didn't notice before was how people just parted to let Everhett pass. There's a certain respect that they have for him, which I envy. A sword can do a lot, but in some cases, words can do much more.

"She's going to take you up to the dorms," Everhett explains, tightening the purple scarf around his neck.

Rosemary comes to a halt in front of us, her breathing heavy. "Sorry about that," she puffs. "The last group I led dropped their books and the pages got trampled in the halls."

She turns to Everhett and bows her head, "I've got it from here." Everhett gives us a farewell, making us promise to talk to him sometime during the Duel. Everhett takes Levi, Makai, and Elias with them.

"Your bags should already be in your rooms," Rosemary says, guiding us through the halls. I notice some of the students who recognize Levi as I watch them walk away. Levi isn't anything flashy like Everhett, but he has a presence that's hard to miss. "I'd recommend changing into something warmer when you go out to watch the Duels. The temperatures here vary a lot, security reasons. Rest a bit and maybe get something to eat. You must be exhausted from your travels."

We follow Rosemary through the winding halls of Alexandra Dominique. The school looks like a huge mansion, unlike a war fort like Grantham. The halls are decorated with crystals and gold leaves, a sharp contrast from our cold stone and ivy. Something about it seems too glamorous for life. If I went here, I would constantly worry about knocking over a priceless vase in between classes.

The exact location of the school is unknown to most, forbidden from being put on a map. People just assume that it's somewhere not on the West Coast, since they're not in our League. A few dragons know how to get there, having exceptional memory. Once you get there,

there's extensive charms around the campus that verify the identity of those that enter.

We climb a grand staircase and walk into a hall of rooms with plaques, just like the stables, with our names on them. "You both will be sharing a room with Eve Elizabeth Valor." She hands us both a pair of old, gold keys. "Get settled, the traditional Dueling Day Gala will be held at 8 p.m. and the Scholar Duels will last from 5:30- 7:00 p.m. The Duel will be held in the North Garden. The schedule for the Duels is in the Main Hall. If you get lost, just hold your key by the string and it will show you where you want to go. I will be your helper during your stay so if you have any questions, send me a Lightning Critter."

"Thank you," I say, giving a small grin. If I'm going to improve my diplomatic skills, I might as well start now. "May I ask how you know Everhett?"

"We have a class together," she explains. She turns to leave, but then remembers something. "Oh! I almost forgot. Just as a warning between us, people are generally pro-Werewolf around here. You know, Royals value loyalty a lot. Try not to draw too much attention."

She gives a glimmering smile to Mia and Austra and skips away. I give my best scowl and hope that it burns a hole through her feathered jacket.

Hermia turns to me, "What was that about?"

Trying to calm myself down, I mutter, "The people here know their politics." Without giving more information, I jab my key into the lock and open the door with a bam.

"Ahhh!" A small girl with pastel purple hair screams and hides under the covers.

"Evie?" Mia scurries up to the bedside. "Don't worry it's just Skye. She's not as scary as you think she is."

Evie peaks at me and then slowly gets out. "Oh! Sorry. I was just startled. That's all."

307

I sigh and start to unpack my things. Everyone's been so on edge lately. I change into dark blue jeans and a black turtleneck sweater with the Grantham symbol over my heart. The four of us rest in the room for a few hours, only getting up for lunch, our muscles sore from dragon riding. Even though they're an efficient way to travel, they aren't the most comfortable.

When the sun starts to descend over the horizon, painting the sky with magnificent colors, I tug on my puffy jacket and pick up a heavy blanket from my bed. "Are you all ready?"

Austra pulls on a jacket that makes her look like a ball and Evie just nods her head, tense. Honestly, am I that scary?

"Why are you scared of me?" I ask her, unable to keep my curiosity to myself. We're the only ones close to the door, the others not hearing my whisper. "You healed me that day when the Malevolents came. I do not repay kindness with violence or hate."

She looks at me strangely and then walks to the door. "Don't worry, I don't fear *you*."

We follow the keys down curved walkways and through golden doors to an open courtyard overlooking a field with hills in the distance. Rosemary was right about the temperature. My breaths turn to crystals in front of my eyes. Hermia, Austra, Evie, and I make a beeline towards the lights. Evie branches out to find Giant near the back and Mia and I run over to our friends who look like they're about to freeze to death.

I sit in between Levi and Elias and drape the blanket over them.

"Thank the Fates, Skye thinks ahead," says Elias, shivering through his thin jacket. Mia hands them all heating packs that she made before we left.

"Huddle together. It'll help," I tell them. Not needing to be asked twice, we form a mass of shivering bodies.

Some of the Alexandra students snicker and laugh at our misery.

"Can't you make it warmer with your gift?" Austra asks Levi. We both wrap an arm around a freezing Elias.

"I guess so," he says. "My teacher gave me a lecture on messing with the natural environment, so I don't think that's the best choice. Austra, can you make a flame or something?"

She nods and takes out a match and lights it, taking the flame from the tip and growing it. The flame floats off her palm to rest just above our laps, radiating heat. With that taken care of, I examine our surroundings.

The stands encircle an oval stage with two Scholars from each school on either side. Cameras make a line behind, broadcasting the Duel across the Six Kingdoms. For normal matches, they don't bother filming it, but once they get higher in the ranks, recruiters for the professional league start to pay attention.

A riddle is projected into the night sky, the Duel having already started. "The first team to answer ten riddles correctly wins," Elias tells us. Grantham is on their fourth and Alexandra is on their third.

The one currently in the stars is:

"I speak the truth and lie, but you can never tell through I,
I have no control, but use can take their toll.
I am stronger with thought then left to fraught.
What am I?"

"A pen," I whisper to Levi.

"You're kidding," Levi laughs, the color slowly coming back to his cheeks. "I don't understand how you do that." My cheeks warm too, but not from the fire. He takes a sharp intake of breath and clutches his chest.

"Are you okay?" I gasp, feeling for anything that might have shot him, but nothing red can be found. Austra, Elias, and Mia look over, concerned.

"It's nothing. Maybe it's the Alexandra Dominique food," he mutters and lays down on my shoulder. "This duel is such a drag."

Levi ends up taking a long nap while I guess the riddles a good three minutes before the Scholars do. Except for the last one, where both teams were tied. The answer ended up being a pine tree.

I nearly lose my hearing when Elias screams at Grantham's victory. Levi jumps, grabbing onto my elbow before tumbling to the ground.

"Does that mean I can go inside now?" Levi asks, still groggy from sleep.

"It's time to get ready for the feast," I say stiffly. They like to call it a Gala, but that reminds me too much of the nightly events at the palace. Once the arrangement was made with Titus, my father said he regretted not teaching me how to be *ladylike*. I hate the thought of having to learn table ettiquette, how to cook–it's just not my style. Some people can do it great, but not me. Whether Titus likes it or not, I'll go into the King's army when I graduate... or Queen's army

The walk back to the dorm is just as confusing as last time. Thankfully, I memorized the twists and turns enough to find our way without the key. Back at the dorm, I brush my hair out, wavy from the braid, and pick out a long, black gown with a high neck. Noting the white line of my scar that trails from my chin, I wince at the memory. I tug on a formal cloak to hide the rest of the scar. Since my dress covers my feet, I pull on my cargo boots, just in case something decides to attack. Gazing into the mirror, I add a gold pin to pull half my hair away from my face.

Hermia pulls on a maroon, long sleeved dress and Evie looks elegant in her white one. When Austra comes back in the room from the bathroom, the three of us take a moment to take her in.

She wears a royal blue dress, made of a light, flowy material that sways when she walks. It's simple yet beautiful, catching her eye when we went into town the week before. Her long, dark brown hair drapes down her back, nearly down to her hips. Her skin glows and her eyes are striking, the eyeliner accentuating the color.

She looks at us questioningly, adjusting her earpiece. "What?"

"You clean up nicely," Evie complements, walking over to touch the dress.

"As do you," she replies, giggling. Austra looks me over and grins, "You look absolutely terrifying, Skye. In a good way."

Smirking, I slip a knife into one of the pockets.

When we're ready, we stride into the hall and into the swarm of girls getting ready for the event. At Grantham Willow, there isn't much need or time to have fancy events like this. Having spent some time at the palace, I'm relatively used to it, but I can see why the others are so excited.

I can't help but notice Evie whose hands shake ever so slightly.

Chapter 40

Skye

Alexandra's version of the Capricorn is a huge ballroom decorated with multiple gold chandeliers with thousands of candles. There are tables of silver all around the room, except for the center which is reserved for dancing. The walls are made of gold and mirrors while the floors are made of solid marble. Music is played by Master violinists, cellists, violists, and bass players.

I walk as gracefully as I can as whispers follow me like a shadow. Let them stare and despise what I was born as. I have nothing to apologize for.

A hand grabs mine and drags me towards the dance floor. The only person that can sneak up to me. "What do you want, Titus?" I hiss, baring my teeth. I try to pull away, but he grips me tight. I suck in a breath and scowl.

"We need to talk," he whispers, looking around at our audience. He talks soft enough so that even Warriors can't hear.

"I've guessed." I roll my eyes, talking equally as quiet. Stepping to the beat of the music, I wrap my arms around his neck. We can't have more rumors floating around than there already is.

His blond hair falls gracefully over his forehead and his eyes are tired. "You heard about the tensions, right? And about Helena?"

Remembering the daughter of a prominent official, I scoff. "Where do you think I live, under a rock?"

"The King didn't want you to know," he whispers, looking over his shoulder. "Especially about Helena."

"I can find things out if I want to." Truth is, the news about the King wasn't the only thing Vesta picked up. Why she told me instead of keeping me in the dark, I don't know. I silently thank the Royal, but the feeling of gratefulness disappears quickly.

"Seriously, do you really think the Valians and Werewolves will start a war?" There's something like legitimate fear in his voice, not something I expected. A part of me always thought that he would do anything to get out of this alliance, including starting a war.

I pause my wave of retorts and regard his question thoughtfully. "No. I don't think so." I gesture between us. "If this works out, then I think that will set an example. An example of peace."

He hangs his head. "I know the Werewolves are trying to make the Valians look bad, just know that that's not my doing. It's someone in the Werewolf Court, I just know it." That would make a select few people.

"Do *you* think we're just blood thirsty animals that do nothing for the world except master the art of killing and rule breaking?" Sometimes whispers and talk about you can be helpful, especially if you can hear each word they say.

"Of course not," he puffs up. His wavy hair brushes his brow. He looks at me again with shining gold eyes. Something about it reminds me of a lost puppy. "Werewolves and Valians hold too many grudges. It's not smart or good for the peace of the Six Kingdoms. It's just... unnecessary. The current King is an Owl shifter so he can't really support either side and chooses to remain neutral. I think he's torn between his best friend's son or his granddaughter."

I examine him again, noticing the harsher cut of his jaw and the lines of worry on his face. He's grown from the last time I talked to him—gotten more mature. If we had this same conversation a year ago, one of us would be bloodied on the floor by now.

"He shouldn't have to choose," I mutter. "I don't particularly like you, but that's not because you're a Werewolf."

"Well, I like you Skye." I give him a sharp look, hiding the surprise I feel. Just a few months ago I sent him to the Infirmary with a broken nose. "I think we can make it work. And when I say that both Werewolves and Valians hold grudges, that includes you." Looking into his face, sometimes I forget that we're both just kids. Him barely seventeen and me freshly fifteen. In another world we would be worrying about college or prom. His voice lowers. "Good luck in the Trials."

With that he leaves me in the middle of the floor, only to get swept up by a tall brunette figure.

"Drama with your boyfriend?" Everhett teases, winking.

"That doesn't even begin to cover it," I sigh and look down at my feet as we dance to the song. Growing up, I would help him with his dancing lessons, him needing a partner. Both of us are expected to attend events like these for the rest of our lives, making me grateful for those classes.

He sobers up and frowns, "Just for the record, I don't think Valians are horrible."

Blinking, I say, "I never thought you would. How did you know that was what we were talking about?" It's true. Everhett likes the truth and doesn't think rumors are the equivalent. Yet another thing I envy him for.

"I'm not doing so bad at Future Telling. I even predicted that Henry Dolly would slip on a banana peel during lunch."

"Good for you," I laugh a full laugh for what feels like the first time in a while, only to be reminded of the reality. "What would the people do *if* I won the Throne Trials and became Queen? Would there be rebellion?"

"As a potential competitor, I would tell you not to compete. But as a friend, I'm telling you to claim your birthright," he smiles, his indigo eyes dancing. "Personally, I believe you would make a great leader. However, be prepared for criticism on the road to getting there."

"Come on, Everhett," I sigh. "We both know you've been cut out for the job since birth. I feel like I'm more of a military leader, not a diplomat."

"Remember, the Fates will weave the Trials so that the competitor that is the best fit will win," he says with a clear voice, deeper from age.

"I admire your faith in the Fates," I grumble.

We descend into a comfortable silence. He lets me sort things out in my mind before saying, "You know, don't you? I predicted it, but the word traveled too slow. They found their home in Egypt in pieces," Everhett's face contorts in regret. For once, the man of resolve crumples.

"No," I say, finding a rather fascinating spot on the ground. "Titus asked me about it, so I played dumb and learned what I needed to. It didn't take much to guess what happened to Helena. She was always such an adventurous girl, too soft for the life she was born into."

"Then you know what that means," he says, losing the playful tone. From what I remember, him and Helena were good friends. When her family heard about the King, they thought their summer home would be safer from the Malevolents than Alexandra. They guessed wrong. "She was your only shot at not being the Representative if she matured as a Warrior. You have to accept the invitation to the Throne Trials. If not for yourself, you need to do it for your people."

I nod my head solemnly. I was afraid he was going to say something like that. "So," I begin, trying to change the subject, "what has happened since we last met?"

"Not too much," he says, tilting his head. "The King and his advisors are going a little crazy with all the conflicts. Dad and Mom don't visit as often anymore. They seem stressed, so maybe you should say hi to them if they visit for the Final Duel. They've always liked you."

"You're not a Dueler?"

He shrugs. "No. The current Royal Duelers don't graduate until I'm in my fifth year." At Grantham there's more competition for the

Dueling spots, so it's not unheard of for a younger student to overtake a spot from someone else. My feeling is that he just doesn't particularly mind not being on the team. The both of us have other things to worry about.

Thinking about it now, Everhett's about two years older than me, the same year as Titus. "You've gotten old," I tease. "You're nearly a grown man."

He laughs. "I'm far from that, Skye! I still feel twelve. You look taller than when I saw you last time–and more mature," he says, his eyes warm. "Titus is a lucky man."

"I'm not a lucky woman," I bite.

"Give the guy a chance," Everhett says with a frown. "He's not too bad. Over the summer he came to the palace with me and he's different, Skye. He still feels bad about telling the Malevolents about you."

"Yeah, we talked about it today." I take a deep breath. "I think it made me realize a few things... I'll think about it."

Soon after that, I tell him that I have to go somewhere and we part ways. He heads in the direction of a group of very powerful children and I head in the direction of the most valuable beings in the Six Kingdoms. What have our lives come to?

Miraculously, Levi and Giant are engaged in civil conversation, for the sake of Evie, who looks much less on edge next to the tall Warrior. They're a strange pair, but have unusual levels of bravery, remembering that day on the cliff. I haven't talked to either of them very much since they're a year above me. There is a certain softness to Giant's face that wasn't there at the beginning of the year.

"Hey, Skye," Levi greets, grimacing slightly at the glare from the Warrior that towers over him.

"Sorry about that," I say to them. "I had to talk to some people."

"Didn't look like they minded," jokes Elias. I scoff. His eyes widen. "Aris! Aspyn! Where were you?" The Wielder of Darkness glides toward us with Aspyn at his elbow. He's as attentive as always, eyes darting around the room whenever he has the chance. Aspyn waves at us, her white dress making the streaks of color in her hair stand out.

"We wanted to explore the school," he says. The corner of his lip turns up. "There aren't many records of what the place looks like, let alone what's on the inside." My heart sinks. If he is allied with the Malevolents, they'll know the layout of the safest school in the world.

"It's fine," Austra says, her voice rising an octave. "You're here now. Let's get some food."

"Wait," Elias exclaims, jumping up and down. "The Duelers are making their entrance."

Through the massive double doors, Duelers enter with grace and power, emanating their dominance. The Sorcerers put a charm on the Grantham Duelers so that they literally glow. The Alexandra Duelers wear their military dress uniforms with too many medals and patches that should be possible for people of their age. I spot Spencer and Lila looking as happy as can be, entering the room arm in arm.

Lila wears a gown that flows like water and Spencer has on a stiff black suit, looking the most put together I've ever seen him. The others come in just as spectacularly.

The occasion is considered more casual than the Six Year Ball, which happens during the opening night of the International Dueling Tournament. I've only ever seen it once, but it was an event to remember. However, that doesn't make this event any less glamorous. One thing Alexandra Dominique knows how to do is make things as glamorous as possible.

My eye catches one of the Circle of Myths, her white hair shining like starlight. She walks over to the other five of the Circle. During the school year, she only participated in a few of the Duels, saying that she had to focus on her studies. With her in the lineup, Grantham is for sure going to put up a good fight during the Sorcerer Duel.

Just behind her walks Topaz Legend, her blue streak of hair blazing like fire as she slides by. Another Myth. She smiles slyly as she passes, her tanned skin and angled face stunning in the light of the crystal chandelier.

Meanwhile, the Alexandra Duelers are decorated in jewels and wealth from head to toe, making me wonder how many college tuitions they could pay for in the Outside world. I bet they could start a scholarship fund only using their jewelry.

Elias points out who's who, giving us a full description of their gifts and strengths. It seems as though the Alexandra Scholars are absent.

The night is filled with ceremonial speeches and toasts. Levi practically eats half the feast while I walk around the room with my father as we meet with the children and parents of power. Most of them I've met when I was a child, like Everhett. Some I've generally forgotten, thinking they're just fluff in the narrative of the time. With the coming war, I hope they prove me wrong.

Before midnight, most of the Duelers go to their dorms to prepare and sleep for the next day. Yawning, I tell the others I'm going to go to sleep. They continue to party and eat, Elias showing off his skills on the dance floor. Austra tells me that she'll make sure the others get back at a reasonable hour.

Just as I exit, someone blocks my path.

"Kalica Time?"

She strokes her long, dark red hair and stares at me with glaring, gold eyes. I trained with this girl when I was a toddler and traveled to Alexandra Dominique. Of course, I would always win, but she never lost her fighting spirit. Her freckles seem to have gotten lighter since we last saw each other, one of us having a large gash in the stomach at the time.

"It's been a while," she sneers. "Pity, I thought you were going to die." Back before we were fully aware of the world around us, we were on good terms. We weren't friends by any means, but we weren't enemies.

"What do you want?" I sigh, wanting to just get some sleep. I put my hands on my hips and tap my foot impatiently.

"Decline your betrothal to my cousin," she says with conviction.

That is not what I was expecting. "Why?"

"I don't want him to spend his life with someone like *you*. This plan will never work anyway. It's been doomed from the moment they decided to pair a Werewolf without a partner with a broken Valian."

When someone loses a partner, you don't speak of it. No matter how much I despise Titus, there are lines that I do not cross. "I'm not a broken Valian," I say with gritted teeth.

"Oh yeah? Last time I checked, you always wear those hideous turtlenecks because of your future husband's mistakes!"

That hit me in the gut. "I have my reasons. I am not ashamed of it."

"Then show it!" With that she grabs the zipper of my jacket and yanks. When we were toddlers, I would always beat her. I have learned that people learn and improve.

Ten years later, she beats me.

...

Levi

I crane my neck to see what the commotion is about, to find Skye and that girl I recognize from Hawkeye Academy. They sneer at each other, shouting, not caring if others hear.

A crowd starts to gather. I hear murmurs of *"what's happening"* and *"about time someone talked down that snob of a werewolf"* or *"that Valian shouldn't even be allowed in the school."* Then without warning, the girl unzips Skye's jacket.

319

I've gotten a glimpse of her scar before. It's thin but long and tells a sad and painful story. Before people can get a good glimpse, Skye's knuckle connects to the girl' cheek, making her fly back. Not a second later, the Werewolf attempts to trip Skye. Skye jumps over it and sends a good kick to the Werewolf's gut.

The Werewolf reels back and Skye steps away, giving her a moment to recuperate. If she wanted to, Skye could end it, sending the girl to darkness. Instead, she hisses at her, her claws long and sharp fangs out. Kalica rises, her canines reflecting the candlelight.

I push through the crowd to stop the fight, but someone gets there before me.

"Kalica, stop this!" Titus looks between the redhead who helped save me in the beginning of the year and his betrothed.

"Titus! Get out of the way," the girl warns, all her teeth now as sharp as razor blades. Titus growls, his hair starting to stand on end.

Then for some reason, I step into the fray. The logical side of me says, *You absolute idiot.* Why in the Six Kingdoms would you step in between a fight with Skye Fervent and two angry Werewolves prompted by a centuries old cold war rooted in deception and thousands of deaths. "Hey," I gulp. "Skye and I need to go."

"Levi," Skye growls, "let me finish this." She starts walking towards Kalica and I grab her shoulders.

"No, Skye. You don't. We should go, *now.*" I attempt to turn her around and out the door, but the Deuxieme's voice booms through the hall.

"What in the Six Kingdoms is happening here?" He stalks in our direction, face red as a strawberry. If not all the people in the hall were watching us, they are now. "Why does Ms. Time have blood dripping from her face?"

Kalica wipes her nose, but only manages to smear it across her face. I sneak a glance at Skye and she lets out a satisfied smirk.

"Can someone please tell me what happened," Premier Citrus glides up to Deuxieme Fervent, with my dad right behind, "from the beginning?"

Skye starts to talk, then Kalica, and then Titus. All tell a chorus of words but not a story. Premier Citrus raises her hand and then points to me. "You, tell the story."

All the eyes in the room turn to me, leaving me gaping.

I look around and then point to myself. "Me?"

"Yes, you."

Scratching my head, I huff a laugh. "Are you really sure about that?"

"I am sure about that."

"I mean, like–"

"Levi, just answer the question," my dad says, running a hand through his slightly gelled hair. Catching himself, he pats his hair back in place. "We just want you to tell it so it isn't biased."

"Um… I'm Skye's friend though. I think that automatically adds a certain bias to it."

"For goodness sake, child! Just tell us," Premier Citrus cries.

"Okay, okay!" I exclaim. "I didn't really see much, but when I started listening, I heard things about, *'you don't deserve him'* and something about Valians being bad. Then Kalica was like, *'Why are you ashamed.'* And Skye was like *'I'm not ashamed'*. Then Kalica unzipped Skye's jacket and then Skye punched her in the face." I look between the people involved and ask, "Did I miss something?"

"Thank you, Levi," Premier Citrus says, letting out a long breath. "That will do. Let me just discuss with your Premier and Deuxieme."

Deuxieme Fervent turns around and shouts, "Get back to your Gala! And can someone please get Ms. Time a tissue."

People start talking amongst themselves, watching us out of the corner of their eyes. A plain pixie comes flying in and hands Kalica a tissue.

Now that I get a good look at the Werewolf, her features are sharp and refined, but there's a certain grit to her that reminds me of Skye. She's maybe a few inches taller than the Valian, lankier. She would be beautiful if she didn't have blood smeared all over her face and that scowl. She does her best with the handkerchief, but just makes the blood spread even more, her red, silk dress stained. She gives me a glare, so I scoot closer to Skye who looks critically at the group of school leaders.

A fourth person joins the circle, probably the Deuxieme of Alexandra. "What do you think they'll do to you?" I ask Skye.

She slants her head, contemplating. "I'm guessing something like being sent home early, extra practice hours, maybe cleaning the dragon stables..." She pursed her lips. "I don't think I've ever had a fight and had the Head Teachers as witnesses. There's a first time for everything, right?"

A clap sounds from the circle and they all turn to face us again. Premier Citrus motions for us to follow her out the ballroom. I sort of stand there awkwardly, wondering if I should follow, when my father pushes me from behind to go along. *Hey Dad,* I whisper to him in his mind, trying to get a bearing on the feeling. Then I remember that I don't have to whisper. *Why do they hate each other so much?*

He jumps and clutches his chest. Alexandra's Deuxieme asks if he's okay, but he just mutters something about being fine. *I need to start getting used to the fact you can do that,* my father says in his head. *It seems to me that the Werewolf Court is trying to get the Six Kingdoms to exile the Valians from the Six Kingdoms. Of course, the current king would never do that and their evidence is vague at best. However, the next king or queen may not be so kind. You've heard about the Throne Trials, correct?*

Stopping myself from nodding, I reply, *I know the general idea.*

He continues, *Skye just so happens to be the only living relative of the first Warrior competitor that has matured into a Warrior and is not a member of any other kingdom. She will compete for the crown when the current King dies.*

Really? I ask, intrigued. *When she was talking about it, it sounded like there were other options.*

The official announcement hasn't been released yet. I'll just tell you now since you'll find out shortly. The only other candidate was killed by the rebels last night. Unless the Fates choose to change the bloodline, it'll be Skye fighting for the throne.

Taking a moment to let that sink in, I rub my temples. *Isn't that a good thing though? If she becomes Queen, then the Valians are set to stay in the Six Kingdoms.*

Yes, but it will be a very hard and perilous journey to get there. Skye is still underaged. If the King dies before her sixteenth birthday, she will not be eligible for the throne. If she dies during the trials, it'll end the Warrior bloodline and the role will be passed onto another family for the first time in history. She could die during the trials.

"Then who would compete?"

"That's up to the Fates. Though the most probable choice is Kalica."

Chapter 41

Levi

If Skye becomes Queen, then she would secure the safety of the Valians, but there will be the threat of a possible uprising by the Werewolves and their allies. There is no doubt the banishment of the Valians would occur if Kalica got the crown, but the Kingdom as a whole might experience less turmoil.

The King is very ill and it looks as though he won't last too long. Thankfully, the best Healing Masters are treating him and they say the process is moving very slow. They estimate he will pass away within the next few years. My father comes up to my side. We make sure to not make eye contact. As far as we know, the Malevolents might not know about my telepathy. Might as well hide it until we can't anymore.

Then how is he very ill if he'll last that long? How old is he anyway?

Six Kingdom sicknesses are different than in the Outside World. The normal ailments that are found in the Outside World do not affect us as much. There are poisons and charms that are more effective. My guess is that he probably got one of the two. To answer your other question, he is 275 years old.

What! I wince as my dad rubs his forehead in pain. *Sorry about that. I need to get used to this mind thing. He's just really old! You told me that people here marry and have kids young because they die young.*

The reason most die is because of Malevolent attacks and murders. Without that risk, members of the Six Kingdoms can live a very long time.

We walk down halls of marble and gold wallpaper with endless twists and turns. The crystals and intricate decor make everything seem alluring. Premier Citrus opens a seemingly plain door, revealing a dark pathway lit by candles. At the end of the hall is a carved iron door that she unlocks with a long steel key. The room we then enter is nothing like the old hall and is bright as day, all the furniture and decor gold or white.

"Please sit down," she gestures to the long plush silk couch where we all cram together, me nearly falling off the edge next to Skye. "One of our biggest school rules during a time of school competition is to keep the peace between students. Therefore, you must understand that this cannot go unpunished."

"Then why are we here?" I ask, pointing between Titus and me.

"You both will be part of the punishments."

"Oh great," I grumble.

"I wouldn't be too worried. At the end of the day, they should be beneficial to you," says the man who I assume is the Deuxieme of Alexandra.

"Just drop the bomb already," groans Kalica like a teenager mad at her parents. If I were in her position, I'd be more cautious. I'm pretty sure I'm the only one that can act like that to a Premier.

"Miss Time," scolds Deuxieme Fervent, "be kinder to your Premier."

All she does is roll her eyes, pressing a bloodied cloth to her nose. The Deuxieme's face turns the color of a beat. "Well," sighs Premier Citrus, "I'll deliver your punishment first if that will make you feel better."

The Premier takes a sip of water before continuing. "We'll need you to help clean the human litter from the Yellow Water Swamps. The swamp pixies have been needing some helpers. You will report to the North Plain every day from now until the end of the school year."

"At least there's only like two weeks left of school," she sighs, looking sadly at her nails. "I'll be counting the days."

"Now onto Ms. Fervent and Mr. Sage. The Six Kingdoms Court recommended that Levi be taught the politics of the palace. It's only fitting that we have the infamous Ms. Fervent do the job," she says. "Although, Premier Sage did object passionately."

"He'll learn soon enough," my father says with a face of stone. "He's barely accustomed to the ways of the Six Kingdom."

"He's the most hunted person in the Six Kingdoms," counters the Alexandra Deuxieme. "In this case, he is more than just your son."

"Deuxieme Ferlidat, I would appreciate it if you would be more respectful to my Premier," hisses Deuxieme Fervent.

He puffs out his chest and begins to say, "I was merely saying—"

Premier Citrus holds up her hand. "That's enough. The point is, we want Skye to use an hour after school every day to teach you more about the various alliances and nuances of the palace. You'll start this when you get back and continue during the summer, since neither of you will be leaving campus. One day, Mr. Sage will be called in and he needs to be prepared."

Skye's eyes widen, "What?"

I sit forward too. Not that I don't like Skye, I just don't like the idea of having to spend an hour every day doing that. From the looks of it, she feels the same.

"I think you heard me just fine, Ms. Fervent."

"No," she clarifies, "I mean, why me? I don't think I'm the most qualified—"

"That is where you are quite wrong. You are the most qualified person in the school to teach young Mr. Sage the skills he will need in the future," Premier Citrus explains. "You know better than anyone the underside of the works of Six Kingdoms politics. You could even teach a class on it one day."

I nudge Skye and give her a small smile. "It's not too bad. Just don't drill me too hard." The looks she gives me tells me the exact opposite.

Titus is given a week of detention which really isn't that bad. The Premier seems to have a soft spot for the Wolf Shifter. We all say a gloomy goodnight and head our separate ways, while the Premiers and Deuxiemes stay behind to discuss something about the upcoming Duels.

When I finally get back, Elias and Makai bombard me with questions. Apparently, we stirred up quite the fuss.

"Most of the kids here were asleep, yet *everybody* seems to know about it now. It hasn't been that way since the Waterfront Attack of Grantham Willow," emphasizes Elias, referencing the attack at the beginning of the school year.

Ruffling his curly hair, Makai murmurs, "I don't get the excitement. It was just a fight."

"It wasn't just a fight, trust me," I tell him with a little smile. "There's a lot to it. Let me catch you up."

I tell them about the Trials and the relations between the Valians and Werewolves. Their faces turn from dread to fear like day and night. I don't finish until the clock strikes twelve, leaving us in an uncomfortable silence.

I look at Elias and Makia expecting more shocked faces, but they just nod their heads tiredly. "Is this not new information for you guys?" I ask, rubbing my neck.

"Nope," sighs Elias with shadows under his eyes. "Unfortunately, Werewolf and Valian politics have always been in the air. I've been thinking that it's just about time that things start to erupt."

"Do you think there will be a civil war?" I ask, afraid of what the answer might be.

"I don't know. But it is a total possibility. We just have to wait it out," Makai replies and settles into his bed. "Sleep on it," he tells me before he pulls a large blanket over himself.

Elias turns to me. "Did you bring the Book of Mysteries?"

I rub my chin. "I think I did. Let me look for it." I hustle over to my bag and scrounge around until my fingers grip the rough leather. I look through it, not finding anything new. I hand it over to Elias and ask, "Why?"

"I just figured that you could ask it about tomorrow?" He scratches his head sheepishly. "Maybe it could tell us who will win the Championships!"

I roll my eyes. "Go ahead then." He's already scrounging around for a pen. While he does that I decide to start changing and getting ready for bed. When I get myself tucked in, Elias lets out a yelp.

"What?" I jump out of bed and look over his shoulder into the book.

In Elias' rough scrawl is his question, *"Who will win tomorrow?"*

Then underneath, the elegant loopy cursive reads,

"The one who may never love."

...

Levi

"Malevolents," Elias whispers, his face lined with panic. "We should warn the Premier."

"Let's not think so rash," I say, pressing down the lump of fear in my chest. "It could mean something else. You know how these prophecy things work. They almost never tell you the straight truth. Let's ask them more questions and see if they answer with something good."

I swipe the pen away and write, *Is that a bad thing?*

We sit in silence for what seems like an eternity before a glow like fire writings in the book by invisible hands.

"No."

I let out a sigh of relief. "See."

"Then what do they mean by someone who might never love?" Elias' skin is paler than before, Makai getting up to see what the commotion is about. "Malevolents can't love!"

"So! They said it's not a bad thing. If they wanted to make it imperative that we know something then they would have spoken first," I counter, fed up with having conflicts today.

"Are you sure?" Elias asks, still not satisfied with my protests. "Wouldn't it be better to be safe than sorry?"

"Let's ask them," I sigh and take the pen from Elias again. "Should I not go to the Duels tomorrow?"

"No."

"See!" I leave them to their scrunched-up faces and tuck myself into bed.

I huff out a sigh of frustration. I've spent my entire life wishing that I wasn't normal, as most people do, and now that I'm not–

I let myself wonder what my life would be like if I was a normal Six Kingdoms child. Maybe I would have lived with my dad in a nice house in the Town of Grantham Willow and met Skye when we were children. Maybe I would have gotten to know Elias and Austra as children. I would know all this political stuff already with the Werewolves and Valians.

"Do you still think we shouldn't warn the Premier?" Elias sets aside the book.

"Maybe in the morning. Those words might refer to a riddle involved in the final duel. You might just be worrying for nothing.

They've never warned us before when something actually happened anyway," I say, turning the other way on my bed.

I sink into the soft mattress and study the intricate designs on the silk curtains of my canopy bed. At Grantham Willow, the beds are surrounded by a light, white curtain and the room has a warm interior. Here, the walls have gold, silver, and emerald colored wallpaper that must cost more than my whole wardrobe. The lights are chandeliers, draped with crystals. Even the bathrooms have faucets of pure gold. I'm afraid to even open my dresser with the fear of dropping one of the china vases. Everywhere you look there's something new.

To me, it's to the point where it just feels like too much. As the Earthen Born Fate, I would be second in command of the Six Kingdoms my whole life. Would that mean I would have to live in a place like this? In a world of politics and complex alliances.

Questions run around my brain like a dozen children playing tag until darkness embraces me.

...

Skye

"What in the Six Kingdoms were you thinking?" My father screams at me, sweat dripping down his forehead. He paces back and forth, his face red with anger.

I do my best to keep a straight face, but I can't help but flinch when he whips himself back to me. "Do you realize all the questions that will be raised when the courts hear about this? You *broke* her nose."

"I don't think it's completely misaligned so it shouldn't show–"

He slams his hand on his desk, sending a boom through the room. "That's enough!" His gold eyes are the brightest I've seen in a very long time. My heartbeat quickens in fear.

Calm down, Skye. Breathe.

330

My eyes open and peer right into my father's. "What did you want me to do?"

"Nothing!" he wails. "Walk away!"

"She insulted my people!"

"It is not your people! It is the court of all the Valians! Victor Kolinski will hear about this." My ears perk up at the name of the leader of the Valians. "The Court also wanted me to inform you that the alliance date has moved up two years."

Dread fills me. "Excuse me?"

"With the recent events that have happened, even before tonight, they figured that it would be best to do it sooner. The tensions are already too high."

"I thought we agreed that they would wait until I graduated?" Panic prickles my senses and my mind runs through alternative possibilities. I have plans and eighteen is too young for me. Others, perhaps not, but not me. I can't fathom that I'll be much different three years from now.

"Titus will have graduated! The Court may do unfair things, but they at least made sure one of you would be out of school."

"We aren't in the 1800s!"

"We are about to be in a time of war!"

"Then why choose people so young and someone who could still have a second chance partner out there?"

"You know why, child," he snaps, making me jump. "I worked so hard to get us high in the Valian's eyes. You may not be pure of blood, but your mother was the daughter of the former Valian Superior! With you being a half born, they see you as disposable, but still valuable enough to form this alliance with! And you know that Second-Chance Partners are rarer than Valian children."

Our blood and authenticity aren't tainted because I'm not of full vampire descent. The Fates made is so that what Kingdom one matures into has nothing to do with genes. My father is the one who still thinks

331

like the old ways. So angry, the nagging question that I never had the urge to ask escapes my lips. "Why did you have me then? If you knew I would be a half born!"

He faces me again with a face of hard stone. "I married for love, child. I was young and naive, and I will *never* make the same mistake again. I will have mercy on you and spare you from the realization."

He grabs me by the collar of my coat and shoves me out the door.

Chapter 42

Skye

I awake to the sound of crying crows. When I see the clock, I cringe. I slept in late.

The first Duel of the day started at around 6:00am. They used the darkness of the morning for the Warrior Duel, which I'm sure Elias didn't miss. The soft snores next to me tell me that I'm not the only one who slept in.

When I came back last night, they saw my face and figured that it was best not to press. When I decide to sulk, I like silence and peace.

When my father gets really mad, he makes me train with the strongest of his students. He brought out a random Warrior from his dorms and ordered us to fight. We walked out into the field, the cold biting at our cheeks and testing our tolerance. The older boy was a statue the entire time, too terrified to go against my father.

When we began, I couldn't find the heart to hurt him, which just made my father madder. After he got a punch to my cheek that sent my head spinning, my father finally let up, sending us both to our rooms.

I open the silk curtains with a swoosh and wince as the bright light blinds me, igniting a headache. I shake it off and get ready for the day. My footsteps echo through the bathroom and get out my toothbrush.

It drops into the sink when I see my face.

I expected a bruise, but nothing like this. The skin on my right cheek turned purple and blue and little dots of indigo are speckled throughout like freckles. I curse in an unladylike manner and look closer into the mirror.

Footfalls sound down the hall and I quickly pull down my hair to cover my face. None other than Vesta Goldfinder walks through the door and eyes me with disgust. "I've heard much about you lately."

"That would be expected," I murmur and continue to brush my teeth. Already grumpy, every move this girl makes pulls at my strings.

"Personally, I never liked Kalica," she says brushing her long chestnut hair. Even in the morning, her beauty compared to the rest of the school stands out. Her mother is just the same, coming from nothing and marrying high. I've heard enough rumors about the family that I sometimes feel pity for them. Sometimes.

I spit spitefully into the sink and start to wash my face, hoping to be left alone.

Vesta oils her hair and minds her own business. Wiping my face dry, a hiss flies out of my mouth when I hit the bruise. I bite my lip and wish she didn't hear but she sharply turns her head and squints at me. "Is that... What is that?" She leads closer and I push away.

"It's nothing," I tell her and pack my stuff up pixie level fast and walk towards the door.

"Wait!" She hustles after me and whispers, "Where did you get it? It looks like grape juice dye sunk into your skin."

"Thanks."

"No, I mean... Kalica couldn't do that. You'd beat her in a fight any day." As if realizing what she said, she points a finger in between my brows. "Don't take that as a compliment."

I give her a look that says, *Do I care?*

She tosses her hair over her shoulder. "Kids of political power know each other. It's common knowledge and I've sparred with Kalica enough to know. They were fleeting moments where I could get hits in. You can beat Titus on any given day. When we would visit your betrothed, Nikolai and I would always be down in a snap of a finger. Even with him, there were still those moments of weakness. With you, there's none."

I feel a little flattered, but she holds up her hand, "Like I said, don't get ahead of yourself. I'm just saying this to prove a point. Kalica didn't do that."

She pauses and puts her hands on her hips expecting an answer. I meet her resolve with silence.

"I was distracted last night, after the fight," I lie. "I went to go train, punching bags. I wasn't used to the weight and it rebounded and hit me in the face." I look her in the eye to say the matter is done and add, "It won't happen again."

She studies me with a critical eye and I give my most convincing poker face. After a few moments, she nods her head. The Royal scrounges through her bag and pulls out a tall but skinny mustard colored vial.

"Put this on when the sun is at its highest." I take the vial, startled at the kindness. "My mother got it for me on the first day of school from the Sun Lias. As you know, she's working out an alliance with them, but they're too suspicious of you Valians." She rolls her eyes and turns back to look at her reflection. My shoulders slump—defeated—and walk towards the door of the restroom.

Looking back at me, she says, "The Night Lias have agreed to the Treaties." I stop walking. "I felt that you should know—considering everything else." The Night Lias are powerful creatures, powerful enough to be a significant ally against the Malevolents.

Her eyes flash with something like pity, but it's quickly replaced by disgust. "Now, go away. I need absolute silence when I do my eyeliner."

...

Skye

335

"You all look dead," I say. Makai and Levi make their way over, looking like zombies that just rose from the dead. "Did you sleep at all?"

"We did," Levi says, yawning. "I just laid awake longer than I would have liked. Also, Elias came running in at 7 a.m. screaming about how the Warriors lost their trials. He didn't shut up for a half an hour."

"I think I slept weird," Makai groans and rubs his neck. "I don't remember Elias coming in though."

Austra frowns, remorse on her face. "I should've watched for Spencer. It was his last Duel, too. It didn't occur to me that they would be eliminated. They usually win their Duels."

"Sorry, Austra. If it makes you feel better, it was pretty close." He turns to us so Austra can't see and mouths, *No, it wasn't.*"

"What happened to your face?" Aris asks, taking a seat across from us.

He squints at me and I look away. "Just ignore it, please. I don't want people thinking Kalica got a hit on me."

I touch my bruise subconsciously and wince at the raised skin. "I was practicing late last night and I made a stupid mistake." It's better than a broken nose, but it's a major hit to my ego.

Levi raises his hand horizontally over the table and his fingers start to twitch. I open my mouth to ask what in the Six Kingdoms he was doing when a miniature cloud forms just below his palm and small snowflakes fall to his empty glass cup. Soon it fills to the top and he hands it to me.

"Here. This should help." He gives me a meaningful look and I can tell he wants me to talk about it later. I return the look that says that he should give me the truth about his lack of sleep. His chin bobs slightly so I take the cup and press it to my cheek.

· · ·

Levi

336

"Hey, Skye," I begin, gripping the Book of Mysteries in my arms. "Do you know where my father would be?"

She eyes the book but doesn't pry "Near the library on the top floor. I'll give you instructions when we get closer."

We walk in a comfortable silence. Not graceful in a doe or rabbit stance, but a predator. I haven't noticed her above average poise much before, but her chin is always held high, her hands are almost always folded neatly behind her back, and her posture is perfect.

When we reach a crossroads in the hall she pauses and says, "Go down the hall to the left and turn right. At the end, there'll be a floor to ceiling mirror. Open it like a door. Don't worry about the desk in front of it. It's nailed to the door, so it'll just move with it. Climb the spiral stairs, it may take a while. But once you get to the top, walk down the hall until you see your father's name on the plaque on the door. Better hurry before the Premiers make their good luck speeches to the Final Duelers."

I nod a thanks and jog down the hall. How she knows this, I don't know, but I find the mirror and the staircase just fine. The walk up seems like an eternity, but it's as beautiful as the rest of the building with golden light pink hues reflecting off the crystal glass and the sparkling robin blue and silver wallpaper. Old pictures line the walls, all strange in their own ways, however a select few catch my eye.

One is of a young boy with overalls and a funny looking cap who grins at the camera. He's sitting next to a beautiful mermaid with golden scales and long brown hair.

I asked Austra once if the mermaids we saw in the bay were Warriors that could turn into fishes. She said that Warriors don't turn into aquatic creatures like fishes, eels, sharks, etc. Mermaids and other like species aren't part of the Six Kingdoms and are instead their own nations that control the sea and some islands. Selkies are an exception, having won their independence from the Six Kingdoms generations before.

The photos, portraits, and framed newspaper clippings fly by as I dash up the stairs. One picture makes me stop in my tracks, nearly tripping over the next step. Breathing heavily, I lean in to get a better look at the frame. The person it depicts is unmistakable. What's my mom's picture doing in Alexandra Dominique?

I study the picture thoughtfully, her devious smile unmistakable. My father has his arm around her, the horrors of life not having tainted his face yet. The Premier of Alexandra sits in front of them, a hawk on her shoulder. I wonder where that hawk is now.

I shake my head and continue up the stairs, eager to finally reach the top. How could the teachers make it up here? My dad's young, but not that young. I sigh in relief when I come across a floor to ceiling mirror and open it like a door. On the other side, I find a hall just as ornate and decorated as everything else and scan the doors for my father's name.

When I finally see the correct engraving, I prepare to knock on the door. Then I hear soft whispers through the wood. Intrigued, I press my ear against the door.

"–a lot of protection is in place already," a voice exclaims. *The Deuxieme of Alexandra.*

"It will never be enough. They already got past the shields in Grantham. Who's to say they can't breach Alexandra?" *My father.*

"Are you suggesting that our security is lacking?" Premier Citrus' serene tone sounds through the room with a bite.

"Of course not," my father retorts. "It's obvious the Malevolents are going to try something tonight and it would be foolish to not take the proper precautions. I know it would not go over well with my son, but I really don't think he or his friends should attend. Or any of the children that are high in political power."

"Then what do you suggest we do?" Premier Citrus asks tiredly. "We can't cancel one of the biggest events of the year just because of something that may or may not happen."

338

"I don't think we should do anything at all," Deuxieme Fervent's deep, harsh voice says defiantly.

A long pause follows only to be broken by my father. "Why in the Six Kingdoms would you think that?"

I, myself, am a bit surprised. I want to go to the Final Duel, but I don't want to go in without protection, let alone have something bad happen. I quiet my breathing and stay as still as a rock, wanting to listen more.

"If the Fates will it, it should happen. If I'm not mistaken, this could very well be the last trial for Ms. Rabid. She has been tested on all the elements except for Earth. I do not have a concrete theory how that will play out, but it cannot happen if we don't let it."

"And let other students get caught in the middle?" The Deuxieme of Alexandra throws his hands in the air in frustration.

"Maybe we should ask the Earthen Born Fate himself," Premier Citrus says. My blood turns cold. Shoot. "You can come in, Mr. Sage."

I take a deep breath, turn the gold knob, and peek into the room tentatively. "Yes?" My father and Deuxieme Fervent look at me with astonishment and the other Deuxieme looks ready to wring my neck.

"You've gotten good at sneaking around, haven't you?" Premier Citrus smiles and then turns serious. "You know what we were talking about, so tell us your views. This is technically *your* mission."

"He's barely matured into a member of the Six Kingdoms," the Alexandra Deuxieme states hotly, making my cheeks redden. I've certainly made the most of my time as part of the Six Kingdoms.

"The Fates have entrusted him with the responsibility of all our Fates and if you don't trust me, trust the Fates." She turns to me and orders, "Answer the question."

I gulp and look at my father and Deuxieme Fervent. "Well, I have the Book of Mysteries here and I asked the Fates whether or not I *should* attend the Duel tonight. They said yes, I should. That sort of answers that question, but I was just coming to tell you anyway. It also said something about how *'the person who cannot love will win.'*"

You could hear a pin drop in the room.

I shrug and hand them the book. Premier Citrus grabs it first, the other adults towering over her shoulder to read like children crowding around someone with a new toy.

"What do you think we should do?" I glance at my father who looks deep in concentration. After a bit, he gives me a nod.

Recognizing that my father is giving me the power to decide my fate, I straighten. "I've never shied down from a fight that I knew I had a chance at winning. We'll go," I say, knowing that I'm speaking for Austra as well. I don't need to consult Austra to know that she would risk it, for me and the Six Kingdoms.

Premier Citrus dips her chin in approval.

"What does the other part mean?" I ask, pointing at the line that disturbs me most.

"The one who may never love."

"It says one. It could be one Malevolent or something else," my father's face is grave. "The best battles fought have their losses and their victories." The Deuxieme places a fist to his lips.

My memory flicks to the Attack of the Fifth Sun, the night Skye was born. Sometimes the Fates are unusually cruel, placing two men, who's partners were killed on the same night, on intertwining paths.

My father adjusts his glasses and rubs his face. "Levi, assemble a team. I recommend that you not only gather your friends, but people who will be effective in a fight. I also ask that you take Deuxieme Fervent, Sylas, and Ms. Everglade. We'll send some of the Duelers with you, just in case something happens."

The Deuxieme doesn't look surprised, as if they'd already talked about what to do in a situation like this. I wouldn't put it past them. "Will you tell the students?"

My father looks at the others. "I think that is a matter of dispute. I believe that we'll lean towards telling the select few whose lives will be in more danger than the others. All the Final Duelers will be aware."

"You better get going," Premier Citrus says, checking the worn, grandfather clock in the corner of her office. "Did you bring your armor with you?"

"I didn't, but Skye probably did. My other friends probably left theirs at home too."

"You can use ours. Ms. Fervent will probably know where the armory is." Premier Citrus hands the Book of Mysteries back to me and I take it, the weight settling into my palms.

"Thank you."

Tonight is certainly going to be a night to remember.

...

Austra

The chandeliers are lit and the fireplaces are crackling, releasing the smoke of pine into the air. Excitement runs through the school as some wealthy upperclassmen place bets on who'll win the Final Duel. Lightning Critters are flying through the air, spreading word of the events of the day. The Final Duel is set to be a close one, as expected. Makai, Elias, and I decided to go down to the Entrance Hall for the free food.

Austra, someone screams into my head. I cover my ears, but that doesn't stop the echo.

What? I say into my head to the only person it could be, Levi.

The seriousness of his tone sets me on edge. *Meet in the armament room, now. I'll send show you the way in your head. Bring Makai and Elias. Make sure that Aris doesn't follow.*

I jump from my comfy spot in front of the fireplace and nudge Elias. "Levi's calling us."

"Why?" Makai groans, content to feast on the assortment of cheeses on the table.

"If only I knew," I sigh. "It sounds important."

Together we jog to our dorms and pass flocks of people, all heading over to watch the Premiers' and Deuxiemes' good luck speeches. But something seems off. The air, the mood, everything. I hadn't noticed it before, but I do now.

By the time we reach the room, my legs are tired and I'm ready to take a nap. My adrenaline starts to pump when I see what's inside.

The room is filled with people scurrying around in the suite's living area. Skye looks decked out in her battle gear and Levi is hustling around with a sword hanging from his belt.

"What in the Six Kingdoms is happening?" I yell into the crowd. All the clanking and voices stop except for Levi, who pushes his way over.

He sets his jaw, determination spelling out the emotions in his face. I find myself rising to the challenge. "The Malevolents are coming. Get ready."

Part III

Chapter 43

Austra

I stand side by side with my friends with armor on my back and a sword in my hand.

Elias has his bow slung over his shoulder, gold arrows shining from his quiver. He stands tall and straight, jaw set and arms ready. Levi is on my other side with a long sword decorated with jeweled rubies, the color of blood. My brother, Spencer, stands close behind, with two swords tied to his back, dangerous even without the ability to turn into a bear.

Levi always wanted to see his morphed form up close. Unfortunately, he might get the chance tonight.

Skye stands in front of the window, watching the last stains of color leave the sky. Her long hair is braided down her back, armor reflecting the last light of the day. Little knives are placed everywhere on her body with the company of one sword down her back. The Valian has a haunted expression on her face, likely wondering what the next hours will bring.

Hermia sits on a sofa, reading a book with an angry expression on her face. When her mother heard that Levi asked Hermia to come, she came running to the Premiers and demanded that she not be allowed anywhere near the vicinity. Not that I blame her, but we'll miss her logical input and knowledge.

Deuxieme Fervent accompanies us as well as Sylas and Phoebe, who volunteered on the spot. The Premiers are needed for visuals at the Duels, so things seem normal.

Titus seemed to have found out about the ordeal and insisted on coming along, somehow convincing the Heads. He watches Skye, not needing to put on armor or weapons. The Werewolf is a jerk, no doubt about it, with an ego the size of Jupiter. With that being said, he's as loyal as can be and powerful. For now, that's what we need.

Makai sits at the other side of the armament room, staring at nothing. We haven't talked much since he found out he was manipulated. I'd imagine it would feel violating to have your mind messed with on top of learning that your hopes of finding true love are ruined.

The Premier of Grantham assured us that he's going to put guards to watch Aris and Aspyn. We told him that we weren't sure about Aspyn, but it's better safe than sorry. My heart cringes at that, reminded of that pain. There's something about this possible betrayal that's different than what I felt with Levi. This one *hurts* rather than making me angry. In more ways than one, this one feels worse.

Premier Sage recommended that Crescent Everlight and Topaz Legend come along. When he sent them, I almost didn't believe it. Elias looked just about to faint, and I wasn't much better. They're called Myths for a reason, their gifts supposed to be mere stories. Yet, here they are, ready to take on Malevolents for the sake of the Six Kingdoms.

Being the fearless one, Skye walked over and asked about the Duels. If something were to happen, they wouldn't be able to compete. The two Myths looked at each other and grinned. The one with the electric blue streak of hair smirked. "If you do not succeed tonight, there will be no more Duels. If we come, there will be next year."

The Valian smiles a dangerous smile, satisfied with the answer. If Skye was a Central, I bet she'd be a Myth as well.

The Deuxieme gets a Lightning Critter and leaves the room, all of us holding our breath. When he returns, he gives us a grave nod. It's time. We head out, all of us following the Deuxieme out of the mansion of wealth and power. It must be quite a sight to some, seeing a few

345

young teenagers following a grown man in full battle gear. Sadly, in the Six Kingdoms, it isn't strange at all.

"Wait!"

Turning to the voice, I recognize Everhett Goldenrise sprinting towards us. He took off the bandage that covered the stitches that run along his forehead. It was Premier Citrus' reasoning for him not to go. Everyone coming with us has to be at their 100%.

Skye comes running forward, her face twisted in confusion. "What in the Six Kingdoms are you here? Didn't everyone leave already?"

"Word finally got to me that Malevolents might attack! For goodness sake."

"It's not surprising," mumbles Levi.

"Agreed," sighs Everhett, a little dejected. "I just have to get over the shock of it. Malevolents, here? That would be a first... in history."

He goes off into a daze for a moment, a look of terror on his face. Just as it's there it's gone. He shakes his head, coming back to the present. "I just wanted to tell you all good luck. All the students flew over safely and the first wave of Final Duelers."

"Good luck to you too." She grimaces. "For all we know, nothing could happen."

"For everyone's sake, I hope nothing does." He looks at his golden watch. "One more thing, a short girl with purple hair found me, practically fanatic. She's a Royal. She said that she had a vision of people covered in mud. If you know her and think she's legit, then hopefully that means something to you."

Skye and I share a look. Evie. Maybe that's why she was so nervous the other day. Not because of Skye, but because of what she saw.

Looking behind him, Everhett says, "I better be going. Just... don't forget to look behind your back." With that he jogs away.

It wasn't a threat, but a warning.

Skye walks to the edge of the tall hill and rests herself on the soft grass to watch the stars, letting her guard down for what might be the last time. Levi does the same, finding his place next to her. A flutter of happiness finds my heart despite what may come.

"Children." The Premier of Alexandra Dominique strides towards us. I clench my teeth. Why does she have to call us *children*? I could tell Titus' feathers are ruffled at the name too. Skye just looks over lazily.

She mumbles, "I literally just sat down."

"Deuxieme Fervent knows the way to the arena. It's just over those hills, beyond our grove of trees." She gives us a sad smile and then turns to Levi. "Your father asked me to tell you that he loves you and not to get killed."

Levi's eyes widen. "He put it a little softer, but that was the general idea." Her green eyes flash when she catches sight of Elias.

"And you," she says to him, "shoot straight. My Deuxieme predicts that you will miss something in the near future." She flicks one of his golden fletches, inspecting them. "I've heard of your aim, child, and I sure hope that was yet another false prediction, but you never know these days," she smiles. "Rest knowing that visions and prophecies are almost never as straightforward as they seem."

As she walks away, Elias' face leeches of color. He joins my side as we walk to the stables. I expect Elias to fill the uneasy silence, but he just strokes the fletching of an arrow. "Are you okay?" Levi asks, patting his back.

He shrugs, deep in thought. "I barely miss, unless it's a near impossible shot. What if I miss a shot that actually matters?"

"Don't worry about Fate," Skye says to him. "You can't change what will happen, just hope it happens in a nonvital situation. All Royals do is predict the inevitable." Stroking one of her knives for comfort, she says, "It doesn't do well to dwell on the impossible."

"I don't think you're talking about Elias now." I didn't even notice Titus come from behind. "Destiny and Fate are strange things. We just have to hope it falls in our favor."

Skye looks at him fully, as if for the first time. I have to admit, that was the most thoughtful thing I've heard the wolf shifter say. "I've read a book that ponders destiny and fate. Most of them say the same thing. Fate is set, but destiny is the journey to your fate. Whether you know your fate or not."

"You're making my head hurt," complains Elias, wincing.

"Then you would not like to be me," Levi laughs. "Thinking about fate and destiny is a common pastime for me."

"I think it's a common pastime for most of us," Skye says playfully.

We walk into the pristine stables, our shoes clanking on the polished floor. Stroking Zafira's head, I tell her about what may come. Her stance does not falter. She even stands straighter, as if to say, "Bring it on."

"Levi," someone cries outside my stall.

"What?" Levi comes running into the hall. Hermia hurtles towards him and hands him a satchel.

"Put this on your horse," she gasps, probably not used to running so much. I know Skye is making a mental note to start creating a workout plan for the young Scholar.

"What in the Six Kingdoms is this?" he asks, looking through it. "There's just a bunch of vials and rocks?"

She rolls her eyes. "There's different potions and charms. Skye knows them pretty well. Not as well as me, but I didn't have time to write a detailed table."

Skye gives a scoff from where she watches, but her face is warmed by a soft smile. That Scholar must have gotten on Skye's good side or she would have been thrown into a pile of dragon manure.

"I'll just show you a couple that could be most useful," she picks out a vial of a powdery yellow substance. "This is *exolimus*. Not too dangerous, but it's good if you need to make a quick getaway without blowing everyone up."

I can't help but notice Skye, who watches Levi. There's a mix of longing and sorrow in her gaze. She shakes her head–probably realizing she was staring– and turns away.

"I think we better get going," Crescent says, her voice light and flowy.

"Coming," Levi says, strapping the bag of potions to Odyssey.

He looks back to Hermia and smiles. "Thank you. I'm positive I'll use it." He leans closer and whispers, "I might use just the sulfur on Austra one day."

"I heard that," I say over my shoulder on my way out.

I haul myself onto my dragon and ride up to Skye and the two Myths. "What happened today?" I mean, what happened between you and Levi?" The Myths, wisely, find something else to talk about.

"You sound like you're a relationship counselor," she jokes bitterly. The Deuxieme is off talking to Phoebe and Sylas, discussing our formation in the air. Looking behind her, Titus is doing final preparations with his dragon.

"You're not answering the question."

Her eyes fixate on me again and she dips her chin. "I had him read something from one of the books I'm reading." Her fingers trace the scales of her dragon lazily. "He seems to think that family and friends are below his mission, which I understand to a certain extent. The way he said it almost confirms one of the theories that I've held for a long time."

"What–?"

"Are we ready?" Levi kicks off the ground and comes towards us on his dragon. Titus and Makai follow suit, riding out of the stables on their mounts. The Werewolf and Skye lock eyes, but she swiftly looks away.

They make me remember Aris and what would've happened if Fate meant for it to be. I spent a lot of time that night with wet eyes, wondering how I let him that close to me. When he first came to Grantham, everyone thought he was bad news. But I was naive and hopeful. If anything, the possibility that Aris is working for the Malevolents just confirms that my future lies with Makai. I'm just not sure Makai thinks the same way. He's been quiet about it lately, meaning he's probably thinking about it. We both have responsibilities to uphold at the expense of our happiness.

I give Levi a curt nod, shooting Alexandra Dominique one final look before the Deuxieme explains the plan.

...

Skye

Halfway there, everything seems to be going according to plan. The Deuxieme and Crescent lead the way, Elias taking their flank. Austra and Levi are in the center, Topaz and Phoebe at their sides. To the back is Sylas, Spencer, Titus, and me.

Every few seconds, I look behind, remembering what Everhett said. *Just... don't forget to look behind your back.*

I've known him long enough to know that something was off. That Royal saw something but didn't feel comfortable telling the group. *Don't forget to look behind your back.* He didn't say anything about *watching* our backs.

The cold air whistles past my ears, the temperature eliciting a sharp pain. My dragon, Tyra, fights against the wind. Based on the bobbing of the others, they're doing the same, grappling on to stay stable.

It couldn't have been this windy when the others crossed across the plain or the weaker fliers would've been knocked out of the air.

The location is too close to use the dragons' full speed, which risks the possibility of interception. Elias has his arrow knocked, watching the ground like a hawk. I make sure to do the same. A wave of relief rolls over me when I see the beginnings of the grove. We're not far.

Just over the hills, I can see the glow of what I assume is where the Final Duel will take place. The cheers echo to my Warrior ears. If only they knew. The King agreed to send some of his legendary warriors to guard the area during the Duels. I've always admired them, their gold armor showing the wealth and might of the Six Kingdoms.

One day I hope to wear that armor and fight by Levi's side in the last battles of the Hundred Wars, if I'm lucky to live that long. If I am destined to die in a field for the lives of millions, then I think that would be a good way to enter the Afterworld.

My mind is on Levi when a wave of wind knocks me out of the sky.

...

Levi

My head aches and the world is dark. Sounds slips away like water, a ringing pounding through my ears. I gulp, but even that hurts.

Groaning, I place a hand on the damp ground and rise.

"Hey," Elias cries out. "What happened?"

"Where are the dragons?" I look at the group, all covered in mud and dirt. "Why are we in a cave?"

Austra takes out a match to produce a flame. Taking the small piece of fire in her palm she enlarges it, so we can see each other and our surroundings. All around us is mud and clay, like we're underground. Thick, pain roots protrude from the sides like they're strangling us.

351

Skye answers, her face scratched and dirty, "A strong wind blew us from the sky and we sank through the ground. I think we're in the tunnels below Alexandra's grove." She points to the roots on the side of the walls, visible now that Austra walked away to make us a campfire.

"My guess is that an Air Elemental sucked us in here." Titus peers at us through the dim light of the fire. "Perhaps an Earth Elemental too, considering how easily we fell through. It rained last night though, so maybe the ground is just soft." Though, all of us know that's unlikely.

Elias and Austra help me up and gather our remaining bags, probably blown off in the wind. Skye finds a vial of liquid from the sac Hermia gave us and pours it over various cuts and I hiss softly. I would much prefer being healed by a Royal.

"Did you try magicking your way out of here using the earth?" I ask Austra hopefully.

She shakes her head. "There's a damper in here. Everything's a little muffled."

Skye shoulders the pack and lifts her chin. "Then we walk."

Titus and Spencer morph into their animal forms. I've always liked the Warrior Kingdom. Before I matured, I thought it would've been cool to be a Warrior. The Deuxieme, however, remains in his proper state of a gentleman and walks past the morphing students.

"Which way?" Sylas asks no one in particular.

"Either way. I don't think it matters at this point. The Malevolents wouldn't stick us in a hole to die or the Fates would've told me to not go to the Final Duel," I say, scratching off the dried mud from my face.

We follow the Deuxieme through the tunnels and listen for any signs of life. New tunnels branch out from this one, but we stay on the main one. The earth is damp, likely from the rain the day before. The water soaks through my shoes, making them slosh with each step.

Something pops out of the wall, springing us into action. Skye ducks just in time as a clay arrow impales itself in the wall behind her. "What in the–?"

Darts fly out of the right wall, aiming for each of us. Sylas pulls out a shield and shelters him and Phoebe.

He should be protecting Austra. I shake my head, surprised at the thought. Distracted, an arrow grazes my shoulder. I sort of expected something soft because of the material, but no. The mud is so compacted, it cuts like metal.

"They're like regular arrows. Don't underestimate them!" I dodge arrow after arrow sprinting forward, trying to get to the next corridor.

"*WOSREL!*" Austra shouts from behind. The arrows slow down, making them easier to dodge. I try to flick away as many as I can using wind and storms. But, my ankles still bleed from getting nicked. My sides, face, and shoulders feel raw. I'm surprised I haven't been impaled yet.

The Deuxieme glides gracefully around dart after dart and Skye follows his lead. The others don't seem to be faring any better than me. Titus lets out a whimper with a dart sticking in his leg, but he keeps plowing ahead, pure adrenaline keeping him on his feet. Sylas helps Phoebe along with one in her shoulder.

In the distance I see a smaller tunnel and sprint to it. I leap inside, away from the darts.

"Oomf," I grunt, colliding with someone.

"Levi?"

"Courtney?"

353

Chapter 44

Austra

"What are you doing here?" Courtney pants in shock. I've always thought the similarities between her and her sister, Hermia, were startling. In the dim light, only seeing the faintest of features, they could be twins.

"What are *you* doing here?" Levi asks, holding on to the wall for support. "We're assuming this is a Trial for Austra." The others from our group come tumbling in behind us.

A familiar Royal comes up behind Courtney.

"Everhett?" Skye covers her mouth in dread. A claw mark runs down his once handsome face. Even the best Royal wouldn't be able to fix that.

"The hint I told you," he rasps, blood dripping off his chin. "The vision was for me–not for you."

Look behind you.

He rushes over and starts healing Phoebe and Titus. Skye rushes to find a healing potion strong enough for Everhett.

Courtney says something under her breath. "Everhett and I missed the last wave of Final Duelers, so we went on our own. My mother was bugging me about the possibility that Malevolents might intervene. I should've listened to her..." Her gaze finds the blood dripping down Phoebe's arm. "We thought we entered the Final Duel by accident," she laughs bitterly. "I guess they mistook us for you."

"What do you know about this place?" Levi asks. "You both have been running around for longer than us."

Titus prowls around the dark section of the tunnel we reside in, limping slightly. Thankfully, the skin is mended, though, the soreness will remain for a few hours. Everhett works quickly. The Werewolf nudges Skye's knee and sniffs her hand. She looks at him, grinning, and strokes his head. If a wolf could purr, he would be.

"Not much," replies Courtney. She draws in the mud with a dislodged root, making a circle with squiggly lines radiating from its sides. "We just know that it looks something like this because we were chased down the tunnel by a mud wolf and passed the same boulder twice." She glances at Everett, grey eyes flashing.

"Have you tried manipulating the Earth?" Courtney asks, looking at me.

"Yes," I sigh. "There's something blocking my gifts, like a curtain."

"There's a charm in this tunnel," says Phoebe, grasping her newly healed arm. "I tried to move the roots around us and the best I could, but it felt like wading through water."

Skye nods, having felt the same thing. "It's like my senses are muddled. Austra, try. It'll seem harder, but we might be able to breach it if you can find the source of the spell."

Nodding, I rip some mud off the wall, dirt digging into my nails. I hold my other hand over the pile and pull at the invisible strings connected to it, trying to feel the power of the earth. Just when I'm about to give up, I find a small tether. Skye's right. It's there, just muted. Listening to someone below water.

I tug and pull and stretch the clay, getting used to the feeling of the power. When it's in the shape I want, I summon heat to dry the moisture. When the smoke dissipates, in my hand stands a sculpture of a unicorn.

"Amazing," grumbles Spencer. "We'll just leave the Malevolents sculptures as we run for our lives."

Skye steps forward. "When it comes time, use them to fight."

355

"What do you mean?"

"Courtney and Everhett were chased by a dirtwolf, and only powerful Sorcerers can make them. You're the Earthen Born Fate's Companion. If a common Sorcerer can do that, then so can you." *What's to say that this is some common Sorcerer?*

"How do you think they did it?" Courtney asks, rubbing her chin. "A Malevolent can't do this. Not unless they used Blood for Blood Magic. There haven't been any missing Earth Elementals as of late."

"We thought they had a Sorcerer spy at Grantham," Levi says. "We thought it was Aris, the Darkness Wielder. But that doesn't solve this or how the rocks were thrown in the air during the Austra's second trial. There has to be an earth and air elemental working with them."

Crescent's face bleaches of color and she takes a seat on the muddied ground, her white hair stained with clay.

"Why do you say *you thought*?"

Skye walks up to the Scholar. "What are you getting at?"

"Well," the Myth says, looking around, "have you noticed how the shadows are darker and deeper? It's as if they cling to the edges, waiting for a moment to strike." We take a moment to look at the dark corners warily, wondering if the shadows live.

"He's a very skilled enchanter," Skye says. "I guess he could have done the spells on the tunnel walls."

Aris taught me once how to detect charms. Physical touch with the object helped me the most. I put my hands on the wall, willing my power to extend through the earth. It's as if the earth shows me the tethers of power to cut like the arteries to its life. "I can undo the spell."

"Really?" Makai exclaims from where he leans against the wall.

Noticing that that same power is connected to the charm that holds up the walls, I frown. "But if I do, the roof will fall on us." In truth, I don't think I have enough power to hold it.

Elias lets out an audible groan and Levi plops down on the ground next to Crescent in disappointment. Skye continues to help Everhett stitch his face together, both consumed in sharp focus.

Out of frustration, Levi shouts into the void, "What do you want us to do?"

"Why?" A deep voice echoes, not seeming to come from a select direction. I yelp in surprise and Elias squeals, covering his ears. "I want many things," he continues. *"I thought you already asked that question, young Levi. Frankly it's getting quite monotonous. You're getting rather predictable."*

"I know you want many things," Levi says, sweat dripping down his temple. "I was merely asking how we can get out of this hole."

"This is a rather nice place to spend eternity, if you ask me. But, to answer, prepare tonight and you will find out tomorrow." We wait for a few breathless moments and realize he's not going to finish the thought.

"They're playing with us," growls Titus, back in his human form.

"What do we have to prepare for?" Crescent asks.

I scowl. He's enjoying this. I look around blankly for anything that could help my sanity and eventually just close my eyes and take deep breaths.

Wait. That's it. He's enjoying this. "Prepare for a battle," I say. "In ancient Greece they would find joy in watching people kill each other. He wants to see us suffer, otherwise we would already be dead or attacked."

Elias says frantically, "We have to kill each other?"

"No! Goodness no," I say. Looking at the endless earth, I reach around me, feeling the lines of power. "We can't fight with this blanket over us."

I'm the Companion of the Earthen Born Fate. If I hope to live past tomorrow, I need to be able to use my power to the best of my

357

ability and so do those around me. I can do this. I know I can. The Fates chose *me*, not whoever's controlling this earth. I *won't* be beaten by a Sorcerer that sides with the Malevolents.

Feeling the connection and the tensions of the tunnels, I gather where each outlet is, where each critical point lies. I raise my hand in the air, rallying my strength, willing my strike to be toned with precision.

Not giving myself a chance to reconsider, I slam my fist into the ground.

My head clears instantly, my power free to wander. At the same time, a weight falls on my power. Gritting my teeth, I rise, the world on my shoulders.

I rotate my head and watch as my friends come back to reality. "What in the Six Kingdoms?" Topaz exclaims, her hands over her pierced ears. Her dark, brown hair lays in fluffy waves over her face, the electric blue glowing in the darkness. Topaz plays with her nose ring and stares at me with anger, "You could have killed us all," she hisses.

She sits down next to Titus and pets his head angrily, but only manages to get a nip. The Myth snatches her hand away and snarls back. "I thought you were Elias' animal for a moment. I should have known better."

"Well," says Phoebe cheerfully, trying to gather the spirits of the group. "We should make camp and prepare ourselves for what's to come."

As the others start to look through their packs for food and sleeping materials. While we settle into a busy moment of peace, I study Topaz more thoroughly. Her skin is tanned and her eyes are a dark, vibrant blue. A topaz blue. Even in a Master's fourth year, it's rare to see them having Mastered something. From the rumors around school, she Mastered before she even got to Grantham Willow.

Levi tilts his head to the side, likely thinking something along the same lines as me. "What did you master in?"

She lifts her eyes lazily to him, "You don't want to know."

He crosses his arms. "Actually, yes. I do."

She shakes her head and looks away. The others watch along tentatively, except for Crescent who seems to have something else to do. "I never see you use your mastery during Duels, but you always seem to win."

"It's a secret," she says, picking at her dirt caked nails.

I walk over to Levi to listen by his side.

"What we're doing is worth more than one secret. If I'm going to help Levi plan any defenses or offenses, I need to know all the strengths and weaknesses on this team," I say.

She scoffs and looks back at me. "You're serious?"

"Very." My voice is steady. "We won't tell anybody."

She studies me for a moment. "Fine then." She takes a long inhale. "I'm a master of gut feeling and instinct."

I pause, searching my memory for something I might've read. "I've never heard of it before." I furrow a brow and she stands up, nearly taller than Levi.

"Then you are lucky." Now, her eyes look like the dark teal of a vicious wave crashing into the cliff of Grantham Willow. She points to her chest. "What I feel in my gut, it is usually very true. I can predict what my opponent is going to do so I know what they are going to do even before they do it."

Tilting my head to the side, I ask, "Why would you think that's a bad gift?"

"I sense feelings as well as actions. It sucks knowing that everyone at one point will hurt me," she huffs a bitter laugh. "I have that feeling with both of you. A feeling of dread, which usually leads to death."

Looking to the side, she says, "Sometimes it's better not to know things like that. The Six Kingdoms think I'm dangerous *and* Malevolents are targeting people that can tell the future." My mind flies to the Future Telling teacher, Mr. Prophetic, who disappeared in the beginning of the year. "My gift isn't meant to be known. Remember that." She storms away, her brown hair flying.

"What did you do to her?" Skye asks, walking over. Even covered in mud, she looks elegant. I wish I could say the same for myself. I feel nasty.

I shrug. "Not quite sure."

Crescent comes up to us, grinning softly. Something about her reminds me of what an angel would look like. Her white hair shines despite the lack of light, no shadow in sight. No shadow.

She doesn't have a shadow.

"I'm assuming you want to know mine," she says, giving us a reassuring twitch of her lips. "You might know the basis of it, but it's best if I tell you my weaknesses and strengths before you find out tomorrow. We can help each other."

She spreads out the blanket in her hands and pats the ground softly. "Take a seat." And we do.

She tells us that she's a Light Wielder, one of three. A true Myth. She says that she's never met the others before but intends to go traveling after she graduates to learn more about her gift. Her power works much like Aris'. She must have a light present to be able to wield it. It can be artificial or natural, but she can't summon it.

"If I lose the light, I am powerless," she says, not meeting our eyes.

That's why she was so scared when she heard our theory about Aris. If he blocks off her light source, then she can't use her gift, which she relies on most during fights and duels. Aris is literally her weakness, probably one of the only people who could take her on and walk away.

Seeing the realization on my face, she grabs my hand, hers warm despite the cold. "In the case he does surround me with darkness, please bring back the light."

Chapter 45

Skye

When I was beginning to learn the layout of Six Kingdoms politics, a girl named Selena Patriarch was selected as my mentor. I was still a bit naive at that age, so I immediately thought she was a friend since she didn't try to kill me. Her stunning straight black hair and green eyes seemed friendly, until she showed me the cliffs of Grantham Willow.

I've lived at Grantham my whole life, but she seemed to know more about my home than I did. On the way to the edge, we saw a water pixie, dehydrated and too far from the stream. I screamed at Selena when she kicked her into the bush.

Scrambling to the creature, I picked the pixie up. Splinting her leg, I found the nearest source of water, making sure the water pixies there helped her. They thanked me and took her beneath the flowing stream. Selena scolded me for stopping, saying that the lives that don't affect ours shouldn't take up our time.

She told me that I was inferior, being a Valian. She said that I was a disgrace to my father and that my mother was weak, dirty. As young as I was, my blood boiled with rage. Yet, the doubt crept into my mind like poison.

When we reached the cliffs, Selena convinced me that the best way to mature into a kingdom was to jump off the cliff. When I objected, she told me that there was a spell that would catch me.

At the time, my father was a bit insistent that I get ahead of everyone. So, I felt the pressure to mature. There was a sliver of hope in me that if I matured, my father would be happy.

I was hesitant, as anyone would be when told to jump off a cliff. When I was about to ask for the fifteenth time whether it was safe, she shoved me into the whistling wind.

I still remember the feeling of falling, of the wind scraping against my soft skin, the feeling of thinking I was going to die. The wind tore at my hair and stretched the skin on my face. I prayed to the Fates and anything that would listen, begging for a chance to live. When I saw the jagged rocks below hurling towards me, something snapped.

It really is hard to explain the feeling–but when it finally happens–the sensation is unforgettable.

The moment was like seeing the world for the first time. *Really* seeing it for the first time. The air was sharper, the microfractures in the cliff were visible, and the smell from the kitchens felt like it was three feet away. It was coupled by a flaming pain in my arms, spine, ears, feet, legs, everywhere. It was blinding, stifling. My screams were heard at the depths of the bay.

If you ask any Warrior, the sensation of morphing for the first time is a pretty memorable one. Not that you really want to remember it. It felt like my whole body was on fire and my body was being bent in ways it shouldn't. My bones cracked into places and my skin turned color and texture and hair grew and disappeared.

There was a point where I thought I crashed to the ground and that was the reason for all the pain. When the sensation ceased, I looked at my arms and saw black leather wings. Not knowing what else to do, I flapped them viciously, praying again to the Fates to not let me fall. Thankfully, I placed my wings in the exact angle to halt my descent.

Thinking about it now, it would have been better to just try and land softly on the sand since I lacked control. Instead, I came barreling into Selena, tearing at her with all my might.

Before I could get any good scratches, hands grabbed me and forced me away. Trust me, I fought hard and strong until I calmed down and morphed back. My dad handed me a cloak, since I didn't have the charm in place that makes the clothes disappear every time I morph.

How my father got there so fast, I may never know. Thinking about it now, Selena must've set something up.

It took me a bit to get used to my surroundings with the Valian senses. I had to force my steps to be slow and steady, my eyes to focus in the right places, and the smells to become less consuming. It was an amazing feeling, but it was also a bit overwhelming.

When I got a hold of myself, I explained what happened. It involved a lot yelling and pointing and rebuttals and insults, but everybody believed Selena's word over mine. The official story was that I slipped off the side of a cliff and I thought that Selena did it.

Later that week, I learned that I was the new Warrior Heir and might eventually compete in the Throne Trials. The last piece of information was more disturbing.

One of my competitors would be Selena Patriarch.

The next few days I spent in my room crying from the betrayal and helplessness. I looked up to her so much, thinking she was better than me at everything, even combat. Everyone loved her, while they feared me. I was only eleven at the time.

She was the beautiful maiden and possible queen and I was the evil Valian trying to rob the throne.

Thinking back on it now, she probably was trying to kill me. Her sister, Helena, was the possible Heir for the Warrior's Competitor. Their family lineage was so perfect and elite, that if she were to mature into a Warrior, we would both be in the running to be chosen for the Throne Trials. If she matured as a Hunter, she would be up against her sister to be picked as the one Hunter Heir.

My father spent hours yelling at me, telling me that I wasn't worthy of the honor, that it should've been him. He said that my mother would have been ashamed to see me. That I was weak. Because Selena said the same thing, doubt took hold again, this time with claws.

A few days later, a water pixie came to my window and told me thank you. The pixie was young, not even a teenager yet. She came with her mother, who stayed a few feet away.

The pixie asked me if I was a queen.

I told her no.

She asked me, "Why not?"

I replied, "Because I'm not good enough." It was the truth.

I remember the confused look on her face. "You seem good to me? That nasty lady, she's not good."

That made me think for a moment.

"I would have to beat her, and I don't know if I can."

"You can," she said with no hesitation. "The pixies believe in Courage, where you believe in Fates. When faced with an eminent end, we are told to make Courage believe. Make the Fates believe, good Queen. Fight for it."

It hit me then. I was not inferior; I was not weak. That day, I learned courage. I learned to fight for the world I want to live in before it's too late.

...

Levi

Time seems to pass in a blur when you're lost in thought.

Deuxieme Fervent does his best to teach Austra how to create creatures out of earth. First, he starts with molding the shape, which Austra masters quickly. Before, she was morphing the clay one point at a time, but after the Deuxieme told her to just visualize the figures, things started moving quicker.

The next step is to make the mud strong, like the darts that flew from the walls. Not only does she have to mold the earth, but she needs to compact it, otherwise it won't do any good.

Skye and I watch them practice. Deuxieme Fervent yells critiques every thirty seconds, yet it's somehow comforting. Both of us have had him as an instructor at some point and it's a reminder of the mundane every day at Grantham.

The feeling of all our friends talking and living fills our souls. It's a bittersweet feeling–cherishing something with the thought that it could cease to exist tomorrow.

When Austra throws a hardened knife of clay that sticks into the wall, we cheer and hoot and holler. Makai even smiles, clapping quietly. She blushes and gives us a wink. The old Austra would've waved off the accomplishment, but she's grown.

She transfers the skill to a clay bunny, then a racoon, then a deer. Soon the wolves she creates have claws and snouts as sharp as knives and as hard as rocks. They prowl and pounce, their movements getting smoother as Austra gets used to controlling multiple mud sculptures at once.

We watch in awe as she adds flames to their hair, illuminating the tunnel with their crackling. She creates a show, directing the dirt wolves in every direction. They push away the shadows that spy on us, burning their edges.

When she's done, we watch in silence as she conjures a flame to keep us warm, the wolves melting into piles of mud behind us. I wrap my cloak closer around my arms and legs and rub my hands together for warmth, grateful for the added heat.

Topaz seems to have come back but stays at the opposite side of the fire as Austra. She stares at the flame, her face figuratively as cold as ice. Skye's on first lookout with Sylas, who spent the last hour looking at a picture of Claire.

Phoebe sharpens her arrows as Deuxieme Fervent does the same to his sword. The Hunter blows a piece of hair from her face, her attention settling on another woman's Master.

Sensing the dampening of spirits, Crescent illuminates the ceiling with pieces of light, mimicking the night sky. "Just in case we don't get to see it again," she says, joy not leaving her grin.

Elias and I huddle together for warmth, Makai snoring like a mammoth. That boy can sleep anywhere. Skye sits a few lengths away, her face illuminated by the crackling fire. The Valian watches everyone, content to sit and observe for the rest of the night.

I squint at Skye's cheek. No bruise.

Something tells me that she didn't willingly go practice after the affair with Kalica. She looked just as exhausted as me that night, the same expression is reflected now. Come to think of it, there's something else that wasn't there before.

Courage.

...

Austra

I sit up and grab my head as a searing pain courses through my temples.

The ground shakes and the air around me is littered with yelps of surprise and alarm. Levi grabs my arm and drags me in a direction. I follow. The others run towards us, away from—what is that?

I try to blink away the sleep, but again the morning grogginess hits hard. The Malevolents even picked up on that weakness.

I nearly trip over my own feet when the ceiling starts to fall.

Chunks of dirt and mud fall from the sky, crashing around us. Then the sound is deafening, like bombs going off every few seconds. I scream as one falls just a few feet away, a few chunks of rock hitting my shins. My breaths start to quicken and I'm taken back to that day in the secret passage in the library. The world is closing in and the world becomes smaller, and smaller, and–

Makai comes charging for me and grasps my shoulders, "Breathe!"

I nod, more to myself than him and close my eyes. I take a few deep breaths as we speed ahead. I imagine myself in a light, airy space, in a meadow without walls and the air clear and fresh. Levi asked me to go to our counselors to talk about it and figure out some exercises I could do. Remembering them now, I go through each one.

I risk a look ahead. A dead end that shouldn't be there comes into view. "Are they trying to trap us or something?" I scream to Levi in panic.

He grunts and shouts, "Use your Elemental Gifts!"

"How?"

"It looks like a blockage! You can control the Earth, for goodness sake," he lets go of me and together we run as fast as we can to the wall.

Last night, before I went to sleep, I made sure to reinforce the tunnels, compacting the mud so that it would stand on its own. It was tedious and took a lot of energy, but I felt where the earth was bending, where it was weak. If I can do that, then I can make a tunnel of my own.

Pulling from that power, I thrust my arms forward and push against the wall. It molds out of our way and we all barrel through. Levi and I fall onto the dirt floor. Shooting out my hands, I enforce the earth around us, making sure roots can't crash through. Once they're secure, I do a headcount.

Three of us are missing.

...

Skye

Courtney and I run side by side. Rocks and debris crash around us, clogging my lungs and coating my tongue with dust. We jump over root after root and dodge over and over again, but the tunnel doesn't stop collapsing.

Austra created a gap in the tunnel just ahead, a safe spot.

Courtney and I make a beeline towards the small opening as the world falls around us. The rocks crash closer each passing second and the mud falls faster.

We're not going to make it.

I start to fall behind the Scholar. Thinking about it now, this wouldn't be a bad way to die. Maybe that's the reason the Malevolents saved me from that creature on the night of the full moon, so I could die a death that would spur the wills of my peers as they prepare for battle. Maybe I wasn't meant to ever fight alongside my friends.

"Run, Fervent. You did not train this hard to die running away. Are you going to let me beat you?" screams Courtney over the falling rocks. She dodges one that barely scrapes her elbow.

Pumping my arms harder, I fight to keep up with her. My lungs burn not only from exertion but also dust and debris. I cough into my arm and blink away the particles that try to blind my eyes.

Over the roar, I hear Austra and Elias screaming at us to run faster. I catch glimpses of my father covering his mouth with his hand and Levi's pale face.

I hear the world falling down behind me just as Courtney and I launch ourselves towards the hole.

...

Austra

The two girls tumble through the entrance just before a chunk of ceiling crashes behind them. Skye and Courtney lay on the ground in complete exhaustion, both coughing up dust and mud. I nearly cry from the stress of it all and take a seat against the wall.

Elias stands holding to his brother as he mumbles something about Phoebe. "She pushed me out of the way." After a few moments, the Master rises and strides towards the deadly crushed mix of roots and mud.

"Don't," Elias says, grabbing his brother's arm. "It's not worth it."

"She might be out there" His voice breaks, struggling against the hold of his brother. "If this was Levi or Makai, you would do the same."

Skye watches, her hand over her mouth. The Duexieme looks just as grave. Topaz and Crescent hold fists to their mouths, a sign of respect but also a farewell.

"You're right," he says, arms wrapped around Sylas' midsection. "I don't have a child coming in a few months. I don't have a wife, who loves me to death. However, I do have a brother who loves me." My friend cries into his brother's shoulder. "I would stay for him."

Together, the two brothers sink to the ground.

Spencer comes behind me and places a hand on my shoulder. Taking a scan of the temporary safe room I made, he says, "Remind me to never get mad at you again for taking my banana and peanut butter sandwiches."

I smile grimly and nod. "I'll remind you the next time you come storming into my room in search for my candy stash." We nearly fall over as a rumble rocks the room. Dust falls from the ceiling and light enters through a crack. Squinting at a small metal object in the rubble, I exclaim, "Is that a camera? Are they filming us?"

"You are a hard lot to kill," a deep voice sounds in my head. I cower to the floor and cover my ears, trying to block the voice from my head. *"Wouldn't it be lovely for the Six Kingdoms to watch you spell their doom. The battle has yet to begin."*

"Who are you," Levi shouts into the void.

"I am Hardorous. The Fate of the Malevolents."

369

The blood leaves my face and the floor starts to tilt. Makai places a hand on my arm and gives me a reassuring nod. I manage a small smile back and a nod in thanks.

"When you're brave enough to show your face, I will fight you," challenges Levi, his face screwed with so much hate, I barely recognize him. In the light, his eyes almost look–red. "And I will win."

The fog over my mind clears and I look frantically to Levi. Everyone else does the same. He meets our eyes and searches our faces. I wonder what he sees. Probably a group of scared teens and adults, preparing to face some of the most formidable opponents known to man and creature.

Instead of the dread I expect to swarm my senses, there's hope.

Yanking his sword from the ground, he says, "Ready yourselves for battle. We're going to show the Malevolents what the Six Kingdoms can do." At this moment he doesn't look like a fifteen-year-old. Maybe it's the look in his eyes or the harshness of his tone...

He looks like the Earthen Born Fate.

Chapter 46

Austra

I take out my sword and start sharpening it, careful not to let my hands shake.

Once again, I try pushing up, trying to break the ceiling. Since the crack I made, the Earth Elemental must've hardened this area. The opening even sealed itself. Relaxing from the strain, I curse. It won't budge.

Topaz comes to sit by me, her steps so silent, I don't notice until she's in front of me. She gives me a sad smile and I raise an eyebrow. What's with the sudden empathy?

She swallows and looks away. "You do good out there, okay? Everyone at one point is scared of dying." The Myth glances at Courtney at the deepest part of the makeshift room. "Sometimes the purpose of living is to die." She leans forward and looks at me–*really* looks at me. "Don't forget to live when you get out of this place."

Ignoring the dark thought of death, I ask, "How do you know if I'll get out?"

She smiles. "I have a gut feeling." Slowly, the smile disappears. "Battles are hard to predict though. I wouldn't want to jinx it."

Taking out her sword, she starts to sharpen hers with me. "Predicting is a hard thing. It's not like what the Royals do. The feeling I get sometimes isn't as black and white as I would like it. There can be bad in the good and there can also be good in the bad. Those are always hard to tell apart." She gives me a glimpse out of the side of her eye. "Just hope I'm right."

I study her blade. It's about two-thirds the length of mine but looks just as deadly. "Why's it so short?" I ask her, taking us off the topic of death.

"When I know what will happen, to a certain extent, I can get closer to my opponent. Why?"

I shrug, "I don't know. I guess the length of the blades I've used have never felt quite right. Maybe I'll try something like that when I get back."

"You won't need to. If we get back, you'll have earned your Staff."

"Oh yeah…" I nearly forgot. The weapon given to the Sorcerer Companion is a staff, a place to channel excess power. Sorcerers usually don't do weapon to weapon combat, relying on their gifts and elements.

Topaz stops and holds up a hand for me to do the same. "Do you hear that?"

I strain my ears for a moment, listening. "No?"

"I thought I heard a–"

"*Help.*"

We dart up, Skye and the Duexieme close behind. We near the exit of the compacted room, following the sound of the pleas. Hope rises in my chest, but I scrunch it down before it gets too high.

The roots stopped moving a few minutes ago, but that doesn't mean they won't move again. When we get close enough to the sound, we walk slowly to the opening. The Deuxieme takes the lead, putting a hand behind him to push us back. When he looks around the corner, he dives for the sound.

"Mr. Goldenrise!" The Deuxieme comes running in, a bloodied Phoebe in his arms. "She needs medical attention now. It doesn't look like there's any large incisions, but she might've taken a hit to the head."

Sylas falls back, consumed with shock and relief. His face falls apart as he thanks the Fates. Elias laughs in disbelief, his face still puffy from earlier and gives Makai a full hug.

Everhett nods, not quite believing it either. He places his hands above her, after Skye's father sets down the Huntress. We all hold our breath until he says, "There isn't anything internal. She has a concussion, but it's minor. She should stay here until we can get her properly checked out."

We give Sylas and Elias some privacy to wonder about the glories of Fate.

...

Austra

Soon after that gift, Levi calls us together.

Skye, Deuxieme Fervent, and Levi discussed strategy. I try to put in my thoughts, but it isn't much use. At first the plan is literally to expect anything. Expect the unexpected. The Deuxieme tells us that when he rushed out to get Phoebe, he saw a small army of dirtwolves. There were other creatures as well, but he didn't get a good enough view of them to tell what they are.

We don't have much to go on. Levi's thinking is that we send out people to scout, to figure out their numbers and what we're up against. Grantham taught us good strategy and the first thing they teach us is to know who we're fighting.

Skye and the Duexieme agree.

"If only Elias could make his roots have eyes," Titus says, laughing to himself.

When he's met with silence, he raises his head, a smile on his lips. When he notices that we're actually contemplating it, his grin falls. "You're joking?"

"No, think about it," Levi says. "We have Elias grow himself some roots he can walk on. If Austra stabilizes the walls so that they can't be manipulated by the Earth Elemental, then we can figure out what we're up against."

"That's too risky," the Deuxieme says. "What if they send a dagger at him like Austra made the other night? There's no telling if they'll notice him or not. If the Aris boy is the traitor, the darkness can see all."

We sit on the thought for a moment. Skye offers to go out flying, which the Deuxieme rejects immediately. Flying above would be too obvious, especially without the cover of the clouds or altitude.

"I'll do it," Elias breathes. He clears his throat and says again, "I'll do it."

"Elias," Sylas warns, his eyes dancing with unshed tears.

Levi's face contorts in pain. "You don't have to–"

Elias shakes his head. "No, I do. I can do it. Just tell me when." He places a hand on Sylas' shoulder, conveying to him with his eyes that words cannot express. Eventually, the Master of Swordsmanship nods.

We send him out within the hour, all of us nervous wrecks. We can't go to the entrance and watch, otherwise we would get a dart to the face. It's a waiting game. Every now and then, the Deuxieme glances outside quickly, checking up on his progress. When the Hunter finally crawls back into the opening, we rush around him, both in relief and anticipation of what he saw.

"It's bad," Elias says, hairline lined with sweat. "There are whole rows of them. Dirtwolves and bears, even about ten dragons."

"Numbers, Mr. Pursue," the Deuxieme stresses.

"About two hundred," Elias says. "There's only about ten of us, with Phoebe down. How are we going to win?"

I rise to my feet, the earth bending to my will.

"We make our own army."

...

374

Skye

Courtney and I sit at the mouth of the small inlet Austra made, taking turns sipping from the one water bottle we have. Both of us let out a dry cough every now and then, but at least we're alive.

"Do you have any regrets, Fervent?"

I look over slowly, hiding my surprise at the question. "I have a few. Why?"

"Well, I have many," she says, a smile playing on her chapped lips. "I regret so many things, I created regrets while trying to fix them."

I stay silent, not knowing the right things to say. If Everhett were here, then he would know what to do

"Hermia's my biggest regret though. If I die today, make sure Hermia knows that I love her. No matter what I said over the past year, she was my sister and always will be." She takes the last gulp of water and goes over to stuff it in Hermia's bag next to a napping Everhett. "No littering here," she says with a grin.

I give a pursed smile back and nod my head. "I'll tell her. But you're not going to die."

"You don't decide that," she says. "And neither do I. I'm not cut out for that Librarian life and I've known that for a while. I've known that Hermia was the perfect candidate for Librarian, so I pushed her. It's only logical Hermia would become the heir; I just didn't know how it would happen. I have accepted my Fate. I just hope it's one Librarians will read for centuries."

...

Austra

The Deuxieme stepped in and ordered Levi and I to stay behind the lines to remain the final defense. We protested furiously, but he

375

wouldn't budge. The others agreed with him. Compared to us, the others were expendable to a certain degree. If one of us dies, it's over.

Levi checks his watch. "Ten minutes." Everyone scrambles to their places. Just like chess.

After Elias came back, Everhett had a vision of the battle, seeing Levi's watch hit noon. It was a hard decision to leave Phoebe in the safe spot, but we made the decision that he was needed on the battlefield. Phoebe regained enough consciousness to watch over both herself.

Everhett stands between Levi and Skye now, a red cross painted on both his shoulders with an unknown substance from Hermia's bag. Since the paint's not smoking or exploding, we assumed it was okay.

It's customary in a battle that the enemy does not attack the medics as long as they have the red cross on their right arm. The same goes for the Six Kingdoms. We just have to hope that the Malevolents follow this code like the rest of the mystical creatures do.

I lick my lips and squeeze my hands into fists to stop the shaking. Noticing the knocking of my knees, I straighten them. "Hey, Levi?"

Without looking at me, he answers, "Yes?" His focus is trained on the rows of mud and clay in front of him.

"Are you scared?"

"Down to the bitter bone."

"Me too." Taking a deep breath, I say, "I just wanted you to know that if I don't make it, please tell everyone I'm sorry."

"Same with me," he says, nonchalantly and smirks. Even at a time like this, he manages some dark humor.

"If either of you die, I'll find you in the Afterworld and make you suffer," growls Skye, her stance emanating a sizzling wrath. I feel sorry for the Malevolents or dirt creatures she comes across.

The ground begins to shake again. Levi remains unfazed. "It's starting."

The light of day blinds me, leaving me blinking rapidly to adjust. Six figures fall from the sky. The ground lowers them to be level with us. Everything else are creatures made of mud and dirt, no beating hearts. The six walk forward, standing a ways behind the last line of dirt dragons.

When they lift their cloaks, the breath gets knocked out of me.

"Aris," I whisper, placing a hand on my chest to stem the sting. We called it, but that doesn't make the sting any better.

Yet there he stands. Despite the light of the sky, his face is still covered by shadows, the darkness under his eyes prominent. I find some satisfaction at how miserable he looks.

"Aspyn," Elias hisses, the raw betrayal on his face deep. The girl with a soft soul regards us with disinterest, picking at a loose thread on her cloak. The girl across the battleground is nothing like the Huntress I've grown to know.

"Miranda," I whisper. The Sorcerer that everyone looked over, assuming she just had a huge infatuation with Levi. From the few times I've seen and talked to her during class, there wasn't anything that made me think this reality was possible... She's a Wind Elemental.

My eyes drift to the other traitor, my heart cracking. Giant stands as tall as ever, his large shoulders prepared to crush my dirt wolves that I've assembled around us. When Evie finds out...

"Zander." Skye looks at the red eyed boy in awe, then rage. Her childhood friend.

I vaguely remember him from when my family and I would visit the school for Spencer's Duels. He was an older, handsome boy with a bright future.

He looks horrible now, pale with dark hair sticking in all directions and covering down to his brows. His red eyes make him look anything but a member of the Six Kingdoms. The Fervent family and his family always thought he would mature into a Valian, both parents being of the sort.

I'm just glad Ms. Valcov can't see him now.

"I suppose no one knows me then," the sixth person says, his voice oddly familiar. The white of his teeth gleams from beneath his hood. "I am Kylen Lenius, the King of the Malevolents."

The Malevolent's eyes flick to Zander, both of them fading away, fragments of mind.

Giant raises his arms, the dirt creatures coming alive.

He smirks, seeing our realization.

Earth Wielder.

Dirt wolves ground their nails into the wet dirt beneath. The bears are so detailed, I can see the hairs of their fur. New human-like figures rise from the ground, as if coming back from the Afterworld. He gives them helmets and swords, their eyes soulless pits.

He holds his arms high and whips them around, sending the creatures forward with a battle cry.

"GO!" Levi screams at our army.

Skye leaps into the air and slashes at a dirtwolf with her razor-sharp wings. It goes down without a head.

The others work against theirs, but the creatures don't slow with minor injuries. Giant conjures their swords like the darts we saw yesterday. They swing, slash after slash and I wince at a yelp of agony.

Crescent yells and raises her arms to the sky. Realizing what's about to happen, I scream, "Everyone close your eyes!" I squeeze my eyes shut, but even then, I see a light flash so blinding, if someone had their eyes open, it would take a while to see clearly again.

"SHOOT!"

Arrows fly towards the traitors who cover their eyes in pain. Elias sends arrow after arrow, too many to dodge. Aris sends a wave of darkness to shield them, but one arrow lodges itself in Aspyn's cat. Sydney.

I vaguely hear a sob through the darkness.

The Duexieme of Alexandra Dominique's prediction came true.

Titus gets treated by Everhett, seething at the five traitors, still untouched.

Aris sends a current of darkness towards Crescent, suffocating her. The sounds of panicked screams consume my senses. Narrowing my eyes, I remember what the Light Wielder told me. *Bring back the light.*

I pull out the match from my pocket, lighting it on the first stroke. Taking the small flame in my hand, I let it explode towards the wall of darkness.

A pale hand reach out of the darkness, towards the heat of the light. When they touch, the world lights up.

Covering my eyes with my cloak, I wait for the world behind my eyelids to come back. Slowly I look up again, the sound of battle continuing. Aris kneels on the ground, his shoulder burned.

Levi points his arm at one creature and a lightning bolt hits it, searing it so it falls into a useless heap. The boom vibrates in my head, dust falling from the hole in the ceiling.

Topaz and Sylas charge into the wave of monsters. Seeing a Myth in action is something I may never forget. She's merely a streak, severing heads with each blow of her sword.

Sylas is just as good, having his Mastery in swordsmanship. His blade finds its target with each arc into the air, revenge alight in his eyes. The look of sure death isn't just for his family above the surface, but for his old friend that defied fate.

Together, the two Masters wreak havoc.

Makai uses his wind to tear the creatures apart before they can touch him.

When he first matured, I remember that kids in our territory would tease him, asking what use wind could possibly be. Despite my lecturing, he started to believe them. When he first met Premier Sage, he was told of the brave Sorcerers before him who've used the wind as a distraction, a ploy. The wind may not be able to sear or drown, but it could clear the way for others.

Makai interpreted the Premier's words as a means to cause trouble and play pranks. Watching him now, I think he's finally understood.

He blows back a whole row of creatures to the ground, leaving them to the newly healed Titus to finish.

Aspyn grasps her hands as if she's grabbing something and yanks to the side. The roots erupt from around us, knocking away lines of my soldiers. I strain, feeling the tethers snap. Not having time to raise more, I force my fighters forward, keeping the line.

The line falters.... and I watch it break.

Chaos surrounds me.

Skye is pinned to the floor by a creature and Titus gets thrown into a wall trying to help. Elias shoots at a creature attacking Topaz, sticking it to the wall. The Deuxieme and his daughter fight back to back, surrounded by more creatures than I can count.

Courtney charges for the fallen Valian, slashing down dirt creatures left and right in her wake. In the chaos, we watch. We watch as the Scholar born with a fighter's heart shows the world what her hard work and grit was for.

The creature on top of Skye didn't get a chance to move before its head was rolling across the floor.

A smile spreads on Skye's face and then twists in horror as a creature tears through Courtney's back from behind. Skye yells a battle cry and hauls herself up to defend Courtney as her blood pools at her feet.

Aris dives into the fray when Topaz breaches the creatures. He dodges a blow by rolling away. He counters with an attack that I know from the months we trained together, but for once Topaz has to block. Levi and I think the same thing, she shouldn't need to block.

Together, the Master of gut feeling and the Wielder of Darkness clash swords, a Myth against a monster.

Elias is tugged from his post that on a root, falling to the ground. Levi sends a bolt of lightning but can't get close enough to Elias to attack the ones holding him. Elias' face turns purple, gasping for air that doesn't come.

From across the way, Miranda holds out her hand, fingers twitching.

I send over some of my own creations to help him, but they're too far away. Sylas looks up from the swarm around him and makes a beeline for his brother. The dread in his face says it all. He'll be too late.

My attention falls again to Topaz, who has blood leaking from her thigh. Aris stands a few feet away, his chest rising up and down slightly. With an injury that deep, even the Myth cannot defeat Aris.

Everhett rushes to me with medicines falling from his arms. "Do something! This is your fight!"

When he leaves, I search desperately through the area while lightning scatters the room.

For months, I've told myself to keep my emotions and my power separate, thinking that it was limiting my power rather than helping it. Over the past couple months, I've been building stamina in my power, using it often.

Aris told me about where he stores his and how he makes it grow. He said that sometimes, emotion can help build that capacity, giving the power a purpose.

Part of me will never understand why he told me these things, why he taught me how to fight. He made me stronger. Now it's time that he pays the price.

Noise erupts around me. I don't know if the shouts are from the others or me.

Whenever I practiced with earth at home, I felt connected to the element to some extent, but it was always my weakest. It was like it hadn't awakened yet. But now, surrounded by it–it feels *alive*.

I unleash the energy that surges through me in a single, blood-curdling scream.

I push on that connection on the nearest creature. There's a link from its heart to Giant. Brushing a hand of power over that link, I smile.

It snaps.

The dirt soldier attacking Skye stops mid swing. It turns away and starts to destroy Giant's wolves. Aspyn points, her face stained with tears, and yells in alarm. Giant holds his temples in concentration and scowls at me.

I smile.

I do the same with the next, and the next. Creature after creature turns, adding to the army I already made. I snap out of my daze, my mind still having a hold on the creatures, but more aware of those around me. Power can be consuming if you lose yourself in it.

One by one, my creatures capture the traitors, starting with Giant, who gets swarmed by his own. I bury him alive, ensuring that he has an opening to breath. I enforce the dirt, making sure he can't leave.

Levi grins slightly as the line straightens back into place. I made sure to break the creatures holding Elias and send one of my dirtwolves to attack Miranda. I order my creatures to capture–not kill–the traitors.

Everhett manages to drag Elias behind us, where Giant's dirt animals can't reach us.

"Is he okay?" I ask, not letting my focus falter.

"You got him just in time. I can heal him, but he'll need to rest. I don't think he'll be able to go back in," Everhett says, breathing heavy. "How are you?"

"I'm fine. I think my power's relieved to be let out," I say steadily.

"I wish I felt the same," Levi huffs, sweat clinging to his brow.

After a few moments, potion bottles clinking, he replies, "It's amazing how you can do that. You certainly are the Earthen Born Fate's Companion."

I manage a small smile; a small amount of that doubt dissipates. "I just hope it's enough."

Everhett runs over and makes Levi drink a potion. He instantly perks up, his eyes less droopy. "Wow! What's in that?"

"An elevated version of coffee," the Royal says, his normally fluffy hair limp. "Look for it next finals week. The Cooking Masters always make sure to brew it."

A cry sounds across the room, snapping our attention.

Topaz sinks to the ground, gasping her midsection. Sylas comes from behind her, getting to Aris before he can finish the job.

Aspyn shoots an arrow right through Sylas' shoulder. Lifting a hand, I raise a portion of the ground and swallow her, stopping her in place. With Giant likely unconscious and immobile, the earth around me recognizes its new master.

Snapping the shaft, Sylas cries a battle cry.

Blow after blow, we watch in horror as Aris does not yield. How a young teenager can keep up with a Master of Swordsmanship, I have no idea. It shouldn't be possible. Yet I've fought with him before. His attacks are just unique, and he has above average speed and reflexes. Sylas just doesn't know the attacks.

I do.

Screaming from exertion, I make the creatures form a path for me. An aisle free for me to walk opens before me, straight towards a fallen Topaz, a near beaten Master, and my former friend.

Chapter 47

Austra

Before I take the first step towards my Fate, Levi grabs my arm. "Don't," he pleads, grimacing. "It's too risky."

I look back at Aris, who backs away from Sylas to watch me. The Master bends on the floor, gasping for air. He spits blood at Aris' feet.

But, there's a tug. I've heard people tell me about the tug from the Fates, saying that sometimes certain decisions just feel right. It's almost like being a puppet–the Fates telling you the path to take. I never quite understood it before, but I do now.

"It's not," I say, the uncertainty gone. "I can do it."

Levi studies my face carefully. Whatever he sees convinces him. Reluctantly, he lets go. "Yes," he breathes. "You can."

The Wielder of Darkness and I walk towards each other, the contact of swords and weapons stopping. There's no reason to fight anymore. Aris is making the last stand for the Malevolents.

A wave of darkness follows him, the edges curling in, begging me to approach it. As tempting as it seems to go into the shadows, I look towards my friends. They're battered and beaten, but their eyes are as bright as ever.

Topaz lies where Aris left her, now being treated by Everhett. Crescent stays by her side, holding her friend's hand. Tears fall down her glowing face freely, pleading for the Fates to give her more time. For her friend to see the light again.

Aris and I meet eyes–friends turned to enemies. There's something like pride in his eyes. As soon as it's there, it fades into an arrogant smirk. My mind's probably playing tricks on me, not letting that last hope die.

The Darkness disappears behind him. The meaning is clear: we fight, just us. No gifts.

My soldiers fall and I toss my matches to the side along with my cloak. Nothing but sheer grit and skill. My final trial.

Once we're a few lengths away, we run towards each other, our swords meeting in the light of the sun.

The first contact sends a jolt down my body, jarring my shoulder. He crashes the sword down, breaking away. We back up, circling each other. My eyes scan his body for injuries: a burn in his left shoulder, the non-dominant side. He still uses both arms even as blood drips down to his hand.

His attacks might get slower and if I can get a blow to that shoulder…

Aris attacks again, using a method he taught me a hundred times before. Muscle memory comes back to me, and I step side easily, throwing up an attack of my own. I refrain from using the ones he taught me, instead using the ones I'd see Skye and Levi do when I watched their practices.

It doesn't faze Aris, probably having watched his own share of them.

We dance, the only sound of our breaths and our swords. Two souls fighting for the future of their people, but for different worlds.

As I fight, I think about my friend's sister, likely dead or dying in a hole in the wall a few feet away. I think about my friend and mentor, who taught me how to fly. I think about the snarky girl with blue hair, cursed with her gift, likely having known she was going to greet death today, but chose to fight anyway. I think about my friends who have stayed by my side when I didn't even know who I was.

I think about the world I want to live in.

My attacks become swift, more exact. With each step back Aris takes, I step forward. With each attack he musters, I counter two.

Aris and I lock eyes for a moment, a small moment between slices through the space between us, when we're at our closest. He looks into mine with something of sorrow, maybe remorse. There's another emotion that I can't pinpoint.

The moment's gone, replaced with his own attack.

This attack is different. It's messy. And I see it.

An opening. In the flurry of blades, there's an opening.

Preparing my strike, I realize something, my hands suddenly cold. I could kill him. I could *kill* the boy I almost kissed the night of New Year's Eve. The boy born into darkness that was found on the side of the road. The boy that enjoyed sitting at the edge of the cliff, content to listen to the sounds of waves and birds for eternity.

Turning my blade at the last minute, I stab him right through the side, the tip of my sword glistening with blood.

...

Levi

Aris looks up at Austra–and *smiles*. Blood coats his teeth from the hit my Companion managed to get in one of her attacks.

Austra looks down, wiping her bloodied nose.

She was unbelievable. Both she and Aris. They were like two sides of the same coin. Each movement one made, the other reflected it, not missing a beat. Not until the end.

"You missed," he says bitterly, grasping the wound at his side. The way he says it throws me off. He doesn't mock her, but says it sadly, as if he was awaiting death.

Skye and Titus stand together, watching the exchange in awe. Looking at me, she nods her head. Austra didn't hit anything vital,

386

nothing that couldn't be repaired with a good Royal Healer. Titus moves to grab her hand.

She doesn't pull away.

I feel that same sharp pain in my heart and grab my chest. Taking a shaky breath, I wave off her look of concern and concentrate on the task at hand.

Austra nods, disbelief clear on her face. "I did."

Groaning, the Darkness Wielder rises. All of us who are standing grab our weapons.

He scans the room, scans our faces. His dark eyes train on Topaz, Everhett still weaving her flesh back together, before turning back to Austra. "Don't miss next time."

With that the tunnel is consumed by darkness. I draw my sword, sweeping it in a circle, preparing for a surprise attack. When Crescent sends the darkness away, he's gone... along with Giant, Aspyn, and Miranda and the body of Sydney.

Austra says in a sort of daze, "They're not in the tunnels. I don't feel them. Aspyn must've carried them to the surface." She falls to the ground, her focus on the pool of blood a few feet away.

Elias comes up to me, whispering into my ear, "Courtney didn't make it."

Sucking in a breath, I wait a few seconds before responding. "She will be remembered."

He presses his lips together, throat bobbing. "Yes. She will."

Crescent sends flares into the sky, signaling for help. Everhett says that Topaz needs blood and fast. Already the Master looks too pale.

I stride over to Austra, placing a hand on the exhausted Sorcerer. Summoning the last bit of positivity on me, I say, "You did it."

"No, I didn't," she says, distraught. "I let him get away. I could've killed him; the blow would've been easy. Now, he's going to go back to his Malevolent masters and tell them all our secrets. He knows the layout of Alexandra Dominique, for goodness sake. This whole school is compromised."

"Hey, hey," I say calmly, not finding it in my heart to tell her about Courtney. "Alexandra Dominique isn't compromised, there's plenty of other security measures. And yes, you could've killed your former friend and mentor, but you would have regretted it until the day you faced the Judges."

Taking a moment to think, I wonder. Some things still don't add up. "Something about Aris doesn't make sense," I mutter. Wiping the mud from my blade, I hold out my hand. "That's a problem we can solve later. Get up. We need to get out of here."

She takes my hand, getting up from the blood and dirt.

We're all covered in mud and desperately need showers. In spite of our sorry appearances, I can't help but marvel at the ensemble before me. Yes, we barely defeated four traitors, but we were at a clear disadvantage, and we survived a nightmare.

Austra puts a hand over her mouth when she sees Courtney, carried away from the place she fell, covered with Sylas' cloak. Phoebe limps out of the room and gives us a grim smile. Skye's handshakes as she places her palm on Courtney's forehead. Closing her eyes, she mutters a few words to the Scholar that saved her life. After a few seconds of silence, she nods to Sylas and Titus to carry her away.

We surround Courtney as Makai wields the wind to carry her home.

...

Levi

When I'm pulled onto the grass, I'm quickly ushered away and fussed over by Master and Royal Healers. They close my wounds and let me take a long, warm bath before giving me a clean cot to sleep on. I drift in and out for a few hours, vaguely hearing the beat of wings and the sound of wind.

I'm laid into another cot, opening my eyes just long enough to notice my surroundings.

Too tired to question how we're back at Grantham, I fall into a fitful sleep, tossing and turning. The images of the battle rage in my in my dreams. On the back of my eyelids, I watch Topaz fall, Courtney's dead body, the rows of creatures of dirt. The memories of helplessness and panic make me scream, my voice becoming scratched and raw.

The next morning, I awake to a blazing headache. A nurse pours me water and my arms so sore I almost spill it on my white gown. The nurse hands me some of my own clothes, maybe my friends got them from the dorm, and I change slowly, wincing at my aching muscles.

When I'm fed and declared healed by Ms. Mendy, a nurse leads me outside. As we walk by, the other beds have curtains around them so I can't tell if people are okay or not.

The fresh air smacks me in the face and I'm enveloped in a hug. "My son."

"Dad?"

He laughs and cries at the same time. I close my eyes, expecting a wave of emotions, but my gut just feels empty. The sadness about Courtney and betrayal of Aris and Aspyn make my insides feel raw. My Dad pulls away and studies my face. "I watched it all."

"How?" I ask.

"The Malevolents thought it would be entertaining to broadcast everything on the Lightning Channels during the time the Final Duel was to be held. I took me a bit of time to remember the roots in the tunnels and realize that the only place they could run so deep and large was the Field of the Lost. But then, seeing how cold you all were down there, I remembered that Alexandra Dominique has a twin tunnel system." He stops to catch his breath and I just look up at him and smile.

He hugs me again. "I'm just glad you made it back. Austra is about to have her Honoring. You must've read in your studies that the tree in the courtyard is where the Sorcerer's Staff is kept, along with the other Weapons of the Champions."

He leads me towards the noise, me asking questions about the others the whole way there. Topaz will make it, but she had to stay at the Infirmary at Alexandra Dominique for a few more days. The others were fine, just some minor injuries and a few broken bones. Phoebe has a concussion, as Everhett diagnosed, not one that will last for too long. Everhett's once perfect face is forever marred, the claw marks too deep to clear. According to my father, the Royal doesn't seem too upset about it. The Duexieme now won't be the only person at parties with a scar down his cheek.

From power exertion, I was out the longest–Austra only waking up a couple hours before me. According to my father, the tree began to bloom silver flowers instead of white this morning, signaling the passing of a Companion to a Chamption.

When we walk through the huge double doors into the Entrance Hall, a roar of cheers erupts all around me. As the Premier and I walk through to the courtyard, the students make a path, showering us with confetti and silver petals.

I spot Hermia and her family in the crowd. Hermia bows her head, tears flowing down her face. There is no doubt in my mind that her lost sister is watching proudly from the Afterworld.

Those who fought in the tunnel make a line around the tree, like the bridesmaids and groomsmen during a wedding. Skye is dressed in a long, yellow dress with her scar down her neck shining so the world can see. Makai and Elias catch my eye, both already bored of standing in the same place for too long. My father said that Elias and his class are going to perform their dance piece early in celebration, which I can't wait to see. Then there's Austra–who stands at the center, staring up at the towering tree.

Her eyes are filled with memories that will torment all of us long after today, but her smile is genuine.

My father nudges me to take my place at her side.

Austra looks to the Premier, thanking him. My father bows his head and walks to his spot in the audience.

She takes a deep breath and places her hand on the rough bark, and I do the same, symbolizing my approval as one of the Fates. The whole tree begins to glow like the sun with ancient magic, far older than the Fates themselves.

I cover my eyes from the light. By the time the glare clears, Austra backs away from the tree, a staff in her hand.

Everyone rejoices and Lightning Critters shoot across the sky, sending news to the far reaches of the world. I hoot and holler along with the crowd. Phoebe and my father have tears streaming down their faces and Spencer looks at his sister with pride.

The Earthen Born Fate's Sorcerer Champion raises her staff in the air in victory.

...

Skye

I find Hermia crying in her bookshelf.

The tears don't fall like streams, just a sniffle here and there. My guess is that she probably got the tears out of her system and now there's the emptiness. At times like this, I prefer the tears.

I hoist myself up to sit next to her, where her legs dangle off the side. We watch as the sun sets which is my favorite pastime. I find that whenever I need to think or ponder, I always find myself gazing out the window. Sunsets have taught me that even endings can be beautiful.

"She said she was proud of you," I say, pushing down the lump in my throat. "She said that she loved you."

"She did?" She wipes her nose.

Nodding my head, I grab her hand. "Yeah."

The Scholar doesn't pull away, but rather scoots closer to me and rests her head on my shoulder. "I'm the new Librarian Heir," she says. The acceptance in her voice sends a wave of emotions through me.

"Yeah," I scratch out. "You know, Austra's brother died just a year ago. I remember the day vividly. She sent me a Lightning Critter and her voice was drowning in tears. I understood what she said."

The Scholar looks up at me. "What'd she say?"

I breathe out a laugh, "She talked about things she didn't care about. She said that she now had to take her brother's position in inheriting the title of future Governor of the Six Kingdom Hawaiian Territories. She explained the situation with Spencer, knowing that his heart wasn't in ruling. She talked about how she would need an arranged marriage to be elected and that she was willing to make that sacrifice."

Looking down at Hermia, a tear escapes my eye. "What she really was saying was that she was hurting and didn't know how to make it stop. She meant to say that there was a hole in her chest that would never be filled again. She meant to say that she was lost and didn't know how to be found."

Tears stream down both our faces, while I wrap the young Scholar in a hug. "I told her that hole will be there always to remind her of that love. I told her that she would find herself, when the time is right." She buries her face in my shoulder, her body shaking. "She found herself yesterday."

Chapter 48

Levi

When I return to my room, I limp over to my bed, exhausted. The others are still out partying the night away, likely until the sun touches the sky.

I still hear the music from the courtyard and the bass pounding through the floor. My heart warms at the thought of other schools across the Six Kingdoms doing the same. I flop onto my bed, not bothering to change out of my clothes, and frown when I hear something crunch beneath me. Pulling out a page of parchment, my happiness curdles at the name at the end. *Aris.*

I slam the letter on my bed, looking around the room for a lingering darkness in the shadows. My breath quickens–but the shadows look like normal shadows.

After concluding that the room is safe and that whatever is on the letter–true or not–is valuable, I lift the letter up and start to read.

Hello Levi Sage,

This is Aris. I know that you might be startled to read something written by someone who tried to kill you, but I implore you to finish reading this letter.

First off, I wish to explain things from the beginning.

I am a Sorcerer born of two Malevolent parents. When I matured, I was thrown out by my mother. A passing soldier is the only reason I am able to walk today. The King took me in, figuring that I might be of use for my ability to call on the Darkness. At his manor, I met Giant, Aspyn, and Miranda, who were all born into a world we had no business being in.

The King taught us how to fight, manipulate, wield our gifts, and everything under the mood. For all intents and purposes, he was a father to me. He told us stories about what the Fates did to them–banishing them. Fooled by his stories, I worked hard so that I could one day be on the level of the Malevolents since the other Kingdoms were considered inferior in their eyes. I've grown up hating the very fiber of the Six Kingdoms, in turn, hating myself.

This isn't the first mission the four of us have been on, but it was the most critical. The King didn't let me go, saying that I was too valuable to lose and that my gifts were too suspicious. Not taking no for an answer, I snuck out and followed them. I was found on the just outside the town, looking for Grantham Willow.

When they realized I was a Sorcerer, I was taken to the Premier and I expected to be tortured and questioned. I was startled to find that all he did was keep me in his office for a few hours, trying to get to know me. The intelligence in his questions surprised me. He didn't speak in a way to trick, but to get me to trust him.

After not getting anything information out of me, he let me go and enrolled me in Grantham Willow. At first, I was so shocked that my plan actually worked, but I suspect the Fates had a role to play.

When the King found out I left, he was furious. If I have survived our encounter, Levi, I will likely pay for my actions soon.

After a few weeks, the King figured that as long as I was here, then I should carry out his plans. Speaking through our minds through Hardorous, he told Aspyn and I to get close to you all, learn about your weaknesses and plans. Miranda and Giant were given the job of watching from afar. Miranda joined the group of kids who noticed the little things, wallflowers. Giant, on the other hand, found the most social, hoping to learn about you by word of mouth.

When we went to save you from the Malevolents, it didn't even occur to me that you were the Earthen Born Fate. However, I knew how sharp Skye was and I was fearful. I made sure that I healed her in a way that would leave her unconscious long enough for me to grow roots in your friendships.

I listened on that night you and Austra snuck out to visit Skye. I heard about Austra's struggles and her dilemma with Makai. I didn't fully hear the conversation. After some research and using the Recollection Charm on Austra during one of our sessions, I figured it out.

Then, on the day the Malevolents attacked Grantham Willow, I used darkness to shield a group of Malevolents. We used the Recollection charm on all who saw us and knowing that you had First Aid that day, they entered the bay. That was all me, the others were on campus, pretending to be helpful. One followed me to the castle in hopes of finding and killing you. I think he might've suspected that I was growing soft and tried to kill me as well. He injured me, so I had to wait for Giant to come find me and perform a healing spell.

For Austra's second trial, Miranda wielded the air to hold Makai in the air, just as Skye guessed. We wanted to carry Makai away so that we could use the Recollection charm, to learn more about you and Austra. But Skye caught us, despite my darkness, and the King saw through our minds what happened and stepped in. We tried to remedy the situation, Miranda throwing rocks using her air. Giant made a tree fall. At the end, it was all in the Fates' plan. I wrote a note and attached it to Makai's wrist. "You are the pawns." Elias liked chess, so I thought it would trigger something.

When Skye guessed that there were traitors in Grantham, Aspyn and I were dumbfounded. We hadn't expected a Warrior so calculating. Frankly, we didn't expect any of you to be as powerful and as smart as you are. The King felt as though Malevolents deserved to rule over the Six Kingdoms, if not eliminate them. We were taught that the Six Kingdoms were inferior, unintelligent.

In spending time with you all, I kept seeing flaws in the King's descriptions of the Six Kingdoms. But my peers were more set in their minds than I was.

I enjoyed the feeling of the sun on my skin, the sound of music and laughing. I was able to feel emotion for the first time without feeling guilty or angry about it. Slowly, I made my decision.

During my sessions with Austra, I taught her everything that I knew. I taught her the attacks that the King taught me, that his guards taught me. I taught her how she could beat me. Levi, have her teach you what she knows. For when the time comes for you to fight him, you must be ready, and you cannot fail.

During her third trial, I lit the fire. I used a starter that can only be found in the caves of Grantham Willow. That day of the trials, I was so angry that she didn't stop the fire sooner. Even though the type of fire spreads fast, it's so much easier to manipulate than a normal flame. She could've stopped it before it destroyed half the school.

On the night of New Year's Eve, I realized that I liked Austra. That I more than just liked Austra. The mark seared itself into my lower back that night. She's my Partner, Levi.

You may ask why I'm writing to you and not her. She can't know about this. Not yet. She has to hate me. You all have to. You may still hate me after reading this and you should. Rage and hate me with all of your being. If you don't, the King will know.

Come in my mind every once in a while, Levi. I will tell you his plans and strategies. I will tell you how to beat the King of the Malevolents because only you can.

- Aris

...

Levi

A few days after the battle, the four of us sit together in Gemini. We've done this before–sit and talk like old friends. Sometimes we talk about the battle, other times we stay quiet. There's something comforting about this, being here with them, together.

We sit in silence now, a question bubbling up in my chest. "Who's Zander?"

Skye grimaces. Hermia gives me a pointed look and then it dawns on me. "You don't have to tell us if you don't want to," I say, quickly. "It might be a good thing to know... just in case we see him again."

Skye just shakes it off. "It's fine. He was a few years older than me, but us Valians stick together." A small smile plays with her lips. "We were like two peas in a pod for many of my younger years and my father and Ms. Valcov were good friends at the time. My mother knew her since bother were Valians. The other kids were too scared to hang out with either of us because of our kind's history. He was my only friend."

She takes a seat next to me, looking as defeated as I've ever seen her. And Skye *hates* being defeated. Not knowing what to do, I place a hand on her shoulder, hoping to bring some level of comfort. I prepare for her to slap me away, but she lets me be.

"I remember the day we found out that he was a Malevolent. The sun finally set and Zander and I were watching hail fall to the ground through an open window. There was something fascinating about watching the ice shatter across the floor, watching something so beautiful getting destroyed." She stares into her empty palms.

"Despite myself, I jumped in surprise when a loud sound erupted through the echoing hall. Both of us immediately scowled at the smell of who stood in the door. One perk of being Valian means that you can smell subtle things like the scent of a werewolf. Keep in mind that this was about two weeks after he betrayed my trust and that mission. Zander knew about it, partially because his mother and father were in high

397

positions and had connections in the government. He also knew because I told him every sick detail. With my overly biased story and the huge pearl white scar running down the whole front of me, Zander finally tipped."

She swallows, pain etched on her face. "One thing that I specifically remember about Zander was that he was very protective over me. This was the first time Titus and he faced each other after the accident and Zander exploded." She laughs at herself. "At the time, it was bittersweet watching a former friend get pummelled by another. But it wasn't until Zander looked up from an unconscious Titus did I see the red. Not only was it coming out of his mouth and nose, but his eyes."

Hermia comes over to hold her hand. "Like an idiot, I just stood there gaping at him. I remember the look of confusion on his face when he asked me what was wrong. He tried to touch me, but I backed up like a coward. Looking back at it now, I should have taken that silver dagger in my jacket and plunged it into his heart to save him from a life as one of them. But, before I could react, he looked above me and the remaining color drained from his face. Behind me was a small mirror and through the reflected glass, my friend saw who he had become."

I rub her back, hoping to make up for the pain of asking her to tell me. "The look on his face is one that I will never forget. The last thing I saw that night was a fist and then–nothing."

She sets her jaw and scowls. "I woke up in the Infirmary a day later to witness my second family fall apart. Zander disappeared that night and the search party never found him. Zander's dad left for Romania in disgrace. Ms. Valcov stayed and we all helped her pick up the broken pieces. But we couldn't help her fractured heart. After a brief hiatus, she returned to teaching."

Her gaze flickers to me for a moment, her eyelashes fluttering. "I've always blamed myself for not seeing it sooner and not helping him see the light. Zander acted strange in the months before all this happened. Some nights he would come back to Grantham Willow with cuts and bruises all over his face, arms, and legs. We had this unspoken agreement between us that we would never ask each other anything. The information that we wanted to say, we would say. Bags under his eyes started to form and I just assumed they were caused by an overload of work."

Her eyes turn misty. "When I matured, I would fly around at night. Sometimes I would see a lantern going down the path through the woods. One night I swooped down out of curiosity and found that it was Zander. I didn't think much of it. I was such a *stupid*, naive—"

"Hey," I say, trying to calm her down. "Even if you did intervene, the Fates always make us mature into what fits our soul. What Zander matured into didn't depend on what you said or did in the couple months before he matured. Hardorous made his decision and it wasn't your fault."

"He's right," says Austra with a sorrowful look on her face. It doesn't take much to guess who she's thinking of now.

A boy whose soul doesn't fit where it was born.

…

Levi

"Have you gotten any more information about them?"

"We looked at their paperwork... all fake. They were so skillfully forged; I still don't know how they did it. It makes me wonder if there are more spies within these walls that we don't even know about," the Premier bristles.

I nod silently as we walk the empty halls of Grantham Willow. A week has passed since the battle in the tunnels. School got out. Of course, being the Premier's son, I stayed. So did Skye and Elias. Sylas looks after his brother when he doesn't have school. Faculty get housing at Grantham all year around, so it's only fitting that at least part of the gang stays together.

Makai, Spencer, and Austra have returned to their homes in Hawaii. Makai and Austra plan to sort out their alliance plans and both of them agreed that the fit might not be right. At least not now, hoping to suspend plans until they grow a bit more. Hermia thinks that they would be a handsome couple, but I know better.

I train with Skye every day, which helps with the memories. A potion hid her bruise that day, so it came back full force after it wore off. It has started to fade, but like everything else, the pain behind it still lingers.

After celebrations came a funeral. Courtney was burned and her ashes were laid alongside others of Librarian blood.

Since Courtney was the first in line to inherit the title of Librarian, the duty now passes onto Hermia. The small Scholar took the title with grace, accepting the responsibility. The family doesn't blame me for the incident, but I can tell there will be a rift there for years to come.

The tunnels were buried both at Grantham Willow and Alexandra Dominique, never to be used again. With the new techniques the Hunters use to tend the trees, they won't be needed anymore.

My father has opened the floodgates for public opinion, giving me a Lightning TV to watch in my dorm room. Every now and then, I reach across the world and ask Austra in her mind how she's doing. She seems to be taking it all pretty well too. However, there's a hidden sorrow I sense each time.

The Trials have made her stronger. Past Austra would have crawled under the covers and felt so guilty, she wouldn't get out of bed for a week. Instead, her and Spencer keep training every evening.

The King called me by Lightning Critter to congratulate me. He said that he watched the whole thing and admired my bravery. I was honored, but I would have been happier if he wasn't coughing through the entire conversation.

Topaz was able to come back to Grantham Willow a few days after the battle. When the Circle of Myths reunited, Crescent and Topaz were consumed in a group hug. They fell into a heap in the courtyard during the celebration after Austra's Honoring. Austra and I watched and Austra shed a tear or two. She and Topaz exchanged addresses so that they could keep in contact over the summer.

"What now?" I ask the Premier. "Now that the first Companion became a Champion, when will the second show up?"

"The Fates will decide that," he sighs. "They may choose to give you a break, wait a few months, a year or two maybe. Time isn't as precious to them as it is to us."

Patting me on the back, he says, "Don't worry too much for now. Focus on training and studying because these Trials will continue to get harder the closer you get towards the Hundred War. They will mess with your mind and test you to your limits," he sighs, stopping his steady pace, "which is why I must bring one weakness to your attention."

Frowning, I ask, "What do you mean?"

He runs a hand over his face and places his hands over the railings of the balcony he led me to.

The week has been just as busy for me as him and dark circles and messy hair proves a lack of sleep. It seems as though every waking moment he has meetings and conferences, constantly traveling back and forth from the capitol to here. "Ms. Fervent is always thinking, calculating. She came to me with a theory that I was playing with as well."

"She's mentioned something before," I say, growing more worried by the second. "About the gifts I have creating an imbalance."

He furrows his brows, watching the waves crash against the cliffs below. "There's a reason I might've been a bit distant these past couple months. I told myself that it was me trying to make sure you didn't notice it before Austra passed her trials, not wanting it to distract you. In reality, it was just me trying to protect myself."

"Spit it out then," I say, leaning on the railing, careful not to crush any of the ivy. I've gotten enough lectures from Elias about hurting the plants.

"The most reliable Royal predicted something like this when you were born. One day Austra mentions how your eyes turn red when you're mad. Then, when you and Austra started to grow stronger and stronger, that was enough for me to believe the theory to be fact."

Taken aback, I say, "I thought that was normal for an Earthen Born Fate."

"To a certain extent, it is. But, it's usually just a portion of the eye, not the whole thing. It shows how dominant that part is in you."

Turning to me, he asks, "Levi, when Austra was put in danger in the tunnels, did you think of her safety to protect a friend or protect a Companion that holds the fate of the Six Kingdoms?"

I stare off at the bay and breathe in the salty air. Did I think of Austra as a friend or a tool? "I don't know," I whisper.

My dad looks at me sadly. "This revelation hit your mother hard, but she understood. I hope that you do too." He takes a deep breath and then says, "You may never know the feeling of love."

...

Zander

The water drips to the ground sending ripples through the puddles that line the walkway. The Malevolents have lived below ground since the First War.

I look at my hands and then back at the man of power before me. He is feared by the Fates and his name is feared by mortals. He is ruthless, taking the lives of so many. That is why Malevolents follow him, not from love or kindness, but for the hate he carries.

"We have had our setbacks," my King sneers. "The four that we sent for the Final Trial failed. Nevertheless, we need them to carry out the rest of the plan. They will be trained harder than before." Aspyn curls on the floor, her face bloodied and her hair covered in mud. The others look just as beaten; their hands tied behind their backs.

Aris stares at the floor, his face void of emotion.

"As punishment, their parents have been sentenced to death."

A roar fills the room as soldiers begin hauling Malevolents to the dais.

The parents of the four look nothing like their children. Some scream and curse at them, blaming their children for their tragic fate.

When a Malevolent is born, they are not a Malevolent. Their eyes are of normal color and when they mature, it turns red. Before maturing, some long for love and kindness as any baby would. Their parents, of course, send them to a trainer by the time they can walk to learn how to kill.

A select few mature into a member of the Six Kingdoms. Four. The beaten down group of children, kneeling on a dirtied stage are the only ones to have matured into Six Kingdoms from Malevolent parents in thousands of years. The King believes them to be the key for defeating the Six Kingdoms.

Their unfortunate parents kneel in front of the crowd. Many fight and scream, snarling through their restraints.

They are bitter until the bitter end.

I turn away and walk in the direction of the dungeons.

Malevolents don't care about living. They care about how tough you are. It's all about if you can survive this, if you can survive a bit longer. The Malevolents about to meet their end are more concerned about their pride then spending the rest of their existence in a limbo, never to enter the Gates.

It has been five years since I slept on a soft bed, been kissed by my mother, praised by my tutors. I remember what it was like to love, but the feeling has never returned for so long.

I make my way over to the prisons where wails and cries scream for help and mercy that will never be granted. The guards let me through the Gates with a sneer. Begging Masters, crying Royals, screaming Elves–nearly every creature you could think of–greet me. I smirk and say, "You miss me?"

The dungeons are foul smelling, damp, and miserable.

"One day, young Malevolent, you will feel the wrath of the Six Kingdoms." Helena Patriarch sneers, her green eyes flickering in the dim light. A freshly burned tattoo is stark against her tanned skin.

The Earthen Born Fate's Huntress Companion.

"I'm sure I will," I say promptly and look through the skylight into the stars. "But first, they will feel ours."

Acknowledgements

First of all, I would like to give a special thanks to Roshni and Rachana for being with me since the beginning. You have read this book when it was in its infancy and listened to my endless questions and plot dilemmas. Roshni, thank you for helping me come up with the title of this book. I will always remember you whenever I say its name. Rachana, thank you for the emotional comments and texts you sent when you were reading the high points of this book. They never failed to make me smile and remind me of why I write. Your perseverance and hard work are woven into each line of this book and our friendship is now written into eternity. I would have never had the strength and confidence to reach this stage of my writing career without you. We did it. Thank you.

I would like to thank my family for teaching me the beauty of storytelling. For my mom for reading to me before bed, introducing me to Nancy Drew and various Japanese folktales. For my grandma and grandpa for raising me to be kind and conscious of those around me. And to my dad, for fueling me with tea and coffee during the evenings when I was consumed by scene development and characters. Thank you.

I would like to thank every single one of my friends for their support and words of encouragement, even if they didn't know the book existed until it was published. I am a reflection of the people I have met and my experiences. This book would not be what it is today without you. To Audrey, thank you for hyping me up when I needed the boost. Your positivity and intelligence make you radiate in a crowd. I am proud and so grateful to call you a friend. To Michelle, for being one of the most understanding and talented individuals I know. Thank you for illustrating the gorgeous cover of the novel. Your creativity and artistry will take you so far and there is no doubt in my mind that you will do amazing things. To The Pack, for being by my side even when it seems like my world is crumpling around me. You all have been my rock, my support, and most importantly, my friends. Since I've known you, I have changed. I have become a better person and friend. You are my people and I am so lucky to be able to say that. I love you all and thank you.

I would like to thank all the mentors and teachers that I have ever had. Your guidance and time that you have invested in me has not gone to waste. This book was inspired by a history lesson in middle school for goodness sake! When I was in elementary school, English was my hardest subject. I remember being behind in my reading level and had to get tutored. School did not show me my weaknesses, but rather gave me the opportunity to improve. When I discovered the *Percy Jackson and the Olympians* series by Rick Riordan in fifth grade, the world of fantasy and adventure consumed me. Reading was no longer something I dreaded, but instead encouraged me to dream. Every teacher reading this, I want you to think about the students that may be struggling in your class, but you see a drive, a passion, in their heart. I implore you not to think of them as a student who may earn a bad grade in your class, but rather someone who will fight. Someone who will persevere and accomplish something beyond what you thought possible. All you have to do is believe in them.

Thank you to everyone who believed in me, even when I did not believe in myself.

Finally, I would like to thank every single reader for giving this book, written by a high schooler, a chance. Whether you enjoyed it or not, I hope you gained something from reading its pages. I have a long journey to come and I can promise that this will not be my last story. You are the reason I have such a love for humanity. The pursuit of knowledge and the initiative that you have gives me reason to believe in a better world.

You have all helped give me the courage and confidence to put this story out there and to make this dream become a reality.

Thank you.

Made in the USA
Middletown, DE
02 October 2020